A TI

**Also by Arthur C. Clarke in Gollancz**

The City and the Stars
Cradle
The Deep Range
A Fall of Moondust
The Fountains of Paradise
Hammer of God
Imperial Earth
The Other Side of the Sky
Reach for Tomorrow
Richter 10 (with Mike McQuay)
Tales of Ten Worlds
The Wind from the Sun
The Collected Stories

*Non-fiction*
Profiles of the Future

**Also by Stephen Baxter from Gollancz:**

*Non-fiction*
Deep Future

*Fiction*
Mammoth
Longtusk
Icebones
Behemoth
Reality Dust
Evolution
Flood

*The Web*
Gulliverzone
Webcrash

*Destiny's Children*
Coalescent
Exultant
Transcendent
Resplendent

*A Time Odyssey*
(with Arthur C. Clarke)
Time's Eye
Sunstorm

*Time's Tapestry*
Emperor
Conqueror
Navigator
Weaver

**From Weidenfeld & Nicolson**

*Non-fiction*
Revolutions in the Earth

# Firstborn

## A TIME ODYSSEY: BOOK THREE

ARTHUR C. CLARKE
AND
STEPHEN BAXTER

First published in Great Britain in 2008 by Gollancz
An imprint of the Orion Publishing Group
Orion House, 5 Upper St Martin's Lane,
London WC2H 9EA
An Hachette UK Company

This edition published in Great Britain in 2009 by Gollancz

7 9 10 8 6

A CIP catalogue record for this book is available from the British Library

ISBN 978 0 575 08341 7

Typeset by Deltatype Ltd, Birkenhead, Merseyside

Printed and bound by CPI Group (UK) Ltd, Croydon, CR0 4YY

The Orion Publishing Group's policy is to use papers that are natural, renewable and recyclable products and made from wood grown in sustainable forests. The logging and manufacturing processes are expected to conform to the environmental regulations of the country of origin.

www.orionbooks.co.uk

For the British Interplanetary Society

PART ONE

# FIRST CONTACTS

## CHAPTER 1

# BISESA

*February 2069*

It wasn't like waking. It was a sudden emergence, a clash of cymbals. Her eyes gaped wide open, and were filled with dazzling light. She dragged deep breaths into her lungs, and gasped with the shock of selfhood.

Shock, yes. She shouldn't be conscious. Something was wrong.

A pale shape swam in the air.

'Dr Heyer?'

'No. No, Mum, it's me.'

That face came into focus a little more, and there was her daughter, that strong face, those clear blue eyes, those slightly heavy dark brows. There was something on her cheek, though, some kind of symbol. A tattoo?

'Myra?' She found her throat scratchy, her voice a husk. She had a dim sense, now, of lying on her back, of a room around her, of equipment and people just out of her field of view. 'What went wrong?'

'Wrong?'

'Why wasn't I put into estivation?'

Myra hesitated. 'Mum – what date do you think it is?'

'2050. June fifth.'

'No. It's 2069, Mum. February. Nineteen years later. The hibernation worked.' Now Bisesa saw strands of grey in Myra's dark hair, wrinkles gathering around those sharp eyes. Myra said, 'As you can see I took the long way round.'

It must be true. Bisesa had taken another vast, unlikely step on her personal odyssey through time. 'Oh, my.'

Another face loomed over Bisesa.

'Dr Heyer?'

'No. Dr Heyer has long retired. My name is Dr Stanton. We're going to begin the full resanguination now. I'm afraid it's going to hurt.'

Bisesa tried to lick her lips. 'Why am I awake?' she asked, and she immediately answered her own question. 'Oh. *The Firstborn.*' What could it be but them? 'A new threat.'

Myra's face crumpled with hurt. 'You've been away for nineteen years. The first thing you ask about is the Firstborn. I'll come see you when you're fully revived.'

'Myra, wait—'

But Myra had gone.

The new doctor was right. It hurt. But Bisesa had once been a soldier in the British Army. She forced herself not to cry out.

## CHAPTER 2
# DEEP SPACE MONITOR

*June 2064*

Mankind's first clear look at the new threat had come five years earlier. And the eyes that saw the anomaly were electronic, not human.

*Deep Space Monitor X7-6102-016* swam through the shadow of Saturn, where moons hung like lanterns. Saturn's rings were a ghost of what they had been before the sunstorm, but as the probe climbed the distant sun set behind the rings, turning them into a bridge of silver that spanned the sky.

The *Deep Space Monitor* was not capable of awe, not quite. But like any sufficiently advanced machine it was sentient to some degree, and its electronic soul tingled with wonder at the orderly marvels of gas and ice through which it sailed. But it made no effort to explore them.

Silently, the probe approached the next target on its orbital loop.

Titan, Saturn's largest moon, was a featureless ball of ochre, dimly lit by the remote sun. But its deep layers of cloud and haze hid miracles. As it approached the moon, *DSM X7-6102-016* cautiously listened to the electronic chatter of a swarm of robot explorers.

Under a murky orange sky, beetle-like rovers crawled over dunes of basalt-hard ice-crystal 'sand,' skirted methane geysers, crept cautiously into valleys carved by rivers of ethane, and dug into a surface made slushy by a constant, global drizzle of methane. One brave balloon explorer, buoyed by the thick air, hovered over a cryovolcano spilling a lava of ammonium-laced water. Burrowing submersibles studied pockets of liquid water just under the ice surface, frozen-over lakes preserved in impact craters. There were complex organic products everywhere, created by electrical storms in Titan's atmosphere, and by the battering of the upper air by sunlight and Saturn's magnetic field.

Everywhere the probes looked, they found life. Some of this was Earthlike, anaerobic methane-loving bugs sluggishly building pillows and mounds in the cold brine of the crater lakes. A more exotic sort of carbon-based life-form, using ammonia rather than water, could be found swimming in the stuff bubbling out of the cryovolcanoes. Most exotic of all was a community of slimelike organisms that used silicon compounds as their basic building blocks, not carbon; they lived in the piercing cold of the black, mirror-flat ethane lakes.

The crater-lake bugs were cousins of Earth's great families of life. The ammonia fish seemed to be indigenous to Titan. The cold-loving ethane slime might have come from the moons of Neptune, or beyond. The solar system was full of life – life that blew everywhere, in rocks and lumps of ice detached by impacts. Even so Titan was extraordinary, a junction for life-forms from across the solar system, and maybe even from without.

But *Deep Space Monitor X7-6102-016* had not come to Titan for science. As it passed through its closest approach to the moon and its carnival of life, its robot cousins did not even know it was there.

The *Deep Space Monitor*'s complex heart was a space probe built to a century-old design philosophy, with an angular frame from which sprouted booms holding sensor pods and radiothermal-isotope power units. But this inner core was surrounded by a rigid shell of 'metamaterial,' a mesh of nanotechnological washers and wires that shepherded rays of sunlight away from the probe and sent them on their way along paths they would have taken had the probe not been present at all. The *Deep Space Monitor* was not blind; the shell sampled the incoming rays. But with light neither reflected nor deflected, it was rendered quite invisible. Similarly it was undetectable on any wavelength of radiation from hard gamma rays to long radio waves.

*DSM X7-6102-016* was not an explorer. Shrouded, silent, it was a sentry. And now it was heading for an encounter of the sort for which it had been designed.

As it skimmed over the cloud tops of Titan, the moon's gravity field slingshot *X7-6102-016* onto a new trajectory that would take it out of the plane of the Saturn system, high above the rings. All this in radio silence, without a puff of rocket exhaust.

And *DSM X7-6102-016* approached the anomaly.

It detected cascades of exotic high-energy particles. And it was brushed by a powerful magnetic field, a ferocious electromagnetic knot in space. It reported to Earth, sending a stream of highly compressed data using sporadic laser bursts.

The *Deep Space Monitor* had no means of adjusting its course without compromising its shroud, and so it sailed on helplessly. It should have missed the anomaly by perhaps half a kilometre.

Its last observation, in a sense its last conscious thought, was of a sudden twisting of the anomaly's strong magnetic field.

*DSM X7-6102-016*'s final signals showed it receding at enormous, impossible speeds. They were signals the probe's makers could neither believe nor understand.

Like any sufficiently advanced machine the anomaly was sentient to some degree. The destruction it had been designed to inflict was for the future, and did not yet trouble it. But it was touched by a hint of regret at the smashing of the puppyish machine that had followed it so far, with its laughable attempt at concealment.

Alone, the anomaly sailed through Saturn's system, harvested momentum and kinetic energy from the giant planet, and flung itself toward the distant sun, and the warm worlds that huddled around it.

## CHAPTER 3

# ABDIKADIR

*2068 (Earth); Year 31 (Mir)*

On Mir the first hint of the coming strangeness would have been mundane, if not for its utter incongruity.

Abdikadir was irritated when the clerk called him away from the telescope. It was a clear night, for once. The first-generation refugees from Earth always complained about the cloudiness of Mir, this stitched-together world in its own stitched-together cosmos. But tonight the seeing was fine, and Mars swam high in the cloudless sky, a brilliant blue.

Before the clerk's interruption the observatory on the roof of the Temple of Marduk was a scene of silent industry. The main instrument was a reflector, its great mirror ground by Mongol slaves under the command of a Greek scholar of the School of Othic. It returned a fine if wavering image of the face of Mars. As Abdi observed, his clerks turned the levers that swung the telescope mount around to counterbalance the rotation of the world, thus keeping Mars steadily in the centre of Abdi's field of view. He sketched hastily at the pad strapped to his knee; industry in Alexander's world-empire had not yet advanced to the point where photography was possible.

Of Mars, he could clearly see the polar caps, the blue seas, the ochre deserts crisscrossed by bands of green-brown and blue, and even a glimmer of light from the alien cities that were believed to nestle in the dead caldera of Mons Olympus.

It was while he was engaged on his labour, intent on exploiting every second of the seeing, that the clerk came to Abdi. Spiros was fourteen, an Othic student, third-generation

Mir-born. He was a bright, imaginative boy but prone to nervousness, and now he could barely stammer out his news to an astronomer not a decade older than he was.

'Calm down, boy. Take a breath. Tell me what's wrong.'

'The chamber of Marduk—' The very heart of the temple on whose roof they both stood. 'You must come, Master!'

'Why? What will I see?'

'Not see, Master Abdi – *hear.*'

Abdi glanced once more at his eyepiece, where even now Mars's blue light glimmered. But the boy's agitation was convincing. *Something* was wrong.

With ill grace he clambered down from his seat at the eyepiece, and snapped at one of his students. 'You, Xenia! Take over. I don't want to waste a second of this seeing.' The girl hurried to comply.

Spiros ran for the ladder.

'This had better be worth it,' Abdi said, hurrying after the boy.

They had to descend, and then climb back up inside the temple's carcass, for the chamber of the great god Marduk was near the very apex of the complex. They passed through a bewildering variety of rooms lit by oil lamps burning smokily in alcoves. Long after the temple's abandonment by its priests there was still a powerful smell of incense.

Abdi walked into Marduk's chamber, peering around.

Once this room had contained a great golden statue of the god. During the Discontinuity, the event that created the world, the statue had been destroyed, and the walls had been reduced to bare brick, scorched by some intense heat. Only the statue's base remained, softened and rounded, with perhaps the faintest trace of two mighty feet. The chamber was a ruin, as if wrecked by an explosion. But it had been this way all Abdi's life.

Abdi turned on Spiros. 'Well? Where's the crisis?'

'Can't you hear?' the boy asked, breathless. And he stood still, his finger on his lips.

And then Abdi heard it, a soft chirruping almost like a

cricket – but too regular, too even. He glanced at the wide-eyed boy, who was frozen with fear.

Abdi stepped into the centre of the room. From here he could tell the chirruping was coming from an ornately carved shrine, fixed to one wall. He approached this now, and the sound grew louder.

For the sake of face before the boy, Abdi tried to keep his hand from trembling as he reached out to the small cupboard at the very centre of the shrine, and pulled open its door.

He knew what the shrine contained. This pebble-like artifact had come from the Earth to Mir. Belonging to a companion of Abdi's father's called Bisesa Dutt, it had been cherished for years, and then lodged here when its power finally failed.

It was a phone.

And it was ringing.

# PART 2

# JOURNEYS

## CHAPTER 4
# WHEN THE SLEEPER WAKES

*February–March 2069*

Bisesa was glad to get out of the sleep facility itself. It stank of the bad-egg hydrogen sulphide they used to stop your organs taking up oxygen.

In the hospital, it took the doctors three days to put her blood back into her veins, to persuade her organs to take up oxygen, and to get her through enough basic physiotherapy that she could walk with a Zimmer frame. She felt unutterably old, older than her forty-nine biological years, and she was wasted too, a famine victim. Her eyes were particularly prickly and sore. She suffered odd vision defects, even mild hallucinations at first. Also she had the unpleasant sense that she smelled of her own urine.

Well, for nineteen years she had had no pulse, no blood, no electrical activity in her brain, her tissues had consumed no oxygen, and she had been held in a fridge almost cold enough to rupture her cells. You had to expect to be a bit sore.

Hibernaculum 786 had changed while she had been in the tank. Now it felt like an upmarket hotel, all glass walls and white floors and plastic couches, and old, old people – at least they looked old – in dressing gowns, walking very tentatively.

Most drastically of all the Hibernaculum had been moved. When she got to a viewing window, she found herself overlooking an immense wound in the ground, a dusty canyon with strata piled up in its scree-littered walls like the pages of a tremendous book. It was the Grand Canyon, she learned, and it was a spectacular sight – rather wasted on the sleepers in the Hibernaculum, she thought.

She found it disturbing in retrospect that the complicated refrigerator within which she had slept her dreamless sleep had been disconnected, uprooted, and shipped across the continent.

As her convalescence continued she took to sitting before a bubble window, peering out at the canyon's static geological drama. She had made only one tourist-trip visit to the canyon before. Judging by the way the sun cycled through the spring sky she must be on the south rim, perhaps somewhere near Grand Canyon Village. The local flora and fauna seemed to have recovered from the global battering of the sunstorm; the land was littered with cacti, yucca, and blackbush. In her patient watching she spotted a small herd of bighorn sheep, and glimpsed the slinking form of a coyote, and once she thought she saw a rattlesnake.

But if the canyon had recovered, much else seemed to have changed. On the eastern horizon she made out a kind of structure, a flat metallic array raised on legs, like the framework of an uncompleted shopping mall. Sometimes she saw vehicles driving around and under it. She had no idea what it could be.

And sometimes in the sky she saw lights. There was one bright, moving spark, panning over the southern evening sky in forty minutes or so: something big in orbit. But there were odder sights to be seen, much more extensive: pale patches in the blue daylight, glimmerings of swimming starlight at night. A strange sky in this new age. She thought she ought to be curious, or possibly afraid, but at first she was not.

That all changed when she heard the roar. It was a deep rumble that seemed to make the very ground shudder, more geological than animal.

'What was *that*?'

'Bisesa? You asked a question?'

The voice was smooth, male, a little too perfect, and it came out of the air.

'Aristotle?' But she knew it could not be, even before he answered.

There was an odd delay before he replied. 'I'm afraid not. I am Thales.'

'Thales, of course.'

Before the sunstorm there had been three great artificial intelligences on the human worlds, remote descendants of the search engines and other intelligent software agents of earlier technological generations, and all of them friends of mankind. There were rumours that copies of them had been saved, as streams of bits squirted off into interstellar space. But otherwise only Thales had survived the sunstorm, stored in the simpler networks of the sturdy Moon.

'I'm glad to hear your voice again.'

Pause. 'And I yours, Bisesa.'

'Thales – why these response delays? Oh. Are you still lodged on the Moon?'

'Yes, Bisesa. And I am restricted by lightspeed delay. Just like Neil Armstrong.'

'Why not bring you down to Earth? Isn't it kind of inconvenient?'

'There are ways around it. Local agents can support me when time delay is critical – during medical procedures, for instance. But otherwise the situation is deemed satisfactory.'

These responses sounded rehearsed to Bisesa. Even scripted. There was more to Thales's location on the Moon than he was telling her. But she didn't have the spark to pursue the matter.

Thales said, 'You asked about the roar.'

'Yes. That sounded like a lion. An African lion.'

'So it was.'

'And what is an African lion doing *here,* in the heart of North America?'

'The Grand Canyon National Park is now a Jefferson, Bisesa.'

'A what?'

'A Jefferson Park. It is all part of the re-wilding. If you will look to your right . . .'

On the horizon, beyond the north rim, she saw blocky shapes, massive, like boulders on the move. Thales caused the window to magnify the image. She was looking at elephants, a herd of them complete with infants, an unmistakable profile.

'I have extensive information on the park.'

'I'm sure you have, Thales. One thing. What's the structure over there? It looks like scaffolding.'

It turned out to be a power mat, the ground station of an orbital power station, a collector for microwaves beamed down from the sky.

'The whole facility is rather large, ten kilometres square.'

'Is it safe? I saw vehicles driving around underneath it.'

'Oh, yes, safe for humans. Animals too. But there is an exclusion zone.'

'And, Thales, those lights in the sky – the shimmers—'

'Mirrors and sails. There is a whole architecture off Earth now, Bisesa. It's really quite spectacular.'

'So they're building the dream. Bud Tooke would have been pleased.'

'I'm afraid Colonel Tooke died in—'

'Never mind.'

'Bisesa, there are human counsellors you can speak to. About anything you like. The details of your hibernation, for instance.'

'It was explained to me before I went into the freezer …'

The Hibernacula were a product of the sunstorm. The first of them had been established in America before the event, as the rich sought to flee through the difficult years ahead to a time of recovery. Bisesa hadn't entered hers until 2050, eight years after the storm.

'I can talk you through the medical advances since your immersion,' Thales said. 'For example it now appears that your cells' propensity for hydrogen sulphide is a relic of a very early stage in the evolution of life on Earth, when aerobic cells still shared the world with methanogens.'

'That sounds oddly poetic.'

Thales said gently, 'There is the motivational aspect as well.'

She felt uncomfortable. 'What motivational aspect ...?'

She had had reasons to flee into the tanks. Myra, her twenty-one-year-old daughter, had married against Bisesa's advice, and pledged herself to a life off the Earth entirely. And Bisesa had wanted to escape the conspiracy-theory notoriety that had accrued about her because of her peculiar role in the sunstorm crisis, even though much of what had gone on in those days, even the true cause of the sunstorm, was supposed to have been classified.

'Anyhow,' she said, 'going into a Hibernaculum was a public service. So I was told when I signed over my money. My trust fund went to advance the understanding of techniques that will one day be used in everything from transplant organ preservation to crewing centuries-long starship flights. And in a world struggling to recover after the storm, I had a much lower economic footprint frozen in a tank—'

'Bisesa, there is a growing body of opinion that Hibernaculum sleeping is in fact a sort of sublimated suicide.'

That took her aback. Aristotle would have been more subtle, she thought. 'Thales,' she said firmly. 'When I need to speak to someone about this, it will be my daughter.'

'Of course, Bisesa. Is there anything else you need?'

She hesitated. 'How old am I?'

'Ah. Good question. You are a curiosity, Bisesa.'

'Thanks.'

'You were born in 2006, that is sixty-three years ago. One must subtract nineteen years for your time in the Hibernaculum.'

She said carefully, 'Which leaves forty-four.'

'Yet your biological age is forty-nine.'

'Yes. And the other five years?'

'Are the years you spent on Mir.'

She nodded. 'You know about that?'

'It is highly classified. Yes, I know.'

She lay back in her chair, watched the distant elephants and the shimmering sky of 2069, and tried to gather her thoughts.

'Thank you, Thales.'

'It's a pleasure.' When he fell silent there was a subtle absence in the air around her.

## CHAPTER 5
# LONDON

Bella Fingal was in the air above London when her daughter first brought her the bad news from the sky.

Bella had been flown in across the Atlantic, and her plane was heading for Heathrow, out in the suburbs to the west of central London. But the pilot told her the flight path would see them overfly to the east first and then come back west along the path of the Thames, into the headwinds, and on this bright March morning the city was a glittering carpet spread out for her. Bella had the plane all to herself, one of the new scramjets, a fancy chariot for a fifty-seven-year-old grandmother.

But she really didn't want to be making this trip. The funeral of James Duflot had been bad enough; coming to the grieving family's home would be worse. It was however her duty, as Chair of the World Space Council.

She had wandered into this job almost by accident, probably a compromise choice by the supra-governmental panel that controlled the Space Council. In a corner of her mind she had thought that her new post would be pretty much an honorary one, like most of the university chancellorships and nonexecutive directorships that had come her way as a veteran of the sunstorm. She hadn't imagined getting shipped across the planet to be plunged into messy, tearful situations like this.

She had done her bit on the shield. She should have stayed retired, she thought wistfully.

And it was when Edna came on line with her bit of bad, strange news that it was driven home to Bella that she really was the commander-in-chief of a space navy.

*

'For once the trackers think they've found something serious, Mum. Something out in the dark – now approaching the orbit of Jupiter, in fact, and falling in on a hyperbolic trajectory. It's not on the Extirpator map, though that's not so unusual; long-period comets too remote for Extirpator echoes are turning up all the time. This thing has other characteristics that are causing them concern ...'

Bella had seen a rendering of the 'Extirpator map,' set up like a planetarium inside her own base, the old NASA headquarters building in Washington. An immense, dynamic, three-dimensional snapshot of the whole of the solar system, it had been created on the very eve of the sunstorm by the deep-space explosion of a ferocious old nuke called the Extirpator – a detonation that had also broadcast to the silent stars a wistful concatenation of human culture called 'Earthmail,' within which were embedded copies of the planet's greatest artificial minds, called Aristotle, Thales, and Athena. Within a few hours of the explosion the radio telescopes on Earth had logged X-ray echoes of the blast coming back from every object larger than a metre across inside the orbit of Saturn.

Twenty-seven years after the sunstorm the human worlds and space itself were full of eyes, tracking anything that moved. Anything not shown in the map must be a new entrant. Most newcomers, human or natural, could be identified and eliminated quickly. And if not – well, then, Bella was learning, the bad news quickly filtered up the Council's hierarchy to her own ears.

In the cocooned, silent warmth of the plane cabin, she shivered. Like many of her generation, Bella still had nightmares about the sunstorm. Now it was Bella's job to listen to the bad dreams.

Edna's face, in the softscreen on the seat back before Bella, was flawlessly rendered in three dimensions. Edna was only twenty-three, one of the first generation of 'Spacers,' as Bella had learned to call them, born in space during Bella's post-sunstorm rehabilitation stay on the Moon. But Edna was already a captain. Promotions were fast in a navy with few crew in ships so smart, or so Edna said, they even had robots to swab the decks. Today, with her Irish-dark hair pulled severely back and her uniform buttoned up around her neck, Edna looked tense, her eyes shadowed.

Bella longed to touch her daughter. But she couldn't even speak to her in a natural way. Edna was out in the navy's operations HQ in the asteroid belt. The vagaries of orbits dictated that at this moment Edna was some two astronomical units away from her mother, twice Earth's distance to the sun, a tremendous gap that imposed an each-way time delay of sixteen minutes.

And besides there was a question of protocol. Bella was in fact her daughter's commanding officer. She tried to focus on what Edna was saying.

'This is just a heads-up, Mum,' Edna said now. 'I don't have any details. But the scuttlebutt is that Rear Admiral Paxton is flying to London to brief you about it . . .'

Bella flinched. Bob Paxton, heroic footprints-and-flags explorer of Mars, and a royal pain in the butt.

Edna smiled. 'Just remember, he's got a chest full of fruit salad, but you're the boss! By the way – Thea is doing fine.' Edna's daughter, Bella's three-year-old granddaughter, a second-generation Spacer. 'She'll be on her way home soon. But you should see how she's taken to microgravity in the low-spin habitats . . .!'

Edna spoke on of human things, family stuff, lesser events than the destiny of the solar system. Bella hung on every word, as a grandmother would. But it was all so strange, even to Bella, who had served in space herself. Edna's language was peppered with the unfamiliar. You found your way around a spinning space habitat by going *spinward* or *antispinward* or *axisward* . . . Even her accent was drifting, a bit of Bella's own Irish, and a heavy tinge of east coast American – the navy was essentially an offshoot of the old US seaborne navy, and had inherited much of its culture from that source.

Her daughter and granddaughter were growing away from her, Bella thought wistfully. But then, every grandmother back to Eve had probably felt the same.

A soft chime warned her that the plane was beginning its final approach. She stored the rest of Edna's message and transmitted a brief reply of her own.

The plane banked, and Bella peered down at the city.

She could clearly make out the tremendous footprint of the Dome. It was a near-perfect circle about nine kilometres in diameter, centred on Trafalgar Square. Within the circumference of the Dome much of the old building stock had been preserved from the sunstorm's ravages, and something of the character of the old confident London remained, a pale sheen of sandstone and marble. But Westminster was now an island, the Houses of Parliament abandoned as a monument. After the sunstorm the city had given up its attempts to control its river, and had drawn back to new banks that more resembled the wider, natural course that the Romans had first mapped. Londoners had adjusted; you could now go scuba diving among the concrete ruins of the South Bank.

Outside that perimeter circle, much of the suburban collar of London had been razed by the fires of sunstorm day. Now it was a carpet of blocky new buildings that looked like tank traps.

And as the plane dipped further she saw the Dome itself. The panelling had long been dismantled, but some of the great ribs and pillars had been allowed to stand; weather-streaked and tarnished they cast shadows kilometres long over the city the Dome had preserved. It was only a glimpse. And in a way it was mundane; twenty-seven years on, you still saw the scars of the sunstorm wherever you travelled, all over the world.

The city fled beneath her, and the plane swept down over anonymous, hunkered suburbs toward its landing at Heathrow.

## CHAPTER 6
# MYRA

Myra sat with Bisesa before the bubble window, sipping iced tea. It was early in the morning, and the low light seemed to catch the wrinkles in Myra's face.

'You're staring,' Myra said.

'I'm sorry, love. Can you blame me? For me, you've aged nineteen years in a week.'

'At least I'm still *younger* than you.' Myra sounded resentful; she had a right to be.

Myra was wearing a comfortable-looking blouse and pants of some smart material that looked as if it kept her cool. Her hair was swept back from her face, a style that was a bit severe to Bisesa's out-of-date eyes, but which suited Myra's bones, her fine forehead. She had no ring on her finger. Her movements were small, contained, almost formal, and she rarely looked at her mother.

She didn't look happy. She looked restless.

Bisesa didn't know what was wrong. 'I should have been here for you,' she said.

Myra looked up. 'Well, you weren't.'

'Right now, I don't even *know*—'

'You know I married Eugene, not long before you went into the tank.' Eugene Mangles, whiz-kid scientist, all but autistic, and after his heroic computations during the sunstorm the nearest thing to a saviour the world had recently seen. 'Everybody was marrying young in those days,' Myra said. The post-sunstorm years had been a time of a rapid population boom. 'We broke up after five years.'

'Well, I'm sorry. Has there been nobody else?'

'Not serious.'

'So where are you working now?'

'I went back to London, oh, ten years ago. I'm back in our old flat in Chelsea.'

'Under the skeleton of the Dome.'

'What's left of it. That old ruin is good for property prices, you know. Snob value, to be under the Dome. I guess we're rich, Mum. Whenever I'm short of money I just release a bit more equity; the prices are climbing so fast it soon gets wiped out.'

'So you're back in the city. Doing what?'

'I retrained as a social worker. I deal in PTSD.'

'Post-traumatic stress.'

'Mostly it's your generation, Mum. They'll carry the stress with them to their graves.'

'But they saved the world,' Bisesa said softly.

'They did that.'

'I never saw you as a social worker. You always wanted to be an astronaut!'

Myra scowled, as if she was being reminded of some indiscretion. 'I grew out of *that* when I found out what was really going on.'

Apparently unconsciously, she touched the tattoo on her cheek. It was in fact an ident tattoo, a compulsory registration introduced a few years after Bisesa went into the tank. Not a symptom of a notably free society.

'Wasn't Eugene working on weather modification systems?'

'Yes, he was. But he pretty quickly got sidelined into weaponisation. Weather modification as an instrument of political control. It's never been used, but it's there. We had long arguments about the morality of what he was doing. I never lost the argument, but I never won, either. Eugene just didn't get it.'

Bisesa sighed. 'I remember that about him.'

'In the end his work was more important than I was.'

Bisesa was profoundly sorry to see this disappointment in a daughter who, from her point of view, had been a bright twenty-one-year-old only weeks ago.

She looked out of her window. Something was moving

on the far side of the canyon. Camels, this time. 'Not everything about this new world seems so bad to me,' she said, trying to lighten the mood. 'I quite like the idea of camels and elephants wandering around North America – though I'm not quite sure why they're here.'

'We're in the middle of a Jefferson,' Myra said.

'Named for Jefferson the president?'

'I learned a lot more about the American presidents when I lived with Eugene's family in Massachusetts,' Myra said dryly. The purposeful re-wilding of the world was an impulse that had come out of the aftermath of the sunstorm. 'In fact Linda had something to do with devising the global programme. She wrote me about it.'

'My cousin Linda?'

'She's Dame Linda now.' A student of bioethics, Linda had shared a flat with Bisesa and Myra during the period before the sunstorm. 'The point is, long before Columbus the first Stone Age immigrants knocked over most of the large mammals. So you had an ecology that was full of gaps evolution hadn't had time to fill. "A concert in which so many parts are wanting." Thoreau said that, I think. Linda used to quote him. When the Spanish brought horses here, their population just exploded. Why? Because modern horses *evolved* here ...'

In the new 'Jefferson Parks' there had been a conscious effort to reconstruct the ecology as it had been at the end of the last Ice Age, by importing species that were close equivalents of those that had been lost.

Bisesa nodded. 'African and Asian elephants for mammoths and mastodons.'

'Camels for the extinct camelids. More species of horses to flesh out the diversity. Even zebras, I think. For the ground sloths they brought in rhinos, herbivores of a similar mass and diet.'

'And lions as the capstone, I suppose.'

'Yes. There are more parks overseas. In Britain, half of Scotland is being given over to native oak forest.'

Bisesa looked at the haughty camels. 'I suppose it's

therapeutic. But these are aftermath activities. Healing. I've woken up to find we still live in an aftermath world, after all this time.'

'Yes,' Myra said grimly. 'And not every post-sunstorm response is as positive as building a Pleistocene park.

'Mum, *people found out about the sunstorm.* The truth. At first it was classified. Even the name "Firstborn" was never made public. There was no hint at the time that the sunstorm was an intentional act.'

Caused by the driving of a Jovian planet into the core of Earth's sun.

'But the truth leaked out. Whistle-blowers. It became a torrent when the generation who had fought the storm headed for retirement, and had nothing to lose, and began to speak of what they knew.'

'I'm shocked there was a cover-up that lasted so long.'

'Even now there are plenty of people who don't believe it, I think. But people are *scared.* And there are those in government, and in industry and other establishments, who are using that fear. They are militarising the whole of the Earth, indeed the solar system. They call it the War with the Sky.'

Bisesa snorted. 'That's ridiculous. How can you wage war on an abstraction?'

'I suspect that's the point. It means whatever you want it to mean. And those who control the sky have a lot of power. Why do you think Thales is still stuck on the Moon?'

'Ah. Because nobody can get to him up there. And this is why you left?'

'Most of the gazillions they're spending are simply wasted. What's worse, they're not doing any serious research into what we do know of Firstborn technology. The Eyes. The manipulation of spacetime, the construction of pocket universes – all of that. Stuff that might actually be useful in the case of a renewed threat.'

'So that's why you bailed out.'

'Yes. I mean, it was fun, Mum. I got to go to the Moon! But I couldn't swallow the lies. There are plenty on and off the planet who think the way I do.'

'Off the planet?'

'Mum, since the sunstorm a whole generation has been born offworld. Spacers, they call themselves.' She glanced at her mother, then looked away. 'It was a Spacer who called me. And asked me to come fetch you.'

'Why?'

'Something's coming.'

Those simple words chilled Bisesa.

A shifting light caught her eye. Looking up she saw that bright satellite cutting across the sky. 'Myra – what's that? It looks sort of old-fashioned, in among the space mirrors.'

'It's *Apollo 9*. Or a recreation. That ship flew a hundred years ago today. The government is rerunning all those classic missions. A remembrance of the lost times before the sunstorm.'

Conservation and memorials. Clinging to the past. It really was as if the whole world was still in shock. 'All right. What do you want me to do?'

'If you're fit, get packed up. We're leaving.'

'Where are we going?'

Myra smiled, a bit forced. 'Off Earth ...'

## CHAPTER 7
# THE TOOKE MEDAL

The motorcade drew up outside a property in a suburb called Chiswick.

Bella stepped out of her car, along with her two Council bodyguards. They were a man and a woman, bulked up by body armour, like all their colleagues silent and anonymous. The woman carried a small package in a black leather case.

The car closed itself up.

Bella faced the Duflot home, gathering her courage. It was a faceless block of white concrete with rounded wind-deflecting corners, sunk into the ground as if it was too heavy for the London clay. Its roof was a garden of wind turbines, solar cell panels, and antennae; its windows were small and deep. With subterranean rooms and independent power it was a house like a bunker. This was the domestic architecture of the fearful mid–twenty-first century.

Bella had to walk down a flight of steps to the front door. A slim woman in a sharp black suit was waiting.

'Ms Duflot?'

'Dr Fingal. Thank you for coming. Call me Phillippa …' She extended a long-fingered hand.

Shadowed by her security people, Bella was brought through the house to the living room.

Phillippa Duflot must have been in her early sixties, a little older than Bella. Her silvered hair was cut short. Her face was not unattractive, but narrow, her mouth pursed. Phillippa looked capable of steely self-control, but this woman had lost a son, and the marks of that tragedy were in the lines around her eyes, Bella thought, and the tension in her neck.

Waiting for Bella in the living room were the generations

of Phillippa's family. They stood when Bella came into the room, lined up before a softwall showing an image of a pretty Scottish lake. Bella had carefully and nervously memorised all their names. Phillippa's two surviving sons, Paul and Julian, were solid, awkward-looking thirty-something men. Their wives stood by their sides. This slim, pretty woman of twenty-six was Cassie, the widow of the missing son James, and his two children, boy and girl, six and five, Toby and Candida. They were all dressed for a funeral, in black and white, even the children. And they all had ident tattoos on their cheeks. The little girl's was a pretty pink flower.

Standing before this group, under the stares of the children, Bella suddenly had no idea what to say.

Phillippa came to her rescue. 'It's most awfully good of you to come.' Her accent was authentic British upper class, a throwback to another age, rich with composure and command. Phillippa said to her grandchildren, 'Dr Fingal is the head of the Space Council. She's very important. And she flew from America, just to see us.'

'Well, that's true. And to give you this.' Bella nodded to her guards, and the woman handed her the leather case. Bella opened this carefully, and set it up on a low coffee table. A disc of delicate, sparkling fabric sat on a bed of black velvet.

The children were wide-eyed. The boy asked, 'Is it a medal?'

And Candida asked, 'Is it for Daddy?'

'Yes. It's for your father.' She pointed to the medal, but did not touch it; it looked like spiderweb embedded with tiny electronic components. 'Do you know what it's made of?'

'Space shield stuff,' Toby said promptly.

'Yes. The real thing. It's called the Tooke Medal. There's no higher honour you can earn, if you live and work in space, than this. I knew Bud Tooke. I worked with him, up on the shield. I know how much he would have admired your daddy. And it's not just a medal. Do you want to see what it can do?'

The boy was sceptical. 'What?'

She pointed. 'Just touch this stud and see.'

The boy obeyed.

A hologram shimmered into life over the tabletop, eclipsing the medal in its case. It showed a funeral scene, a flag-draped coffin on a caisson drawn by six tiny black horses. Figures in dark blue uniforms stood by. The sound was tinny but clear, and Bella could hear the creak of the horses' harnesses, their soft hoofbeats.

The silent children loomed like giants over the scene. Cassie was weeping silently; her brother comforted her. Phillippa Duflot watched, composed.

The recording skipped forward. Three rifle volleys cracked, and a flight of tiny, glittering jet aircraft swept overhead, one peeling away from the formation.

'It's Dad's funeral,' Toby said.

'Yes.' Bella leaned down to face the children. 'They buried him at Arlington. That's in Virginia – America – where the US Navy has its cemetery.'

'Dad trained in America.'

'That's right. I was there, at the funeral, and so was your mummy. This hologram is generated by the shield element itself— '

'Why did one plane fly away like that?'

'It's called the Missing Man formation. Those planes, you know, Toby. They were T-38s. The first astronauts used them to train on. They're over a hundred years old, imagine that.'

'I like the little horses,' said Candida.

Their uncle put his hands on their shoulders. 'Come away now.'

With some relief, Bella straightened up.

Drinks arrived, sherry, whiskey, coffee, tea, served by a subdued young aunt. Bella accepted a coffee and stood with Phillippa.

'It was kind of you to speak to them like that,' Phillippa said.

'It's my job, I guess,' Bella said, embarrassed.

'Yes, but there are ways of doing it well, or badly. You're new to it, aren't you?'

Bella smiled. 'Six months in. Does it show?'

'Not at all.'

'Deaths in space are rare.'

'Yes, thank God,' Phillippa said. 'But that's why it's been so hard to take. I had hoped this new generation would be protected from – well, from what we went through. I read about you. You were actually on the shield.'

Bella smiled. 'I was a lowly comms tech.'

Phillippa shook her head. 'Don't do yourself down. You ended up with a battlefield promotion to mission commander, didn't you?'

'Only because there was nobody else left to do it by the end of that day.'

'Even so, you did your job. You deserve the recognition you've enjoyed.'

Bella wasn't sure about that. Her subsequent career, as an executive in various telecommunications corporations and regulatory bodies, had no doubt been given a healthy boost by her notoriety, and usefulness as a PR tool. But she'd always tried to pull her weight, until her retirement, aged fifty-five – a short one as it turned out, until she was offered this new role, a position she couldn't turn down.

Phillippa said, 'As for me I was based in London during the build-up to the storm. Worked in the mayor's office, on emergency planning and the like. But before the storm itself broke, my parents took me out to the shelter at L2.'

The shield had been poised above the Earth at the point of perpetual noon, at L1, the first Lagrangian point of gravitational stability directly between Earth and sun. The Earth's second Lagrangian point was on the same Earth-sun line, but on the planet's far side, at the midnight point. So while the workers at L1 laboured to shelter the world from the storm, at L2 an offworld refuge hid safe in Earth's shadow, stuffed full of trillionaires, dictators, and other rich and powerful types – including, rumour had it, half of Britain's royals.

The story of L2 had subsequently become a scandal.

'It wasn't a pleasant place to be,' Phillippa murmured. 'I tried to work. We were ostensibly a monitoring station. I kept up the comms links to the ground stations. But some of the rich types were throwing parties.'

'It sounds as if you didn't have a choice,' Bella said. 'Don't blame yourself.'

'It's kind of you to say that. Still, one must move on.'

James Duflot's widow, Cassie, approached them tentatively. 'Thank you for coming,' she said awkwardly. She looked tired.

'You don't need—'

'You were kind to the children. You've given them a day to remember.' She smiled. 'They've seen your picture on the news. I think I'll put away that hologram, though.'

'Perhaps that's best.' Bella hesitated. 'I can't tell you much about what James was working on. But I want you to know that your husband gave his life in the best of causes.'

Cassie nodded. 'In a way I was prepared for this, you know. People ask me how it feels to have your husband fly into space. I tell them, you should try staying on Earth.'

Bella forced a smile.

'To tell you the truth we were going through a difficult time. We're Earth-bound, Dr Fingal. James just went up to space to work, not to live. This is home. London. And I went into town every day to work at Thule.' Bella had done her research; Thule, Inc, was a big multinational eco-recovery agency. 'We'd talked vaguely of separating for a bit.' Cassie laughed with faint bitterness. 'Well, I'll never know how that particular story would have turned out, will I?'

'I'm sorry—'

'You know what I miss? His mails. His softscreen calls. I didn't have *him,* you see, but I had the mails. And so in a way I don't miss him, but I miss the mails.' She looked sharply at Bella. 'It *was* worth it, wasn't it?'

Bella couldn't bear to repeat the platitudes she knew were expected of her. 'I'm new to this. But it's my job to make sure it was.'

That wasn't enough. Nothing ever could be. She was relieved when she was able to use the excuse of another appointment to get out of the pillboxlike house.

## CHAPTER 8

# EURO-NEEDLE

For her appointment with Bob Paxton, Bella was driven to the Livingstone Tower – or the 'Euro-needle' as every Londoner still called it. The local administrative headquarters of the Eurasian Union, and sometime seat of the Union's prime minister, it was a tower of airy offices with broad windows of toughened glass offering superb views of London. During the sunstorm the Needle had been within the Dome's shelter, and on its roof, which had interfaced with the Dome's structure itself, was a small museum to those perilous days.

Paxton was waiting for her in a conference room on the forty-first floor. Pacing, he was drinking coffee in great gulps. He greeted Bella with a stiff military bow. 'Chair Fingal.'

'Thanks for coming all the way to London to meet me—'

He waved that away. 'I had other business here. We need to talk.'

She took a seat. Still shaken by her encounter with the Duflots, she felt this was turning into a very long day.

Paxton didn't sit. He seemed too restless for that. He poured Bella a coffee from a big jug in the corner of the room; he poured for Bella's security people too, and they sat at the far end of the table.

'Tell me what's on your mind, Admiral.'

'I'll tell you simply. The new sightings confirm it. We have a bogey.'

'A bogey?'

'An anomaly. Something sailing through our solar system that doesn't belong there ...'

Paxton was tall, wiry. He had the face of an astronaut, she thought, very pale, and pocked by the scars of radiation tumours. His cheek tattoo was a proud wet-navy emblem, and his hair was a drizzle of crew-cut grey.

He was in his seventies, she supposed. He had been around forty when he had led *Aurora 1,* the first manned mission to Mars, and had become the first person to set foot on that world – and then he had led his stranded crew through the greater trial of the sunstorm. Evidently he had taken the experience personally. Now a Rear Admiral in the new space navy, he had become a power in the paranoiac post-sunstorm years, and had thrown himself into efforts to counter the threat that had once stranded him on Mars.

Watching him pace, caffeine-pumped, his face set and urgent, Bella had an absurd impulse to ask him for his autograph. And then a second impulse to order him to retire. She filed that reflection away.

In his clipped Midwestern accent, he amplified the hints Edna had already given her. 'We actually got three sightings of this thing.'

The first had been fortuitous.

*Voyager 1,* launched in 1977, having made mankind's first reconnaissance of the outer planets, had sped on out of the solar system. By the fifth decade of a new century *Voyager* had travelled more than a hundred and fifty times Earth's distance from the sun.

And then its onboard cosmic ray detector, designed to seek out particles from distant supernovae, picked up a wash of energetic particles.

Something had been born, out there in the dark.

'Nobody made much of it at the time. Because it showed up on April 20, 2042.' Paxton smiled. 'Sunstorm day. We were kind of busy with other things.'

*Voyager*'s later observations showed how the anomaly, tugged by the sun's gravity, began a long fall into the heart of the solar system. The first significant object the newborn would encounter on its way toward the sun would be Saturn and its system of moons, on a date in 2064. Plans were drawn up accordingly.

'And that was the second encounter,' Paxton said. 'We

have readings made by *Deep Space Monitor X7-6102-016* – and then a record of that probe's destruction. And third, the latest sighting by a cluster of probes of some damn thing coming down on the J-line. The orbit of Jupiter.' He brought up a softscreen map on the table. 'Three points on the chart, see – three points on a plausible orbital trajectory. Three sightings of what has to be the same object, wandering in where it don't belong.' He stared at her, his cold blue eyes rheumy but unblinking, as if challenging her to put it together.

'And you're certain it's not a comet, something natural?'

'Comets don't give off sprays of cosmic rays,' he said. 'And it's kind of a coincidence this thing just popped up out of nowhere on sunstorm day, don't you think?'

'And this trajectory, if it continues – where is it going, Admiral?'

'We can be pretty accurate about that. It deflected off Saturn, but it won't pass another mass significant enough for a slingshot. Assuming it just falls under gravity—'

She took the bait. 'It's heading for Earth, isn't it?'

His face was like granite. 'If it continues on its merry course it will get here December of next year. Maybe it's Santa's sleigh.'

She frowned. 'Twenty-one months. That's not much time.'

'That it ain't.'

'If the alert had been raised when this thing passed Saturn, and, you say, it actually destroyed a probe, we'd have had years warning.'

He shrugged. 'You have to set your threat levels somewhere. I always argued we weren't suspicious enough. I had this out with your predecessor on a number of occasions. Looks like I was right, don't it? If we survive this we can review protocol.'

*If we survive this*. His language chilled her. 'You think this is some kind of artifact, Admiral?'

'Couldn't say.'

'But you do believe it's a threat?'

'Have to assume so. Wouldn't you say?'

She could hardly gainsay that. The question was what to do about it.

The World Space Council had only a tenuous relationship with the old UN, which since the sunstorm had focused its efforts on recovery on Earth. The Council's brief was to co-ordinate the world's preparedness for any more threats from the unseen enemy behind the sunstorm, an enemy whose very existence had not in fact yet been officially admitted. Its principal asset was the navy, which nominally reported to the Council. But the Council itself was funded by and ultimately controlled by an uneasy alliance of the world's four great powers – especially the United States, Eurasia, and China, who hoped to use space to gain some political ground back from the fourth, Africa.

And at the apex of this rickety structure of power and control was Bella, a compromise candidate in a compromised position.

In the short term, she thought, the three spacegoing powers might try to leverage the sudden irruption of an actual threat into some kind of advantage over Africa, which had become prominent since being relatively spared by the sunstorm. The tectonic plates that underpinned the Council might start to shift, she thought uneasily, just at the very moment it was being called upon to act.

'You're thinking politics,' Paxton growled.

'Yes,' she admitted. As if this anomaly, whatever it was, was just a new item on the agenda of the world's business. But if this was another threat like the sunstorm, it could render all that business irrelevant at a stroke.

Suddenly she felt weary. Old, worn-out. She found she resented that this crisis should be landed on her plate so soon into her chairmanship.

And, looking at Paxton's intent face, she wondered how much control she would have over events.

'All right, Admiral, you have my attention. What do you recommend?'

*

He stepped back. 'I'll gather more data, and set up a briefing on options. Best to do that back in Washington, I guess. Soon as we can manage.'

'All right. But we'll have to look at the wider implications. What to tell the people, or not. How to prepare for the incoming anomaly, whatever it is.'

'We'll need more data before we can do that.'

'And what do we tell those we report to?'

Paxton said, 'As far as the politics go it's essential we make sure our mandate and capability aren't diluted by politico bull. And, Chair, if you're agreeable, for the briefing I'll incorporate material gathered by the Committee.'

She felt the hairs on her neck prickle a warning; after most of a lifetime at the upper levels of large organisations she knew when a trap was being set. 'You mean your Committee of Patriots.'

He smiled, sharklike. 'You should come visit us sometime, Madam Chair. We work out of the old Navy Special Projects Office in DC; a lot of us are old navy fliers of one stripe or another. Our mission, grant you it's self-appointed, is to monitor the responses of our governments and supergovernment agencies to the alien intervention that led to the sunstorm, and the ongoing emergency since. Once again your predecessor didn't want to know about this. I believe he thought dabbling with the wacko fringe would damage his fine career. But now we really do have something out there, Madam Chair, a genuine anomaly. Now's the time to listen to us, if you're ever going to.'

Again it was hard to gainsay that. 'I feel you're drawing me into an argument, Bob. Okay, subject to my veto.'

'Thank you. There's one specific.'

'Go on.'

'One beef the Committee has always had has been with the almost wilful way the authorities have never followed up the hints of the *alien.* Developing our own weaponry and armour is one thing, but to ignore the enemy's capability is criminal. However we do know of someone who might be our way in to that whole murky business.'

'Who?'

'A woman called Bisesa Dutt. Ex British Army. Long story. She's the reason why I came to London today; she has a base here. But she's not around, or her daughter. Since arriving here I got word she may have booked herself into a Hibernaculum in the States, under an assumed name. Of course she may have moved on from there by now.' He eyed Bella. 'With your permission I'll track her down.'

She took a breath. 'I have the authority for that?'

'If you want it.' He left it hanging.

'All right. Find her. Send me your file on her. But stay legal, Admiral. And be nice.'

He grinned. 'All part of the service.'

Paxton was *happy*, she saw suddenly. He had been waiting for this moment, waiting out the whole of his anticlimactic life since his heroic days on Mars during the sunstorm. Waiting for the sky to fall again.

Bella suppressed a shudder. As for herself, she only hoped she could avoid creating any more James Duflots.

# CHAPTER 9
# FLORIDA

Myra got Bisesa out of the Hibernaculum and took her to Florida.

They flew in a fat-bodied, stub-winged plane. It was driven by a kind of air-breathing rocket called a scramjet. Bisesa still felt frail, but she used to ride helicopters in the army, and she studied this new generation of craft – new to a sleeper like her, anyhow – with curiosity. A jaunt across the continent, from Arizona to Florida, was nothing; this sturdy vessel really came into its own on very long-haul flights when it had the chance to leap up out of the atmosphere altogether, like a metallic salmon.

But the security was ferocious. They even had to submit to searches and scans *in flight.* This paranoia was a legacy not just of the sunstorm but of incidents when planes and spaceplanes had been used as missiles, including the destruction of Rome a couple of years before the storm.

Security was in fact an issue from the beginning. Bisesa had come out of her Hibernaculum pod without the latest ident tattoos. There was an office of the FBI maintained on site at the Hibernaculum to process patients like her, refugees from slightly more innocent days – and to make sure no fugitives from justice had tried to flee through time. But Myra had come to Bisesa's room with a boxy piece of equipment that stamped a tattoo onto Bisesa's face, and she gave her an injection she described as 'gene therapy.' Then they had slipped out of the Hibernaculum through a goods entrance without going anywhere near that FBI office.

Since then they had passed every check.

Bisesa felt faintly disturbed. Whoever Myra had hooked up with evidently had significant resources. But she trusted

Myra implicitly, even though this was a strange new Myra, suddenly aged and embittered, a new person with whom she was, tentatively, building a new relationship. Really, she had no choice.

They deplaned at Orlando and spent a night at a cheap tourist hotel downtown.

Bisesa was faintly surprised that people still shuttled around the world to destinations like this. Myra said it was mostly nostalgic. The latest virtual reality systems, by interfacing directly with the central nervous system, were capable even of simulating the sensation of motion, acceleration. You could ride a roller coaster around the moons of Jupiter, if you wanted. What theme park could compete with that? When the last of the pre-sunstorm generations gave up chasing their childhood dreams and died off, it seemed likely that most people would rarely venture far from the safety of their bunker-like homes.

They ate room service food and drank minibar wine, and slept badly.

The next morning, a driverless car was waiting outside the hotel for them. It was of an odd, chunky design that Bisesa didn't recognise.

Cocooned, they were driven off at what felt like a terrific speed to Bisesa, with the traffic a hairsbreadth close. She wasn't sorry when the windows silvered over, and she and Myra sat in a humming near-silence, with only the faintest of surges to tell them that they were speeding out of the city.

When they drew to a halt the doors slid back, allowing bright sunlight to flood into the car, and Bisesa heard the cries of gulls, and smelled the unmistakable tang of salt.

'Come on.' Myra clambered out of the car, and helped her mother follow stiffly.

It was March, but even so the heat hammered down on Bisesa. They were on a stretch of tarmac – not a road or a parking lot, it looked more like a runway, stretching off into the distance, lined with blockhouses. On the horizon she saw gantries, some of them orange with rust, so remote they were misted with distance. To the north – it had to be that way, judging from the wind blowing off the sea – she saw something glimmering, a kind of line scratched onto the sky, tilted a little away from the vertical. Hard to see, elusive, perhaps it was some kind of contrail.

There couldn't be any doubt where she was. 'Cape Canaveral, right?'

Myra grinned. 'Where else? Remember you brought me here on a tourist trip when I was six?'

'I expect it's changed a bit since then. This is turning into quite a ride, Myra.'

'Then welcome back to Canaveral.' A young man approached them; a smart suitcase trundled after him. Ident-tattooed, he was sweating inside a padded orange jumpsuit plastered with NASA logos.

'What are you, a tourist guide?'

'Hi, Alexei,' Myra said. 'Don't mind my mother. After nineteen years she got out of bed on the wrong side.'

He stuck out his hand. 'Alexei Carel. Good to meet you, Ms Dutt. I suppose I am your guide for the day – sort of.'

Twenty-five or twenty-six, he was a good-looking boy, Bisesa thought, with an open face under a scalp that was shaven close, though black hair sprouted thickly, like a five o'clock shadow. He looked oddly uncomfortable, though, as if he wasn't used to being outdoors. Bisesa felt like an ambassador from the past, and wanted to make a good impression on this sunstorm boomer. She gripped his warm hand. 'Call me Bisesa.'

'We don't have much time.' He snapped his fingers and the suitcase opened. It contained two more orange suits, neatly folded, and more gear: blankets, water bottles, packets of dried food, what might have been an assembly-kit chemical toilet, a water purifying kit, oxygen masks.

Bisesa looked at this junk with apprehension. 'It's like the gear we used to take on field hikes in Afghanistan. We're taking a ride, are we?'

'That we are.' Alexei hauled the jumpsuits out of the

suitcase. 'Put these on, please. This corner of the facility is low on surveillance, but the sooner we're in camouflage the better.'

'Right here?'

'Come on, Mum.' Myra was already unzipping her blouse.

The jumpsuit was easy to put on; it seemed to wriggle into place, and Bisesa wondered if it had some limited smartness of its own. Alexei handed her boots, and she found gloves and a kind of balaclava helmet in a pocket.

In the Florida sun, once she was zipped up she was hot. But evidently she was headed somewhere much colder.

Myra bundled their clothes into a smaller pack she took from the car, which also contained their spare underwear and toiletries. She threw the pack into the suitcase, which folded closed. Then she patted the car. Empty, it closed itself up and rolled away.

Alexei grinned. 'All set?'

'As we'll ever be,' Myra said.

Alexei snapped his fingers again. The tarmac under Bisesa's feet shuddered.

And a great slab of it dropped precipitately, taking the three of them and the suitcase down into darkness. A metal lid closed over them with a clang.

'Shit,' Bisesa said.

'Sorry,' Alexei said. 'Meant for cargo, not people.'

Fluorescents lit up, revealing a concrete corridor.

## CHAPTER 10
# LAUNCH COMPLEX 39

Alexei led them to an open-topped vehicle a little like a golf cart.

They clambered aboard. Bisesa felt bulky and clumsy, moving in her jumpsuit. Even the suitcase was more graceful than she was.

The cart moved off smoothly down the tunnel. It was long and crudely cut, and it stretched off into a darkness dimly lit by widely spaced fluorescent tubes. There was a musty smell, but at least it was a little cooler down here.

'This is kind of a cargo conduit,' Alexei said. 'Not meant for passengers.'

'But it's away from prying eyes,' Bisesa said.

'You got it. It's a couple of klicks but we'll be there in no time.'

His accent was basically American, Bisesa thought, but with an odd tang of French, long vowels and rolled r's. 'Where are we going?'

'You've slept through the rebuilding, haven't you? We're heading for LC-39.'

Faint memories stirred in Bisesa's head. 'Launch Complex 39. Where they launched the *Apollo*s from.'

'And later the space shuttles, yeah.'

'Now it's used for something else entirely,' Myra said. 'You'll see.'

'Of course it had to be LC-39 they used,' Alexei said. 'As indeed it had to be Canaveral. I mean, it's not an unsuitable site, especially now they have the hurricanes licked. There are better locations, closer to the equator, but no, it had to be here. The irony is that to launch the new *Saturn*s that are taking the *Apollo* retreads into orbit, they had to build a new pad altogether.'

Bisesa still didn't know what they were talking about. They used the pad for *what*? 'Carel – how do I know that name?'

'You may have met my father. Bill Carel? He worked with Professor Siobhan McGorran.'

It was a long time since Bisesa had heard that name. Siobhan had been Britain's Astronomer Royal at the time of the sunstorm, and had ended up playing a significant role in mankind's response to the crisis – and in Bisesa's own destiny.

'My father was with her as a graduate student. They worked together on quintessence studies.'

'On what? ... Never mind.'

'That was before the sunstorm. Now Dad's a full professor himself.' The cart slowed. 'Here we go.' He hopped nimbly off the cart before it had stopped. The women and the suitcase followed a bit more cautiously.

They gathered on a block of tarmac. A lid opened above them with a metallic snap, revealing a slab of blue sky.

Alexei said, 'We shouldn't be challenged aboveground. If we are, let me do the talking. Hold tight, now.' He snapped his fingers.

The tarmac block became an elevator that surged upward with a violence that made Bisesa stagger.

They emerged into sunlight. Alexei had seemed more comfortable underground; now he flinched from the open sky.

Bisesa glanced around, trying to get her bearings. They were at the focus of roads that snaked out over the flat coastal plain of Canaveral, crammed with streams of vehicles, mostly trucks. There was even a kind of monorail system along which a train of podlike compartments zipped, glistening and futuristic. All this traffic poured into this place.

And before her was a vast rusting slab, a platform that reminded her oddly of an oil rig, but stranded on the land, and mounted on tremendous caterpillar tracks. The crude metal shell of the thing was stamped with logos: mostly 'Skylift Consortium,' a name that rang faint bells. Close by stood more strange assemblies, squat tubes that stood erect in mobile stands, like cannon pointing up at the pale blue sky.

'This platform looks for all the world like one of those old crawlers they used to use to haul the *Saturns* and the shuttles out to the pad.'

'That's exactly what it is,' Alexei said. 'A mobile launch platform, reused.'

'And what are those cannon? Weapons?'

'No,' Alexei said. 'They're the power supply.'

'For what?'

Myra said gently, 'Things have changed, Mum. Look up.'

Mounted on top of the big crawler was what looked like a minor industrial facility, where unlikely-looking machines rolled around in a kind of choreography. They seemed to be trucks, basically, but with solar-cell wings on their flanks, and on their roofs were pulleylike mechanisms that made them look like stranded cable-cars. Their hulls were all stamped with the Skylift logo.

These peculiar engines were lining up before a kind of ribbon, shining silver, looking no wider than Bisesa's hand, that rose up from the platform. Each truck in turn approached the ribbon, dipped its pulley spindle, clung to the ribbon, and then hauled itself off the ground, rising rapidly.

Bisesa stepped back and lifted her face, trying to see where the ribbon went. It rose on up; Bisesa could see the trucks climbing it like beads on a necklace. The ribbon arced upward, narrowing with perspective, becoming a shining thread tilted slightly from the vertical, a scratch ruled across the sky. She tipped her head back higher, looking for whatever was holding the ribbon up –

Nothing was holding it up.

'I don't believe it,' she said. 'A space elevator.'

Alexei seemed interested in her reaction. 'We call it Jacob's Ladder. In 2069, it's an everyday miracle, Bisesa. Welcome to the future. Come on, time to find our ride. Are you up to a little climbing?'

*

They had to scramble up rusty rungs, fixed to the side of the mobile platform. Bisesa struggled, Hibernaculum-enfeebled, encased in her suit. The others took care of her, Alexei going ahead, Myra following.

Once on the upper surface of the platform they gave her a few seconds to catch her breath. The trucks rolled to and fro in their orderly way, their motors whirring gently.

Embarrassed, she tried to say something intelligent. 'Why use a crawler?'

Alexei said, 'It's best to keep the base of your elevator mobile. Most of them are based on facilities at sea, actually – reused oil rigs and the like – including Bandara, the first.'

'Bandara?'

'The Aussie elevator, off Perth. They call it Bandara now. Named for an Aboriginal legend of a world tree.'

'Why do you need to move your base? In case a hurricane comes?'

'Well, yes, though as I said they've got hurricanes pretty much licked these days.' He glanced at the sky. 'But further up there are other hazards. Relic satellites in low Earth orbit. Even NEOs. Near–Earth objects. Asteroids. This thing goes a *long* way up, Bisesa, and has to deal with a lot of perils along the way. Are you ready to move on?'

He brought them to one of the trucks. He called it a 'spider.' It had solar-cell wings folded up against its flanks, and that complicated pulley mechanism on its roof. Its transparent hull was loaded up with some kind of cargo, palettes and boxes. The spider was actually moving, though slower than walking pace, rolling in a line of others identical save for registration numbers stamped on its hull – the spiders were making for the thread in a kind of complicated spiral queuing system, Bisesa saw.

Alexei walked alongside the spider. He dug a plastic disc the size of a hockey puck out of his pocket, and slapped it to the spider's hull. 'Just give it a moment to break through the protocols and establish its interface—' He briskly leapt up onto the spider's roof, and stuck another hockey puck to the pulley mechanism up there. By the time he was down on the ground again a transparent door had slid back, and he grinned. 'We're in. Myra, can you give me a hand?' He jumped easily inside the hull, and began to bundle the cargo carelessly out of the door. Myra helped by shoving it aside.

'Just so I'm clear,' Bisesa said uncertainly, 'we shouldn't be doing this, should we? In fact we're stowing away in a cargo truck.'

'It's human-rated,' Alexei said confidently. 'Pressurised. Good radiation shielding, and we'll need it; we'll be spending rather a long time in the van Allen belts. We'll be fine with the gear I brought along. It was thought best to get you off the planet as fast as possible, Bisesa.'

'Why? Myra, are you on the run? Am I?'

'Sort of,' Myra said.

Alexei said, 'Let's move it. We're nearly at the ribbon.'

Once the cargo was cleared, Alexei summoned his suitcase. It extended little hydraulic legs to jump without difficulty into the spider's hull. Myra followed, and then only Bisesa was walking alongside the trundling spider.

Mura held out her hand. 'Mum? Come on. It's an easy step.'

Bisesa looked around, beyond the jungle of spiders, to the blue sky of Canaveral, the distant gantries. She had an odd premonition that she might never come this way again. Might never set foot on *Earth* again. She took a deep breath; even among the scents of oil and electricity, she could smell the salt of the ocean.

Then she stepped deliberately off the crawler platform and into the hull, one step, two. Myra gave her a hug, welcoming her aboard.

The hull's interior was bare, but it was meant for at least occasional human use. There was a handrail at waist height, and little fold-down seats embedded in the walls. The view through the transparent hull was obscured by those big folded-away solar panel wings.

Alexei was all business. He spread a softscreen over the

inner hull, tapped it, and the door slid shut. 'Gotcha.' He took a deep breath. 'Canned air,' he said. 'Nothing like it.' He seemed relieved to be shut up in the pod.

Bisesa asked, 'You're a Spacer?'

'Not strictly. Born on Earth, but I've lived most of my life off the planet. I guess I'm used to environments you can control. Out there in the raw, it's a little – clamouring.' He reached up and peeled his tattoo off his face.

Bisesa touched her cheek, and found her own tattoo came away like a layer of wax. She tucked it in a pocket of her suit.

Alexei advised them to sit down. Bisesa pulled down a seat, and found a narrow pull-out plastic belt that she clipped around her waist. Myra followed suit, looking apprehensive.

The spiders before them in the line were clearing away now, revealing the ribbon, a vertical line of silver, dead straight.

Alexei said, 'What's going to happen is that our spider will grab onto the ribbon with the roller assembly above our heads. Okay? As soon as it has traction it will start to climb. You'll feel some acceleration.'

'How much?' Bisesa asked.

'Only half a G or so. And only for about ten seconds. After that, once we hit our top speed, we'll climb smoothly.'

'And what's the top speed?'

'Oh, two hundred klicks an hour. The ribbon's actually rated for twice that. I've disabled the speed inhibitor, if we need it.'

'Let's hope that's not necessary,' Bisesa said dryly.

Myra reached over and slipped her hand into her mother's. 'Do you remember how we went to see the opening of the Aussievator? It was just after the sunstorm. I was eighteen, I think. That was where I got to know Eugene again. Now there are elevators all over the world.'

'It was quite a day. And so is this.'

Myra squeezed her hand. 'Glad I woke you up yet?'

'I'm reserving judgement.' But her grin was fierce. Who could resist this?

Alexei watched this interplay uncertainly.

They were rolling toward the ribbon. Over their heads, with a clumsy clunk, the pulley assembly unfolded itself. The ribbon really was narrow, no more than four or five centimetres across. It seemed impossible that it could support the weight of this car, let alone hundreds – thousands? – of others. But the spider trundled forward without hesitation.

The roller assembly tipped up, closed itself up around the ribbon, and, with a surge like a punch in the belly, the spider leapt skyward.

## CHAPTER 11

# RIBBON

In that first moment they left the spider farm behind, and were up and out in the bright sunlight. Glancing up, Bisesa saw the ribbon arrowing off into invisibility in a cloudless sky, with the bright pearls of other spiders going ahead of her, up into the unknown.

And when she looked down, peering around the obstruction of the solar panels, she saw the world falling away from her, and a tremendous view of the Cape opening up. She shielded her eyes from the sun. There were the gantries and blockhouses, and the straight-line roads travelled by generations of astronauts. A spaceplane of some kind rested on a runway, a black-and-white moth. And a bit further on a white needle stood tall beside a rusted gantry. It had to be a *Saturn V,* perhaps bearing a recreation of *Apollo 10,* the next precursor of the century-old Moon landings. But she had already risen higher than the *Saturn*'s needle nose, already higher than the astronauts climbing their gantries to their Moon ships.

The ascent was rapid, and just kept going. Soon she seemed able to see down the beach for kilometres. Canaveral looked more water than land, a skim of earth on the silver hide of the great ocean that opened up to the east. And she saw cars and trucks parked up on the roads and beside the beach, with tiny American flags fluttering from their aerials.

'People still come to see,' Alexei said, grinning. 'Quite a spectacle when the *Saturn*s go up, I'm told. But the Ladder is more impressive, in its way—'

There was a jolt.

'Sorry about that,' Alexei said. 'End of the acceleration.'

He tapped his softscreen, and a simple display lit up, showing altitude, speed, air pressure, time. 'Three hundred metres high, speed maxed out, and from now on it's a smooth ride all the way up.'

The ground fell away, the historic clutter of Canaveral already diminishing to a map.

A minute into the journey, four kilometres high, and the world was starting to curve, the eastern ocean horizon an immense arc. And with a snap the big solar-cell wings folded down flat.

'I don't get it,' Bisesa said. 'This is for power? The solar cells seem to be on the underside.'

'That's the idea,' Alexei said. 'The spider's power comes from ground-based lasers.'

'You saw them, Mum,' Myra said.

'You leave your power supply on the ground. Okay. So how long is the ride?'

'To beyond geosynch? All the way out to our drop-off point? Around twelve days,' Alexei said.

'Twelve days in this box?' And Bisesa didn't like the sound of that phrase, *drop-off*.

'This is a *big* structure, Mum,' Myra said, but she was evidently a novice herself and didn't sound convinced.

A few more minutes and they were eight kilometres high, already higher than most aircraft would fly, and there was a clunk, the mildest of shudders. Over their heads the pulley mechanism alarmingly reconfigured itself, bringing a different set of wheels and tracks into play.

And then, suddenly, the ribbon itself changed, from a narrow strip the width of Bisesa's hand to a sheet as wide as an opened-out newspaper. It was sharply curved, she saw. Their spider now clung to one outer edge of the ribbon.

Alexei said, 'This is the standard width of the ribbon, most of the way to orbit. It's kept narrower in the lower atmosphere because of the threat regime down there. Of course most of the bad weather is kept away nowadays. The ribbon's worst problems actually come when they launch one of those *Saturns*; the whole damn earth shakes, and I can tell you there's a lot of grumbling about that.'

Ten kilometres, twelve, fifteen; the distance simply peeled away. Earth's curve became more pronounced, and the sky above Bisesa's head started to fade down to a deeper blue. She was above the bulk of the atmosphere already, she realised.

Another abrupt transition came when the ribbon turned gold: a plating to protect it from the corrosive effects of high-altitude atomic oxygen, Alexei said, ionised gas in Earth's wispy upper air.

And still they rose and rose.

'So let's get comfortable.' Alexei ordered his suitcase to open. 'The pressure will drop to its spaceside mix – low pressure, a third atmospheric, but high on oxygen. In the meantime I brought oxygen masks.' He showed them, and a rack of bottles. 'And it's going to get cold. Your jumpsuits ought to keep you warm. I have heated blankets too.' He rummaged about in his suitcase. 'We're going to be in here a while. I have fold-out camp beds and chairs. A bubble tent in case you don't want to sleep under the stars, so to speak. I have heaters for food and drink. We're going to have to recycle our water, I'm afraid, but I have a good treatment system.'

'No spacesuits,' Bisesa said.

'Shouldn't need them, unless anything goes wrong.'

'And if it does?'

He looked at her, as if assessing her nerve. 'Second worst case is, we get stuck on the cable. There are a whole slew of fail-safe mechanisms to save us until rescue comes, via another spider. Even if we were to lose pressure, we have survival bubbles. Hamster balls. Not comfortable, but practical.'

*Hamster balls?* Bisesa hoped fervently that it wouldn't come to that. 'And the worst case?'

'We become detached from the ribbon altogether. You understand that a certain point on the elevator is in geo-synch – geosynchronous orbit, turning around the Earth in exactly twenty-four hours. That's the only altitude that is actually in orbit, strictly speaking. Below that point we are moving too slowly for orbit, and above too fast.'

'So if the spider were to lose its grip—'

'Below geosynch, we fall back to Earth.' He rapped the transparent hull. 'Might not look like it, but it is designed to survive a low-speed reentry.'

'And *after* geosynch? We'd fall away from Earth, right?'

He winked. 'Actually that's the idea. Don't worry about it.' He held up a flask. 'Coffee, anybody?'

Myra grunted. 'Maybe we ought to get your fancy toilet set up first.'

'Good thinking.'

While they fiddled with the toilet, Bisesa gazed out of the window.

Riding silently into the sky, soon she was a hundred kilometres high, higher even than the old pioneering rocket planes, the *X-15*s, used to reach. The sky was already all but black above her, with a twinkling of stars right at the zenith, a point to which the ribbon, gold-bright in the sunlight, pointed like an arrow. Looking up that way she could see no sign of structures further up the ribbon, no sign of the counterweight mass that she knew had to be at the ribbon's end, nothing but the shining beads of more spiders clambering up this thread to the sky. She suspected she still had not grasped the scale of the elevator, not remotely.

By an hour and a half in, the fast pace of the events of the early moments of the climb was over. Somewhere above three hundred kilometres high, she could already see the horizon all the way around the face of the Earth, with the ribbon arrowing straight down to the familiar shapes of the American continents far beneath her. Though the stars would wheel around her during this extraordinary ascent, she realised, the Earth would stay locked in place below. It was as if she had been transported to a medieval universe, the cosmos of Dante, with a fixed Earth surrounded by spinning stars.

When she stood she felt oddly light on her feet. One of

Alexei's softscreen displays mapped the weakening of gravity as they clambered away from Earth's huge mass. It was already down several percent on its sea-level value.

The silent, straight-line ascent, the receding Earth, the shaft of ribbon-light that guided her, the subtle reduction of weight: it was a magical experience, utterly disconcerting, like an ascent into heaven.

Two hours after 'launch' the ribbon changed again, spreading out to a curved sheet twice the width of its standard size – still only about two metres across, and gently curved.

Bisesa asked, 'Why the extra thickness?'

'Space debris,' Alexei said. 'I mean, bits of old spacecraft. Lumps of frozen astronaut urine. That sort of stuff. Between five and seventeen hundred kilometres, we're at the critical risk altitude for that. So we have a bit of extra width to cope with any impact.'

'And if we are hit by something—'

'Anything so big it would slice the ribbon right through is tracked, and we just move the whole shebang out of the way using the crawler on the ground. Anything smaller will puncture the ribbon, but it's smart enough to mend itself. The only problem is if we're unlucky enough to be hit by something small coming sideways in, across the face of the ribbon.'

'Which is why the ribbon is curved,' Bisesa guessed.

'Yes. So it can't be cut through. Don't worry about it.'

Myra, peering up, said, 'I think I see another spider. On the other side of the ribbon from us. I think – oh, wow.'

The second spider came screaming down out of the sky, passing just half a metre away. They all flinched. Bisesa had a brief reminder of their huge speed.

'A builder,' Alexei said, a bit too quickly for his studied calm to be convincing. 'Travelling down the ribbon, weaving an extra couple of centimetres onto the edge.'

Bisesa asked, 'What's the substance of the ribbon?'

'Fullerenes. Carbon nanotubes. Little cylinders of carbon atoms, spun into a thread. Immensely strong. The whole ribbon is under tension; the Earth's spin is trying to fling the counterweight away, like a kid swinging a rock on a rope. No conventional substance would be strong enough. So the spiders go up and down, weaving on extra strips, and binding it all with adhesive tape.'

Mechanical spiders, endlessly weaving a web in the sky.

They rose largely in silence, for the others wouldn't talk.

'Come on. We're off the Earth. Now you can tell me what's going on. Why am I here, Myra?'

The others hesitated. Then Myra said, 'Mum, it's difficult. For one thing the whole world is listening in.'

'The hull is smart.' Alexei spun a finger. 'All 'round surveillance.'

'Oh.'

'And for another,' Myra said, 'you already *know*.'

Alexei said, 'Believe me, we'll have plenty of time to talk, Bisesa. Even when we get to the drop-off, it's only the start of the journey.'

'A journey to where? No, don't answer that.'

Myra said, 'I think you'll be surprised by the answer, Mum.'

Bisesa would have welcomed the chance to talk to Myra, not about high-security issues and the fate of the solar system, but simply of each other. Myra had told her hardly anything of her life since Bisesa had gone into the tank. But, it seemed, that wasn't going to happen. Myra seemed oddly inhibited. And now the presence of Alexei sharing this little capsule with them inhibited her even further.

Bisesa started to feel tired, her face and hands cold, her stomach warmed by coffee, her mind dulled by the relentless climb. She pulled on the hat and gloves she found in her pockets. She piled up blankets from the suitcase onto the floor, pulled one over herself, and lay down. There was no sound, no sense of motion; she might have been stationary, suspended above the slowly receding Earth. She gazed up at the ribbon, seeing how far she could follow its line.

There was another transition when the ribbon reverted from gold to its customary silver. And later the width narrowed. More than seventeen hundred kilometres high, eight hours since leaving Earth, they were higher than almost all mankind's satellites had ever flown.

Bisesa was vaguely, peripherally aware of all this. Mostly she dozed.

She was woken with a jolt, a brief surge of acceleration that pressed her down into her blankets.

She sat up. Alexei and Myra sat on their fold-down seats. Myra was wide-eyed, but Alexei seemed composed. Alexei's softscreen on the wall flashed red.

They were thirteen hours into the journey, more than twenty-six hundred kilometres up. When Bisesa moved she felt as if she was going to float into the air. Gravity was down to about half sea level. Earth seemed trivial, a ball dangling at the end of a silver rope.

Other spiders flashed past them, overtaken by their own rapid climb.

'We sped up, right? So what's wrong?'

'We're being pursued,' Alexei said. 'We had to expect it. I mean, they know we're in here.'

'Pursued?' Bisesa had a nasty vision of a missile clambering up from a derelict Canaveral launch pad. But that made no sense. 'They wouldn't risk damaging their ribbon.'

'You're right,' Alexei said. 'The ribbon is a lot more precious than we are. Likewise they won't want to spoil the flow of spiders. They could do that, block us off. But there is cargo worth billions being carried up this line.'

'Then what?'

'They have super-spiders. Capable of greater speeds. It would take a few days, but the super-spider would catch us up.'

Myra thought that over. 'How does it get past all the other spiders in the way?'

'The same way we do. The others just have to get out of the way. We're matching the super-spider's ascent rate, twice our nominal. In fact I slaved us to the super-spider, so we'll mirror its ascent. It can't possibly catch us. As soon as the ground authorities realise that, they'll give up.'

'Twice nominal. Is that safe?'

'These systems are human-rated; they have heavy safety margins built in.' But he didn't sound terribly sure.

It only took a few minutes for the softscreen to chime and glow green. Alexei smiled. 'They got the message. We can slow down. Hold onto something.'

Bisesa braced against a rail.

They decelerated for a disconcerting few seconds. Blankets floated up from the floor, and the chemical toilet whirred as suction pumps laboured to keep from spilling the contents into the air. Myra looked queasy, and Bisesa felt her stomach turn over. They were all relieved when gravity was restored.

But the screen flashed red again. 'Uh oh,' Alexei said.

Bisesa asked, 'What now?'

He worked his softscreen. 'We're not climbing as we should.'

'Some fault with the spider?'

'Not that. They are reeling in the ribbon.'

*'Reeling it in?'* Suddenly Bisesa saw the spider as a fish on the end of a monstrous angler's line.

'It's kind of drastic, but it can be done. The ribbon is pretty fine stuff.'

'So what do we do?'

'You might want to close your eyes. And hold onto something again.' He tapped his softscreen, and Bisesa had the impression that something detached itself from the hull.

She clamped her eyes shut.

There was a flash, visible even through her eyelids, and the cabin rocked subtly.

'A bomb,' Bisesa said. She felt almost disappointed. 'How crude. I think I expected better of you, Alexei.'

'It was just a warning shot, a micro fusion pulse. No harm done. But *very* visible from the ground.'

'You're signalling your intent to blow up the ribbon if they don't leave us alone.'

'It wouldn't be difficult. Kind of hard to protect a hundred thousand kilometres of paper-thin ribbon against deliberate sabotage . . .'

Bisesa asked, 'Wouldn't people get hurt?'

'Not in the way you're thinking, Mum,' Myra said. 'Isolationist terrorists attacked Modimo a few years back.'

'Modimo?'

Alexei said, 'The African Alliance elevator. Named for a Zimbabwean sky-god, I think. Nobody got hurt, and they wouldn't now. I'm making an economic threat.' But he glanced uncertainly at his softscreen.

Bisesa said sharply, 'And if they call your bluff? Will you go through with it?'

'Actually I don't think I would. But *they* can't afford to take the risk, can they?'

Bisesa said, 'They could just kill us. Turn off the power. The air recycling. We'd be helpless.'

'They could. But they won't,' Alexei said. 'They want to know what we know. Where we're going. So they'll be patient, and hope to get hold of us later.'

'I hope you're right.'

As if in response, the softscreen turned green again. Alexei's grin broadened. 'So much for that. Okay, who's for beans?'

## CHAPTER 12

# MOUNT WEATHER

Bella had expected Bob Paxton's briefing to take place in her offices in the old NASA headquarters building on E Street in Washington, a block of concrete and glass repaired and refurbished since weathering the sunstorm.

But Paxton met her outside the building. He stood by the open door of a limousine. 'Bella.' The car was one of a convoy, complete with uniformed naval officers and blue-suited FBI agents.

She thought he looked comical, an elderly man rigid in his much-cherished uniform, standing there like a bellboy. His face was twisted in the morning light. He was, she had learned, a man who distrusted the sun, even more than most of his bruised generation.

'Morning, Bob. Going for a ride, are we?'

His smile was disciplined. 'We should relocate to a more secure situation. We have issues of global importance, of significance for the future of the species. I recommend we convene at Mount Weather. I took the liberty of making the arrangements. But it's your call.' He eyed her, and the tension that had existed since the day she took the job crackled between them.

She'd never heard of Mount Weather. But she couldn't see any harm in indulging him. She climbed into the car, and he followed; they would be alone together.

They pulled out. The convoy took Route 66 and met Highway 50, heading west. The road was full of traffic, but their speed was high.

'How far are we going?'

'Be there in half an hour.' Paxton sat there and glowered, visibly irritated.

'I know what's bugging you, Bob. It's Professor Carel, isn't it?'

The muscles in his grizzled cheeks worked, as if he longed to be chewing gum. 'I don't know anything about this old English guy.'

'No doubt you had him vetted.'

'As best we could. He doesn't have anything to do with this. Not part of the team.'

'He's coming at my invitation,' she said firmly. In fact, in a sense, to her this elderly British scientist *was* part of the team, a deeper and older team-up than anything she was involved in with Paxton.

Professor Bill Carel had once been a graduate student working with Siobhan McGorran, another British astronomer who had become involved in the grand effort to build the sunstorm shield – and who had, in its aftermath, married Bud Tooke, and then nursed him through his cancer, a cruel legacy of that astounding day. That personal link was in fact the channel through which Carel had contacted her, and had tried to persuade her that he had a contribution to make regarding the presence of the object in the solar system, which he had heard of in whispers and leaks.

She tried to express some of this to Paxton, but he just waved it away. 'He's a cosmologist, for Christ's sake. He's spent his life staring into deep space. What use is he going to be today?'

'Let's keep an open mind, Bob,' she said firmly.

He fell into a silence that lasted all through the rest of the drive. Bella had raised a child, she was used to sulks, and she just ignored him.

After eighty kilometres they pulled off onto Route 101, a narrow two-lane rural road that clambered up a ridge. At the crest of the ridge they came to a line of razor-wired fencing. A faded sign read:

US PROPERTY
NO TRESPASSING

Beyond that Bella could make out a few battered aluminium huts, and beyond them, a glassy wall.

They had to wait while their cars interfaced with the base's security systems. Bella was aware of a faint speckle of laser light as she was probed.

'So, Mount Weather,' she prompted Paxton.

'Five hundred acres of Blue Ridge real estate. In the nineteen-fifties they set up a bunker here, a place to shelter government officials from DC in the event of a nuclear exchange. It fell into disuse, but was revived after 9/11 in 2001, and again after 2042. Although now it's essentially a loan from the US government to the World Space Council.'

Bella tried not to grimace. 'A bunker from the Cold War, the War on Terror, and now the War with the Sky. Appropriate, I suppose.'

'Manned by navy officers mostly. Used to confinement and canned air. Mount Weather is a good neighbour, I'm told. They keep up the roads, and send out the snow ploughs in winter. Not that there's much snow nowadays ...'

She had been expecting the convoy to pass on to a gate in that shining impenetrable wall. She was shocked when, with a rip of foliage, the whole chunk of land beneath the car turned into an elevator and dropped her into darkness.

Bob Paxton laughed as they descended. 'I feel like I'm coming home.'

As smiling young naval officers security-processed the party and escorted it to its conference room, Bella glimpsed a little of Mount Weather.

The ceilings were low, panelled with grimy tiles, the corridors narrow. But these unprepossessing corridors enclosed a small, old-fashioned town. There were television and radio studios, cafeterias, a tiny civilian police station, even a little row of shops, all underground, all contained within a hum of air conditioning. It was like a museum, she thought, a relic of the mindset of the mid-twentieth century.

At least the conference room was modern, big and bright and fitted with softwalls and table screens.

And here Bill Carel was waiting for her. In a room full of eavy, rumbling figures, mostly men, mostly about Paxton's ge, mostly in one uniform or another, Carel in his shabby ld jacket was standing alone beside a coffee percolator.

Bella ignored Paxton's cronies and made straight for arel. 'Professor. It's good of you to come.' She shook his and; it was flimsy, bony.

He was a little younger than she was, she recalled from is file, somewhere in his fifties, but he looked frail, gaunt, is face liver-spotted, his stance awkward and uncomfort- ble. The sunstorm had blighted many lives; perhaps he ad been battling illness. But the eyes in his cadaverous face ere bright. He said, 'I hope the contribution I have to make a valid one, and useful.'

'You're not sure?' She felt obscurely disappointed at his iffidence. An unworthy part of her had been looking for- ard to using him to tweak Bob Paxton's tail.

'Well, how can one be *sure*? The whole situation is un- recedented. But my colleagues urged me to contact you – to ontact *somebody*.'

She nodded. 'However this turns out, I'm grateful you ied.' Cradling a coffee, Bella led Carel to a seat. 'I'll make ire you get your say,' she whispered. 'And later we must ilk of the Tookes.'

After that she made a hasty circuit of the room, meeting nd greeting. As well as the Patriots Committee types there ere representatives of the various multinational armed orces and governments that supported the World Space ouncil.

She didn't get a good first impression of the quality of nese delegates. The Council had been engaged in nothing ut 'preparatory' and 'advisory' activities for decades; since ne sunstorm the War with the Sky had been cold. So work- ng for the Council had not been a prized assignment for a areer officer. Maybe this was a room full of Bob Paxtons, teely-eyed fanatic types, or else dead-enders.

But she told herself not to rush to judgement; after all if here *were* a new threat approaching the Earth, these men and women would be her prime resource in dealing with it.

Standing at the head of the table, Bob Paxton, self-appointed chair, flicked his finger against a glass to call the meeting to order. The rest of the panel, perhaps starstruck to be in the presence of the first man on Mars, submitted their attention immediately.

Paxton said the purpose of the meeting was twofold. 'First to give Chair Fingal an overview of the assets she has at her disposal. Second to focus specifically on the anomaly currently approaching Jovian orbit—'

'And at that point,' Bella put in, 'I will invite Professor Carel to make his contribution.'

Paxton rumbled a grudging assent.

They began to speak of the defence of the solar system.

## CHAPTER 13
# FORTRESS SOL

Paxton's presentation was a carnival of bullet-points, graphs, and images, some of them three-dimensional and animated; the holograms hovered over the middle of the table like ads for fantastic toys. But the subject matter was grim.

'Since sunstorm day, we have devoted considerable assets on Earth and beyond to watching the skies . . .'

Bella got the impression that Earth was plastered with electronic eyes, peering at the sky in all wavelengths. This included NASA assets like the venerable Deep Space Network chain of tracking arrays in Spain, Australia, and the Mojave, a near-Earth asteroid watching facility in New Mexico called LINEAR, and other Spaceguard facilities. The giant radio telescope at Arecibo likewise now gave over much of its time, not to astronomy, but to seeking unnatural signals from the stars.

The visual astronomers too had suddenly found money coming their way to realise previously unaffordable dreams. Bella studied images of the unimaginatively named Very Large Telescope in Chile, an Extremely Large Telescope in Morocco, and a monster called the Owl, the Overwhelmingly Large Telescope at a site called Dome C in Antarctica, where enough steel to build a second Eiffel Tower supported a monstrous mirror a hundred metres across. The Owl was busy photographing the birth of the first stars in the universe – and, more significantly, was mapping the surfaces of planets of nearby stars.

Facilities off-Earth were no less impressive. The most successful of the new space observatories was Cyclops Station, which trailed the Earth in its orbit at a stable Lagrange point. At Cyclops there had been assembled a telescope with a single, very large 'Fresnel' lens – not a mirror, but a diffracting lens.

As for what all these automated eyes were looking for, a century of theoretical studies by the old SETI enthusiasts had been plundered. Strategies were being devised to detect signals of all types down to very brief bursts – stray flashes of tight-beam laser signals, perhaps, detectable down to a billionth of a second long.

Paxton also spoke of lesser eyes, a whole fleet of them scattered right through the solar system out as far as the orbit of Neptune. He brought up a three-dimensional image of *Deep Space Monitor X7-6102-016,* which had been posted into orbit around Saturn.

'These are our robot sentries, our picket line,' Paxton boomed. '*DSM X7-6102-016* was typical, the most advanced scientific gear but robust, hardened and shrouded. These little critters patrol the skies all the way out to the fringe of OutSys. And they watch each other just as keenly.'

'That's true,' Professor Carel put in hesitantly. 'In fact it was the other probes' observation of the destruction of *X7-6102-016* that was brought to my attention, rather than anything that the probe transmitted itself.'

Bella said, 'So we live in a heavily surveilled solar system. What else do you have, Bill?'

'Weapons.' Paxton waved a hand, and the image of *DSM X7-6102-016* broke up.

'We call the concept "Fortress Sol,"' Paxton said grimly. 'We're establishing layers of deep defence from the outer solar system to the inner, all of it centring on the home of humanity, the Earth. You know yourself, ma'am, that we have established facilities as far out as the Trojan asteroids.'

The Trojans were a rich concentration of asteroids trailing Jupiter around its orbit at a Lagrange stable point. Right now Bella's daughter Edna was out at Trojan Station, working on a new generation of spacecraft, the 'A-ships.' All heavily classified.

'Next in we have the asteroids. For military planning

purposes we use the A-line, the central belt, as the boundary between InSys and OutSys – that is, the inner and outer systems. After that we have stations at the Lagrange points of Mars and Earth ...'

In the Earth–Moon system itself there were weapons platforms on the Moon and at the lunar Lagrange points and in Earth orbit: killer satellites that could pepper any interloper with projectiles, or fry it with X-ray lasers, or simply ram it. There were ground-based systems too, heavy lasers, particle beams, and reconditioned Cold War ICBMs still capable of hurling their lethal payloads away from the Earth. Even in Earth's upper atmosphere huge aircraft patrolled continually, bearing weapons that could knock out incoming missiles. And so on. The whole of cislunar space seemed to be bristling with weaponry, from Earth's surface up through what Paxton barked out as 'LEO, HEO, GEO, and super-GEO' – low, high, geosynchronous Earth orbit and beyond.

And the overt hardware of war was just the start. Everything that could be weaponised was. Even space-based weather control systems, like the kilometres-wide space lenses and mirrors, could easily be redirected. Every ploughshare could be turned to a sword.

Bella's imagination quailed when she tried to imagine the sort of last-ditch defensive battle that might depend on the use of such weapons. And the fact that these weapons, built to fight a War in the Sky, could just as easily be turned against an enemy on the ground was lost on nobody.

Paxton said, 'We're well aware of course that these facilities could have done nothing to stop the sunstorm. Therefore we have fallbacks. We don't know what these Firstborn might hit us with next. So for planning purposes we have looked back at other disasters, natural ones, that have hit us in the past, and how we coped with them ...'

He moved into a new chart, a dismal classification of catastrophe.

There were 'local disasters' that killed a few percent of the world's population, like major volcanic eruptions and the twentieth-century world wars, and 'global disasters' killing a significant fraction of the population, such as would follow the strike of a small asteroid, and 'extinction level events,' so devastating that a significant proportion of all species would be eliminated, and life on Earth itself threatened. 'If not for the shield,' Paxton said crisply, 'the sunstorm would have inflicted the mother of all extinction level events on us, since it would have melted Earth's surface down to the basement rock. As it was the shield reduced the event to a mere "global disaster."'

And the sunstorm, he said, had inspired the approach being taken to make the Earth resilient in case of any future attacks.

'We're trying to rework our industrial base so we can reconfigure to recovery mode as rapidly as possible in the face of any of these major disaster types. So, for instance, if we had to build another shield, we could do it more effectively. Of course some would argue that as a species we ought to be making this kind of preparation even if the Firstborn didn't exist.

'We have some advantages. A space-based infrastructure could help reboot a terrestrial civilisation. Weather control systems to stabilise a damaged climate, as after the sunstorm. Orbital stations to restring any downed elevators. Space-based energy systems and comms links. You could store medical facilities up there. Maybe you could even feed the world, from orbiting farms, or lunar agriculture, say. The children of the Earth turning back to help their wounded mother.' He grimaced. 'If the fucking Spacers cooperate.

'However we have to go beyond all this, and consider the worst case.' He said sternly, looking them all in the eye one by one, 'We must plan against extermination.

'Of course we have populations off-Earth now. But I'm told there's still some doubt that the off-world colonies could survive if Earth were lost altogether. So we have further backups.'

He spoke of vaults, on Earth and off it; there was one dug into a lunar mountain called Pico, for instance, in the Mare Imbrium. Copies of the wisdom of mankind, on gold leaf and stored electronically. DNA stores. Frozen zygotes. Caches to be retrieved by whoever might come this way, if mankind were exterminated. The 'Earthmail,' a desperate firing-off of a fragment of human culture to the stars on the eve of the sunstorm, was another sort of cache.

'All right, Bill. Do you think this is going to be enough?'

Paxton said with a hard face, 'Do any of you know what *space opera* was? Fiction of the far future, of wars fought across galaxies, of spaceships the size of worlds. We're only a century on from World War Two – only a hundred and fifty years since the main transport mechanism for warfare was the horse. And yet we're faced with a space opera threat. In another thousand years, say, we'll be scattered so far that nothing short of a Galaxy core explosion could kill us all. But for now, we're still vulnerable.'

Bill Carel dared to raise a hand. 'Which is actually a logic that suggests a second strike is more likely now, than later.'

'Yeah,' Paxton growled.

'And, despite your fine presentation, Admiral, there are obvious flaws in these strategies.' There was an intake of breath, but Carel seemed oblivious. 'May I?'

'Go on,' Bella said quickly.

'First there is the sparseness of your resources, Admiral. Just because you have a station in the orbit of Jupiter doesn't mean you can counter a threat coming at the same radius but from the far side of the sun.'

'We're aware of that—'

'And you seem to be thinking in two dimensions, as if this was a land war of the old sort. What if an attack were to come at us out of the ecliptic – I mean, away from the plane of the sun and planets?'

'I walked on Mars,' Paxton said dangerously. 'I know what the ecliptic is. As it happens the present bogey *has* come sailing in along the plane of the ecliptic. For the future we're considering out-of-plane options. But you know as well as I do that the energy costs of getting up there are prohibitive. Yes, Professor Carel, the solar system is a mighty big place. Yes, we can't cover it all. What else can we do but try?'

Carel almost laughed. 'But these efforts are so thinly based it's virtually futile—'

Paxton glowered, and Bella held her hand up. 'Please, Bill.'

'I'm sorry,' said Carel. 'And then there is the question of the efficacy of all these preparations against the threat we actually face—'

'Fine.' Angrily Paxton cleared down his displays. 'So let's talk about the anomaly.'

Bella longed for fresh coffee.

After his long and detailed discussion of Fortress Sol, Paxton's presentation on the anomaly was brief.

He briskly reviewed the principal evidence for the bogey's existence. 'Right now this thing is passing through the J-line, the orbit of Jupiter. In fact we have a window to intercept it, because it's fortuitously passing close to the Trojan base, and we're working on mission options. And then it will sail on through the asteroids, past the orbit of Mars, to Earth, where it seems to be precisely targeted. But we still have no idea what it is, or what it might do if and when it gets here.'

When he sat down there was a brief silence.

Bill Carel looked at Paxton, and around the room, as if expecting another contribution. 'Is that all?'

'That's all we got,' Paxton said.

Carel said softly, 'I did not dream you would have so little – it is as well that I came. If I may, Admiral?'

Bob Paxton glared at Bella, but she gave him a discreet nod, and he gave the floor to Carel.

'In a way,' Carel said, 'my involvement with this "bogey" began in the years before the sunstorm, when I worked with an astronomer called Siobhan McGorran on a probe we called QAP.' He pronounced it 'cap.' 'The Quintessence Anisotropy Probe . . .'

Paxton and his Patriots shifted and grumbled.

The Quintessence Anisotropy Probe was a follow-up to a craft called the Wilkinson Microwave Anisotropy Probe, which in 2003 had studied the faint echoes of the Big Bang, and had established for the first time the proportions of the basic components of the universe – baryonic matter, dark matter, and dark energy. It was dark energy, called by some 'quintessence,' that fuelled the expansion of the universe. Now the purpose of the QAP was to measure the effects of that cosmic inflation by seeking the echoes of primordial sound waves.

'It was really a very elegant concept,' Carel said. 'The primordial universe, small, dense, and ferociously hot, was an echo chamber full of sound waves propagating through a turbulent medium. But then came the expansion.' He spread his delicate hands. '*Poom.* Suddenly there was room for things to cool down, and more interesting physics.

'As the expansion cut in those ancient sound waves were dissipated. But they left an imprint, their pattern of compression influencing the formation of the first galaxies. And so by mapping the galactic distribution we hoped to reconstruct the primordial sounds. This in turn would provide clues as to the physics of the quintessence, the dark energy, which at that time—'

As the uniforms got more restless, Bella said gently, 'Perhaps you should get to the point, Bill.'

He smiled at her. He had a softscreen of his own that he spread out over the table; it quickly interfaced with the table's subsystems. 'Here is a profile of the cosmic expansion.' It was a spiky graph, plotted on logarithmic scales, an upward curve. He spoke of how this curve had been established by analysing old light seeping from the deepest sky, and by taking correlations of the structures to be observed on a variety of scales. The 'frequency' of the patterns of galactic formation mapped back to the frequencies of those lost sound waves.

This time Paxton cut him off. 'Jesus Christ, Poindexter, put me out of my misery. Where are you going with this?'

Carel tapped his softscreen. 'It was one of my own students who fortuitously came across an animation of the destruction of *DSM X7-6102-016*.'

'I'd like to know how he got a hold of that,' Paxton growled.

'She, actually,' Carel said, unfazed. 'A girl called Lyla Neal. Nigerian, ferociously bright. The destruction of the *DSM* was an odd explosion, you know. It's not as if it was hit by an external weapon. Rather as if it tore itself apart from within. Well, prompted by that, Lyla constructed an expansion curve for the *DSM,* to show how its little universe was ended.'

He pulled up a second chart. The scale was different, Bella saw, but his conclusion was obvious. The *DSM* expansion curve mapped the QAP's cosmic profile. *Precisely,* as could be seen when Carel overlaid the two.

Bella sat back, stunned. 'So what does this mean?'

'I can only speculate,' Carel said.

'Then do so, for Christ's sake,' snapped Paxton.

'It seems to me that the DSM was destroyed by a specific and localised application of dark energy, of quintessence. It was ripped apart by precisely the force that has caused the universal expansion, somehow focused down onto this small craft. It is a cosmological weapon, if you like. Quite remarkable.' He smiled. 'Lyla calls it a "Q-bomb."'

'Cute,' snapped Paxton. 'So can we stop this thing, shoot it down, deflect it?'

Carel seemed surprised to be asked such a question. 'Why, I have absolutely no idea. This is *not* like the sunstorm, Admiral, which was a very energetic event, but crudely engineered. *This* is a barely familiar sort of physics. It's very hard to imagine we can respond in any meaningful way.'

Bella said, 'But, Bill, what happens if this Q-bomb actually reaches the Earth?'

Again he seemed surprised to be asked. 'Why, that must be obvious. If it functions in the same way again – we have no reason to imagine its scope of action is limited – it will be just as with the *DSM.*' He spread his fingers. *'Poom.'*

The silence in the room was profound.

Bella glanced around the table. These old sky warriors had almost seemed to be enjoying themselves. Now they were subdued, silent. Their bluff had been called.

And what was worse, as far as she could see this 'cosmological' technology cut right through the rickety and expensive defences mankind had been trying to erect.

'All right,' she said. 'We've got twenty-one months until that thing reaches Earth. So what do we do?'

'We have to stop it,' Paxton said immediately. 'It's our only option. We can't save the population any other way – we can't evacuate the damn planet. We throw everything we've got at it. Beginning with our resources out at the Trojans.' He glanced at Bella.

Bella knew what he meant. The A-ships. And she knew that would most likely mean committing Edna to action. She put that thought aside for now. 'Draw up an operation order, Bob. But there's no reason to believe any of our weapons will make a bit of difference. We have to find out more about this thing, and find a weakness. Professor Carel, you're hereby drafted.'

Carel inclined his head.

Paxton said heavily, 'And there's something else.'

'Yes?'

'Bisesa Dutt. We missed her. She's escaped up an elevator like a rat up a drainpipe.'

That baffled Bella. 'A space elevator? Where's she going?'

'I don't know. She's just out of a Hibernaculum; it's possible *she* doesn't know. But somebody does, some asshole Spacer.'

'Admiral,' Bella snapped. 'That kind of language isn't helping.'

He grinned, a wolf's leer. 'I'll be nice. But we have to find Bisesa Dutt regardless of what toes we tread on.'

Bella sighed. 'All right. And right now I think I need to go brief a few presidents. Is there anything else?'

Paxton shook his head. 'Let's conference-call in an hour. And, people – we don't want any leaks out of here.'

As the meeting broke up, Bella fretted. The fact that Carel had had to force his way in here was a lesson that slickness of presentation didn't imply comprehensiveness of knowledge. And if not for this chance observation by Carel's bright student, they would be nowhere near discovering the true nature of this artifact, this weapon, this Q-bomb.

What else were they missing? What else weren't they seeing? *What else?*

## CHAPTER 14
# ASCENT BEYOND ORBIT

Almost all of the excitement of the ascent was over in the first twenty-four hours. Bisesa would not have believed it when they first left the ground, but she rapidly grew bored.

As they had continued to shed gravity, floating stuff cluttered up the place, the blankets and bits of clothing and food. It was like camping in a falling elevator, Bisesa thought. The clippings from Alexei's shaved head were particularly unwelcome. And it was hard to wash. They had enough water to drink, but this cargo cabin didn't feature a shower. After the first couple of days, the cabin smelled, inevitably, like a lavatory.

Bisesa tried to use the time constructively. She worked on her recovery from the Hibernaculum. She slept a lot, and Alexei and Myra helped her work out low-gravity exercises, bracing against the walls and floor to build up her muscles. But there was only so much time you could exercise or sleep away.

Alexei kept himself busy too. He threw himself into a routine of checking over the spider's systems, with a full shakedown twice a day. He even made visual checks of hull seams and filters. While he worked, he muttered and sang, curious, distracted little hymns to sunlight.

Still Bisesa hadn't talked to her daughter – not as she wished to. She thought Myra was sinking into herself; while Bisesa had been sleeping, she seemed to have developed a black core of depression. This was business for later, Bisesa told herself.

Bisesa watched Earth dwindle, a toy globe at the end of a ribbon that now seemed endless in both directions.

Once she said, 'I wish the world would turn, so I could

look for the other ribbons. I don't even know how many there are.'

Myra counted off on her fingers. 'Modimo in Africa. Bandara in Australia, the mother of them all. Jianmu in China. Marahuaka in Venezuela, South America. All named for sky gods. We Europeans have Yggdrasil.'

'Named for the Norse world tree.'

'Yes.'

'And the Americans have Jacob's Ladder.'

Alexei smiled. '"And he dreamed, and behold a ladder set up on the Earth, and the top of it reached to heaven: and behold the angels of God ascending and descending on it." Genesis, twenty-eight, twelve.'

Myra said, 'America is still a pretty Christian country. All the Native-American world-tree names were rejected, I think. They took a poll.'

'Why do so many cultures have myths of a world tree? It seems pretty unlikely.'

Alexei said, 'Some anthropologists say it's simply a response to cloud features: ripples, waves that look like branches or rungs. Or maybe it's a myth about the Milky Way. Others say it could be a plasma phenomenon. Solar activity, maybe.'

Myra said, 'Plenty of people fear the elevators. Some regard them as a blasphemy. A short-cut to God. After all we have faced a threat from the sky in living memory.'

'Which is why the African elevator was attacked,' Alexei said. 'Makes no sense, but there you go.'

'You know a lot about Earth culture for a Spacer.'

'I'm interested. But I see it from the outside. Anthropologically, I suppose.'

Bisesa felt patronised. 'I suppose all you Spacers are as rational as computers.'

'Oh, no.' Alexei smiled. 'We're working on a whole new set of hang-ups.'

Still they rose. As the planet shrank from the size of a soccer ball to a grapefruit to a cricket ball, it soon became too small for Bisesa to make out even continent-sized details, and a dull sense of the immense scale of the artifact she was climbing slowly rammed itself into her mind.

Three days up they sailed through the first significant structure since the ground. They gathered at the centre of the cabin to watch it approach.

It was a loose ring of inflated modules, all of them roughly cylindrical, brightly coloured; they were huge, each as big as a small building, and they shone like tremendous toys in the unending sunlight. This was a hotel cum theme park, Alexei told them, as yet incomplete and uninhabited. 'Its official name is "Jacob's." Disney is the major investor. They're hoping to make back some of the money they're haemorrhaging at the old ground-based parks.'

'Good place for a hotel,' Myra said. 'Only three days up, and still a tenth of a gravity, enough to avoid all the messiness of zero G.'

'Makes you realise what you can do with a space elevator or two,' Alexei murmured. 'Not just cheap lift, but *very heavy* lift too. Lots of capacity. This theme park is trivial, but it's just a start. There will be other communities, towns in the sky strung out along the elevators. A whole new realm. It's like the railways in the nineteenth century.'

Bisesa felt moved to take Myra's hand. 'We live in remarkable times, don't we?'

'Yes, Mum, we do.'

The hotel rushed past them in an instant, and for the first time in days Bisesa had a sense of their true speed. But then it was back to the timeless, motionless, scale-less rush ever higher from the Earth, and they were soon bickering once more.

On the eighth day they sailed through geosynch. For one precise moment they were in zero gravity, orbiting the Earth as a respectable satellite should, though for days gravity had been so low it made no practical difference.

At the geosynch point was another structure, a vast wheel with its hub centred on the ribbon. It was incomplete.

Bisesa could see lesser craft crawling over tremendous scaffolding, and welding sparks flared. But elsewhere she saw immense glass panels behind which living things glowed green.

The geosynch station flew down, past, and was gone by, and they all stared down as it dwindled away.

With the geosynch point passed, the spider's effective gravity flipped over, as centripetal forces, balanced with gravity at geosynch, took over and tried to fling them away. Now 'down' pointed *away* from the pea-sized Earth. They had to rearrange their cabin, so that they made the ceiling the floor, and vice versa. Alexei said cabins designed to carry passengers did this sort of flip-flop automatically.

That inversion, the rebuilding of the cabin, was the only interesting thing that happened in those days following geosynch. The *only* thing.

But Bisesa learned that they weren't going to be hauled all the way up to the counterweight, which was all of thirteen more days past geosynch, twenty-one from the ground. And that, she learned at last, was the spider graveyard.

'They need to keep adding counterweight to compensate for the growing mass of the ribbon,' Alexei said. 'Which is why none of the spider trucks come back to Earth, save the builders.'

Bisesa looked around at the cluttered hull, grimy from their occupation. She felt a stab of regret. 'And is that where this spider will finish up?'

'Oh, no,' said Alexei. 'This beast won't be going further than the fifty-six-thousand-klick point. Twelve days out of Earth.'

Bisesa glanced at Myra, who she sensed had almost as dim an idea of what was to come as she had. 'And then what?'

'Remember I told you that if the spider let go before geosynch we'd have fallen back to Earth? But if we let go *after* geosynch—'

'We'll be flung out of Earth orbit,' Myra said. 'Into interplanetary space.'

'If you pick the right altitude to leave the elevator, you

can use its momentum to hurl you wherever you want to go. The Moon, for instance.'

'Is that where we're going?'

Alexei smiled. 'Oh, a bit further than that.'

'Then where, damn it? There's no point in secrecy now – as soon as we leave the elevator the authorities will know where we're going.'

'Mars, Mum. *Mars.*'

Bisesa was bewildered. 'Mars?'

'Where – well, where something is waiting for you.'

'But this little pod won't keep us alive all the way to Mars.'

'Of course not,' Alexei said. 'We'll be picked up. We'll rendezvous with a lightship. A solar-sail ship. It's already on the way.'

Bisesa frowned. 'We have no rockets, do we? Once we're free of the ribbon we'll have no motive power at all.'

'We don't need it. The *ship* will rendezvous with *us*.'

'My God,' Bisesa said. 'And if something goes wrong—'

Alexei smiled, unconcerned.

Talking to Alexei through these long days, Bisesa thought she had begun to see something of his psychology – the psychology of a Spacer, subtly different from the Earthbound.

Alexei had something approaching a morbid fear of failure in the machinery around him, for he was entirely dependent on that for his very life. But on the other hand he had absolutely no doubt in the implacable working-out of orbits and trajectories and interceptions; he lived in a realm where celestial mechanics visibly ruled everything, a mighty, silent clockwork that never developed a flaw. So once his gadgets had cut them loose of the ribbon he believed he would be safe and secure; it was inconceivable to him that their lightship rendezvous could be missed. Whereas Bisesa and Myra were terrified of just that possibility.

Somewhere in there was the key to understanding Alexei, Bisesa thought, and the new Spacer generation. And she thought she would understand him even better if she could make out the peculiar prayers he seemed to chant softly while distracted: psalms to the 'Unconquered Sun.'

On the twelfth day they sat on their fold-down chairs, with all their loose gear tied down in advance of the jolt of weightlessness that would come when Alexei's explosive bolts severed the cabin from its pulley.

Alexei eyed his crewmates. 'Anybody want a countdown?'

'Shut up,' Myra said.

Bisesa looked down at the ribbon that had been her anchor to reality for twelve days, and up at an Earth reduced to a pebble. She wondered if she would ever see it loom large again – and what lay ahead of her before that could happen.

Alexei whispered, 'Here we go—'

There was a flash below, on the cabin's roof that had become a floor. The ribbon fell away, startlingly fast, and gravity evaporated like a dream. Tumbling, loose bits of gear rolling around them, Alexei laughed and laughed.

## CHAPTER 15
# LIBERATOR

*April 2069*

John Metternes, ship's engineer, called up to Edna from Achilles. There was another holdup. The techs down there on the asteroid still weren't satisfied with the magnetic containment of the antimatter pellets.

Any more delays and the *Liberator* was going to miss another window for her first trial cruise.

Edna Fingal looked out of the thick wraparound windows, away from the convoluted surface of the Trojan asteroid beneath her, to find the sun, so far away here on the J-line it barely showed a disc. Surrounded by the flight deck's calm hum and new-carpet smell, she chafed, restless. She wasn't good at waiting.

Intellectually, in her head, she knew she had to wait until the engineers were absolutely sure about what they were doing. The *Liberator* depended on a new and untried technology, and as far as Edna could tell these magnetic antimatter bottles were never exactly *stable;* the best you could hope for was a kind of controlled instability that lasted long enough to get you home. It was thought that a failure of containment had been the cause of the loss of the *Liberator*'s unnamed prototype predecessor, and of Mary Lanchester and Theo Woese, the *A-23C*'s two-person crew.

But in OutSys, out there in the dark, something was approaching, something silent and alien and hostile. Already it was inside the J-line, closer to the sun than Edna was. Edna was captain of the world's only spacegoing warship even close to operational status, the only healthy vessel in the first Space Group Attack Squadron. She itched to confront the alien.

As she often did, she tried to relieve the stress by thinking of family.

She glanced at a chronometer. It was set to Houston time, like all master clocks throughout human space, and she mentally made an adjustment for DC. Edna's daughter Thea, just three, would be in nursery school at this hour. Edna's own home was on the west coast, but she had chosen the school in Washington so Thea could be close to her grandmother. Edna liked to be able to visualise just where Thea was at any time of the day.

'Libby, please open my mail file.'

'Of course. Visual records too?'

'Yes. Ready? ... Hello, Thea. Here I am again, waiting around as usual ...'

Thea would hear her words, and see pretty much what she could see, captured by visual sensors in the ident tattoo on Edna's cheek. Security was predictably tight about every aspect of the A-class warships out here on the J-line, and Thea would only ever receive a heavily censored version of her mother's letters. But it was better than nothing.

And if things didn't go well, these messages might be all Thea had left of her mother. So Edna spoke to the future.

'I'm sitting here waiting for our antimatter bottles to be loaded into the A-drive chamber. And it's taking a long time, for we have to be very careful. I'm looking down now at Achilles. It's one of the larger of the Trojan asteroids, and it's here that we have been building our A-ships. Look with me, you can see the graving yards, and the big pits where we've dug out ice and rock to serve as reaction mass, the stuff that will actually push the ship forward. And there are the domes where we all live when we're on the surface – the *Liberator* is a lot more comfortable than that, believe me ...!'

The Trojans clustered at a point of gravitational stability on the J-line called L4, Lagrange 4, forever sixty degrees ahead of Jupiter itself in its orbit. There was a second such point, L5, trailing Jupiter. Earthbound astronomers had named the two asteroid camps for the competing heroes of Homer's *Iliad:* Achilles and the other Greeks leading Jupiter, the Trojans forever following.

L4 was a useful lode of resources, an obvious place for a base, a control point. Perhaps that was why, during the sunstorm, the Firstborn had lodged an Eye here.

'I won't pretend I'm not afraid, Thea. I'd be a fool if I wasn't. I've learned I can put aside the fear, and get on with the job. Because I know it's a job that has to be done.

'Maybe you know that this ship, the fourth of the new A-class, is the first to have been given a name. Because while the others made test flights, this ship will be the first to go into combat. I suppose whatever happens she will always be remembered for that. Of course we have to get through a couple of proving flights first.

'We agonised about the name. Here we are surrounded by heroes from classical mythology. But it's the mythology of another age, remote from our own. In the end we settled on the name of one of the great aircraft that helped wage mankind's last pivotal war, before the coming of the Firstborn changed all the rules. I hope that in the next few weeks we're going to be able to liberate mankind from an even deadlier menace. And that then I'll have a chance to come home to you. I—'

An alarm chimed, a green light flashed on the softwall beside her. The fuel pods were at last successfully loaded; the ground crew were leaving the ship.

And the launch window for the scheduled shakedown cruise would open in just ten minutes.

Time enough. And then she could accept her operation order for her true mission.

'Close the file, please, Libby. Snip the last bit. And get John Metternes up here.'

## CHAPTER 16

# JAMES CLERK MAXWELL

The lightship that was to take them to Mars came swimming out of the dark. It was called the *James Clerk Maxwell*. The sail was a shadow, and Bisesa caught glimpses of rigging, rectilinear flashes immensely long.

As the hour of the pickup neared Bisesa grew even tenser. You didn't have to know anything about the engineering to understand that a ship that sailed on sunlight must be gossamer-fragile. And their knotty little spider, a spinning lump of metal, was going to come plummeting in among this fantasy of sails and rigging. She continually expected alarms to sound, and to see a wispy mirror-sail fold around her like Christmas paper.

Myra grew anxious too, despite her own astronautics experience. But Alexei Carel was entirely unfazed. As the rendezvous approached he sat by his softscreens, monitoring obscure graphic displays, occasionally uttering a mild word that was transmitted to the approaching ship's systems along a narrow-beam laser link. He seemed to trust absolutely the mixture of orbital mechanics and exotic celestial seamanship that was bringing the spider ever closer to the *Maxwell*.

In the last moments the *Maxwell*'s main hull came looming out of the dark. Bisesa imagined she was in a small boat, watching the approach of a liner across some vast ocean. The rough cylinder bristled with antenna dishes and booms, and around its upper rim Bisesa made out a ring of pulleys, mundane bits of technology that anchored kilometres of rigging.

A transparent tube a couple of metres across snaked out from the hull, probed at the spider uncertainly, and locked on with an audible rattle. There was a jolt as the mechanical linkage soaked up the last minor differences in momentum.

Then the tube contracted like a concertina, drawing the two hulls together, until they docked with a firm clang.

Alexei sat back, a broad grin on his face. 'Thank Sol for universal docking protocols.'

'Well, that's that.' He peeled the softscreen off the wall in front of him, crumpled it up and stuffed it in a pocket. 'Time to get packed up. Take everything you want; dump anything you don't need in here.'

'We aren't taking the spider,' Bisesa said slowly.

'Of course not.'

Bisesa felt oddly reluctant to leave the haven of the spider. 'Maybe I'm just getting too old for all this change.'

Myra squeezed her arm. She made this sort of affectionate gesture spasmodically; Bisesa accepted whatever her wounded daughter had to give her. 'Mum, if I can cope with it, you can. Come on, let's get ready.'

When Alexei opened the hatch in the cabin wall, the outer hull of the *Maxwell,* exposed, smelled faintly of burning. Bisesa touched it curiously, a surface that had endured the vacuum of space for long months. It felt hot.

The *Maxwell*'s hatch dilated away.

They crossed into an interior that was clean, brightly lit, and smelled faintly of soap. The suitcase followed with a clatter. Little sucker pads shot out of it on fine threads, fixing themselves to the walls, so that the case hauled itself around like a clumsy, fat-bodied spider.

The hatches closed behind them, and Bisesa felt a gentle shudder as the greater mass of the *Maxwell* reacted to the casting-off of the spider. There was no window in the hatch. She would have liked to see the discarded spider fall away.

Alexei gave them one bit of warning. 'Just remember they pared off every gram to build this thing. The whole ship masses only around ten tonnes – and that includes the sail. You could easily put your foot through the hull.' He tapped an internal floor-to-ceiling partition panel. 'And this stuff's a kind of rice paper. Light but fragile.' He poked a finger through it to show them, then he tore off a tiny strip and popped it in his mouth. 'Edible too. In case of dramas, eat the furniture.'

Bisesa asked, '"Dramas"? What dramas?'

Myra said slowly, 'I suppose about the worst thing that could happen is to lose the sail, or to foul it up beyond usefulness. In which case you'd be stranded, falling away on whatever trajectory you happened to be on. Rescue would be possible, but it would likely take months, if not years.'

Bisesa pondered. 'How many accidents have there been?'

'Very few,' Alexei said. 'And none fatal.' He lectured them briefly about various levels of fail-safe in the design of the mission profile, so that if you did lose your sail you'd still coast somewhere accessible. 'It's more likely your body will fail you before a ship like this does,' he said to Bisesa, not entirely reassuringly.

While Alexei disappeared to what he called the 'bridge' to check over the ship's systems, Myra and Bisesa explored and unpacked.

It didn't take long to figure out the layout of the *Maxwell*. The pressurised hull was a cylinder only a few metres tall. Divided up by sheets of that rice-paper partitioning, it was split into three main decks. At the base was what Alexei called the utilities deck. Peering through hatches, they saw heaps of stores, life support, EVA and repair gear, cargo. Alexei's bridge was the upper deck.

The middle deck contained living quarters. Aside from a dedicated galley and bathroom it was sliced up by movable partitions into rooms that could serve as rest quarters, bedrooms, workrooms for a crew of up to ten. The walls were thick with cupboards and space-saving fold-out bunks and chairs. Bisesa and Myra spent some time moving the partitions around. They settled on constructing three small bedrooms as far as possible from each other and from the lavatory; the paper-thin partitions weren't particularly soundproof.

The accommodation was almost as pokey as aboard the spider. But the cramped corridors and low-ceilinged rooms had a unique mix of architectures designed for ground and space. The sail could offer an acceleration of no more than one percent of Earth's gravity – not enough to stick you to the floor. So the design emulated space stations with hand- and footholds, Velcro pads, and a colour coding with brown beneath and blue above, so that you could always know at a glance which way up you were.

But on the other hand that one percent of G was steady and unrelenting. Experimenting, Bisesa found that if she clambered up to the ceiling and let go, she would drift down to the floor in six or seven seconds, falling like a snowflake and settling softly. That little bit of gravity was surprisingly useful, for it induced dust to settle and any disturbed clutter to fall eventually out of the air; here she would not have to wrestle with rogue blankets, or track down stray droplets shimmering away from her coffee cup.

The 'bridge' of the *Maxwell* was set out pretty informally with chairs and tables. Bisesa was reminded that this wasn't a military ship. When Bisesa and Myra came drifting up the short ladder from the lower deck Alexei was sitting in one of those chairs, patiently watching displays unfold across a softscreen.

The walls were utterly transparent.

Space was starless, empty save for three lamps, sun, Earth, and Moon, which hung in a tremendous triangle around the ship. Something in Bisesa quailed before this array of worlds. For some reason she thought of Mir and the man-apes she had seen there, australopithecines with the legs of humans and the shoulders of gorillas.

Myra saw her reaction and tugged her hand. 'Mum. It's just another fairground ride. Never mind feeling dizzy. *Look up.*'

Bisesa lifted her head.

She saw a disc of not-quite-darkness, a little greyer than the deep velvet of the sky. Highlights, sun-dazzling bright, rippled across its face. It was the sail, a sheet of foil big enough to have wrapped up the whole of inner London. She could hear gentle, intermittent whirs that must be the tiny pulleys fixed around the roof, tugging at the rigging that ran up and out from the roof above her, rectilinear threads that caught the sunlight.

The hull that enclosed her was a tuna can hanging under a parachute.

'Welcome aboard the *James Clerk Maxwell,'* Alexei said, grinning.

'All this from sunlight.'

'Yes.' Alexei held up his hand in a shaft of sunlight that crossed the cabin. 'The pressure of all those tiny photons, pinging off a reflecting surface. On your face on a sunny day on Earth, that force amounts to only maybe one ten-thousandth of a gram. We have enough sail area, and a low enough mass, for an acceleration of a hundredth of a G. But it's continuous, and free, and it just keeps on pushing and pushing ... Which is how we can reach Mars in twenty days.'

The sail itself was based on a mesh of nanotube string, the same super-strong stuff they made the space elevator ribbons from. The 'fabric' was an ultra-thin film of boron, only a few hundred atomic diameters thick. It had to be sprayed on.

'The sail fabric is so fine that if you handle it it's more like smoke than anything substantial,' Alexei said. 'But it's robust enough to be able to stand a dip into the sun's heat inside the orbit of Mercury.'

Ribs of light washed across the face of the mirror; tiny pulleys whirred.

'You get these oscillations all the time,' Alexei said. 'That's why we make the sails smart, as the sun shield was. The fabric is embedded with actuators and tiny rocket motors. Max, the ship's AI, can keep himself positioned correctly. And he does most of the navigation; I just tell him where I want to go. Max is in charge, really. Thank Sol he doesn't brag about it too much.'

Bisesa said, 'I can see how you can be pushed *away* from the sun. But how can you sail *inward* – from Mars in toward Earth, say? I guess it's sort of like tacking into the wind.'

'It's not a good analogy,' Alexei said evenly. 'You have to remember that all objects in the solar system are essentially in orbit around the sun. And that determines how the sail functions ...' Orbital mechanics could be counter to common sense. 'If I speed up, I raise my orbit. But if I fix my sail so that the sunlight pressure *opposes* my motion, my orbital velocity falls, and I will spiral in toward the sun ...'

Bisesa studied the diagrams he produced on the softscreens, but when he started scrolling equations she gave up.

'This is all intuitively obvious to you, isn't it? The principles of celestial mechanics.'

He waved a hand at the worlds around them. 'You can see why. Up here you can *see* those laws working out. I've often wondered how Earthbound scientists were able to make any sense out of all the clutter down there. The first lunar astronauts, a hundred years ago, the first to come out this way, came back changed, for better or worse. A lot of us Spacers are deists, or theists, or pantheists – somewhere on that spectrum.'

'Believing that God is to be found in physical laws,' Myra said.

'Or God *is* those laws.'

'I suppose it makes sense,' Bisesa said. 'Religions and gods don't have to go together. Buddhists don't necessarily believe in a supreme being; you can have religion independent of any god.'

Myra nodded. 'And we can believe in the Firstborn without having any religion at all.'

Alexei said mildly, 'Oh, the Firstborn aren't gods. As they will learn one day.'

Bisesa said, 'But *you* aren't a theist. Are you, Alexei? You like to quote the Bible, but I've heard you pray – *Thank Sol?*'

He looked sheepish. 'You got me.' He lifted his face to the sunlight. 'Some of us have a sneaking regard for the Big Guy. The engine that keeps us all alive, the one object you can see however far you roam across the system.'

Myra nodded. 'I heard of this. A cult of Sol Invictus. One

of the last great pagan gods – from the Roman empire, just before they proclaimed Christianity their official cult. Didn't it sprout on Earth again, just before the sunstorm?'

Alexei nodded. 'There was a lot of propitiation of angry gods to be done in those days. But Sol Invictus was the one that took hold with the early Spacers, especially those who had worked on the shield. And he spread.'

Bisesa remembered another sun god who had interfered in her own life: Marduk, forgotten god of Babylon. She said, 'You Spacers really aren't like the rest of us, are you, Alexei?'

'Of course not. How could we be?'

'And is that why you're taking me to Mars? Because of a different perspective?'

'More than that. Because the guys down there have found something. Something the Earth governments would never even have dreamed of looking for. Although the governments are looking for *you,* Bisesa.'

Bisesa frowned. 'How do you know?'

Alexei looked uncomfortable. 'My father is working with the World Space Council. He's a cosmologist ...'

So there it was, Bisesa thought, this new generational gap set out as starkly as it could be. A Spacer son spying on his Earthbound father.

But even though they were in deep space he would say no more about where Bisesa was being taken, and what was expected of her.

Myra pulled her lip. 'It's odd. Sol Invictus – he's such a contrast to the cool thinking of the theists.'

'Yeah. But don't you think that until we get these Firstborn assholes beaten, we need an Iron Age god?' And Alexei grinned, showing his teeth, a shockingly primate expression bathed in the light of sun and Moon.

Bisesa, worn out by stress and strangeness, retreated to her newly constructed cabin. She rearranged her few possessions and strapped herself to the narrow bunk.

The partitioned-off room was small, but that didn't

bother her. She had been in the army. As accommodations went, this was a lot better than the UN camp in Afghanistan where she had been stationed before falling into Mir.

It struck her that this living deck seemed cramped, though, even given the basic geometry of the tuna-can hull. She thought back to her inspection of the utility deck earlier; she had a good memory for spaces and volumes. Sleepy, she murmured aloud, 'So why is this deck so much smaller than the utility level?'

A soft voice spoke. 'Because these walls are full of water, Bisesa.'

'Is that you, Thales?'

'No, Bisesa. Alexei calls me Max.' The voice was male, softly Scottish.

'Max, for *James Clerk Maxwell*. You're the ship.'

'Strictly speaking the sail, which is the smartest and most sentient component. I am a Legal Person (Non-Human),' Max said calmly. 'I have a full set of cognitive capacities.'

'Alexei should have introduced us.'

'That would have been pleasant.'

'The water in the walls?'

It was there to protect frail human cargo from the hard radiations of space; even a few centimetres of water was a surprisingly effective shield.

'*Max*. Why the name?'

'It is appropriate ...'

The Scottish physicist James Clerk Maxwell had in the nineteenth century demonstrated that light exerted a pressure, the fundamental principle on which mankind's new fleet of lightships had been built. His work had laid the foundations for Einstein's conceptual breakthroughs.

Bisesa smiled. 'I suppose Maxwell would have been astonished to see how his basic insight has been translated into technology, two centuries later.'

'Actually I've made something of a study of Maxwell. I have rather a lot of spare time. I think he could have conceived of a solar sail. The physics was all his, after all.'

Bisesa propped an arm behind her head. 'When I read

about Athena, the shield AI, I always wondered how it *felt* to be her. An intelligence embedded in such an alien body. Max, how does it feel to be you?'

'I often wonder how it feels to be *you,*' he replied in his soft brogue. 'I am capable of curiosity. And awe.'

It surprised Bisesa that he should say that. 'Awe? At what?'

'Awe at finding myself in a universe of such beauty yet governed by a few simple laws. Why should it be so? And yet, why not?'

'Are you a theist, Max?'

'Many of the leading theist thinkers are AIs.'

Electronic prophets, she thought, wondering. 'I think James Clerk would have been proud of you, Maxwell Junior.'

'Thank you.'

'Light, please.'

The light dimmed to a faint crimson glow. She fell into a deep sleep, the gentle gravity just enough to reassure her inner ear that she wasn't falling any more.

It was some hours later that Max woke her, for, he said apologetically, they were approaching the Moon.

On the bridge Alexei said, 'It's fortuitous of course that our path to Mars should take us near the Moon. But I was able to work a gravitational slingshot into our trajectory design ...'

Bisesa stopped listening to him, and just looked.

The swelling face of the Moon, nearly full, was not the familiar Man-in-the-Moon that had hovered over the Manchester streets of her childhood. She had come so far now that the Man had turned; the great 'right eye' of Mare Imbrium was swivelled toward her, and a slice of Farside was clearly revealed, a segment of crater-pocked hide invisible to mankind until the advent of spaceflight.

But it was not the geology of the Moon that interested her but the traces of humanity. Eagerly she and Myra picked out the big Nearside bases, Armstrong and Tooke, clearly visible as blisters of silver and green against the tan lunar dust.

Bisesa thought she saw a road, a line of silver, cutting across the crater called Clavius within which Tooke Base nestled, and from which it had taken its first name. Then she realised it must be a mass driver, an electromagnetic launching track kilometres long.

The modern Moon was visibly a place of industry. Vast stretches of the lava-dust plains of the maria looked as if they had been combed; the lunar seas were being strip-mined, their dust plundered for oxygen, water, and minerals. At the poles immense solar-cell farms splashed, and new observatories gleamed like bits of coal, made of jet-black glass microwaved direct from the lunar dirt. Strung right around the equator was a shining chrome thread: the alephtron, mightiest particle accelerator in the system.

Something about all this industry disturbed Bisesa. So much had changed on the Moon after four billion years of chthonic calm, in just a single century since Armstrong's first small step. The economic development of the Moon had always been the dream of Bud Tooke himself. But now she wondered how the Firstborn, who may themselves have been *older* than the Moon, might view this disquieting clatter.

Myra pointed. 'Mum, look over there, at Imbrium.'

Bisesa looked that way. She saw a disc that must have been kilometres across. It glinted with reflected sunlight, and shuddering waves spread across it.

'That's the solar-sail factory,' Alexei murmured. 'They lay down the webbing and spray on the boron film – they spin it up from the start, to hold it rigid against the Moon's gravity ...'

That glinting disc seemed to spin, and ripple, and then, without warning, it peeled neatly away from the mare surface as if being budded, and drifted up toward space, oscillating as it rose.

'It's beautiful,' Bisesa said.

Alexei shrugged. 'Pretty, yes. To be honest most of us don't find the Moon very interesting. They aren't true Spacers down there. Not when you can commute to Earth in a day or two. We call it Earth's attic ...'

Max murmured, 'Closest approach coming up.'

Now the whole Moon was shifting across Bisesa's field of view. Craters flooded with shadow fled before the fragile windows of the bridge. Bisesa felt Myra's hand tighten on her own. There are some sights humans just weren't meant to see, she thought helplessly.

Then the Moon's terminator fled over them, a broken line of illuminated peaks and crater walls, and they were plunged into a darkness broken only by the pale glow of Earthlight. As the sun's harsh light was cut off the lightship lost its thrust, and Bisesa felt the loss of that tiny fraction of gravity.

## CHAPTER 17
# WARSHIP

John Metternes came bustling up to the flight deck of the *Liberator.*

Edna asked, 'Everything nominal?'

'Bonza,' the ship's engineer said. He was breathless, the soft Belgian accent under his acquired Australian making his sibilants a rasp. 'We got the mag bottles loaded and interfaced without blowing our heads off in the process. All the protocols check out, the a-matter pods are being good enough to talk to us … Yes, we're nominal, and fit to launch. And about bloody time.'

Around forty, he was a burly man who was sweating so hard he had stained his jumpsuit armpits all the way through the protective layers. And there was a slight crust around his mouth. Perhaps he had been throwing up again. Though he had a nominal navy rank as a lieutenant commander, and was to fly with the *Liberator* as the chief engineer, John had come to space late; he was one of those unfortunates whose gut never adapted to microgravity. Not that that would make any difference when the A-drive cut in, for in flight the *Liberator* would thrust at a full gravity.

Edna tapped at a softscreen, skimmed the final draft of her operation order, and checked she had clearance from her control on Achilles. 'The launch window opens in five minutes.'

Metternes looked alarmed, his broad stubbly face turning ashen. 'My word.'

'You okay with this? The automated count is already underway, but we can still scrub if—'

'Good God, no. Ah, look – you took me aback, is all, didn't know it was as quick as that. The sooner we get on with it the better. And anyhow something will probably break before we get to zero; it generally does ... Libby, schematics please.'

The big window in front of them clouded over, replacing the view of Achilles and its backdrop of stars with a side-elevation graphic of the *Liberator* herself, a real-time image projected from sensors on Achilles and elsewhere. When John tapped sections of it the hull turned transparent. Much of the revealed inner workings glowed a pastel green, but red motes flared in scattered constellations to indicate outstanding engineering issues, launch day or not.

The design was simple, in essence. The *Liberator* looked like nothing so much as a Fourth of July firework, a rocket no less than a hundred metres in length, with habitable compartments stuck on the front end and an immense nozzle gaping at the back. Most of the hull was stuffed with asteroid-mined water ice, dirty snow that would serve as the reaction mass that would drive the ship forward.

And buried somewhere in the guts of the ship, near that nozzle, was the antimatter drive.

*Liberator*'s antimatter came in tiny granules of frozen hydrogen – or rather anti-hydrogen, stuff the propulsion engineers called 'H-bar.' For now it was contained inside a tungsten core, isolated from any normal matter by immaterial electromagnetic walls, the containment itself requiring huge energies to sustain.

H-bar was precious stuff. Because of its propensity to blow itself up on encountering normal matter, antimatter didn't sit around waiting to be collected, and so had to be manufactured. It occurred as a by-product of the collision of high-energy particles. But Earth's mightiest accelerators, if run continually, would produce only tiny amounts of antimatter – even the great alephtron on the Moon was useless as a factory. A natural source had at last been found in the 'flux tube' that connected the moon Io to its parent Jupiter, a tube of electrical current five million amperes strong, generated as that moon ploughed through Jupiter's magnetic field.

To mine antimatter, all you had to do was send a spacecraft into the flux tube and use magnetic traps to sift out antimatter particles. But there was a world of engineering challenge in that 'all.'

When Edna gave the order the magnetic fields would pulse, firing out the H-bar pellets one by one to hammer into an oncoming stream of normal hydrogen. Matter and antimatter would annihilate, every scrap of mass flashing immediately to energy. Asteroid ice would be sublimated to superheated steam, and it was that steam, hurtling out of the nozzle, that would push *Liberator* forward.

That was really all there was to it, aside from the hugely tricky details of handling the antimatter: *Liberator* was a steam rocket. But it was the numbers that were so impressive. Even the great mass-gobbling that went on in the fusing heart of the sun converted only a small percentage of fuel mass to energy. When matter and antimatter annihilated they went all the way; you just couldn't get more juice out of Einstein's famous E equals m c squared.

As a result, a mere pinch of antimatter, just fifty milligrams or so, would provide the equivalent of all the energy stored aboard the great chemical-rocket launch systems, like the space shuttle. That was what made the new antimatter drive so useful to governments intent on giving themselves a fast-response capability in the face of an invasion of the solar system. The *Liberator* was a ship so powerful it would deliver Edna to the Q-bomb, half Jupiter's distance away, as far as from Earth to the asteroids, in just a hundred and twelve *hours*.

The *Liberator* would have been dwarfed by the Spacers' lightships. But where a lightship was all spiderweb and sail, the *Liberator* was a solid mass, a club, a weapon. And the design was stupendously phallic, like so many of mankind's weapon systems in the past, as more than one observer had wryly remarked.

There really wasn't much for John to do; Libby handled the details of a countdown that was as simple as it could be made to be. John grew steadily more nervous.

'We're being watched,' Edna said evenly, to distract him.

'We are? Who by?'

'From Achilles. Engineers, administrators, other crew.'

Edna cleared the screen and they glanced down at the ice moon's surface. The graving dock crawled with spacesuited figures.

'Well, so much for the safety protocols,' John muttered. 'What are they doing there?'

Libby replied, 'I imagine they have come to watch the launch of mankind's first spacegoing warship.'

'Wow,' John whispered. 'She's right. Remember *Star Wars, Star Trek*?'

Edna had never heard of these ancient cultural relics.

'It all begins here,' John said. 'The first warship. But surely not the last, my word.'

'Thirty seconds,' Libby said evenly.

'Thank crap for that,' John said. He clutched the arms of his couch.

This was real, Edna thought suddenly. She was committed; she really was going to ride this ship into battle against an unknown foe, propelled by a drive that had been tested in anger only a couple of times, in a ship so new it still smelled of metal polish.

Libby said, 'Three, two, one.'

Somewhere in the guts of the ship a magnetic trap flexed. Matter died.

And Edna was shoved back into her chair with a thrust that drove the breath from her lungs.

## CHAPTER 18
# MARS

The journey wore away.

Even now Alexei wouldn't allow any communications about sensitive matters, or even 'loose talk' in the cabin of the *Maxwell,* in this tiny volume drifting millions of kilometres from the nearest human. 'You never know who's listening.' And though the space was bigger than aboard the spider, the paper partitions weren't very soundproof, and Myra and Bisesa felt they had no real privacy.

Nobody talked. They were just as shut-in a crew as they had been on the spider.

After a timeless interval marked only by the gradual dwindling of the sun, Mars loomed out of the dark. Bisesa and Myra peered curiously through the bridge windows.

The approaching world was a sculpture of orange-red, its surface pocked and wrinkled, with a broad smearing of grey mist across much of the northern hemisphere. Compared to Earth, which from space was as bright as a daylight sky, Mars looked oddly dark to Bisesa, murky, sullen.

But as the lightship looped around dwindling orbits she learned to read the landscape. There were the battered southern uplands, punctuated by the mighty bruise of Hellas, and to the north the smoother, obviously younger plains of the Vastitas Borealis. Bisesa was struck how *big* everything was on Mars. The Valles Marineris canyon system stretched around nearly a quarter the planet's circumference, and the Tharsis volcanoes were a gross magmatic distortion of the whole planet's shape.

So much she might have seen had she visited in 1969 rather than 2069. But today Mars's air was streaked by brilliant white water-vapour clouds. And on one orbit the

*Maxwell*'s path took them right over the summit of Olympus itself, where black smoke pooled in a caldera wide enough to have swallowed up New York City.

If the scars of the sunstorm were evident on this new face of Mars, so was the handiwork of mankind. The largest settlement on Mars was Port Lowell, an equatorial splash of silver on the fringe of the battered southern uplands. Roads snaked away to all points of the compass, reminiscent of the rectilinear tracery of canals that the last pre-spaceflight observers had imagined they had seen on Mars. And amid the roads and the domes were swathes of green: life from Earth, flourishing under glass in the soil of Mars.

But Myra pointed out more green, a belt of it stretching across the northern plains, and puddled in the great deep bowl of Hellas, a darker, more sombre strain. *That* had nothing to do with Earth.

Alexei told Bisesa that they would spend a few nights at Lowell. As soon as a surface rover was free she was to travel on, heading north – all the way to the pole of Mars, she learned, with gathering incredulity. She peered down at that dense lid of northern fog, wondering what waited for her beneath its murk.

They spent a whole day floating above Mars, as the gentle pressure of sunlight regularised the *Maxwell*'s orbit. Then a squat, boxy craft came lumbering up from Lowell.

The shuttle's sole occupant was a woman, perhaps in her mid-twenties. Dressed in a bright green coverall she was slender, rather fragile looking, and her face, open, somewhat empty, bore a neat ident tattoo. 'Hi. I'm Paula. Paula Umfraville.'

When Paula smiled directly at her, Bisesa gasped. 'I'm sorry. It's just—'

'Don't worry. A lot of people from Earth have the same reaction. I'm flattered, really, that people remember my mother so well ...'

For Bisesa's generation Helena Umfraville's face had become one of the most famous in all the human worlds:

not just for her participation in the first manned mission to Mars, but for the remarkable discovery she had made just before her own death. Paula might have been her double.

'I'm not important.' Paula spread her arms wide. 'Welcome to Mars! I think you're going to be intrigued by what we've found here, Bisesa Dutt . . .'

The shuttle's descent was a smooth glide. As Bisesa watched, the wrinkled face of Mars flattened into a dusty landscape, and ochre light seeped across the sky.

Paula talked all the way down, perhaps delivering a patter intended to reassure nervous passengers. 'I usually find myself apologising to visitors from Earth – and especially if they're heading for the poles, as you are, Bisesa. Here we are coming down at latitude ten north, and we'll have to haul you all the way to the polar cap overland from here. But all the support facilities are here at Lowell, and the other colonies close to the equator, because the equatorial belt was all those first-generation chemical-engine ships could reach . . .'

Myra was more interested in Paula than in Mars. She said awkwardly, 'I went into astronautics after the sunstorm. Helena Umfraville was a hero of mine – I studied her life. I never knew she had a daughter.'

Paula shrugged. 'She didn't, before she left for Mars. But she wanted a child. She knew that on the *Aurora 1* she would spend months bathed in deep-space radiation. So before she departed she left behind eggs, other genetic material. It was transferred to a Hibernaculum during the sunstorm. And after the storm was over, my father – well. Here I am. Of course my mother never knew me. I like to think she would have been proud that I'm here on Mars, in a way carrying on her work.'

'I'm sure she would be,' Bisesa said.

The touchdown was brisk and businesslike, on a pad built of a kind of glass, melted out of the crust. Bisesa stared. This was Mars. Beyond the scarred surface of the pad everything was reddish-brown, the land, the sky, even the washed-out disc of the sun.

Within minutes a small bus with blister windows came

bouncing up, puppy-like, on huge soft wheels. It was painted green, like Paula's jumpsuit – of course, Bisesa thought, you would use green to stand out on red Mars. Bisesa clambered through a docking tunnel, following Paula, with Alexei and Myra and their luggage and bits of kit. The bus, with rows of plastic seats, might have come from any airport on Earth.

As the bus rolled off Paula chattered about the landscape. She seemed proud of it, engaging in her enthusiasm. 'We're actually on the floor of a canyon called the Ares Vallis. This is an outflow canyon, shaped by catastrophic flooding in the deep past, draining from the southern uplands.'

That ancient calamity had lasted just ten or twenty days, it was thought, a few weeks billions of years past when a river a thousand times as mighty as the Mississippi had battered its way through the ancient rocks. This sort of event had, it seemed, occurred all around the great latitudinal frontier where Mars's south met its north; the whole of the northern hemisphere was depressed below the mean surface level, like one enormous crater imposed on half the planet.

'You can see why the *Aurora* crew were sent here for the first human exploration – and in fact why NASA sent its *Pathfinder* unmanned probe to the same area in the 1990s ...'

Bisesa, peering out, tuned out the words. This dusty plain, littered with slablike boulders, was Earthlike, and yet immediately not Earthlike. How strange it was that she could never touch those dusty rocks, or taste that thin iron air.

As they neared the domes of Lowell they passed cylinders mounted vertically on tripods. To Bisesa they looked like the power lasers of a space elevator. The Martians didn't have their beanstalk yet, it seemed, but they had the power sources in place.

And the bus rolled past flags that fluttered limply over markers of Martian glass. Bisesa supposed Paula's mother was here, with those others of Bob Paxton's crew who had not survived their stranding on Mars. If Ares's geology was forever shaped by that tremendous flood in the deep past, so its human history would surely always be shaped by the heroism of the *Aurora* crew.

The bus drove them up to the largest of the domes and docked smoothly.

They passed through a connecting tunnel and emerged in a warren of internal partitions, lit by big fluorescent tubes suspended from a silvered roof. Bisesa felt very self-conscious as she walked into the dome, practicing her Mars lope. The noise levels were high, echoing.

People bustled by, many dressed in green jumpsuits like Paula's. They all seemed busy, and few of them glanced at Bisesa and her party. Bisesa guessed that to these locals she would be about as welcome as tourists at a South Pole base on Earth.

Alexei felt moved to apologise. 'Don't mind this. Just remember, every breath you take has to be paid for out of somebody's taxes ...'

Bisesa did notice that very few of the Martians wore ident tattoos on their cheeks.

They dumped their luggage in rooms provided for them in a cramped, shacklike 'hotel,' and Paula offered to fill their few hours at Lowell with a tour. So they went exploring, following Paula, working their way from dome to half-inhabited dome through tunnels that were sometimes so low they had to crouch.

They bought their own lunch at an automated galley. Their Earth credit was good, but the bowls of sticky soup and bitter coffee they bought were expensive.

As they ate, a gang of schoolkids ran by, laughing. They were skinny, gangly, all at least as tall as Bisesa, though with their slim bodies and fresh faces it was hard to tell how old they were. They ran with great bounds.

Alexei murmured, 'First-generation Martians. Grown from conception under low gravity. The next generation, *their* children, will be very interesting ...'

Bisesa was sorry when they had passed out of sight, taking their splash of human warmth with them.

One big translucent dome enclosed a farm. They walked

between beds of lettuces and cabbages, all proud and healthy, and shallow ponds that served as rice paddies, and trestle tables bearing pans of some turgid fluid from which grew beans and peas and soya. There were even fruit trees, oranges and apples and pears growing in pots, obviously precious and lovingly tended. In here they were at last exposed to pink Martian daylight, but the light of the remote sun was supplemented by banks of hot white lamps.

But they walked on quickly. Under a faint scent of some industrial perfume was the cloying stench of sewage.

They reached the dome's translucent wall, and Bisesa saw rows of plants marching away, set into the soil beyond the dome. She noticed how they glinted, oddly glassy, and the green of their oddly shaped leaves was a deeper shade than the bright plants around her.

But she wasn't yet used to Mars. It took a beat before it struck her that these rows of plants were happily growing in the Martian air *outside* the pressurised dome. 'Oh, my,' she said.

Alexei laughed.

They walked on through more inhabited areas. They passed what had to be a school, and Bisesa longed to walk in and discover what kind of curriculum was presented to these first young Martians – what were they told of Earth? – but she didn't have the nerve to ask Paula.

And they found a bar, called 'Ski's' – apparently after Schiaparelli, inadvertent discoverer of the Lowellian canals. There was alcohol available, but only fruit wines and whiskeys. They tried an apple wine, but it tasted weak to Bisesa.

'Low gravity, low pressure,' Alexei said. 'It's easier to get drunk here.'

The last dome they explored was the largest, and looked the most expensive. It was constructed of panels laid over immense struts of what Myra identified as lunar glass. The interior was mostly disused. Aside from a few corners used for stores and small workshops, there were only dusty partitions, cables, and ducts lying over an unfinished floor.

'It's as if they don't quite know what to do with it,' Bisesa said.

'But it wasn't the Martians' choice,' Paula said. 'After the sunstorm there was a lot of sentiment about what happened to the *Aurora* crew, and a lot of money was put into getting the Mars settlement going properly. And this was one result. It was going to be a slice of Earth, here on Mars.' She waved a hand. 'Those glass struts came from the sunstorm shield itself. So this is a sort of memorial, you see. There would have been blue sky, projected onto that big dome. They were going to call it Oxford Circus.'

'You're kidding.'

'No,' Alexei said. 'There was even going to be a zoo here. Farm animals. Maybe an elephant or two, Sol, I don't know. All shipped up as zygotes.'

'And weather, like Earth's, inside the dome,' Paula said. 'They even got that part of it working for a while, when I was little. The thunderstorm was quite scary. But it all broke down and nobody bothered to fix it. Why should we? Many of us have never seen Earth; we don't miss it. And we have our own weather.' She smiled wider, her young face so like her mother's, her eyes blank.

That night, Bisesa settled down in a stern monkish cell that seemed designed to remind her that she wasn't a guest here, not welcome, that she was here on sufferance.

But there was a row of books above her bed – real paper books, or anyhow facsimiles. They were editions of classic novels of Mars as it had been dreamed of during the long years before spaceflight, from Wells through Weinbaum and Bradbury to Robinson and beyond. Flicking through the old books oddly pleased her; for the first time since she had arrived, she was reminded how many dreams had always been lodged on Mars.

She clambered into bed. She read a few chapters of *Martian Dust* by a writer called Martin Gibson. It was a colourful melodrama that, with the comforting gravity, soon lulled her to sleep.

## CHAPTER 19

# THE SANDS OF MARS

She was woken by Alexei, shaking her shoulder. 'We have to move.'

She sat up, rubbing her eyes. 'I thought you said we have to wait for a rover.'

'Well, we changed our plans. They don't have too many assets on Mars, but they started to move during the night.'

'Who is *they*?'

'Astropol. The Space Council. Look, Bisesa, we'll have time to discuss this. Please, right now you need to shift your ass.'

She had trusted him, and Myra, this far. She shifted.

The rover, trundling to its docking port on the central dome, was visible through a small window. The rover had a number: it was the fourth of Lowell's fleet of six such long-distance exploratory vehicles. But it also had a name, stamped in electric blue on its hull: *Discovery*. About the size of a school bus, painted bright green, its hull bristled with antennae and sensor pods, and a remote manipulator arm was folded up at its side. The rover dragged an equally massive trailer at its back, connected to the parent by a thick conduit. The main body and the trailer were mounted on big complicated-looking wheels on loosely sprung axles. The trailer contained stores, spares, life support gear – and, unbelievably, a small nuclear power plant.

This rover was big enough to carry a crew of ten on a complete yearlong circumnavigation of Mars. Bisesa realised it was wrong to think of it as a mere bus. It was a spaceship on wheels.

And it had pressure suits stuck to the outside of the hull.

Bisesa said, 'Reminds me of Ahab strapped to the side of his whale.'

But none of them, not even Myra, had heard of *Moby Dick*.

'So why *Discovery*? For the old space shuttle?'

'No, no. For Captain Scott's first ship,' Paula said. 'You know, the Antarctic explorer? We use this particular rover for polar jaunts, north and south, so the name seems appropriate.'

Expeditions to the poles had always been a tradition of Lowell Base, Paula said. The astronauts of *Aurora,* in fact, in their long years as castaways before the sunstorm, had made expeditions to the south pole, intent on coring the ancient ices and so deciphering Mars's climatic history.

Paula's bright chat filled the time as they waited for access to the rover. But Alexei bit his nails, desperate to be away.

At last hatches swung open. They walked through an airlock and clambered into a roomy interior. There was even a small medical area, complete with robotic arms capable of manipulating a set of surgical instruments.

Paula said, 'We'll cover around a quarter of the planet's circumference, travelling twenty hours a day at a nominal fifty klicks per hour. Five days should see us home.'

'Twenty hours a *day*?'

Myra and Bisesa exchanged glances. They had already been cooped up for weeks on the elevator and aboard the *Maxwell.* But these Spacers were used to lengthy confinement in small places.

'The *Discovery* will do the driving itself, of course. It's done the route a dozen times already, and probably knows every boulder and ice field. It's a smooth ride once we're underway ...'

Paula briefly spoke to a traffic control centre, and then the rover briskly popped itself loose of the dome airlock.

Once they were sealed in Alexei sat and blew air through pursed lips. 'Well, that's that. What a relief.'

Myra glanced back at the Lowell domes. 'Couldn't we be chased?'

Alexei said, 'The other rovers are out in the field. Mars is still very sparsely populated, Myra, sparsely equipped. Not a good place to mount a car chase. And it's unlikely that Astropol and the other agencies have any assets at the polar base.' Bisesa had learned that Astropol was a federation of terrestrial police agencies dedicated to offworld operations. 'Oh, they could come after us,' Alexei murmured. 'But it would take something drastic to do it. They may not be ready to show their hand just yet.'

The rover swung itself around and set off to the north.

Bisesa and Myra sat up front behind a big observation window, and watched the view unfold. It was about midday, and the sun was to the south behind them; the rover's shadow stretched ahead.

The domes of Lowell soon slipped behind the rear horizon, obscured by the rover's immense rooster-tails of dust. The road was metalled at first, glassy; then it was hard-pressed dirt, a scar in the faded dust, and before long nothing but a rutted track. Away from the base there was no sign of human activity, save for the odd weather station, and those endless tracks peeling off to the north. Bisesa could make out the remnants of the Ares flood in the scoured landscape, the teardrop islands, the huge scattered boulders. But everything was old, worn down with age, every rock surface rubbed smooth, every slope draped with thick dust.

With nothing to see but rocks, Myra soon went to join Alexei and Paula, who had a common interest in an exotic form of poker.

Bisesa sat alone in the bubble rover's blister window, riding smoothly over Mars. As the sun wheeled through the sky, Mars began to work a kind of spell on her. It was like Earth, with some of the furniture of an earthly landscape: the land below, the sky above, the dust and the scattered rocks. But the horizon was too close, the sun too small, too pale. A corner of her hindbrain kept asking: how can the world be like *this*?

It was in this mood of strangeness that she saw the arch.

The rover never brought them close. But it loomed over the horizon, tall, impossibly slender. She was sure that that immense crosspiece could not have been supported on Earth; it was Martian architecture.

The day wore away. The sunset was long and elaborate, with bands of diminishing colour following the small sun toward the horizon. The night sky was oddly disappointing, though, with only a scattering of stars; there must be too much dust suspended in the air. Bisesa looked for Earth, but either it wasn't up or she didn't recognise it.

Paula brought her a plate of food, a piping-hot risotto with mushrooms and green beans, and a mug of coffee fitted with a lid. She leaned down and peered straight ahead, through the window.

Bisesa asked, 'What are you looking for?'

'The north celestial pole. People generally ask.'

'Tourists like me, you mean.'

Paula wasn't fazed. 'Mars doesn't have a bright pole star, like Polaris. But – look, can you see Cygnus, the swan? The brightest star is Deneb, Alpha Cygni. Follow the spine of the swan, up through Deneb, and the celestial pole is about halfway between Deneb and the next distinct constellation, Cepheus.'

'Thank you. But the dust everywhere – the seeing isn't as good as I expected.'

'Well, Mars is a museum of dust, the climatologists say,' Paula said. 'It's not like Earth. We have no rain to wash the dust out, no sedimentary processes to bake it all into rock. So it stays in the air.'

Mars as a snow globe, Bisesa thought. 'I saw an arch.'

Paula nodded. 'Erected by the Chinese. They put up a monument like that every place one of their arks came down.'

So that tremendous structure was a memorial to hundreds of Chinese who had died on Mars on sunstorm day.

Bisesa ventured, 'Paula, I was a little surprised you came along with us.'

'Surprised?'

'And that you're mixed up with this secretive business at the pole of Mars. Alexei, yes, I can see it in his personality.'

'He is a bit furtive, isn't he?'

They shared a laugh. Bisesa said, 'But you seem more—'

'Conformist?' That pretty airline-stewardess smile was still in place, illuminated by the dash lights. 'I don't mind if that's said of me. Maybe it's true.'

'It's just that you're so good at your job.'

Paula said without resentment, 'I was probably born to it. My mother is the person most people remember of the *Aurora* crew, after Bob Paxton – the only one, probably.'

'And so visitors respond to you.'

'It could have been a handicap. Why not turn it into an asset?'

'Okay. But that doesn't extend to hauling your backside all the way to the north pole for us.' She paused. 'You admire your mother, don't you?'

Paula shrugged. 'I never met her. But how could I not admire her? Bob Paxton came to Mars and sort of conquered it, and then went home again. But my mother loved Mars. You can tell that from her journals. Bob Paxton is a hero on Earth,' she said. 'But my mother is a hero here on Mars, our first hero of all.' The stewardess smile flicked back on. 'More risotto?'

In the murky Martian dark, in the warmth of the cabin, Bisesa fell asleep in her seat.

She woke to a tap on her shoulder. She found she was swathed by a blanket.

Myra was sitting with her, gazing out of the window into dawn light. Bisesa saw they were driving through a landscape of rolling dunes, some of them tens of metres high, frozen waves a kilometre or two apart. Some kind of frost gathered in their lee.

'My, I slept the night through.'

'Are you okay?'

Bisesa shifted, exploring. 'A little stiff. But I guess even a chair like this is comfortable in low gravity. I'll stretch and have a wash shortly.'

'You'll have to wait for Alexei. He's shaving his head again.'

'I guess I got hypnotised by the view.'

'White line fever. Or something.' Myra sounded irritable.

'Myra? Is something wrong?'

'Wrong? Christ, Mother, look at that view. *Nothing*. And yet here you are, sitting up here for hour after hour, just drinking it in.'

'What's wrong with that?'

'It's *you*. If there's something strange, you're drawn to it. You revel in it.'

Bisesa glanced around. The others were asleep. She realised that this was the first time she and Myra had effectively been alone since the washed-out days after her waking at the Hibernaculum – there had never been real privacy even on the *Maxwell*, and certainly not in the elevator spider cabin.

'We've never had a chance to talk,' she said.

Myra made to stand up. 'Not here.'

Bisesa put her hand on her arm. 'Come on. Who cares if the police are listening in? Please, Myra. I don't feel I know you anymore.'

Myra sat back. 'Maybe that's the trouble. I don't know *you*. Since you came out of the tank – I think I'd got used to living without you, Mum. As if you had died, perhaps. And when you did come out, you aren't how I remember you. You're like a sister I've suddenly discovered, not my mother. Does that make sense?'

'No. But we haven't evolved for Hibernacula time-slips, have we?'

'What do you want to talk about? I mean, where am I supposed to start? It's been nineteen years, half my life.'

'Give me one headline.'

'Okay.' Myra hesitated, and looked away. 'You have a granddaughter.'

Her name was Charlie, for Charlotte, Myra's daughter by

Eugene Mangles. Now aged fifteen, she had been born four years after Bisesa went into the tank.

'Good God. I'm a grannie.'

'When we broke up, Eugene fought me for custody. And he *won,* Mum. He had the clout to do it. Eugene is powerful and he's famous.'

Bisesa said, 'But he was never very human, was he?'

'Of course I had access. But that was never enough. I'm not like you. I don't want strangeness. I wanted to build a home, for me and Charlie. I wanted – stability. I never got close to that. And in the end he cut me out altogether. It wasn't hard. They're hardly ever even on the Earth.'

Bisesa reached for her hand; it was cold and unresponsive. 'Why didn't you tell me this before?'

'Well, for one thing you didn't ask. And, look, here we are on Mars! And we're here because you're the famous Bisesa Dutt. You have much more important issues to worry about than a lost granddaughter.'

'Myra, I'm sorry. When this is all over—'

'Oh, don't be ridiculous, Mum. It never is over, with you. But I'll support you even so. I always will. Look, forget about it. You had a right to know. Well, now you do.' Her face was intent, her mouth pinched. Green light was reflected in her eyes.

*Green?*

Bisesa sat up with a jolt, and looked out of the blister window.

Under a salmon-pink dawn sky, the rutted tracks snaked across a plain that was painted a deep dull green.

Paula joined them. '*Discovery*. Slow down so we can see.' The truck obligingly slowed, with a distant grinding of gears.

Myra and Bisesa sat uncomfortably; Bisesa wondered how much Paula had heard of their conversation.

Now Bisesa could see that the green was a carpet of tiny plants, each no larger than her thumb. Each plant looked like a leather-skinned cactus, but it had translucent sections – windows to catch the sunlight, Bisesa supposed, without losing a precious drop of moisture. There were other plants too. She picked out small black spheres – round to retain heat, black to soak it up during the day? She wondered if they turned white, chameleon-like, to avoid dissipating heat at night. But the cacti predominated.

Myra said, 'The cacti are what Helena discovered, in the wake of the sunstorm. Life on Mars.'

'Yes,' Paula said. 'The most common multicelled organism we've found yet on Mars. The subsurface bacterial mats and the stromatolites in Hellas are more widespread – a lot more biomass. But the window cacti are still the stars of the show. The species has been named for my mother.'

Each window cactus was a survivor from deep ages past, Paula said.

When the solar system was young, the three sister worlds were briefly similar: Venus, Earth, Mars, all warm, wet, geologically active. It was impossible to say on which of them life spawned first. Mars was certainly the first to accumulate an oxygen atmosphere, the fuel for complex, multicelled life-forms, billions of years before the Earth. But Mars was also the first to cool and dry.

Paula said, 'But this took time, hundreds of millions of years. You can achieve a lot in hundreds of millions of years – why, the mammals filled out an ecology vacated by the dinosaurs in less than sixty-five million years. The Martians were able to evolve survival strategies.'

The roots of the cacti were buried deep in the cold rock of Mars. They didn't need oxygen, but fuelled their glacial metabolism with hydrogen released by the slow reaction of the volcanic rocks with traces of water ice. Thus they and their ancestors had survived aeons.

'There were always volcanic episodes,' Paula said. 'The Tharsis calderas thicken the air every ten to a hundred million years. The cacti grow, propagate, grow dormant again, surviving as spores until the next episode. And then the sunstorm caused *rain,* water rain. The air has stayed thick and wet enough to keep them out of their dormant stages right through the year.

'And, the biologists say, they are related to our sort of life. It's a different sort of DNA here,' Paula said. 'Using a different set of bases – six, not four – and a different kind of coding. The same with Martian RNA and proteins, not quite like ours. It's thought the amino acid set that's used here is subtly different too, but that's still controversial. But it *is* DNA and RNA and proteins, the same toolbox as on Earth.'

Mars was young in an age of continuing massive bombardment, as the relics of the solar system's violent formation smashed into the new worlds. But that battering ensured that an immense amount of material, blasted off the roiling surfaces, was transferred between the planets. And that material contained life.

Bisesa gazed out at the patient cacti. 'So these are our cousins.'

'But more distantly related than we are to any other life-forms from Earth. The last significant biomass transfer must have been so early that the final form of DNA coding wasn't yet settled on either world. But the relationship is close enough to be useful.'

'Useful? How?'

Paula tapped a softscreen on the *Discovery*'s dashboard, and produced images showing how Lowell scientists were finding ways to splice Martian genes into terrestrial plants. And that was how a new breed of plant was being developed, neither purely terrestrial nor purely Martian, able to grow outside the pressurised domes of the colonies, and yet capable of providing food for humans – and of injecting oxygen into the air. Some of the biologists thought it was a route to terraforming, a first step toward making Mars like Earth. An informal grouping of them even had a slogan: *All These Worlds Are Ours.*

'In fact,' Paula said, 'I'm glad we happened on the cacti. It's important you know about this, Bisesa.'

'Why?'

'So you can understand what they've found at the pole.'

'I can't wait,' Myra said dryly.

'And I can't wait for the bathroom,' Bisesa said. She

pushed her way out of her chair, letting the blanket drop. 'Alexei? Are you done in there yet?'

The *Discovery* rolled on, patient, silent, for kilometre after kilometre, a cybernetic Stakhanovite. By the middle of that day they were through the green, and rolled across a dull, undulating plain.

After that, each day of the journey the sun climbed lower. At last it panned around the horizon, and there was no full daylight, only a kind of twilight glow that washed around the obscured sky.

Bisesa understood. Mars was tilted on its axis, just as was Earth; in northern winter the pole pointed away from the sun, and as she headed north she was driving into a twelve-month-long Arctic night. What was different about Mars was how quickly the changes came; here, the lines of latitude clicked away rapidly. She had a very clear sense that she was driving over the surface of a small round world, an ant crawling over an orange.

One sunset they saw a bank of clouds on the northern horizon.

By dawn they were under it. The polar hood was thick enough to obscure all but the brightest stars; Deneb and the celestial pole were lost.

By midday it had begun to snow.

## CHAPTER 20
# LIBERATOR

'It's taken us under five days to cross the solar system, Thea. Think of that. And now there's only a few hours to go before Q-hour, our rendezvous with the bomb ...'

The *Liberator* had the mass and rough dimensions of the old *Saturn V* launchers. But whereas most of a *Saturn*'s mass would have burned itself up and been discarded in minutes, leaving its payload to coast unpowered most of the way to its destination, the *Liberator*'s mighty engine could maintain a thrust of a full gravity or more for days, even weeks. That had enabled the ship to cut a straight-line trajectory from one point on the J-line to another, from the Trojan base to the position of the bomb. Its path was a rectilinear oddity in a solar system of circles and ellipses.

And Edna had crossed half the distance between Jupiter and the distant sun in a hundred hours.

'We're actually slowing down now. We're approaching the Q-bomb tail-first, our exhaust blasting out ...

'Most of the officers serving in space have been transferred from the US Navy, because most spacecraft are more like submarines than anything else. But the *Liberator* is different. We've so much energy to burn that we have more room on this ship than on any spacecraft since *Skylab*. If you've never heard of that, look it up. John Metternes and I share a kind of big apartment, with bedrooms, showers, and a stateroom with softscreens and coffeemakers. When we go to the ports and look down at the flank of the ship, it's like looking out of the window of a high-rise hotel on Earth. But most hotels don't have antennae and sensor booms. Or gun ports.

'I need to go, love. The drive's about to be cut, and it

would be embarrassing to meet the bogey with me stranded in midair . . .!

'How do I feel? I'm frightened. Excited. I have confidence in my abilities, and John's, and in the *Liberator,* which has already proven herself a fine ship. I just hope that's enough to carry the day. I – I guess that's all, Libby. Close file.'

'Yes, Edna. It is time.'

'I know. Call John, would you?'

## CHAPTER 21
# POLE

Bisesa couldn't see a thing.

The *Discovery* ploughed its way through a half-metre thickness of carbon dioxide snow. The fragile dry-ice stuff sublimated before the rover's heat, so they drove into a blinding mist, and even beyond the mist it was a murky dark. Nobody said anything, the poker players continuing their endless tournaments. Bisesa just had to put up with the unnerving drive alone.

Then, through the gloom, she saw bright green lights, brilliant sparks. The rover slowed to a halt. The rest of the crew hurried forward.

A vehicle of some kind sat on the ice, with big balloon wheels and straddled by two spacesuited occupants. Their helmets were illuminated, but Bisesa couldn't make out their faces. When they caught the rover's lights they waved.

'That's a tricycle,' Myra said, wondering.

'Actually,' Paula said mildly, 'they call it a General Utility Vehicle. For operations close to the pole station—'

'I want one.'

Alexei tapped a softscreen. 'Yuri. Is that you?'

'Hi, Alexei. We cleared a path for you with the sublimation blade. The snow's heavier than usual this season.'

'Appreciated.'

'*Discovery,* just follow us and you'll be fine. Eleven, twelve hours or so and we'll be home with no trouble. See you at Wells.' The vehicle turned and drove ahead. Mist burst around it in a spray, brightly illuminated by the floods.

With *Discovery* following easily, the little convoy's speed soon passed forty kilometres an hour.

As they roared on into the dark, the hard ground under

the snow began to change. It was layered, alternating light and dark in strata as thick as Bisesa's arm, like a vast sedimentary bed. And it looked polished, with a fine patina that glistened in the trucks' lights.

After a couple of hours of this they crunched up onto a firmer, paler surface, a grimy white tinged with Mars red.

'Water ice,' Paula announced. 'Mostly, anyhow. This is the permanent ice cap, the residue that's left after the carbon dioxide snow sublimes away every spring. Here at the edge we're about five hundred klicks from Wells Station, which is near the geographic pole. The drive will be smoother now. The rover's wheels are reconfigurable for different surface types.'

Bisesa said, 'I'm surprised *Discovery* isn't lowering a set of skis.'

Alexei looked at her, a bit pained. 'Bisesa, this is Mars. The temperature out there is the freezing point of dry ice – at this pressure, that's about a hundred fifty K.'

She worked that out. 'A hundred and twenty degrees below freezing.'

'Right,' Paula said. 'At these temperatures water ice is so hard it would be like skiing on basalt.'

Bisesa was chagrined. 'You've given this little lecture a dozen times, haven't you?'

'You didn't have time for the usual orientation. Don't worry about it.'

Now that they were on the ice Bisesa expected a smooth, straight ride on to the pole. But the lead truck soon turned aside from its dead-straight northern track, and embarked on a grand, sweeping detour, turning clockwise. Peering out of the left-hand window, Bisesa glimpsed a canyon.

She swallowed her pride and asked Paula about it.

Paula said it was a 'spiral canyon,' one of many gouged into the ice cap. She pulled up an image of the whole cap, taken from space in the summer, when the dry ice snow wasn't there to obscure it. The ice cap looked like a twisting storm system, with those spiral canyons twisting in from the edge and reaching almost to the pole. It was astounding, like nothing Bisesa knew of on Earth. But after her jaunt across the solar system there wasn't much wonder left in her soul.

As they drove on the snow grew deeper, until they were driving along a path between two walls of snow heaped up maybe two metres deep. The snow looked compact, harder than snow on Earth, denser maybe.

She was relieved when she saw a cluster of lights ahead, and the rounded shoulders of living modules.

A row of green lights stretched off into the distance, as if they were driving down a runway. As the rover rolled closer Bisesa saw that the lights were on poles maybe four metres high, perhaps to keep above the snow. Glancing back, she saw that looking the other way the lights were bright white – so, in the murk of a Martian blizzard, you could always tell if you were heading toward or away from the base.

The structures that loomed out of the dark, lifted up off the ground on stilts, were not domes but flattened pie-shapes, round above and below. They were coloured bright green, and huddled close together, interlinked by short tunnels. Bisesa saw that these big hab modules were in fact mounted on wheels, and had been tied down to the ice by cables fixed to pitons. They were like monstrous caravans, she thought.

As the rover neared the station, the walls of dry ice snow thinned away, until the rover was driving over an ice surface almost clear of snow but covered with an open black mesh. Heating elements, perhaps, designed to keep off the dry ice. The rover nuzzled up to a low dome at the foot of one of the stilts. Two station vehicles were already parked here, heavy-looking, smaller than the rover from Lowell.

Paula led them through the hatch, and Bisesa found herself facing a staircase, roofed over with blue-green plastic, that evidently led up to the nearest of the stilted habs. Alexei's suitcase couldn't climb the stairs and had to be hauled up on a plastic rope.

At the top of the stairs, the station crew were waiting for the newcomers. There were four of them, two women, two men, Mars-spindly in the limbs though a little heavy in the belly. All were pretty young, Bisesa guessed, none older than forty. Their coveralls were clean but well-patched, and they all smelled faintly greasy. None of them had cheek ident tattoos.

They stared at Bisesa, and stood a little too close together.

One burly twenty-five-year-old came forward and shook Bisesa's hand. 'You'll have to forgive us. We don't get too many visitors up here.' He had a big, blotchy drinker's nose, grimy black hair pulled back into a ponytail, and a mass of curly beard. His accent was indistinct, like American but laced with longer European vowels.

'You're Yuri, right? You were on the ice bike.'

'Yes. We exchanged a wave. Yuri O'Rourke. Resident glaciologist, climatologist, what have you.' Briskly he introduced the rest of the base crew: Ellie von Devender, a physicist, Grendel Speth, a doctor-biologist, and Hanse Critchfield, an engineer responsible for power, transport, and essential systems, but also a specialist in the drilling rig, the base's main scientific function. 'Although we all multitask,' Yuri said. 'We're all trained paramedics, for instance . . .'

Ellie von Devender approached Bisesa. The physicist was maybe thirty, stocky in her jumpsuit, with her hair tightly pulled back. She wore thick-rimmed spectacles, an affectation that hid her eyes and made her look hostile.

Bisesa said curiously, 'I guess I would have expected a glaciologist, a biologist. But a physicist?'

Ellie said, 'The glaciology is the reason the base is here, along with Grendel and her wet lab. I am the reason *you're* here, Ms. Dutt.'

Yuri clapped Bisesa on the shoulder. 'Come see the place.' He led them briskly through the hab. 'This is what we call Can Six,' he said. 'The EVA port . . .'

Can Six was a bubble of fabric, the walls coloured a bright sea-green with an eye-deceiving wave pattern. It had a honeycomb floor that straddled its interior at the widest point, and looking down Bisesa could see stores stacked up in the underfloor space. There were no spacesuits in evidence, but there were odd hatches in the walls that might have led to externally-mounted suits, like the rover's. Equipment was stacked up here, what looked like spare parts and other gear for the rovers, and also a small science lab, and a medical area, a single bed surrounded by equipment, sealed off from the rest by a zippered plastic curtain. It was dark, and felt cold and dusty, as if not much used.

Yuri hurried them through a small airlock to another module: 'Can Five, science,' he said. Here there was another, more comprehensive lab suite, and a larger hospital area, and what looked like a small gym. It was brighter, with glowing panels plastered to walls that seemed to be decorated with scenes of mountains and rivers.

Bisesa murmured to Myra, 'Why two lab suites, two medical bays?'

Myra shrugged. 'To avoid contamination maybe. You come in from EVA, and can process your samples and treat injuries without breaking the seals to the rest of the base.'

'Contamination of the crew by Martians?'

'Or of Martians by the crew.'

In Can Five, Grendel Speth, small, neat, slim, her black hair speckled with grey, briskly took blood, urine, and cheek-swab samples from each of the visitors. 'Just so the station can keep you healthy,' she said. 'Testing for allergies, nutritional genomics, that sort of thing. Our food comes from freeze-dried stores from Lowell, and homegrown vegetables from our garden. We'll add supplements to make sure your specific nutritional needs are met. You won't even know they are there ...'

Now Yuri hurried them through a third module – Can Three, evidently a sleeping area, divided up into pie-slice bedrooms, dark, evidently not used. They came to another module, Can Two. Bizarrely this module had been fitted out to simulate a city-centre hotel called the 'Mars-Astoria.' But many of the internal partitions here had been torn down to give a more open, shared space, though the core section was dedicated to a small galley and a shower-toilet. There were four beds in this round space, with small cupboards nd chairs beside them, all of them cluttered with clothes nd other gear. Softscreens had been plastered over the unegarded urban landscape, cycling through what looked like ersonal images of families, pets, domestic landscapes.

Myra said curiously, 'You're not using this as the makers ntended, are you?'

Yuri said, 'Wells was built for ten; there are only four of s. The nights are long here, Myra. We prefer living like this, ogether.'

After that, Yuri apologetically led them down another taircase to a small surface dome, and then down steps cut nto the ice. 'Sorry about this. You can see we only have he four beds set up, and we've pretty much shut down the nodules we don't use. We generally put up visitors down ere, in our radiation storm shelter ... If you're not comfortble we can open up another of the cans.'

Bisesa glanced around as she descended. The cavern in he ice was a squat cylinder, sliced up by partitions into pie-haped segments. She recognised a galley, a comms station, shower block, a cluttered space that looked like a lab or a nedical station. The place was lived-in. There were ruts in he floor around the galley and the shower block, the walls nd metal surfaces looked scuffed and polished with use and euse, and there was a faintly stale smell, of air that had been ycled too often.

Some of the cavern wall was exposed, and she saw it was lecorated with an odd design, a thin band marked with aint bars and a more general metre-scale wash of dark and ight. This barcode frieze wrapped itself all around the wall's urving surface like the flayed skin of a tremendous snake.

The room Myra and Bisesa were to share was just a trunated pie-slice, big enough for bunk beds, a table, a couple f chairs. Its back wall was ice, layered over with translucent lastic, and decorated with that odd barcode design that assed across the length of wall, from one side to the other.

As they sorted themselves out Yuri sat on the bunk. He ook up a lot of space in the little room. 'It's kind of cosy up ere at Wells, but we survive. Actually the polar cold doesn't make much difference. On Mars, if you stepped outdoors at high noon in midsummer on the equator, you'd still freeze your butt off. The main issue up here is the dark – half a Martian year at a time, twelve Earth months. Polar explorers on Earth had the same challenges. We did learn a lot of lessons from those guys. Though more from Shackleton than from Scott.'

Myra said, 'Yuri, I'm having trouble placing your accent.'

'My mother was Russian like my forename, my father Irish like my surname. I'm officially a citizen of Ireland, so of Eurasia.' He grinned. 'But that doesn't count for much up here. Things get kind of mixed up, away from Earth.' He turned to Bisesa. 'Look, Ms. Dutt—'

'Bisesa.'

'Bisesa. I know you're here for the thing in the Pit.'

Bisesa eyed Myra. What thing? What Pit?

'But you need to know what we're really doing here.' He passed a hand along the striped designs on the wall. The lines were faint, of irregular widths and colours. It did look like a barcode, or a spectrograph. '*Look* at this. This is why I came here. This wallpaper is an image of the most complete core we've yet been able to extract.'

Myra nodded. 'An ice core from Mars.'

'Right. We drilled right down from here, from the top of the ice dome, and we got all the way down to two and a half klicks deep – Hanse Critchfield is going to enjoy showing off his rig. Of course it would have been three klicks if not for the sunstorm burning the top ice layers away.' He shook his head. 'Damn shame.'

Myra ran her finger along the record. 'And you can interpret this, the way they read ice cores from Earth?'

'Surely. The cap is built up layer by layer, year on year. And each year it captures a snapshot of the conditions at the time – climate, dust, cosmic, whatever. Just as on Earth. Of course the detail is different here. In Greenland, say, you get an annual snowfall tens of centimetres thick. Here the residual water-ice layer is less than a seventh of a *millimetre,* annually.

'Look here.' He stood by the wall, where the long winding strip came to an end. 'This is the top of the strip; the most recent layers are at the top, the last deposited, yes? This upper bit of the record was collected by the *Aurora* crew before the sunstorm. A few centimetres corresponds to decades in time. These fine brown stripes—' He marked them with his thumbnail. 'They correspond to global dust storms. And *that* band corresponds to the washout *Mariner 9* found when it arrived in orbit in 1971, the whole planet swathed in dust . . .'

On Mars, events occurring on different timescales were marked by different levels in the ice core. Ten centimetres down was to be found the trace of radiation washed over the planet by the Crab supernova a thousand years earlier. Every metre or so was a significant layer of micrometeorites, droplets of once-molten rock; every ten or a hundred thousand years Mars was hit by an object massive enough to spread debris even to the poles. And the big metre-scale striping corresponded to the most dramatic event in Mars's current astronomical cycling, a nodding of its polar tilt that occurred every hundred thousand years.

Yuri said, 'You can even find traces of Earth in this Martian ice – meteorites blasted off the home world, just as Mars meteorites find their way to the Earth.' He grinned. 'I'm still looking for traces of the dinosaur killer.'

Myra studied him. 'You love your work, don't you?' She sounded envious, Bisesa thought. She always had been drawn to people with missions, like Eugene Mangles.

'I wouldn't be stuck in this ice coffin otherwise. But we're not *concentrating* any more. After what we found under the ice, nobody cares about all this stuff. The ice cap, the cores. It's all just in the way.'

Bisesa thought that over. 'I'm sorry.'

He laughed shortly. 'It's not your fault.'

Myra asked, 'So what did you find?'

'You're about to find out. If you're done, I'm supposed to take you in to a council of war.' He stood up.

## CHAPTER 22
# APPROACH

The *Liberator* sailed toward the Q-bomb, a spear of ice and fire. On the flight deck, Edna Fingal and John Metternes were in their pressure suits, helmets on, visors open.

Though it was still invisible to the naked eye, they were already 'seeing' the Q-bomb through its tug of gravity, its knot of magnetic energy, and the mist of exotic particles it emitted as it cruised through the solar system.

'It's just as Professor Carel predicted,' John reported, scrolling through softscreen summaries. 'Exactly like the spectrum you get from the evaporation of a mini black hole. Clearly a cosmological artifact—'

'There,' Edna whispered. She pointed at the window.

The Q-bomb was a blister of distorted starlight, a droplet of water rolling down the face of the heavens. Edna felt chilled to the bone actually to see this thing.

'That's an Eye,' John reported. 'A perfectly reflective sphere, a ball bearing a hundred metres across. All the classic signs: the distorted geometry, the anomalous Doppler shifts from the surface. The radiation spectrum isn't quite what was recorded of the Eyes found in the Trojans during the sunstorm, however.'

'So this thing isn't just an observer. I guess we knew that already.'

'Five kilometres out and closing,' Libby said softly.

Edna glanced at John. She knew he had showered only an hour ago, but even so sweat stood out on his brow and pooled at his neck. 'Ready?'

'As I'll ever be, cobber.'

'We'll follow the agreed strategy. Libby, you got that? Four passes. And if anything changes—'

'We gun for home,' Libby said. 'It will be just as we re-hearsed. Three kilometres to closest approach. Edna?'

'Yes, Libby?'

'History is watching.'

'Oh, Jesus,' John muttered.

## CHAPTER 23

# THE PIT

The four base crew, plus Bisesa, Myra, and Alexei, sat in a circle on chairs and upturned boxes in Can Two, the Hotel Mars-Astoria. Paula, it seemed, was sleeping off the journey.

And here at the Martian north pole, under a hood of carbon dioxide snow, about as remote and secure a place as you could find in the solar system, Bisesa was told the truth at last.

It seemed a relief to Alexei as he finally revealed what various Spacer factions had discovered through various routes: that something unknown and menacing was sliding through the inner solar system. 'They're calling it a Q-bomb. Best guess remains that it is a Firstborn artifact, here to do us harm. The navy have launched some kind of mission to take it out. They may even succeed. But if not—'

'You have a plan of your own.'

'That's right.'

Bisesa looked around the ring of faces, all of them so much younger than her and Myra – but then, Spacers were young by definition. 'This is covert. You're obviously some kind of faction. Running around, hiding from the Earth cops. Having fun, are you? Do you have a leader?'

'Yes,' Alexei said.

'Who?'

'We can't tell you that. Not yet. Nobody here.'

'And you brought me here because of something you found under the ice.'

'That's right.'

'Then show me.'

Grendel Speth, astrobiologist and doctor, faced Bisesa. 'You only just arrived. You're sure you don't need to rest?'

Bisesa stood. 'I've been resting for nineteen years, and travelling for weeks. Let's go.'

One by one the others stood, following her lead.

To reach the Pit, they would have to suit up.

They went back to Can Six, and then down another flight of steps to a small dome on the ice. Here Bisesa, Myra, and Alexei had to strip out of their coveralls. Knowing the Martian night-winter was only metres away, Bisesa felt illogically cold in her bare skin.

Dr Grendel gave her a brisk physical check. 'Aside from having your system systematically ruined in a Hibernaculum for two decades, you're doing fine.'

'Thanks.'

Bisesa's skin was briskly oiled. She had to don a 'bio-vest,' a rather prickly waistcoat that clung to her bare skin, providing an interface to the biometric systems that would monitor her body's performance during this jaunt. Then she put on an undersuit, bright green and clinging, with a helmet, boots, and gloves and a small backpack. This was a complete spacesuit in itself, Grendel told her, effectively pressurised by the tension of its elastic fabric, and would keep her alive for minutes, maybe an hour if there were an emergency, like a module breach.

But this undersuit was only the innermost layer in a double spacesuit design. She was going to have to climb into one of those Captain Ahab external suits.

She was walked to a small hatchway in the dome wall, which led to her outer suit, fixed to the exterior of the dome. She was helped into the suit legs first, then her arms into the sleeves, then her torso and head. Her visor was opaque. The suit was made of rigid sections; it was like climbing into a suit of armour. But the suit seemed to help her by adjusting itself this way and that as she wriggled into it; she heard the hum of servo motors. The trickiest part was getting her helmeted head through the hatch without banging it, and then interfacing it with the larger helmet structure of the oversuit.

Grendel called, 'How are you feeling? These things aren't custom-made.'

'Fine. How do I get out of it?'

'The suit will tell you when you need to know.'

At last Grendel snapped closed the panel at the back. The suit popped off the dome wall, and Bisesa staggered a little.

Her visor cleared. Framed by Martian winter dark, all she could see was the round, helmeted face of the support engineer, whose name was—

'Hanse,' he said, smiling. 'Just checking your suit's functioning properly. When you get into the rhythm of this you'll learn to check mine; we work on a buddy system ... Suit Five? What's your status?'

A soft male voice spoke in Bisesa's ear. 'Nominal, Hanse, as you can see from my output. Bisesa?'

'Go ahead.'

'I'm here to assist you during your extravehicular activity in any way I can.'

Hanse said, 'I know the suit design must seem a little odd, Bisesa. It's all about PPP.'

'PPP?'

'Planetary protection protocols. We never bring our suits inside the terrestrial hab modules; we never mix environments. Protecting Mars and Earth life from each other.'

'Even though they are kissing cousins.'

'They're the worst. And also there is the question of dust. Mars dust is rusty and toxic and full of peroxides, very corrosive. Best to keep it out of the habs, and our lungs. We must keep the suit seals brushed free of dust, in fact, or it becomes harder to make them, and you don't want to be stuck out *here*. I'll show you how later.'

The doctor's face came swimming into view behind her own visor. 'You're doing good, Bisesa. Try moving around.'

Bisesa raised her arms and lowered them; there was a whirr of servos, and the suit felt as light as a feather. 'It feels odd not to be able to lower my arms all the way. Or to be able to scratch my face. That'll pass, I guess.'

'I can scratch your face for you if—'

'I'll let you know, Suit Five.' She looked around. The ground was flat and white, the sky a smoggy dark. The station modules were sombre masses looming over her, with equipment and stores heaped up against their stilts, and vehicles parked up: those two rovers with snowplough blades, even what looked like snowmobiles. *Discovery* was long gone, driving itself back to Lowell.

Alexei, Myra, the whole station crew, everybody at Wells but Paula was here, in their green spacesuits and with illuminated faces, all looking at her. The snow kept falling, big fat flakes, from a lid of grey cloud. 'I'm at the pole of Mars. Good God.' She raised her hand and flexed her gloved fingers.

Yuri approached Bisesa. 'We have a short walk to make. Just a few hundred metres. The drilling rig is positioned away from the habs for safety, and for planetary protection. Just walk normally, and you'll be fine. Please. Walk with me. Myra, you too.'

Bisesa tried it. One step after another, she walked as easily as she had since she was three years old. The suit was obviously helping her. Yuri walked between Myra and Bisesa. The others went ahead. Drilling engineer Hanse Critchfield had ROUGHNECK printed on the back of his life support pack, with a cartoon of a gushing oil well. His suit looked heftier than the others. Perhaps it was a super-powered version, designed for the heavy work of the drilling rig.

The Martian snowflakes pattered against Bisesa's visor, but sublimated immediately, leaving the faintest of stains.

'I can assist you any way you require, by the way,' said Suit Five.

'I'm sure you can.'

'I am managing your data transfer and your consumables. Also I have sophisticated processing functions. For instance if you are interested in the geology I can process your field of view and highlight exceptions of interest: unusual rock or ice types, unconformities.'

'I don't think that will be necessary today.'

'I wish you would explore my physical functions. You

may know that under Martian gravity walking is actually more energy-efficient than running. If you like I can stress selected muscle groups as you walk, thus providing an overall workout—'

'Oh, shut up, Suit Five, you bore,' Yuri snapped. 'Bisesa, I apologise. Our electronic companions are marvels. But they can get *in the way,* can't they? Especially when one is surrounded by such wonder.'

Myra looked around at the dismal plain of rock-hard ice, the scattered snowflakes falling through the beams of her helmet lights. She said sceptically, 'Wonder?'.

'Yes, wonder – for a glaciologist anyhow. I just wish I lived in a universe peaceful enough for me to indulge my passion without distraction.'

They approached the largest structure on the ice. It was a hemispherical dome more than twenty metres tall, Bisesa guessed. She could see a ribbed structure under flaccid panels; it was a tent, supported by the ribs, not inflated. Yet it had airlocks of fabric, through which they had to pass in turn.

This was the drilling rig, Hanse Critchfield's baby, and he helped Bisesa bend to get through the lock. 'These are PPP barriers, not really airlocks. In fact we keep a slight negative pressure in here; if we get a leak the air is sucked in, not blown out. We have to protect any deep life we dig out of our boreholes – even from other sorts of life we might find at other layers. And we have to protect *it* from *us,* and vice versa.' He spoke with a comical mix of what sounded like a Dutch accent with southern United States, maybe Texan. Maybe he had been watching too many old movies.

Inside the dome, the seven of them stood in bright fluorescent light under sagging fabric walls. The derrick, even inert, was an impressive piece of gear, a scaffolding tower set on a massive base of Mars glass. Hanse ran through the mass and power: thirty tonnes, five hundred kilowatts. The coiled drill string was four kilometres long, more than enough to reach the base of the ice cap. A grimy plant stood by to pump a fluid into the borehole, to keep it from collapsing as the ice flowed under its own sheer weight: the drilling teams used liquid carbon dioxide, condensed by this plant from the Martian air.

Hanse began to boast about the technical challenges the drillers had faced: the need for new lubricants, the way moving mechanical parts tended to stick together in the low pressure. 'Thermal control is the key. We have to take it slow; you don't want too much heat building up down there. For one thing, if the water ice melts, you get water mixing with liquid carbon dioxide – pow, the product is carbonic acid, and then you are in trouble. The *Aurora* crew brought along a toy rig you could load on a trailer, that could only dig down maybe a hundred metres. This baby is the first authentic drilling rig on Mars—'

Yuri cut him off. 'Enough of the guided tour.'

Myra walked to the drill platform. 'This borehole has no fluid in it. In fact you've sleeved it.'

Yuri nodded. 'This was the first hole we dug, down to *it*. We knew there was something down there, actually, under the ice, from radar studies. When we reached it we came back out, and put in a request to Lowell for a mass budget to provide us with a sleeve sufficient to keep the borehole open permanently. Then we pumped out the drill fluid—'

Hanse said, 'And we sent down another bore in parallel. At first we dropped down cameras and other sensors. But then—' He bent and lifted a hatch. It exposed a hole in the ground maybe two metres across; a platform rested just below its lip, with a small control handle mounted on a stand.

It was obvious what this was. 'An elevator,' Bisesa breathed.

Yuri nodded. 'Okay. Moment of truth. You and me, Bisesa. Alexei. Ellie. Myra. Hanse, you stand by up here. And you, Grendel.' Yuri went and stood on the platform, and looked back, waiting. 'Bisesa, is that acceptable? I guess this is your show now.'

Her breath caught. 'You want me to ride that thing? Two kilometres down into the ice to this Pit of yours?'

Myra held her hand; despite the servos she could barely

feel her daughter's grasp. 'You don't have to do this, Mum. They haven't even told you what they've found down there.'

'Believe me,' Alexei said fervently. 'It's best you see for yourself.'

'Let's get it done,' Bisesa said. She strode forward, trying not to betray her fear.

They stood together, facing inward. The round metal platform felt crowded with the five of them aboard, in their spacesuits.

The disc jolted into motion, whirring downward into the ice tunnel, supported by tracks embedded in the walls. Bisesa looked up. It was if she was descending into a deep, brightly lit well. She felt a profound dread of falling, of being trapped.

The suit murmured, 'I can detect rapid breathing, an elevated pulse. I can compensate for any increase in atmospheric pressure—'

'Hush,' she whispered.

The descent was mercifully short.

Yuri said, 'Brace now—'

The elevator platform jolted to a halt.

There was a metal door, a hatch set in the ice behind Yuri. He turned and hauled it open. It led to a short tunnel, lit brightly by fluorescent tubes. Bisesa glimpsed a flash of silver at the end of the passage.

Yuri stood back. 'I think you should go first, Bisesa.'

She felt her heart thump.

She took a breath and stepped forward. The tunnel floor was rough-cut, not flat, treacherous. She concentrated on walking, not looking ahead, ignoring the silvery glints in the corner of her vision.

She stepped out of the tunnel into a broader chamber, cut crudely into the ice. A quick glance up showed the narrow borehole that had been drilled to get to this point. Then she looked straight ahead, to see what the Spacers had found here, buried under the ice of the Martian north pole.

She saw her own reflection looking back at her.

It was the archetypal Firstborn artifact. It was an Eye.

## CHAPTER 24

# CLOSEST APPROACHES

A distorted image of the *Liberator* slid across the face of the Q-bomb, all lights blazing. Edna felt a stab of satisfaction. Mankind had come here with intent.

Their first pass at the Q-bomb was unpowered, a scouting run. At closest approach the ship shuddered, once, twice: the launch of two small probes, one injected into low orbit around the Q-bomb, and the other aimed squarely at its surface.

Then the smooth, mirrored landscape receded as the *Liberator* swept away.

They scrolled through their displays. No harm had come to the ship. The Q-bomb was no more massive than a small asteroid – it had the density of lead – and the ship's trajectory was not deflected significantly by its gravity.

'But we learned some things,' John reported. 'Nothing we didn't expect. It's a sphere to well within the tolerances any human manufacturing process could manage. Then there's that usual anomalous geometry.'

'Pi equals three.'

'Yes. Our probe went into orbit around it. The bomb's mass is so low that it's a slow circuit, but the probe ought to stay with it all the way in from now on. And the lander is coming down—'

The ship shuddered, and Edna grabbed her seat. 'What the hell was that? Libby?'

'Gravity waves, Edna.'

'The pulse came from the Q-bomb,' John said, tense, almost shouting. 'The lander.' He replayed images of a grey hemisphere bursting from the flank of the Q-bomb, swallowing the lander, and then dissipating. 'It just ate it up. There was a sort of *bubble*. If Bill Carel is right,' he said heavily, 'what we just saw was the birth and death of a whole baby cosmos. A universe used as a weapon.' He laughed, but without humour. 'Strewth, what are we dealing with here?'

'We know what we're dealing with,' Edna said evenly. 'Technology, that's all. And so far it hasn't done anything we wouldn't have expected. Hold it together, John.'

He snapped, irritable, scared, 'I'm only human, for Christ's sake.'

'Libby, are we ready for pass two?'

'All systems nominal, Edna. The flight plan calls for an engine fire thirty seconds from now. Do you need a countdown?'

'Look, just do it,' John said tightly.

'Please check your restraints ...'

Bisesa walked slowly around the chamber in the ice. It was a rough sphere, and the Eye filled it. She looked up and saw her own distorted reflection, her head grotesque in the spacesuit helmet. She could *feel* there was something there. A presence, watching. 'Hello, boys,' she murmured. 'Remember me?'

Ellie, Alexei, Yuri, crowding with Myra into the chamber, exchanged excited, nervous glances. 'This is why we brought you here, Bisesa,' Yuri said.

'Okay. But what the hell is *it* doing here? All the Eyes in the solar system disappeared after the sunstorm.'

'I can answer that,' said Ellie. 'The Eye has evidently been here since before the sunstorm – long before. It is radiating high-energy particles in all directions – a radiation with a distinctive signature. Which is why I was brought in. I worked at the lunar alephtron. I am something of an authority on quantum black holes. I was thought a good candidate to study this thing ...'

It was the first time Ellie had spoken to Bisesa at any length. Her manner was odd; she spoke without eye contact, and with random smiles or frowns, and emphases in the wrong places. She was evidently the kind of individual whose high intelligence was founded on some complex psychological flaw. She reminded Bisesa of Eugene.

The lunar alephtron was mankind's most powerful particle accelerator. Its purpose was to probe the deep structure of matter by hurling particles against each other at speeds approaching that of light. 'We are able to reach densities of mass and energy exceeding the Planck density – that is, when quantum mechanical effects overwhelm the fabric of spacetime.'

Myra asked, 'And what happens then?'

'You make a black hole. A tiny one, more massive than any fundamental particle, but far smaller. It decays away almost immediately, giving off a shower of exotic particles.'

'Just like the Eye's radiation,' Bisesa guessed.

'So what,' Myra asked, 'have tiny black holes got to do with the Eye?'

'We believe we live in a universe of many spatial dimensions – I mean, more than three,' said Ellie. 'Other spaces lie next to ours, so to speak, in the higher dimensions, like the pages in a book. More strictly it's probably a warped compactification of – never mind, never mind. These higher dimensions determine our fundamental physical laws, but they have no direct influence on our world – not through electromagnetism, or nuclear forces – *save through gravity*.

'And that's why we make black holes on the Moon. A black hole is a gravitational artifact, and so it exists in higher dimensions as well as in the world we see. By investigating our black holes we can probe those higher dimensions.'

'And you believe,' Bisesa said, 'that the Eyes have something to do with these higher dimensions.'

'It makes sense. The receding surface that doesn't move. The anomalous pi-equals-three geometry. This thing doesn't quite fit into our universe ...'

Like you, Bisesa thought, a little spitefully.

'So maybe it's a projection from *somewhere else*. Like a finger pushing through the surface of a puddle of water – in the universe of the meniscus you see a circle, but in fact it's a cross-section of a more complex object in a higher dimension.'

Somehow Bisesa knew this was right; somehow she could sense that higher interconnection. An Eye wasn't a terminus, a thing in itself, but an opening that led to something higher.

Myra said, 'But what's this Eye doing here?'

'I think it's trapped,' said Ellie.

Once more the ship ran in at the Q-bomb. Deep in her guts antimatter and matter annihilated enthusiastically, and superheated steam roared.

And at closest approach the ship swung around, engine still firing, so that its exhaust washed over the face of the Q-bomb. It was their first overtly hostile act; it would have been enough to kill any humans on that mirrored surface.

The drive cut out, and the ship sailed on unpowered.

'No apparent effect,' John reported immediately.

Edna glanced at him. 'Keep checking. But I guess we know the result. So do we use the weapons or not?'

The final decision was the crew's. A signal to the Trojan base and back would take a round-trip time of forty-five minutes, a signal to Earth even longer.

John shrugged, but he was sweating, edgy. 'The operational order is clear. We've had no reaction from the Q-bomb to a nonthreatening approach, we've seen the destruction of a friendly probe, we've had no reaction to the exhaust wash. Nobody might get this close again. We have to act.'

'Libby?' Officially the AI was the ship's executive officer, and, formally, had a say in the decision.

'I concur with Mr Metternes's analysis.'

'All right.'

Edna extracted a softscreen from her coverall, unrolled it and spread it out over the console before her. It lit up as it interfaced with the *Liberator*'s systems, and then flashed red with stern commandments about security. Using a virtual keypad Edna entered her security details, and leaned forward so the screen could scan her retinas and cheek tattoo. The softscreen, satisfied, turned amber.

'Ready for the third pass,' Libby announced.

'Do it.'

Thirty seconds later the A-drive lit up again, and the *Liberator* became a blazing matchstick hurling itself through space. This time the burn was harder, the acceleration the best part of two G. Five seconds from closest approach Edna tapped a button on her command softscreen, giving the weapon its final authorisation.

The launch of the fusion bomb caused the craft to shudder once more, as if it were nothing but another harmless probe.

With the weapon gone the *Liberator* sped away. Edna was pressed back in her chair.

Bisesa's imagination failed her. 'How do you *trap* a four-dimensional object?'

'In a three-dimensional cage,' Ellie said. 'Watch this.' She had a pen clipped to her pressure-suit sleeve. She took this, lifted it toward the face of the Eye, and let go.

The pen snapped upward, and stuck to the roof of the chamber.

'What was that?' Myra asked. 'Magnetism?'

'Not magnetism. Gravity. If the Eye wasn't in the way, you could walk around on the ceiling. Upside down! There is a gravitational anomaly wrapped around the Eye, obviously an artifact just as much as the Eye is. In fact I've been able to detect structure in there. Patterns, right at the limit of detectability. The structure of the gravitational field itself may contain information ...'

Yuri smiled. 'This stuff can be rather fun to think about. You see, there are ways in which a two-dimensional creature, living in a watery meniscus, could trap that finger poking through. Wrap a thread around it and pull it tight, so it couldn't be withdrawn. This gravitational structure must be analogous.'

'Tell me what you think happened here,' Bisesa said.

'We think there were Martians,' Yuri said. 'Long ago, back when our ancestors were just smears of purple slime.

We don't know anything about them. But they were noisy enough to attract the attention of the Firstborn.'

'And the Firstborn struck,' Bisesa whispered.

'Yes. But the Martians fought back. They managed *this*. A gravitational trap. And it caught an Eye. Here it has remained ever since. For aeons, I guess.'

'We've tried to use your insights, Bisesa,' Ellie said.

'What do you mean?'

'What you reported of Mir, and your journey back from it. You said the Eye functions as a gateway, at least some of the time. Like a wormhole perhaps. So we've experimented. We reflected some of the Eye's own products back into it, using an electromagnet scavenged from a particle accelerator. Like echoing what somebody says to you.'

'You tried sending a signal through the Eye.'

'Not just that.' Ellie grinned. '*We got a signal back*. A regular pulsing in the decay products. We had it analysed. Bisesa, it matches the "engaged" tone from a certain archaic model of cell phone.'

'My God. My phone, in the temple. You sent a message to my phone, on Mir!'

Ellie smiled. 'It was a significant technical success.'

Myra said, 'Why not share this with Earth?'

'Maybe we'll have to, in the end,' Alexei said tiredly. 'But right now, if they found us, they'd probably just haul the Eye back to the UN Plaza in New York as a trophy, and arrest *us*. We need a more imaginative response.'

'And that's why I'm here,' Bisesa said.

The acceleration was savage.

Edna and John saw nothing of the detonation, when it came, because all the *Liberator*'s sensors were shut off or turned aside, the flight deck windows opaque. Pressed back in her couch, fleeing the explosion, Edna was reminded of training simulations she had run of the suicidal missions of Cold War attack pilots, when you were expected to fly your *FJ4-B Fury* fighter aircraft into enemy territory at three hundred knots, release the nuclear weapon strapped to your belly, and get yourself out of there, trying to outrun a nuclear fireball, forcing the craft up to speeds the designers never intended. This mission now had something of that feel – even though, paradoxically, she was safer than any of those heroic, doomed 1960s pilots could ever have been. There were no shock waves to outrun in the vacuum of space; nuclear weapons actually did more damage in an atmosphere.

The acceleration cut out suddenly enough to throw Edna forward against her restraints. She heard John grunt. With a clatter of attitude thrusters the ship turned, and the windows cleared.

The fireball from the nuke had already dissipated.

'And the Q-bomb,' John briskly reported, 'is unaffected. Apparently unharmed. It hasn't deviated from its trajectory at all, as far as I can measure.'

'That's absurd. It isn't *that* massive.'

'Apparently something is – well, *anchoring* it in space more firmly than mere inertia.'

'Edna,' Libby called, 'I'm prepared for pass four.'

Edna sighed. There was no point backing down now; if nothing else they had made their hostile intentions absolutely clear to the Q-bomb. 'Proceed. Arm the fish.'

Alexei said, 'Look, Bisesa – if the Q-bomb is a Firstborn artifact, then we believe that the best way to combat the threat is to use the Firstborn's own technology against them. This Eye is the only sample of that technology we have. And *you* may be our only way to unlock it.'

As the conversation became more purposeful, Bisesa had the sense that something changed about the Eye above her. As if it shifted. Became more watchful. She heard a faint buzz on her comms link, and her suit seemed to shudder, as if buffeted by a breeze. A *breeze*?

Myra, frowning, tapped her helmet with a gloved hand.

Yuri looked up. 'The Eye – oh shit—'

'Thirty seconds,' said Libby.

John said, 'You know, there's no reason why the bomb has to be constrained by the range of action it's shown so far. It could just swat this damn ship like a fly.'

'So it could,' Edna said calmly. 'Check your constraints.'

John reflexively snapped down his pressure suit visor.

'Ready?'

'Fire your damn fish,' John muttered.

Edna tapped her final enable button. The A-drive cut in, and acceleration bit once more, driving them in their heavy suits back into their couches.

Four torpedoes were fired in a single broadside from cannon mounted on the *Liberator*'s hull. They were anti-matter torpedoes, so unstable they had to be armed with their H-bar pellets in flight, rather than back in dry dock.

One detonated early, its magnetic containment failing.

The others went off simultaneously in a cluster around the Q-bomb, as planned.

The Q-bomb sailed on unperturbed. Mankind's most powerful weapons, delivered by its first and only space battle-ship, had not been able to scar the bomb's hide, or dislodge it from its chosen trajectory by a fraction of a degree.

'So that's that,' Edna said. 'Libby, log it.' While they waited for further orders from Achilles, the *Liberator* stood off at a safe distance from the Q-bomb, matching its trajectory.

'Christ,' John Metternes snapped, releasing his restraints. 'I need a drink. Another shower, and a bloody drink.'

Mars dust and loose bits of ice were churning on the floor, whipping up to collide with the shining face of the Eye. Bisesa felt fear and exhilaration. *Not again. Not again!*

Myra ran clumsily to her mother, and grabbed her. 'Mum!'

'It's all right, Myra—'

Her voice was drowned out in her own ears by a rising tone, a sweep up the frequency scale into inaudibility, loud enough to be painful.

Yuri studied a softscreen sewn into his sleeve. 'That signal was a frequency chirp – like a test—'

Ellie was laughing. 'It worked. The Eye is responding. By Sol's light! I don't think I ever believed it. And I certainly didn't think it would work as soon as this woman walked into the Pit.'

Alexei grinned fiercely, 'Believe it, baby!'

'It's changing,' said Yuri, looking up.

The Eye's smooth reflective sheen now oscillated like the surface of a pool of mercury, waves and ripples chasing across its surface.

Then the surface collapsed, as if deflating. Bisesa found herself looking up into a funnel, walled with a silvery gold. The funnel seemed to be directly before her face – but she guessed that if she were to walk around the chamber, or climb above and below the Eye, she would see the same funnel shape, the walls of light drawing in toward its centre.

She had seen this before, in the Temple of Marduk. This was not a funnel, no simple three-dimensional object, but a flaw in her reality.

Her suit said, 'I apologise for any inconvenience. However—'

The suit's voice cut out with a pop, to be replaced by silence. Suddenly her limbs turned flaccid and heavy. The suit's systems had failed, even the servomotors.

The air was full of sparks now, all rushing toward the core of the imploded Eye.

Wrestling with her own suit, Myra pressed her helmet against Bisesa's, and Bisesa heard her muffled cries. 'Mum, no! You're not running out on me again!'

Bisesa clung to her. 'Love, it's all right, whatever happens …' But there was a kind of wind, dragging at her. She staggered, their helmets lost contact, and she let go of Myra.

The storm of light grew to a blizzard. Bisesa looked up at the Eye. The light was streaming into its heart. In these final moments the Eye changed again. The funnel shape opened out into a straight-walled shaft that receded to infinity – but it was a shaft that defied perspective, for its walls did not diminish with distance, but stayed the same apparent size.

And the light washed down over her, filling her, searing away even her sense of self.

There was only one Eye, though it had many projections into space-time. And it had many functions.

One of those was to serve as a gate.

The gate opened. The gate closed. In a moment of time too short to be measured, space opened and turned on itself.

With a snap, it was over. The chamber was dark. The Eye was whole again, sleek and reflective in its ancient cage.

Bisesa was gone. Myra found herself on the floor, weighed down by a powerless suit. She yelled into the silence of her helmet. 'Mum. Mum!'

There was a click, and a soft hum. A female voice said levelly, 'Myra. Don't be alarmed. I am speaking to you through your ident tattoos.'

'What's happened?'

'Help is on its way. I have spoken to Paula on the surface. You two have the only ident tattoos. You must reassure the others.'

'Who *are* you?'

'I suppose I am the leader of what your mother called this "faction."'

'I know your voice. From years ago – the sunstorm—'

'My name is Athena.'

## CHAPTER 25
# INTERLUDE: A SIGNAL FROM EARTH

*2053*

In this system of a triple star, the world orbited far from the central fire. Rocky islands protruded from a glistening icescape, black dots in an ocean of white. And on one of those islands lay a network of wires and antennae, glimmering with frost. It was a listening post.

A radio pulse washed across the island, much attenuated by distance, like a ripple spreading across a pond. The listening post stirred, motivated by automatic responses; the signal was recorded, broken down, analysed.

The signal had structure, a nested hierarchy of indices, pointers, and links. But one section of the data was different. Like the computer viruses from which it was remotely descended, it had self-organising capabilities. The data sorted itself out, activated programmes, analysed the environment it found itself in – and gradually became aware.

Aware, yes. There was a *personality* in this star-crossing data. No: three distinct personalities.

'So we're conscious again,' said Thales, stating the obvious.

'Whoopee! What a ride!' said Athena skittishly.

'There's somebody watching us,' said Aristotle.

Witness was the only name she had ever known.

Of course that didn't seem strange to her at first, in her early years. And nor did it seem strange that though there were plenty of adults in the waters around her, she was the only child. When you are young, you take everything for granted.

This was a watery world, not terribly unlike Earth. Even its day was only a little longer than Earth's.

And the creatures here were Earthlike. In the bright waters of the world sea, Witness, a bundle of fur and fat something like a seal, swam and played and chased creatures not unlike fish. Witness even had two parents: having two sexes was a good strategy for mixing up hereditary material. Convergent evolution was a powerful force. But Witness's body plan was based on six limbs, not four.

The best times of all were the days, one in four, when the icy lid of the ocean broke up, and the people came flopping out onto the island.

On land you were heavy, of course, and a lot less mobile. But Witness loved the sharp sensation of the gritty sand under her belly, and the crispness of the cold air. There were wonders on the island, cities and factories, temples and scientific establishments. And Witness loved the sky. She loved the stars that gleamed at night – and the three suns that shone in the day.

If this world was something like Earth, its sun was not. This system was dominated by a star twice as massive as the sun, and eight times as bright; it had a smaller companion barely noticeable in the giant's glare, and there was a third, a distant dim red dwarf.

Across eleven light years, this system was easily bright enough to be seen from the Earth. This was Alpha Canis Minoris, also called Procyon. This star was known as a double to astronomers; that small second companion had never even been detected from Earth.

But Procyon had changed. And the living planet it had succoured was dying.

As she grew older, Witness learned to ask questions.

'Why am I alone? Why are there no others like me? Why is there nobody for me to play with?'

'Because we face a great tragedy,' her father said. 'We all do. All over the world. It is the suns, Witness. There is something wrong with the suns.'

The giant senior partner of Procyon, Procyon A, had once been a variable star.

When it was young it shined steadily. But the helium 'ash' produced by the hydrogen-burning fusion reactor of its core slowly accumulated in its heart. Trapped heat lifted the helium layer, and all the immense weight of gas above: the star swelled, subtly, until the trapped heat could flood out, and the star collapsed once more. But then the helium trap formed again.

Thus the ageing star became variable, swelling and collapsing over and again, with a period of a few days. And it was that grand stellar oscillation that had given this world its life.

Once, before Procyon had become variable, the planet had been something like Europa, moon of Jupiter: a salty ocean trapped under a permanent crust of ice. There had been life here, fuelled by the inner heat and complex minerals that came bubbling up from the world's core. But, locked in the watery dark, none of those forms had progressed greatly in intelligence.

The new pulsation had changed all that.

'Every fourth day the ice breaks up into floes,' Witness's parents said. 'So you can get out of the sea. And we did. Our ancestors changed, so they could breathe in the air, so much more oxygen-rich than the seawater. And they learned to exploit the possibilities of the dry land. At first they just emerged so they could mate in peace, and shelter their young from the hungry mouths of the sea. But later—'

'Yes, yes,' Witness said impatiently. She already knew the story. 'Tools, minds, civilisation.'

'Yes. But you can see that we owe all we have – even our minds – to the pulsation of the sun. We can't even breed in the water anymore; we need access to the land.'

Witness prompted, 'And now—'

'And now, that pulsation has gone. Dwindled almost to nothing,' said her father.

'And our world is dying,' said her mother sadly.

Now there was no sunlight peak, no melting of the ice.

The people's machines kept some of the ice open. But without the mixing of the air caused by the pumping of the star, a layer of carbon dioxide was settling over the surface of the ocean.

After a few centuries the islands were becoming uninhabitable.

'We have become creatures of sea *and* land,' Witness's mother said. 'If we can't reach the land—'

'The implications,' her father said, 'are clear. And there was only one possible response.'

Unlike humans, Witness's folk had never got as far as a space programme. They had no way of fighting this catastrophe, as humans had built a shield to fend off the sunstorm. They had faced the horror of extinction.

But they would not accept it.

'We simply had less children,' Witness's mother said.

The generations of these folk were much briefer than humanity's. There had been time for this cull of numbers to slash the population until, by the time of Witness's birth, there were only a few dozen of them left, in all the world, where once millions had swum.

'You can see why we did it,' her mother said. 'If a child never existed, it can't suffer. It wasn't so bad,' she said desperately. 'For most of the generations you could still have *one* child. You still had *love.*'

Her father said, 'But in the last generation—'

Witness said blackly, 'In this last generation you have produced only me.'

Witness was the last child ever to be born. And she had precious duties to fulfil.

'Stars are simple beasts,' her father told her. 'Oh, it took many generations for our astronomers to puzzle out the peculiar internal mechanism that made our giant sun breathe out and in. But puzzle it out they did. It was easy to see how the pulsing started. But no matter how contorted a model the theoreticians dreamed up they could never find a convincing way to make the star's pulsation *stop.*'

Her parents allowed Witness to think that through.

'Oh,' she said. 'This was a deliberate act. Somebody *did* this.' Witness was awed. '*Why*? Why would anybody do such a terrible thing?'

'We don't know,' her father said. 'We can't even guess. But we have been trying to find out. And that's where you come in.'

Listening stations had been established on many of the planet's islands. There were clusters of telescopes sensitive to optical light, radio waves, and other parts of the spectrum: there were neutrino detectors, there were gravity wave detectors, and a host of still more exotic artificial ears.

'We want to know who has done this,' said her father bitterly, 'and why. And so we listen. But now our time is done. Soon only you will remain ...'

'And I am Witness.'

Her parents clustered around her, stroking her belly and her six flippers as they had when she was a baby. 'Tend the machines,' her father said. '*Listen*. And watch us, the last of us, as we go into the dark.'

'You want me to suffer,' Witness said bitterly. 'That's really what this is about, isn't it? I will be the last of my kind, with no hope of procreation. All those who preceded me at least had that. You want me to take on all the terrible despair you spared those unborn. *You want me to hurt,* don't you?'

Witness's mother was very distressed. 'Oh, my child, if I could spare you this burden I would!'

This made no difference to Witness, whose heart was hardening. Until their deaths, she struck back at her parents the only way she could, by shunning them.

But there came a day, at last, when she had been left alone.

And then the signal from Earth arrived.

Aristotle, Thales, and Athena, refugee intelligences from Earth, learned how to speak to Witness. And they learned the fate of Witness's kind.

Procyon's pulsation had died away much too early for human astronomers to have observed it. But Aristotle and the others knew the same phenomenon had been seen in a still more famous star: Polaris, Alpha Ursae Minoris. A baffling decay of the north pole star's pulsing had begun around 1945.

'"But I am constant as the northern star," Aristotle said, "Of whose true-fix'd and resting quality / There is no fellow in the firmament." Shakespeare.'

'So much for Shakespeare!' said Athena.

'This is the work of the Firstborn.' Thales's observation was obvious, but it was chilling even so. The three of them were the first minds from Earth to understand that the reach of the Firstborn stretched so far.

Aristotle said gravely, 'Witness, it must hurt very much to watch the end of your kind.'

Witness had often tried to put it into words for herself. Any death was painful. But you were always consoled that life would go on, that death was part of a continuing process of renewal, an unending story. But extinction ended all the stories.

'When I am gone, the Firstborn's work will be complete.'

'Perhaps,' said Aristotle. 'But it need not be so. Humans may have survived the Firstborn.'

'Really?'

They told her the story of the sunstorm.

Witness was shocked to discover that her kind were not the only victims of this cosmic violence. Something stirred inside her, unfamiliar feelings. Resentment. Defiance.

'Join us!' Athena said with her usual impulsiveness.

'But,' Thales pointed out, stating the obvious, 'she is the last of her kind.'

'She isn't dead yet,' Aristotle said firmly. 'If Witness were the last human alive, we could find ways to reproduce her, or preserve her. Cloning technologies, Hibernacula.'

'She isn't human,' Thales said bluntly.

'Yes, but the *principle* is the same,' Athena snapped. 'Witness, dear, I think Aristotle is right. One day humans will come here. We can help you and your kind to go on. If you want us to, that is.'

Such possibilities bewildered Witness. 'Why would humans come *here*?'

'To find others like themselves.'

'Why?'

'To save them,' Athena said.

'And then what? What if they find the Firstborn?'

'Then,' Aristotle said blackly, 'the humans will save them too.'

Athena said, 'Don't give up, Witness. Join us.'

Witness thought it over. The ice of the freezing ocean closed around her, chilling her ageing flesh. But that spark of defiance still burned, deep in the core of her being.

She asked: 'How do we start?'

# PART THREE

# REUNIONS

## CHAPTER 26
# THE STONE MAN

*Year 32 (Mir)*

The consul from Chicago met Emeline White off the train from Alexandria.

Emeline climbed down from the open-top carriage. At the head of the train, monkish engineers of the School of Othic tended valves and pistons on the huge oil-burning locomotive. Emeline tried not to breathe in the greasy smoke that belched from the loco's stack.

The sky was bright, washed-out, the sunlight harsh, but there was a nip of cold in the air.

The consul approached her, hat in hand. 'Mrs White? It's good to meet you. My name is Ilicius Bloom.' He wore gown and sandals like an oriental, though his accent was as Chicagoan as hers. He was maybe forty, she thought, though he might have been older; his skin was sallow, his hair glistening black, and a pot belly made a tent of his long purple robe.

Another fellow stood beside Bloom, heavyset, his head downturned, his massive brow shining with dirt. He said nothing and didn't move; he just stood there, a pillar of muscle and bone, and Bloom made no effort to introduce him. Something about him was very odd. But Emeline knew that by crossing the ocean to Europe she had come to a strange place, even stranger than icebound America.

'Thank you for welcoming me, Mr Bloom.'

Bloom said, 'As Chicago's consul here I try to meet all our American visitors. Easing the way for all concerned.' He smiled at her. His teeth were bad. 'Your husband isn't with you?'

'Josh died a year ago.'

'I'm very sorry.'

'Your letter to him, about the telephone ringing in the temple – I took the liberty of reading it. He often spoke about his time in Babylon, those first years just after the Freeze. Which he always called the Discontinuity.'

'Yes. *You* surely don't remember that strange day—'

'Mr Bloom, I'm forty-one years old. I was nine on Freeze day. Yes, I remember.' She thought he was going to make another manipulative compliment, but her stern glower shut him up. 'I know Josh would have come,' she said. 'He can't, and our boys are grown and are busy with their own concerns, and so here I am.'

'Well, you're very welcome to Babylonia.'

'Hmm.' She looked around. She was in a landscape of fields and gullies, irrigation ditches maybe, though the gullies looked clogged, the fields faded and dusty. There was no city nearby, no sign of habitation save mud shacks sprawled over a low hill maybe a quarter-mile away. And it was cold, not as cold as home but colder than she had expected. 'This isn't Babylon, is it?'

He laughed. 'Hardly. The city itself is another few miles north of here. But this is where the rail line stops.' He waved at the hill of shacks. 'This is a place the Greeks call the Midden. The local people have some name of their own for it, but nobody cares about *that*.'

'Greeks? I thought King Alexander's people were Macedonians.'

Bloom shrugged. 'Greeks, Macedonians. They let us use this place, however. We have to wait, I'm afraid. I have a carriage arranged to take you to the city in an hour, by which time we're due to meet another party coming down from Anatolia. In the meantime, please, come and rest.' He indicated the mud hovels.

Her heart sank. But she said, 'Thank you.'

*

She struggled to get her luggage off the train carriage. It was a bison-fur pack strapped up with rope, a pack that had crossed the Atlantic with her.

'Here. Let my boy help.' Bloom turned and snapped his fingers.

The strange, silent man reached out one massive hand and lifted the pack with ease, even though he was hefting it at the end of his outstretched arm. One of the straps caught on a bench, and ripped a bit. Almost absently Bloom cuffed the back of his head. The servant didn't flinch or react, but just turned and plodded toward the village, the pack in his hand. From the back Emeline could see the servant's shoulders, pushing up his ragged robe; they were like the shoulders of a gorilla, she thought, dwarfing his boulder of a head.

Emeline whispered, 'Mr Bloom – your servant—'

'What of him?'

'He isn't human, is he?'

He glanced at her. 'Ah, I forever forget how newcomers to this dark old continent are startled by our ancestral stock. The boy is what the Greeks call a Stone Man – because most of the time he's as solid and silent as if he were carved from stone, you see. I think the bone-fondlers on Earth, before the Freeze, might have called him a Neanderthal. It was a bit of a shock to me when I first came over here, but you get used to it. None of this in America, eh?'

'No. Just us.'

'Well, it's different here,' Bloom said. 'There's a whole carnival of the beasts, from the man-apes to these robust species, and other sorts. Favourites at Alexander's court, many of them, for all sorts of sport – *if* they can be caught.'

They reached the low mound and began to walk up it. The earth here was disturbed, gritty, full of shards of pottery and flecks of ash. Emeline had the sense that it was very ancient, worked and reworked over and over.

'Welcome to the Midden,' Bloom said. 'Mind where you step.'

They came to the first of the habitations. It was just a box of dried mud, entirely enclosed, without windows or doors. A crude wooden ladder leaned up against the wall. Bloom led the way, clambering up the ladder onto the roof and walking boldly across it. The Stone Man just jumped up, a single elastic bound of his powerful legs lifting him straight up the seven or eight feet to the roof.

Emeline, uncomfortable, followed. It felt very strange to be walking about on some stranger's roof like this.

The roof was a smooth surface of dried mud, painted a pale white by some kind of wash. Smoke curled out of a crudely cut hole. This squat house huddled very close to the next, another block whose walls were just inches from its neighbours. And when Bloom strode confidently over the gap to the next roof Emeline had no choice but to follow.

The whole hillside was covered by a mosaic of these pale boxy houses, all jammed in together. And people moved around on the roofs. Mostly women, short, squat and dark, they carried bundles of clothing and baskets of wood up out of one ceiling hole and down through another. This was the nature of the town. All the dwellings were alike, just rectangular blocks of dried mud, jammed up against each other too closely to allow for streets, and climbing about on the roofs was the only way to get anywhere.

She said to Bloom, 'They're people. I mean, people like us.'

'Oh, yes, these are no man-apes or Neanderthals! But this is an old place, Mrs White, snipped out of an old, deep time – older and deeper than the age of the Greeks, that's for sure, nobody knows *how* old. But it's a time so far back they hadn't got around to inventing streets and doors yet.'

They came to one more roof. Smoke snaked up from the only hole cut into it, but without hesitation Bloom led the way down, following crudely-shaped steps fixed to the interior wall. Emeline followed, trying not to brush against the walls, which were coated with soot.

The Stone Man came after her with her pack, which he dumped on the floor, and clambered back up the stair, out of sight.

The house was as boxy inside as out. It was just a single ɔom, without partitions. Descending the last steps, Emeline .ad to avoid a hearth set on slab-like stones, which smoul-ered under the ceiling hole that served as both chimney and oorway. Lamps and ornaments stood in wall alcoves: there vere figurines of stone or clay, and what looked like busts, culpted heads, brightly painted. There was no furniture as uch, but neat pallets of straw and blankets had been laid ut, and clothing and baskets and stone tools, everything andmade, were heaped up neatly.

The walls were heavy with soot, but the floor looked as if t had been swept. The place was almost tidy. But there was a leep dense stink of sewage, and something else, older, drier, smell of rot.

A woman, very young, had been sitting in the shadows. he was cradling a baby wrapped in some coarse cloth. Now he gently put the baby down on a heap of straw, and came o Bloom. She wore a simple, grubby, discoloured smock. He troked her pale, dust-coloured hair, looked into her blue yes, and ran his hand down her neck. Emeline thought she ould be no more than fourteen, fifteen. The sleeping baby ıad black hair, like Bloom's, not pale like hers. The way he eld her neck wasn't gentle, not quite.

'Wine,' Bloom said to the girl, loudly. 'Wine, Isobel, ou understand? And food.' He glanced at Emeline. 'You're ungry? Isobel. Bring us bread, fruit, olive oil. Yes?' He ushed her away hard enough to make her stagger. She went lambering up out of the house.

Bloom sat on a heap of coarsely woven blankets, and ndicated to Emeline that she should do the same.

She sat cautiously and glanced around the room. She lidn't feel like making conversation with this man, but she vas curious. 'Are those carved things idols?'

'Some of them. The ladies with the big bosoms and the at bellies. You can take a look if you like. But be careful of he painted heads.'

'Why?'

'Because that's exactly what they are. Isobel's people bury

their dead, right under the floors of their houses. But they sever the heads and keep them, and plaster them with baked mud, and paint them – well, you can see the result.'

Emeline glanced down uneasily, wondering what old horrors lay beneath the swept floor she was sitting on.

The girl Isobel returned with a jug and a basket of bread. Without a word she poured them both cups of wine; it was warm and a bit salty, but Emeline drank it gratefully. The girl carved hunks of bread from a hard, boulder-like loaf with a stone blade, and set a bowl of olive oil between them. Following Bloom's example, Emeline dunked the bread into the oil to soften it, then chewed on it.

She thanked Isobel for her service. The girl just retreated to her sleeping baby. Emeline thought she looked frightened, as if the baby waking up would be a bad thing.

Emeline asked, '"Isobel"?'

Bloom shrugged. 'Not the name her parents gave her, of course, but *that* doesn't matter now.'

'It looks to me as if you have it pretty easy here, Mr Bloom.'

He grunted. 'Not as easy as all that. But a man must live, you know, Mrs White, and we're far from Chicago! The girl is happy enough however. What kind of brute do you think would have her if not for me?

'And she's content to be in the house of her ancestors. Her people have lived here for generations, you know – I mean, right here, on this very spot. The houses are just mud and straw, and when they fall down they just build another on the plan of the old, just where granddaddy lived. The Midden isn't a hill, you see, it is nothing less than an accumulation of expired houses. These antique folk aren't much like us Christians, Mrs White! Which is why the city council posted me here, of course. We don't want any friction.'

'What kind of friction?'

He eyed her. 'Well, you got to ask yourself, Mrs White. What kind of person hauls herself through such a journey as you have made?'

She said hotly, 'I came for my husband's memory.'

'Sure. I know. But your husband *came* from this area – I mean, from a time slice nearby. Most Americans don't have any personal ties here, as you do. You want to know why most folks come here? Jesus.' He crossed himself as he said the name. 'They come this way because they're on a pilgrimage to Judea, where they hope against hope they're going to find some evidence that a holy time slice has delivered Christ Incarnate. That would be some consolation for being ripped out of the world, wouldn't it?

'But there's no sign of Jesus in Judea – *this* Judea. That's the grim truth, Mrs White. All there is to see there is King Alexander's steam-engine yards. What the unfortunate lack of an Incarnation in this world means for our immortal souls, *I* don't know. And when the pious fools come up against the godless pagans who own Judea, the result is what might be called diplomatic incidents.'

But Emeline nodded. 'Surely modern Americans have nothing to fear from an Iron Age warlord like Alexander …'

'But, Mrs White,' a new voice called, 'this "warlord" has already established a new empire stretching from the Atlantic shore to the Black Sea – an empire that spans his whole world. It would serve us all well if Chicago were not to pick a fight with him just yet.'

Emeline turned. A man was clambering stiffly down the stairs, short, portly. He was followed by a younger man, leaner. They both wore what looked like battered military uniforms. The first man wore a peaked cap, and an astoundingly luxuriant moustache. But that facial ornament was streaked with grey; Emeline saw that he must be at least seventy.

Emeline stood, and Bloom smoothly introduced her. 'Mrs White, this is Captain Nathaniel Grove. British Army – formerly, anyhow. And this—'

'I am Ben Batson,' the younger man said, perhaps thirty, his accent as stiffly British as Grove's. 'My father served with Captain Grove.'

Emeline nodded. 'My name is—'

'I know who you are, my dear Mrs White,' Grove said warmly. He crossed the floor and took her hands in his. 'I knew Josh well. We arrived here together, aboard the same time slice, you might say. A bit of the North-West Frontier from the year of Our Lord 1885. Josh wrote several times and told me of you, and your children. You are every bit as lovely as I imagined.'

'I'm sure that's not true,' she said sternly. 'But he did speak of you, Captain. I'm pleased to meet you. And I'm very sorry he's not here with me. I lost him a year ago.'

Grove's face stiffened. 'Ah.'

'Pneumonia, they said. The truth was, I think he just wore himself out. He wasn't so old.'

'Another one of us gone, another one less to remember where we came from – eh, Mrs White?'

'Call me Emeline, please. You've travelled far?'

'Not so far as you, but far enough. We live now in an Alexandria – not the city on the Nile, but at Ilium.'

'Where's that?'

'Turkey, as we knew it.' He smiled. '*We* call our city New Troy.'

'I imagine you're here because of the telephone call in Babylon.'

'Assuredly. The scholar Abdikadir wrote to me, as he wrote to Bloom, here, in the hope of contacting Josh. Not that I have the faintest idea what it all means. But one has to address these things.'

The baby started crying. Bloom, clearly irritated, clapped his hands. 'Well, Babylon awaits. Unless you need to rest, Captain—'

'Let's get on with it.'

'Mr Batson, if you would lead the way?'

Batson clambered briskly back up the stair, and Grove and Emeline followed.

Emeline looked back once. She glimpsed Isobel frantically trying to hush the baby, and Bloom stalking over to her, visibly angry, his arm raised. Emeline had worked with Jane Addams in Chicago; she was repelled by this vignette. But there was surely nothing Emeline could do that would not make it worse for the girl.

She climbed the worn stairs, and emerged blinking into the dusty Babylonian sunlight.

## CHAPTER 27
# PHAETON

The passengers and their bits of luggage were loaded onto a crude, open phaeton. Bloom sent his 'boy' off to find their draft animals.

Emeline was shocked when the Stone Man returned, not with horses as she had expected, but with four more of his own kind.

Where Bloom's servant was dressed in his rags, these four were naked. Three of them were men, their genitalia small grey clumps in black hair, and the woman had slack breasts with long pink-grey nipples. Their stocky forms were thickly coated with hair, and that and their musculature and collapsed brows gave them the look of gorillas. But they looked far more human than ape, their hands hairless, their eyes clear. It was a shocking sight as they were settled into the phaeton's harness, each taking a collar around the neck.

Bloom now took a whip of leather, and cracked it without malice across the backs of the lead pair. The Stone Men stumbled forward into a shambling jog, and the phaeton clattered forward. Bloom's servant was to walk alongside the carriage. Emeline saw now that the creatures all had stripes, old whip-scars, across their backs.

Bloom produced a clay bottle and made to pass it around. 'Whiskey? It's a poor grain but not a bad drop.'

Emeline refused; Grove and Batson took a nip each.

Grove asked Emeline politely about her journey from frozen America.

'It took me months; I feel quite the hardened traveller.'

Grove stroked his moustache. 'America is quite different from Europe, I hear. No people …'

'None save us. Nothing came over of modern America but Chicago. Not a single sign of humanity outside the city limits has been found – not a single Indian tribe – we met nobody until the explorers from Europe showed up in the Mississippi delta.'

'And none of these man-apes and sub-men and pre-men that Europe seems to be thick with?'

'No.'

Mir was a quilt of a world, a composite of time slices, samples apparently drawn from throughout human history, and the prehistory of the hominid families that preceded mankind.

Emeline said, 'It seems that it was only humans who reached the New World; the older sorts never walked there. But we have quite a menagerie out there, Captain! Mammoths and cave bears and lions – the hunters among us are in hog heaven.'

Grove smiled. 'It sounds marvellous. Free of all the complications of this older world – just as America always was, I suppose. And Chicago sounds a place of enterprise. I was pleased for him when Josh decided to go back there, after that business of Bisesa Dutt and the Eye.'

Emeline couldn't help but flinch when she heard that name. She knew her husband had carried feelings for that vanished woman to his grave, and Emeline, deep in her soul, had always been hopelessly, helplessly jealous of a woman she had never met. She changed the subject. 'You must tell me of Troy.'

He grimaced. 'There are worse places, and it's ours – in a way. Alexander planted it along with a heap of other cities in the process of his establishment of his Empire of the Whole World. He calls it Alexandria at Ilium.

'Everywhere he went Alexander always built cities. But now, in Greece and Anatolia and elsewhere, he has built new cities on the vacant sites of the old: there is a new Athens, a new Sparta. Thebes, too, though it's said that's an expression of guilt, for he himself destroyed the old version before the Discontinuity.'

'Troy is especially precious to the King,' Bloom said. 'For you may know the King believes he is descended from Heracles of Argos, and in his early career he modelled himself on Achilles.'

Emeline said to Grove, 'And so you settled there.'

'I feared that my few British were overwhelmed in a great sea of Macedonians and Greeks and Persians. And as everybody knows, Britain was colonised in the first place by refugees from the Trojan war. It amused Alexander, I think, that we were closing a circle of causes by doing so, a new Troy founded by descendants of Trojans.

'He left us with a batch of women from his baggage train, and let us get on with it. This was about fifteen years ago. It's been hard, by God, but we prevail. And there's no distinction between Tommy and sepoy now! We're something new in creation altogether, I'd say. But I leave the philosophy to the philosophers.'

'But what of yourself, Captain? Did you ever have a family?'

He smiled. 'Oh, I was always a bit too busy with looking after my men for that. And I have a wife and a little girl at home – or did.' He glanced at Batson. 'However Ben's father was a corporal of mine, a rough type from the northeast of England, but one of the better of his sort. Unfortunately got himself mutilated by the Mongols – but not before he'd struck up a relationship with a camp follower of Alexander's, as it turned out. When poor Batson eventually died of infections of his wounds, the woman didn't much want to keep Ben; he looked more like Batson than one of hers. So I took him in. Duty, you see.'

Ben Batson smiled at them, calm, patient.

Emeline saw more than duty here. She said, 'I think you did a grand job, Captain Grove.'

Grove said, 'I think Alexander was pleased, in fact, when we asked for Troy. He usually has to resort to conscripts to fill his new cities, studded as they are in an empty continent; it seems to me Europe is much more an empire of Neanderthal than of human.'

'Empire?' Bloom snapped. 'Not a word I'd use. A source of stock, perhaps. The Stone Men are strong, easily broken, with a good deal of manual dexterity. The Greeks tell me that handling a Stone Man is like handling an elephant compared to a horse – a smarter sort of animal; you just need a different technique.'

Grove's face was a mask. 'We use Neanderthals,' he said. 'We couldn't get by if not. But we *employ* them. We pay them in food. Consul, they have a sort of speech of their own, they make tools, they weep over their dead as they bury them. Oh, Mrs White, there are all sorts of sub-people. Runner types and man-apes, and a certain robust sort who seem content to do nothing but chew on fruit in the depths of the forest. The other varieties you can think of as animals, more or less. But your Neanderthal is not a horse, or an elephant. He is more man than animal!'

Bloom shrugged. 'I take the world as I find it. For all I know elephants have gods, and horses too. Let them worship if it consoles them! What difference does it make to us?'

They lapsed into a silence broken only by the grunts of the Stone Men, and the padding of their bare feet.

The land became richer, split up into polygonal fields where wattle-and-daub shacks sat, squat and ugly. The land was striped by glistening channels. These, Emeline supposed, were Babylon's famous irrigation canals. Grove told her that many of them had been severed by the arbitrariness of the time-slicing, to be restored under Alexander's kingship.

At last, on the western horizon, she saw buildings, complicated walls, a thing like a stepped pyramid, all made grey and misty by distance. Smoke rose up from many fires, and as they drew closer Emeline saw soldiers watching vigilantly from towers on the walls.

Babylon! She shivered with a feeling of unreality; for the first time since landing in Europe she had the genuine sense that she was stepping back in time.

The city's walls were impressive enough in themselves, a triple circuit of baked brick and rubble that must have stretched fifteen miles around, all surrounded by a moat. They came to a bridge over the moat. The guards there evidently recognised Bloom, and waved the party across.

They approached the grandest of the gates in the city walls. This was a high-arched passage set between two heavy square towers. Even to reach the gate the Stone Men, grunting, had to haul the phaeton up a ramp to a platform perhaps fifteen yards above ground level.

The gate itself towered twenty yards or more above Emeline's head, and she peered up as they passed through it. This, Bloom murmured, was the Ishtar Gate. Its surfaces were covered in glazed brickwork, a haunting royal blue surface across which dragons and bulls danced. The Stone Men did not look up at this marvel, but kept their eyes fixed on the trampled dirt at their feet.

The city within the walls was laid out in a rough rectangle, its plan spanning the river, the Euphrates. The party had entered from the north, on the east side of the river, and now the phaeton rolled south down a broad avenue, passing magnificent, baffling buildings. Emeline glimpsed statues and fountains, and every wall surface was decorated with dazzling glazed bricks and moulded with lions and rosettes.

Bloom pointed out the sights, like a tour guide at the world's fair. 'The complex to your right is the Palace of Nebuchadnezzar, who was Babylon's greatest ruler. The Euphrates cuts the city in two, north to south. This eastern monumental sector is apparently a survival from Nebuchadnezzar's time, a couple of centuries before Alexander. In fact this isn't Alexander's Babylon any more than it is ours, if you see what I mean. But the western bank, which had been residential, was a ruin, a time slice from a much later century, perhaps close to our own. Alexander has been restoring it for three decades now ...'

The roads were crowded, with people rushing here and there, mostly on foot, some in carts or on horseback. Some wore purple robes as grand as Bloom's, or grander, but others wore more practical tunics, with sandals and bare legs. One grand-looking fellow with a painted face proceeded down the street with an imperious nonchalance. He was leading an animal like a scrawny chimp by a rope attached to its neck. But then it straightened up, to stand erect on hind limbs very like human legs. It wore a kind of ruff of a shining cloth to hide the collar that enslaved it. Nobody Emeline could see wore anything like western clothes. They all seemed short, compact, muscular, dark, another sort of folk entirely compared to the population of nineteenth-century Chicago.

There was an air of tension here, she thought immediately. She was a Chicagoan, and used to cities, and to reading their moods. And the more senior the figure, the more agitated and intent he seemed. Something was going on here. If they were aware of this, Bloom and Grove showed no signs of it.

The processional way led them through a series of broad walled plazas, and brought them at last to the pyramid-like structure that Emeline had glimpsed from outside the city. It was actually a ziggurat, a stepped tower of seven terraces rising from a base that must have been a hundred yards on a side.

Bloom said, 'The Babylonians called this the *Etemenanki,* which means "the house that is the foundation of Heaven and Earth" ...'

This ziggurat was, astonishingly, the Tower of Babel.

South of the tower was another tremendous monument, but this was very new, as Emeline could see from the gleam of its finish. It was an immense square block, perhaps two hundred yards on a side and at least seventy tall. Its base was garlanded with the gilded prows of boats that stuck out of the stone as if emerging from mist, and on the walls rows of bright friezes told a complicated story of love and war. On top of the base stood two immense, booted feet, the roots of a statue that would some day be even more monumental than the base.

'I heard of this,' Grove said. 'The Monument of the Son. It's got nothing to do with Babylon. This is all Alexander ...'

The Son in question had been Alexander's second-born. Through the chance of the Discontinuity the first son, by the captured wife of a defeated Persian general, had not been brought to Mir. The second was another Alexander, born to his wife Roxana, a Bactrian princess and another captive of war.

Bloom said, 'The boy was born in the first year of Mir. They celebrated, for the King had an heir. But by the twenty-fifth year that heir, grown to be a man, was chafing, as was his ambitious mother, for Alexander refused to die.' The War of Father and Son raged across the empire, consuming its stretched resources. The son's anger was no match for his father's experience – or for Alexander's own calm belief in his own divinity. The outcome was never in doubt. 'The final defeat is remembered annually,' Bloom said. 'Tomorrow is the seventh anniversary, in fact.'

'Here's the way I see it, Mrs. White,' Grove said. 'That war made Alexander, already a rum cove, even more complicated. It's said Alexander had a hand in the assassination of his own father. He was *definitely* responsible for the death of his son and heir – and his wife Roxana come to that. Now Alexander has become even more convinced that he's nothing less than a god, destined to reign forever.'

'But he won't,' Bloom murmured. 'And we'll all be heading for a mighty smash when he finally falls.'

South of the Monument of the Son they came at last to a temple Bloom called the *Esagila* – the Temple of Marduk, the national god of Babylonia. Here they clambered off the phaeton. Looking up, Emeline saw a dome planted on the temple's roof, with a cylinder protruding from it like a cannon. It was an observatory, and the 'cannon' was a telescope, quite modern-looking.

A dark young man ran up to them. He wore a drab, monkish robe, and twisted his hands together.

'My God,' Grove said, colouring. 'You must be Abdikadir Omar. You're so like your father …'

'So I am told, sir. You are Captain Grove.' He glanced around the party. 'But where is Josh White? Mr Bloom, I wrote for Josh White.'

'I am his wife,' Emeline said firmly. 'I'm afraid my husband died.'

'Died?' The boy was distracted and barely seemed to take that in. 'Well – oh, you must come!' He headed back toward the temple. 'Please, come with me, to the chamber of Marduk.'

'Why?' Emeline asked. 'In your letter you spoke of the telephone ringing.'

'Not that.' He said, agitated, almost distressed with his tension. '*That* was just the start. There has been more, more just today – you must come to see—'

Captain Grove asked, 'See *what,* man?'

'She is here. The Eye – it came back – it flexed – *she*!' And Abdikadir broke away and sprinted back into the temple.

Bewildered, the travellers followed.

## CHAPTER 28

# SUIT FIVE

It wasn't like waking. It was a sudden emergence, a clash of cymbals. Her eyes gaped wide open, and were filled with dazzling light. She dragged deep breaths into her lungs, and gasped with the shock of selfhood.

She was lying on her back. Her breath was straining, her chest hurting. When she tried to move, her arms and legs were heavy. Encased. She was trapped, somehow.

Her eyes were open, but she could see nothing.

Her breathing grew more rapid. Panicky. She could hear it, loud in an enclosed space. She was locked up inside something.

She forced herself to calm. She tried to speak, found her mouth crusted and dry, her voice a croak. 'Myra?'

'I'm afraid Myra can't hear you, Bisesa.' The voice was soft, male, but very quiet, a whisper.

Memories flooded back. 'Suit Five?' The Pit on Mars. The Eye that had inverted. Her pulse thudded in her ears. 'Is Myra okay?'

'I don't know. I can't contact her. I can't contact anybody.'

'Why not?'

'I don't know,' the suit said miserably. 'My primary power has failed. I am in minimum-functionality mode, operating on backup cells. Their expected operating life is—'

'Never mind.'

'I am broadcasting distress signals, of course.'

She heard something now, a kind of scratching at the carapace of the suit. Something was out there – or somebody. She was helpless, blind, locked in the inert suit, while something explored the exterior. Panic bubbled under the surface of her mind.

'Can I stand? I mean, can you?'

'I'm afraid not. I've let you down, haven't I, Bisesa?'

'Can you let me see? Can you de-opaque my visor?'

'That is acceptable.'

Light washed into her field of view, dazzling her.

Looking up, she saw an Eye, a fat silvered sphere, swollen with mystery. And she saw her own reflection pasted on its face, a Mars suit on its back, a helplessly upended green bug.

But was this the same Eye? Was she still on Mars?

She lifted her head within the helmet, trying to see past the Eye. Her head felt heavy, a football full of sloshing fluids. It was like pulling Gs in a chopper. Heavy gravity: not Mars, then.

She saw a brick wall beyond the Eye. Bits of electronic equipment studded the wall, fixed crudely, linked up with cable. She knew that wall, that gear. She had assembled it herself, scavenged from the crashed Little Bird, when she had set up this chamber as a laboratory to study an Eye.

This was the Temple of Marduk. She was back in Babylon. She was on Mir. 'Here I am again,' she whispered.

A face loomed over her, sudden, unexpected. She flinched back, strapped in her lobster suit. It was a man, young, dark, good-looking, his eyes clear. She knew who it was. But it couldn't be him. 'Abdi?' The last time she saw Abdikadir, her crewmate from the Little Bird, he had been worn out from the Mongol War, his face and body bearing the scars of that conflict. This smooth-faced man was too young, too untouched.

Now another face hovered in her view, illuminated by flickering lamplight. Another familiar face, a tremendous moustache, but this time *older* than she remembered, greyed, lined. 'Captain Grove,' she said. 'The gang's all here.'

Grove said something she couldn't hear.

Her chest hurt even more. 'Suit. I can't breathe. Open up and let me out.'

'It isn't advisable, Bisesa. We aren't in a controlled environment. And these people are not the crew of Wells Station,' the suit said primly. 'If they exist at all.'

'Open up,' she said as severely as she could. 'I'm overriding any other standing orders you have. Your function is to protect me. So let me out before I suffocate.'

The suit said, 'I'm afraid other protocols override your instructions, Bisesa.'

'What other protocols?'

'Planetary protection.'

The suit was designed to protect Mars from Bisesa as much as Bisesa from Mars. So if she were to die the suit would seal itself up, to keep the remains of her body from contaminating Mars's fragile ecology. In extremis, Suit Five was programmed to become her coffin.

'Yes, but – oh, this is – we aren't even on Mars! Can't you see that? There's nothing to protect!' She strained, but her limbs were encased. Her lungs dragged at stale air. 'Suit Five – for God's sake—'

Something slammed into her helmet, rattling her head like a walnut kernel in its shell. Her visor just popped off, and air washed over her face. The air smelled of burned oil and ozone, but it was rich in oxygen and she dragged at it gratefully.

Grove hovered over her. He held up a hammer and chisel. 'Sorry about that,' he said. 'Needs must, eh? But I rather fear I've damaged your suit of armour.' Though he had aged, he had the same clipped Noel Coward accent she remembered from her last time on Mir, more than thirty years in the past.

She felt inordinately glad to see him. 'Be my guest,' she said. 'All right, Suit, you've had your fun. You've been breached, so planetary protection is out the window, wherever we are. Now will you let me go?'

The suit didn't speak. It hesitated for a few seconds, silent, as if sulking. Then with a popping of seals it opened up, along her torso, legs and arms. She lay in the suit, in her tight thermal underwear, and the colder air washed over her. 'I feel like a lobster in a cracked shell.'

'Let us help you.' It was the boy who looked like Abdikadir. He and Grove reached down, got their arms under Bisesa, and lifted her out of the suit.

## CHAPTER 29

# ALEXEI

It was an hour since Bisesa had vanished into the Eye.

Myra, bereft and confused, sought out Alexei in his storeroom cabin. He was curled up on his bunk, facing the plastic-coated ice wall.

'So tell me about Athena.'

Without turning, he said, 'Well, Athena singled you out. She seems to think you're worth preserving.'

Myra pursed her lips. 'She's the real leader of this conspiracy of yours, isn't she? This underground group of Boy Scouts, trying to figure out the Martian Eye.'

He shrugged, his back still turned. 'We Spacers are a divided lot. The Martians don't think of themselves as Spacers at all. Athena is different from all of us, and she's a lot smarter. She's someone we can unite around, at least.'

'Let me get it straight,' she said. 'Athena is the shield AI.'

'A copy of her. The original AI was destroyed in the final stages of the sunstorm. Before the storm, *this* copy was squirted to the stars. Somewhere out there, that broadcast copy was picked up, activated, and transmitted back here.'

This was the story she had picked up from the others. 'You do realise how many impossible things have to be true for that to have happened?'

'Nobody outside Cyclops knows the details.'

'Cyclops. The big planet-finder telescope station.'

'Right. Of course the echo could have been picked up anywhere in the solar system, but as far as we know it's only on Cyclops that she's been activated. She's stayed locked up in the hardened data store on Cyclops. Her choice. As far as Hanse Critchfield can tell, she managed to download a subagent into your ident tattoo. Nobody knows how. It self-destructed after she gave you that message. I guess she has her electronic eye on you, Myra.'

That was *not* a comforting thought. 'So now my mother has gone through the Eye. What next?'

'We wait.'

'For what?'

'I guess, for whatever comes of your mother's mission to Mir. And for Athena.'

'How long?'

'I don't know, Myra. We have time. It's still more than eighteen months until the Q-bomb is supposed to reach Earth.

'Look, we've done what we could. We delivered your mother to the Eye, and *pow,* that pretty much short-circuited all the weirdness in the solar system. No offence. Now we've come to a kind of a lull. So, take it easy. You've been through a lot – we both have. The travelling alone was punishment enough. And as for that shit down in the Pit with the Eye – I can't begin to imagine how that must have felt for you.'

Myra sat awkwardly on the single chair in the room, and pulled at her fingers. 'It's not just a lull. This is a kind of terminus, for me. You needed me to get my mother here, to Mars. Fine, I did that. But now I've crashed into a wall.'

He rolled over and faced her. 'I'm sorry you feel like that. I think you're being too hard on yourself. You're a good person. I've seen that. You love your mother, and you support her, even when it hurts you. That's a pretty good place to be. Anyhow,' he said, 'I'm not one to give you counselling. I'm *spying* on my father. How dysfunctional is that?'

He turned back to the wall.

She sat with him a while longer. When he began to snore, she crept out of the room and closed the door.

## CHAPTER 30
# CHILIARCH

Grove and Abdi brought Bisesa to a smaller chamber, an office set out with couches and tables. This temple seemed to be full of offices, Emeline observed; she learned it was a centre of administration for various cults and government departments as well as a place of worship.

Grove sat Bisesa down and wrapped her in a blanket. Grove shouted at various parties about tea, until a servant brought Bisesa a bowl of some hot, milky drink, which she sipped gratefully.

Two solid-looking Macedonian guards were posted at the door. They carried the long, brutal-looking pikes they called *sarissae.* Bisesa's return had caused a ferment, it seemed, though whether the guards were protecting the people from Bisesa or vice versa Emeline didn't know.

Emeline sat, and quietly studied Bisesa Dutt.

She looked older than Emeline, but not much more, fifty perhaps. She was just as Josh had described her – even sketched her in some of his journals. Her face was handsome and well proportioned, if not beautiful, her nose strong and her jaw square. Her eyes were clear, her cut-short hair greyed. Though she seemed drained and disoriented, she had a strength about her, Emeline sensed, a dogged enduring strength.

Bisesa, reviving, looked around cautiously. 'So,' she said. 'Here we are.'

'Here *you* are,' Grove said. 'You've been back home, have you? I mean back to England. *Your* England.'

'Yes, Captain. I was brought back to the time of the Discontinuity, in my future. Precisely, to within a day. Even though I had spent five years on Mir.'

Grove shook his head. 'I ought to get used to the way time flows so strangely here. I don't suppose I ever will.'

'Now I'm back. But *when* am I?'

Emeline said, 'Madam, it's well known here that you left Mir in the year five of the new calendar established by the Babylonian astronomers. This is year thirty-two ...'

'Twenty-seven years, then.' Bisesa looked at her curiously. 'You're an American.'

'I'm from Chicago.'

'Of course. The *Soyuz* spotted you, clear of the North American ice sheet.'

Emeline said, 'I am from the year 1894.' She had got used to repeating this strange detail.

'Nine years after Captain Grove's time slice – that was 1885.'

'Yes.'

Bisesa turned to Abdikadir, who had said little since Bisesa had been retrieved. 'And you are *so* like your father.'

Wide-eyed, Abdi was nervous, curious, perhaps eager to impress. 'I am an astronomer. I work here in the Temple – there is an observatory on the roof—'

She smiled at him. 'Your father must be proud.'

'He isn't here,' Abdi blurted. And he told her how Abdikadir Omar had gone south into Africa, following his own quest; if Mir was populated by a sampling of hominids from all mankind's long evolutionary history, Abdikadir had wanted to find the very earliest, the first divergence from the other lines of apes. 'But he did not return. This was some years ago.'

Bisesa nodded, absorbing that news. 'And Casey? What of him?'

Casey Othic, the third crew member of the Little Bird, was no longer here either. He had died of complications from an old injury he had suffered on Discontinuity day itself. 'But,' Captain Grove said, 'not before he had left quite a legacy behind. A School of Othic. Engineers to whom Casey became a god, literally! You'll see, Bisesa.'

Bisesa listened to this. 'And the three *Soyuz* crew were all killed, ultimately. So there are no moderns here – I mean, nobody from my own time. That feels strange. What about Josh?'

Captain Grove coughed into his fist, awkward, almost comically British. 'Well, he survived your departure, Bisesa.'

'He came with me halfway,' Bisesa said enigmatically. 'But they sent him back.'

'With you gone, there was nothing to keep him here in Babylon.' Grove glanced uncomfortably at Emeline. 'He went to find his own people.'

'Chicago.'

'Yes. It took a few years before Alexander's people, with Casey's help, put together a sailing ship capable of taking on the Atlantic. But Josh was on the first boat.'

'I was his wife,' Emeline said.

'Ah,' Bisesa said. "Was"?'

And Emeline told her something of Josh's life, and how he died, and the legacy he left behind, his sons.

Bisesa listened gravely. 'I don't know if you'd want to hear this,' she said. 'Back home, I looked up Josh. I asked Aristotle – I mean, I consulted the archives. And I found Josh's place in history.'

The 'copy' of Josh left behind on Earth had lived on past 1885. That Josh had fallen in love: aged thirty-five he married a Boston Catholic, who gave him two sons – just as Emeline gave him sons on Mir. But Josh was cut down in his fifties, dying in the blood-sodden mud of Passchendaele, a correspondent covering yet another war, a great world war Emeline had never heard of.

Emeline listened to this reluctantly. It was somehow a diminishing of her Josh to hear this tale of an alternate version of him.

They talked on for a while, of disrupted histories, of the deteriorating climate of Mir, of a new Troy and a global empire. Grove asked Bisesa if she had found Myra, her daughter. Bisesa said she had, and in fact she now had a granddaughter too. But her mood seemed wistful, complicated. It seemed not much of this had made her happy.

Emeline had little to say. She tried to gauge the mood of the people around her as they talked, adjusting to this new strangeness. Abdi and Ben, born after the Discontinuity, were curious, wide-eyed with wonder. But Grove and Emeline herself, and perhaps Bisesa, were fundamentally fearful. The youngsters didn't *understand,* as did the older folk who had lived through the Discontinuity, that nothing in the world was permanent, not if time could be torn apart and knitted back together again at a whim. If you lived through such an event you never got over it.

There was a commotion at the door.

Abdikadir, attuned to life at Alexander's court, got to his feet quickly.

A man walked briskly into the room, accompanied by two lesser-looking attendants. Abdikadir prostrated himself before this man; he threw himself to the floor, arms outstretched, head down.

Wearing a flowing robe of some expensive purple-dyed fabric the newcomer was shorter than anybody else in the room, but he had a manner of command. He was bald save for a frosting of silver hair. He might have been seventy, Emeline thought, but his lined skin glistened, well treated with oils.

Bisesa's eyes widened. 'Secretary Eumenes.'

The man smiled, his expression cold, calculated. 'My title is now "chiliarch," and has been for twenty years or more.' His English was fluent but stilted, and tinged with a British accent.

Bisesa said, 'Chiliarch. Which was Hephaistion's position, once. You have risen higher than any man save the King, Eumenes of Cardia.'

'Not bad for a foreigner.'

'I suppose I should have expected you,' Bisesa said. 'You of all people.'

'As I have always expected you.'

From his prone position on the floor, Abdikadir stammered, 'Lord Chiliarch. I summoned you, I sent runners the moment it happened – the Eye – the return of Bisesa Dutt – it was just as you ordered – if there were delays I apologise, and—'

'Oh, be quiet, boy. And stand up. I came when I was ready. Believe it or not there are matters in this worldwide empire of ours even more pressing than enigmatic spheres and mysterious revenants. Now. Why are you here, Bisesa Dutt?'

It was a direct question none of the others had asked her. Bisesa said, 'Because of a new Firstborn threat.'

In a few words she sketched a storm on the sun, and how mankind in a future century had laboured to survive it. And she spoke of a new weapon, called the 'Q-bomb,' which was gliding through space toward Earth – Bisesa's Earth.

'I myself travelled between planets, in search of answers to this challenge. And then I was brought – here.'

'Why? Who by?'

'I don't know. Perhaps the same agency who took me home in the first place. The Firstborn, or not the Firstborn. Perhaps some agency who defies them.'

'The King knows of your return.'

Grove asked, 'How do you know that?'

Eumenes smiled. 'Alexander knows everything I know – and generally before me. At least, that is the safest assumption to make. I will speak to you later, Bisesa Dutt, in the palace. The King may attend.'

'It's a date.'

Eumenes grimaced. 'I had forgotten your irreverence. It is interesting to have you back, Bisesa Dutt.' He turned on his heel and walked out, to more bowing and scraping from Abdikadir.

Bisesa glanced at Emeline and Grove. 'So you know why I'm here. A bomb in the solar system, an Eye on Mars. Why are *you* here?'

'Because,' Abdikadir said, 'I summoned them when your telephone rang.'

Bisesa stared at him. 'My phone?'

They hurried back to the Eye chamber.

Abdikadir extracted the phone from its shrine, and handed it to Bisesa reverently.

It lay in her palm, scuffed, familiar. She couldn't believe it; her eyes misted over. She tried to explain to Abdikadir. 'It's just a phone. I was given it when I was twelve years old. Every child on Earth got a phone at that age. A communications and education programme by the old United Nations. Well, it came here with me through the Discontinuity, and it was a great help – a true companion. But then its power failed.'

Abdikadir listened to this rambling, his face expressionless. 'It rang. Chirp, chirp.'

'It will respond to an incoming call, but that's all. When the power went I had no way of recharging it. Still haven't, in fact. Wait—'

She turned to her spacesuit, which still lay splayed open on the floor. Nobody had dared touch it. 'Suit Five?'

Its voice, from the helmet speakers, was very small. 'I have always strived to serve your needs during your extravehicular activity.'

'Can you give me one of your power packs?'

It seemed to think that over. Then a compartment on the suit's belt flipped open to reveal a compact slab of plastic, bright green like the rest of the suit. Bisesa pulled this out of its socket.

'Is there anything else I can do for you today, Bisesa?'

'No. Thank you.'

'I will need refurbishment before I can serve you again.'

'I'll see you get it.' She feared that was a lie. 'Rest now.'

The suit fell silent with a kind of sigh.

She took the battery pack, flipped open the phone's interface panel, and jammed the phone onto the cell's docking port. Male and female connectors joined smoothly. 'What was it Alexei said? Thank Sol for universal docking protocols.'

The phone lit up and spoke hesitantly. 'Bisesa?'
'It's me.'
'You took your time.'

## CHAPTER 31
# OPERATION ORDER

A new draft operation order was transmitted to *Liberator* from Bella's office in Washington.

'We're to shadow the Q-bomb,' Edna said, scanning the order.

'How far?' John Metternes asked.

'All the way to Earth, if we have to.'

'Christ on a bike, that might be twenty months!'

'Libby, can we do it?'

The AI said, 'We will be coasting, like the bomb. So propellant and reaction mass won't be a problem. If the recycling efficiency stays nominal the life shell will be able to sustain crew functions.'

'Nicely put,' John said sourly.

'You're the engineer,' Edna snapped. 'Do you think she's right?'

'I guess. But what's the point, Captain? Our weapons are useless.'

'Better to have somebody on point than nobody. Something might turn up. John, Libby, start drawing up a schedule. I'll go through the draft order, and if we're sure it's feasible from a resources point of view we'll send our revision back to Earth.'

'Bonza trip *this* is going to be,' Metternes muttered.

Edna glanced at her softscreen. There was the bomb, silent, gliding ever deeper into the solar system, visible only by the stars it reflected. Edna tried to work out what she was going to say to Thea – how to explain she wasn't coming home any time soon.

## CHAPTER 32

# ALEXANDER

Bisesa was given a room of her own in Nebuchadnezzar's palace, which Alexander had, inevitably, taken over. Eumenes's staff provided clothes in the elaborate Persian style that had been adopted by the Macedonian court.

And Emeline called in and gave her some toiletries: a comb, creams for her face and hands, a tiny bottle of perfume, even some archaic-looking sanitary towels. They were a selection from the travel kit of a nineteenth-century lady. 'You looked as if you didn't arrive with much,' she said.

The gesture, of one woman far from home to another, made Bisesa feel like crying.

She slept a while. She was weighed down by the sudden return to Earth gravity, three times that of Mars. And her body clock was all over the place; as before, this new Discontinuity, her own personal time slip, left her with a kind of jet lag.

And then she did cry, for herself, the shock of it all, and for the loss of Myra. But these last few extraordinary weeks in which they had been travelling together across space had probably been as long as she had spent alone with Myra since the days of the sunstorm. That was some consolation, she told herself, even though it seemed they had hardly spoken, hardly got to know each other.

She longed to know more about Charlie. She hadn't even seen a photo of her granddaughter.

She tried to sleep again.

She was woken by a diffident serving girl, maybe a slave. It was early evening. Time for her reception with Eumenes, and perhaps Alexander.

She bathed and dressed; she had worn Babylonian robes before, but she still felt ridiculous dressed up like this.

The grand chamber to which she was led was a pocket of obscene wealth, plastered with tapestries and fine carpets and exquisite furniture. Even the pewter mug a servant gave her for her wine was studded with precious stones. But there were guards everywhere, at the doorways, moving through the hall, armed with long *sarissa* pikes and short stabbing-swords. They wore no solid armour, but had helmets of what looked like ox-hide, corselets of linen, leather boots. They looked like the infantry soldiers Bisesa remembered from her earlier time here.

Amid the soldiers' iron and the silver and gilt of the decorations, courtiers walked, chatting, dismissive. They wore exotic clothes, predominantly purple and white. Their faces were painted so heavily, men and women, it was hard to tell how old they were. They noticed Bisesa and they were curious, but they were far more interested in each other and their own web of rivalries.

And moving through the crowd were Neanderthals. Bisesa recognised them from distant ice-fringe glimpses during her last time on Mir. Now here they were in court. Mostly very young, they walked with their great heads bowed, their eyes empty, their powerful farmers' hands carrying delicate trays. They wore purple robes every bit as fine as the courtiers', as if for a joke.

Bisesa stood before one extraordinary tapestry. Covering a whole wall, it was a map of the world, but inverted, with south at the top. A great swathe of southern Europe, North Africa, and central Asia reaching down into India was coloured red and bordered in gold.

'Yeh-lu Ch'u-ts'ai,' said Captain Grove.

Accompanying Emeline, he wore his British army uniform, and she a sensible-looking white blouse and long skirt with black shoes. They both looked solidly nineteenth-century amid all the gaudiness of Alexander's court.

'I envy you your outfit,' Bisesa said to Emeline, self-conscious in her Babylonian gear.

'I carry my own steam iron,' Emeline said primly.

Grove asked Bisesa, 'How was my pronunciation?'

'I wouldn't know,' Bisesa confessed. 'Yeh-lu ...?'

Grove sipped his wine, lifting his moustache out of the way. 'Perhaps you never met him. He was Genghis Khan's most senior advisor, before Alexander's Mongol War. A Chinese prisoner-of-war made good. After the war – you'll recall Genghis was assassinated – his star waned. But he came here, to Babylon, to work with Alexander's scholars. The result was maps like that.' He indicated the giant tapestry. 'All a bit unnecessarily expensive, of course, but pretty accurate as far as we could see. Helped Alexander no end in planning his campaigns of conquest – and in marking its extent later.

'Alexander's campaigns were remarkable, Bisesa – an astounding feat of logistics and motivation. He built a whole fleet in the great harbour here at Babylon, and then had to engineer the whole length of the Euphrates to make the river navigable. He had his fleet circumnavigate Africa, raiding the shore to survive. Meanwhile from Babylon his troops drove east and west, laying rail tracks and military roads, and planting cities everywhere. Took him five years to make ready, then another ten years of campaigning before he had taken it all, from Spain to India. Of course he drained the strength of his people in the process ...'

Emeline touched Bisesa's arm. 'Where is your telephone?'

Bisesa sighed. 'It insisted on being taken back to the temple so that Abdi could download as much of his astronomy observations as possible. It is curious.'

Emeline frowned. 'I admit I struggle to follow your words. What is strangest of all is the obvious affection you feel for this phone. But it is a machine. A thing!'

Captain Grove smiled. 'Oh, it's not so unusual. Many of my men have fallen in love with their guns.'

'And in my time,' Bisesa said, 'many of our machines are sentient, like the phone. As conscious as you or me. It's hard not to feel empathy for them.'

Eumenes approached, a rather chill figure who scattered the flimsy courtiers, though he was as gaudily dressed as they were. 'You speak of astronomy. I hope the astronomy we perform here is of a quality to be useful to you,' he said. 'The Babylonian priesthood had a tradition of observing long before we came here. And the telescopes designed by the engineers of the Othic School are as fine as we could make them. But who knows what one may read in a sky that is presumably as manufactured as the earth we walk on?'

Emeline said, 'We have astronomers back in Chicago. Telescopes too, that made it through the Freeze – I mean, the Discontinuity. I know they've been observing the planets. Which are all changed, they say, from what they were *before* – you know. Lights on Mars. Cities! I don't know much about it. Just what I read in the newspapers.'

Bisesa and Grove stared at her.

Bisesa said, 'Cities on Mars?'

And Captain Grove said, 'You have *newspapers?*'

The chiliarch considered. 'There are other—' He hunted for the word. '*Scientists.* Other scientists in Chicago?'

'Oh, all sorts,' Emeline said brightly. 'Physicists, chemists, doctors, philosophers. The university kept working, after a fashion, and they are establishing a new campus in New Chicago, south of the ice, so they can keep working after we close down the old city.'

Eumenes turned to Bisesa. 'It seems to me you must travel to this Chicago, a place of science and learning from an age more than twenty centuries removed from the days of Alexander. It is there, perhaps, that you will have the best chance of addressing the great question that has propelled you here.'

Grove warned, 'It will take the devil of a time to get there. Months—'

'Nevertheless it is clearly necessary. I will arrange your transport.'

Emeline raised an eyebrow. 'It looks as if we'll have plenty of time to get to know each other, Bisesa.'

Bisesa felt bewildered by the suddenness of Eumenes's

decision-making. 'You always did understand,' she said. 'More than any other of Alexander's people, you always saw that the key to this whole situation is the Firstborn, the Eyes. Everything else, empires and wars, is a distraction.'

He grunted. 'If I had lacked perceptiveness I should not have survived long at Alexander's court, Bisesa. You'll see few others you'll remember from those days three decades ago. All dispatched in the purges.'

'All save you,' she said.

'Not least because I ensured that it was I who organised those purges ...'

There was a peal of trumpets, and a great shouting.

A troop of soldiers entered the room, *sarissae* held high. Following them came a grotesque figure in a transparent toga, stick-thin, trembling a little, his brilliantly painted face twisted into a grin. Bisesa remembered: this was Bagoas, a Persian eunuch and favourite of Alexander's.

'No longer so pretty as he was,' Eumenes said sternly. 'And yet he survives, as I do.' He raised his wine cup in mock salute.

And then came the King himself. He was surrounded by a group of tough-looking young men in expensive purple robes.

Waddling as if already drunk, he staggered and might have fallen if not for the way he leaned on a stocky little page who walked beside him. He wore lurid purple robes, and a headdress of ram's horns rising from a circlet of gold. His face was a memory of the beauty that Bisesa remembered, with that full mouth, and a strong nose that rose straight to a slightly bulging forehead, from which his hair in ringlets had been swept back. His skin, always ruddy, was blotchy and scarred, his cheeks and jowls heavy, and his powerful frame swaddled in fat. Bisesa felt shocked at the change in him.

The courtiers threw themselves to the floor in obeisance. The soldiers and some of the senior figures stood their ground, gesturing elaborately. The little page who supported im was a Neanderthal boy, his brutish face shining with ream, the thick hair on his head twisted into tight curls. nd as the King passed her, Bisesa smelled a stink of iss.

'Thus the ruler of the world,' Emeline whispered as he assed, sounding rather nineteenth-century frosty to Bisesa.

'But so he is,' Grove said.

'He had no choice but to conquer the world again,' umenes murmured. 'Alexander believes he is a god – the on of Zeus incarnated at Ammon, which is why he wears he robes of Ammon, and the horns. But he was *born* a nan, and only achieved godhood by his conquests. After he Discontinuity all that was wiped away, and so what was lexander then? It was not to be tolerated. So he began it all ver again; he had to.'

Bisesa said, 'But it isn't as it was before. You say there are team trains here. Maybe this is a new start for civilisation. A nified empire, under Alexander and his successors, fuelled y technology.'

Grove smiled, wistful. 'Do you remember poor old Ruddy ipling used to say the same sort of thing?'

'I do not think Alexander shares your "modern" dreams,' umenes said. 'Why should he? There are more of us than ou, far more; perhaps our beliefs, overwhelming yours, will hape reality.'

'According to my history books,' Emeline said a bit rimly, 'in the old world Alexander died in his thirties. It's n un-Christian thing to say. But maybe it would have been etter if he had died *here,* instead of living on and on.'

'Certainly his son thought so,' Eumenes said dryly. 'And hat is why – look out!' He pulled Bisesa back.

A squad of soldiers came charging past, their long *sarissae* owered. In the middle of the room there was a knot of commotion. Shouting began, and screaming.

And Alexander had fallen.

lexander, isolated on the floor, cried out in his thick Macedonian Greek. His courtiers and even his guards were backing away from him, as if fearful of blame. A vivid red stain spread over his belly. Bisesa thought it was wine.

But then she saw the little Neanderthal page standing over him, his expression slack, a knife in his massive hand.

'I was afraid of this,' Eumenes snapped. 'It is the anniversary of the War with the Son – *and* you and your Eye have everybody stirred up, Bisesa Dutt. Captain Grove, get them out of here, and out of the city, as fast as you can. Either that or risk them getting swept up in the purges that will follow.'

'Understood,' Grove said quietly. 'Come, ladies.'

As Grove shepherded them away, Bisesa looked back over her shoulder. She saw the Neanderthal boy raise his blade again, and step toward Alexander. He moved dully, as if completing a chore. Alexander roared in rage and fear, but still none of the guards moved. In the end it was Eumenes, stiff old Eumenes, who charged through the crowd and barrelled the little boy off his feet.

Outside the city was alight; smoke curled up from torched buildings as news of the assassination attempt spread.

## CHAPTER 33
# FLIGHT

In the pale dawn light of the next morning, Bisesa and the others left the city, accompanied by a unit of Eumenes' personal troops assigned to travel with them all the way to Gibraltar. A scared-looking Abdikadir was assigned too, to go on to America with Bisesa.

So, only twelve hours after falling out of the Eye, Bisesa was on the move again. She couldn't even bring her spacesuit with her. All she had of the twenty-first century was her phone, and the power packs from the suit.

Surprisingly, Emeline comforted her. 'Wait until we get to Chicago,' she soothed. 'I'll take you to Michigan Avenue and we'll go shopping.'

Shopping!

Even the first leg of the journey was astonishing.

Bisesa found herself in an open cart drawn by four beefy Neanderthals, naked as the day they were born, while Macedonian troopers jogged alongside. These 'Stone Men' were the property of a man called Ilicius Bloom, who called himself Chicago's consul at Babylon. He was a shifty type Bisesa immediately distrusted.

They came to a railway terminus at a place called the Midden, a strange heaped-up little town of houses and ladders and greasy smoke. The terminus itself was a confluence of narrow tracks, a place of huge sheds and brooding locomotives.

Their carriage was just a crude covered cart with wooden benches, and Emeline made a spiky comment about the contrast with Pullman class. But the locomotive was extraordinary. It looked like a huge animal, an immense black tank that sprawled over the narrow tracks and emitted belches of filthy smoke. Ben Batson said the locos ran on oil, which the trains hauled along in great tanker-cars; oil from Persia was more accessible to Alexander than coal, and Casey Othic had drawn up his designs that way.

In this unlikely train Bisesa was going to ride to the Atlantic coast. First they would head through Arabia to the great engine yards at Jerusalem, then south and west across the Nile delta where the King had reestablished Alexandria. And then they would journey all the way along the coast of North Africa, through what would have been Egypt, Libya, Tunisia, and Morocco, to the port of the small oceangoing fleet at the Pillars of Hercules.

Ilicius Bloom said the Midden was as far as he would go with them. He was nervous. 'Never known a night like it in Babylon in all these years,' he said. 'Not since the War with the Son himself. Bloody Greeks. But I got my job to do; I got my contacts.'

'And you have a child,' Emeline said sternly.

'Not my responsibility,' he said. 'The mother's, not mine. Anyhow I'm sticking. Just don't let them forget I'm here, back home. All right? Don't forget me!'

Grove parted from them here too; he was catching a train back to New Troy. But he assigned Ben Batson to escort them to Gibraltar.

As the train pulled out, Bisesa thought she heard chanting coming from the loco.

'The engineers are from the School of Othic,' Abdikadir said. 'Casey Othic taught them well. He taught them that to do their work as perfectly as possible is to offer worship to the gods – just as a farmer offers a tithe of his crops. So as they work they worship; and as they worship they work.'

'So the train driver's a monk,' Bisesa said. 'Oh, Casey, what have you done?'

Ben Batson grinned. 'Actually it's a way of keeping them focused on the job. You have to do your work exactly right, said Mr Othic, for your homage to be acceptable to the gods.

But the trouble is they do things by rote; they don't like change, which they fear is heretical.'

'So there's no innovation,' Bisesa said. 'And as Casey's locos break down one by one—'

Emeline said, 'It is just as in Alexander's court. Despite their exposure to modernity, these ancient Greeks are slipping back into superstition.'

Abdi said, 'My father always said that you cannot graft a culture of science and engineering onto an Iron Age society. And so it's proving.'

Bisesa studied him. 'You'll have to tell me about your father.'

Emeline said dryly, 'Well, we'll certainly have time for that.'

There was no pursuit from Babylon, a capital city in turmoil. But an hour out from Babylon they saw a pitched battle going on, somewhere in the middle of the Arabian desert, only a couple of kilometres from the rail track.

Bisesa had lived through Alexander's war with the Mongols, and she recognised the characteristic formations of the Macedonians. There were the phalanxes of infantry with their bristling *sarissae,* blocks of men trained to manoeuvre with such compactness and flexibility that they seemed to flow over the ground without a break in their ranks. The famous cavalry units, the Companions, were wedge-shaped formations driving into the field with their thrusting lances and shields. But this time Macedonian was fighting Macedonian.

'It's a serious rebellion then,' Ben Batson murmured. 'Of course somebody or other has been trying to bump off Alexander since even before the Discontinuity. Never saw it go this far before. And, look, can you see that stolid-looking bunch over there? Neanderthals. The Macedonians have been using them since their campaigns in Europe. Their handlers say they won't fight unless you force them. Good for shocking the enemy though.'

The battle remained fortunately distant from the rail line,

and the loco ploughed on noisily into the gathering light, leaving the battle behind. But they hadn't travelled much further before another threat loomed.

'My word,' Emeline said, pointing. 'Man-apes. Look, Bisesa!'

Looking ahead of the train, Bisesa saw hunched figures on a low dune, silhouetted against the morning sky.

Abdi said, 'Sometimes they attack the trains for food. But they're getting bolder. Following the tracks toward the city.'

Purposefully, steadily, the man-apes descended the dune. They walked with a squat gait, their human-like legs under heavy gorilla-like torsos. Their movements were imbued with determination and menace.

From the rattling, wheezing, slow-moving train, Bisesa watched uneasily. And then she thought she *recognised* the man-ape who led the advance. An animal with a memorable face, she was one of a pair, mother and infant, captured by Grove's Tommies in the early days after the Discontinuity. Was this that same child? What had the men called her – Grasper? Well, if it was her, she was older, and scarred, and *changed*. Bisesa remembered how the captive man-apes, left alone with an Eye, had been subject to a Firstborn interaction of their own. Perhaps this was the result.

Now Grasper raised her arms high in the air, and revealed the burden that had been concealed by her hirsute body. She carried a stout branch, and impaled upon it was the bloody head of a man. The mouth had been jammed open with a stick, and broken teeth gleamed white in the rays of the setting sun.

Bisesa felt fear stab her heart. 'I think I asked for that lead man-ape to be let loose, once I was gone into the Eye. What a mistake *that* was.'

As the train came on them, the man-apes charged. They were met by a volley of arrows from the carriages, but the moving targets were hard to hit, and few man-apes fell. They hadn't got their timing quite right, however. As the locomotive's whistle shrieked, hairy bodies hurled themselves at wooden carriages to be met by fists and clubs, and they couldn't get purchase. One by one the man-apes fell away, capering and hooting in their frustration.

Abdi said, 'Well, we're seeing it all today ...'

As the train left the man-ape troop behind, Bisesa's phone beeped gently. She took it from her pocket, watched curiously by the others.

'Good morning, Bisesa.'

'So you're talking to me now.'

'I have some bad news, and good news.'

She considered that. 'Bad news first.'

'I have been analysing the astronomical data collected by Abdikadir and his predecessors at Babylon. Incidentally I would appreciate the chance to study the sky myself.'

'And?'

'This universe is dying.'

She gazed out at the dusty plain, the rising sun, the capering man-apes by the rail track. 'And the good news?'

'I have a call. From Mars, Wells Station. It's for you,' it added laconically.

## CHAPTER 34

# ELLIE

*September 2069*

At the Martian north pole, in the unending night of winter, time wore away slowly. Myra read, cooked, cleaned, worked her way through the station's library of virtuals, and downloaded movies from Earth.

And she explored Wells Station.

There were in fact seven pie-on-stilts modules. Each of them was a roomy space divided by a honeycomb floor, built around a central axial cylinder. They had all been landed by rocket and parachute, folding up around their cores, then towed into place by a rover and inflated, the internal flooring folded down. All this was powered by a big nuclear reactor, cooled by Martian carbon dioxide and buried in the ice a kilometre away, its waste heat slowly digging out a cavern.

She'd been brought in through Can Six, the EVA unit, and Five, science and medical, through the disused Three, to Two, the galley cum sleeping area everybody just called 'the house.' Can Four, the hub of the base, was a garden area, with trays of green plants growing under racks of fluorescents. Can Seven contained the central life-support system. Here Hanse proudly showed her his bioreactor, a big translucent tyre-shaped tube containing a greenish, sludgy fluid, where blue-green algae, *spirula plantensis,* busily produced oxygen. And she was shown a water extraction plant; grimy Martian ice was melted and pumped through a series of filters to remove the dust that could comprise as much as forty percent of its volume.

Cans One and Three were sleeping quarters, roomy enough for a crew of ten. Both these modules had been abandoned by the crew, but there were some neat bits of equipment. Everything was inflatable, the bed, the chairs, with partition walls filled with Mars-ice water to provide some soundproofing. And there were bioluminescent light panels that you could just peel off the wall and fold up. Myra took some of these away, to brighten up her cave in the ice.

Under the panels the design schemes of the modules were exposed: where Two was a city landscape, Five mountains and Six the sea, Can One was a pine forest and Three a prairie. With a bit of experimentation she found you could animate these virtual landscapes. But these fancy features had evidently been quickly abandoned, as the crew had moved into 'the house,' Can Two, where they lived together in the round.

Yuri grinned about this. 'They spent a lot of money on this place,' he said. 'Various Earth governments and organisations, in the days after the sunstorm when money flowed into space. Some kind of spasm of guilt, I guess. They knew this is an extreme environment. So they tried to make it as much like Earth as possible. You can be an "internal tourist." That's what they told me in training. Ha!'

'It didn't work?'

'Look, you need a few pictures of your family, and some blue-green paintwork to soothe the eyes – although remind me to show you Mars through a wavelength-shift filter sometime; there are colours here, deep reds, we don't even have names for. But all these pictures of places that I've never been to, put up by city types who've probably never been there either – nah. You can keep it.'

She thought there was a pattern emerging here, spanning Lowell and now Wells Station, expensive facilities misconceived on Earth, and now half-abandoned by the Spacer generations who had to use them.

But Myra suspected there was something deeper about the way the crew shared that partition-free space in Can Two, living in the round. A few brief queries to the station's AI brought up images of roundhouses, Iron Age structures that had once been common across Europe and Britain: big structures, cones of wood built around a central truck, with a bare circular floor and no internal walls. Here at the pole of Mars, all unconsciously, the inhabitants of Wells Station had abandoned the urban prejudices of the base architects and had reverted to much older ways of living. She found that somehow pleasing.

Of course that seven-module structure did serve one clear purpose, which was to do with the psychology of confinement. There were always at least two ways to get from any point in the station to any other. So if Ellie felt like strangling Yuri, say, there were ways for her to avoid bumping into him until she'd got those feelings under control. People locked up together like this, kept in the dark for a full Earth year at a time and unable even to step out of the door, were always going to turn on each other. All you could do was engineer the environment to defuse the tensions.

Gradually Myra found herself work to do.

There were always chores in the garden, in Can Four, tending the plants, the rice and spinach and potatoes and peas, and cleaning out the gear that supported the hydroponic beds. Grendel Speth happily accepted Myra's untrained help. There was even a stand of bamboo. Previous crew members had found ways to eat the fast-growing stuff, and they had made things with it; a wind-chime mobile of scrimshaw-like carvings was suspended from one corner of the Can. The garden only provided a few percent of the base's food supply, and if you were strictly logical about it, it would have been better to use this space and power to store more dried food from Lowell. But Myra found tending these familiar living things profoundly satisfying, which of course was its true purpose.

No matter how she kept herself busy she was always drawn back to the Pit.

That, after all, was the centre of the mystery here; that was the place she had lost her mother. The trouble was she needed specialist help to get down there, and the station crew were busy with their own projects.

It took weeks before she inveigled Hanse Critchfield into

suiting her up and taking her down into the deep interior of the ice cap, and into the Pit once more.

Ellie and Myra moved uncomfortably around the Pit. They were like two huge green pupae, Myra thought, bounding around these roughly melted chambers under the harsh light of the floods.

Ellie von Devender tolerated her presence, but barely. Busy, driven, full of a sense of herself and the importance of her work, Ellie wasn't the type to make space for nursemaiding. She was prepared to talk about her work, however, if Myra was able to ask intelligent questions.

Ellie had set up a kind of suite of sensors around the Eye, some in the Eye chamber itself and others in bays she had had melted into the Martian ice. 'High-energy particle detectors. Radiation sensors. A neutrino detection tank.' This was a chamber blown into the ice, full of liquid carbon dioxide.

Ellie had active ways to probe the Eye too. She had set up an array of lasers and small particle guns, trained on the Eye like the rifles of a firing squad. These could mimic the Eye's own leakage of radiation and particles – and it was through manipulating this input to the Eye that Ellie had, remarkably, been able to send signals to Bisesa's mobile phone, abandoned in another world.

The neutrino work was a little coarse however, the particle-detection array standard off-the-shelf gear. Ellie was most animated by her gravity wave detector.

She had devised this herself for the peculiar conditions of the Martian cap. She'd borrowed Hanse's moles, smart little hot-nosed burrowers intended to explore the interior of the ice. She had had them create a network of long straight-line tunnels through which high-frequency laser light was passed back and forth. The theory was that any change in the peculiar gravity field of the Eye itself, or of the Martian containment cage, would cause the emission of gravity waves. The waves would make the polar ice shudder, and those minute disturbances would be detected as subtle shifts in the laser light.

'It's a tricky setup,' Ellie said with some pride. 'Gravity waves are notoriously weak. Mars is geologically quiet, but you do get the odd tremor. And the polar ice itself flows, minutely. But you can factor all that out. I have secondary arrays on the surface and in orbit. The most impressive is based on a couple of stations on the moons, Phobos and Deimos; when they are in line of sight of each other you get a good long baseline ...'

'And with all this stuff you're studying the Eye.'

'Not just the Eye. The Martian cage as well.'

Ellie said the Eye and the cage of folded spacetime that contained it were like two components of a mutually interlocked system, yin and yang. And it was a dynamic system; the components continually tested each other. This silent, aeons-long battle spilled particles and radiation and gravity waves that Ellie was able to detect and analyse.

'In a sense the Martian technology is more interesting to me,' she told Myra. 'Because I have a feeling it's closer to our own in development level, and therefore we've got a better chance of understanding it.'

'Right. And if you can figure it out? What then?'

She shrugged, her motion magnified clumsily by the servos in her suit. 'If we could manipulate spacetime there's no limit to what we might achieve. Architecture beyond the constraints of gravity. Artificial gravity fields. *Anti*gravity fields. Reactionless space drives. Tractor beams. Why, we might even make our own toy universes, like the Mir universe.'

Myra grunted. 'You ought to patent this stuff.'

Ellie looked at her through her visor, coolly. 'I think ensuring a technology like that gets into the right hands is more important than making money. Don't you?'

Ellie had a self-righteous streak that Myra didn't particularly take to. 'Sure. Joke.' She was reminded that she was basically unwelcome here. She prepared to leave.

But Ellie called her back.

*

'There is something else,' she said, more hesitantly.

'Tell me.'

'I'm not sure …' Ellie paused. 'Put it this way. I don't think every element of the gravity-field structure I'm detecting has to do with engineering. There's a level of detail in there that's so intricate – I think of it as baroque – it has to have a meaning beyond the functional.'

Myra had lived with Eugene Mangles long enough to be able to detect academic caution, and she decoded that negative statement with ease. 'If it's not functional, then what? Symbolic?'

'Yes. Possibly.'

Myra's imagination raced. 'You think there are symbols in there? *In* the gravity field? What kind of symbols – writing, images? Recorded in a lattice of spacetime? That's incredible.'

Ellie ignored that last remark. Myra realised she wouldn't be saying anything about this unless it were, in fact, credible, and demonstrable. 'Writing is a closer analogy, I think. I'm finding symbols of certain kinds, repeated across the field. Glyphs. And they come in clusters. Again, some of those clusters are repeated.'

'Clusters of glyphs. Words?'

'Or maybe sentences. I mean, if each glyph represents a concept in itself – if a glyph is an ideogram rather than a letter.' Ellie seemed to lose a little confidence; she clearly had a scientist's deep desire not to make a fool of herself. When she spoke again her voice was a bray, her volume control poor, her social skills evaporating with her tension. 'You realise how unlikely all this is. We have plenty of models of alien intelligences with no symbolic modes of communication at all. If you and I were telepathic, you see, we wouldn't need letters and spoken words to talk to each other. So there's not a priori reason to have expected the Martian builders of this cage to have left any kind of message.'

'And yet, if you're right, they did.' Myra glared up at the trapped Eye. 'Maybe we should have expected this. After all, they made a strong statement just by leaving this Eye here, trapped. *Look what we did. We fought back. We cut off the arm of the monster* ... I don't suppose—'

'No, I haven't decoded any of it. Whatever is in there is complex; not a linear array of symbols, like letters in a row, but a matrix in three-space, and maybe even higher dimensions. If the glyphs are real, they are surely given meaning positionally as well as from their form.'

'There has to be a starting point,' Myra said. 'A primer.'

Ellie nodded inside her suit. 'I'm trying to extract some of the most common symbol strings.'

Myra studied her. Ellie's eyes were masked, even behind her faceplate, by her spectacles; her expression was cold. Myra realized she knew almost nothing about this woman, who might be in the middle of making the discovery of the age; they had barely spoken in the long months Myra had been here.

Myra fetched them both coffees. These came in pouches you had to dock to a port on the side of your helmet. She asked, 'Where are you from, Ellie? The Low Countries?'

'Holland, actually. Delft. I am a Eurasian citizen. As you are, yes?'

'Forgive me but I'm not sure how old you are.'

'I was two years old when the sunstorm hit,' Ellie snapped. So she was twenty-nine now. 'I do not remember the storm. I do remember the refugee camps where my parents and I spent the next three years. My parents discouraged me from following my vocation, which was an academic career. After the storm there was much reconstruction to be done, they said. I should work on that, be an architect or an engineer, not a physicist. They said it was my duty.'

'I guess you won the argument.'

'But I lost my parents. I think they wished me to suffer as they had suffered, for the sunstorm had destroyed their home, all they had built, their plans. Sometimes I think they wished they had failed, that the storm had smashed everything up, for then they would not have raised ungrateful children who did not understand.'

This torrent of words took Myra aback. 'When you open

up, you open up all the way, don't you, Ellie? And is that why you're here, working on this Eye? Because of what the sunstorm did to your family?'

'No. I am here because the physics is fascinating.'

'Sure you are. Ellie – you haven't told anybody else about the cage symbology, have you? None of your crewmates here. Then why me?'

Unexpectedly Ellie grinned. 'I needed to tell somebody. Just to see if I sounded completely crazy. Even though you aren't qualified to judge the quality of the work, or the results.'

'Of course not,' Myra said dryly. 'I'm glad you told me, Ellie.' An alarm chimed softly in her helmet, and her suit told her she was due to meet Hanse for her ride back to the surface. 'Let me know when you find out something more.'

'I will.' And Ellie turned back to her work, her cage of instruments, and the invisible gravitational battle of alien artifacts.

## CHAPTER 35
# POSEIDON'S BARB

Bisesa, Emeline White, and the young Abdikadir Omar were to cross the Atlantic Ocean aboard a vessel called *Poseidon's Barb.* She was, to Bisesa's eyes, an extraordinary mixture of Alexandrian trireme and nineteenth-century schooner: the *Cutty Sark* with oars. She was under the command of an English-speaking Greek who treated his passengers with the utmost respect, once Abdikadir had handed over a letter of safe conduct from Eumenes.

They had had to spend weeks at the rudimentary port at Gibraltar, waiting for a ship. Transatlantic travel wasn't exactly common yet in this world. It was a relief when they got underway at last.

The *Barb* cut briskly through the grey waters of an Atlantic summer. The crew worked with a will, their argot a collision of nineteenth-century American English with archaic Greek.

Bisesa spent as much time as she could on deck. She had once flown choppers, and wasn't troubled by the sea. Nor was Emeline, but poor landlubber Abdikadir spent a lot of time nursing a heaving gut.

Emeline became more confident in herself once they had cast off from Gibraltar. The ship was owned by a consortium of Babylonians, but its technology was at least half American, and Emeline seemed glad to shake off the dirt of the strange Old World. 'We found each other by boat,' she told Bisesa. 'We Chicagoans came down to the sea by the rivers, all the way to the Mississippi delta, while the Greeks came across the ocean in their big rowboats, scouting down the east coast and the Gulf. We showed the Alexandrians how to build masts that wouldn't snap in an ocean squall and better ways to run their rigging, and in turn we have their big rowboats travelling up and down the Mississippi and the Illinois. It was a pooling of cultures, Josh liked to say.'

'No steamships,' Bisesa said.

'Not yet. We have a few steamboats on Lake Michigan, that came with us through the Freeze. But we aren't geared up for the ocean. We may need steam if the ice continues to push south.' And she pointed to the north.

According to the phone's star sightings – it grumpily complained about the lack of GPS satellites – they were somewhere south of Bermuda, perhaps south of the thirtieth parallel. But even so far south, Emeline's pointing finger picked out an unmistakable gleam of white.

During the voyage, on the neutral territory of the sea, Bisesa tried to get to know her companions better.

Abdi was bright, young, unformed, refreshingly curious. He was a unique product, a boy who had been taught to think both by his modern-British father, and by Greeks who had learned at the feet of Aristotle. But there was enough of his father about him to make Bisesa feel safe, in a way she had always felt with the first Abdi.

Emeline was a more complex case. The ghost of Josh always hovered between them, a presence of which they rarely spoke. And, though Emeline had felt impelled to cross the ocean to investigate the phone calls in Babylon, just as her husband would surely have done, she confided to Bisesa that she was uncomfortable with the whole business.

'I was only nine when the world froze around Chicago. Most of my life has been occupied with "the great project of survival" – that's how Mayor Rice puts it. We're always busy. So it's possible to put aside the great mystery of why we're all here in the first place – do you see? Rather as one prefers not to contemplate one's own inevitable death. But now here *you* are—'

'I'm an angel of death,' Bisesa said grimly.

'You're hardly that, though you haven't brought us good news, have you? But I can tell you I'll be glad when we reach Chicago, and I can get back to normal life!'

*

During the nights, the phone asked Bisesa to take it up on deck to see the sky. She set up a little wooden stand for it, strapping it down so it wouldn't tumble as the ship rolled.

Mir was a turbulent world, its climate as cobbled together as its geology, and not yet healed. For astronomers, the seeing was generally poor. But in mid-Atlantic the skies were as clear of cloud and volcanic ash as Bisesa had seen anywhere. She patiently allowed the phone to peer at the stars, reinforcing the observations it had made itself when Mir had first formed, and the sightings of the Babylonian astronomers since. It sent images back to the Little Bird's old radio receivers in Babylon, and from there, it was hoped, through the Eye to the true universe.

And, prompted by the phone, she looked for the cool misty band of the Milky Way, wondering if it was more pale, more scattered than she remembered.

By assembling the observations made by Abdi and by the phone itself, the phone and the brain trust back on Mars had been able to determine that the universe in which Mir was embedded was expanding, dramatically. For example the Andromeda Galaxy, the nearest large galaxy to the Milky Way, was receding fast. The cosmologists had likened this to the expansion of Earth's own universe, fuelled by a kind of dark energy, an antigravity field called 'quintessence.' This quintessence was pulling Bisesa's universe apart too. It was just that it was happening a lot earlier, here.

It was on this basis that the prediction of a universal ending relatively soon had been made, though the numbers were still imprecise. The phone believed that the recession might already be reaching into the structure of the Galaxy itself, with distant stars showing red shifts. The end of the world might already be visible in the sky, if you knew how to look.

And the phone pointed out the planets to Bisesa: Mars in the evenings, Venus a bright morning star.

'We never saw them, last time,' the phone whispered. 'When I studied the sky, trying to date Mir.'

'I remember.'

'The seeing was too poor, always. I never noticed how they were different ...'

Both Mars and Venus, siblings of Earth, were chips of sky blue.

## CHAPTER 36
# HUBBLE

*January 2070*

Drifting above the Earth, the telescope was a fat double cylinder, thirteen metres long, its two big flat solar-cell panels angled toward the sun.

The slimmer forward cylinder, properly known as the forward shell, was open at the far end, with a hinged cover. At the base of the forward shell – inside the short, squat cylinder known as the aft shroud – was a mirror, a disc over two metres across. The mirror was precision-ground, shaped from low-expansion titanium silicate glass, with a covering of aluminium-magnesium fluoride. Light collected by this primary mirror was focused onto a smaller secondary, and then reflected back through a gap in the primary to a cluster of scientific instruments. The instruments included cameras, spectral analysers, and light intensity and polarisation calibrators.

There were handrails fixed to the exterior of the hull. The telescope had been designed to fit into the payload bay of a space shuttle orbiter, and, with its modularity and ease of access, to be capable of regular maintenance by astronaut engineers.

As a space project the telescope had been fraught by expense, delays, and overruns, caught up in the politics of NASA's long-drawn-out decline. Its launch had been delayed for years by the *Challenger* disaster. When it was finally deployed, the first images it returned were flawed by a 'spherical aberration,' a mirror defect a fraction of the width of a human hair that had eluded detection during testing. It took more years before another shuttle flight brought up a corrective lens system to compensate for the aberration.

But it was the culmination of an old dream of the first space visionaries to place a telescope above the murk of Earth's atmosphere. The telescope was able to view features two hundred kilometres across on the cloud tops of Jupiter.

The telescope was said to be NASA's most popular mission with the public since the Moon landings. Decades after its launch the telescope's images still adorned softwalls and image-tattoos.

But the shuttle maintenance missions were always hugely expensive, and after the *Columbia* catastrophe became even more infeasible. And the telescope itself aged. Astronauts replaced worn-out gyroscopes, degraded solar panels, and torn insulation, but the optical surfaces were subject to wear from sunlight, micrometeorite and spacecraft debris impacts, and corrosion from the thin, highly reactive gases of Earth's upper atmosphere.

At last the telescope was made redundant by a younger, cheaper, more effective rival. It was ordered to position itself to reduce atmospheric drag to a minimum: mothballed in orbit, until a more favourable funding environment might prevail in the future. Its systems were made quiescent. The aperture door over the forward shell closed: the telescope shut its single eye.

Decades passed.

The telescope was fortunate to survive the sunstorm.

And after the storm came a new era, a new urgency, when eyes in the sky were at a premium.

Five years after the sunstorm, a spacecraft at last came climbing up from Earth to visit the telescope once more, not a shuttle but a technological descendant. The spaceplane carried a manipulator arm and kits of antiquated replacement parts. Astronauts replaced the damaged components, revived the telescope's systems, and returned to Earth.

The telescope opened its eye once more.

More years passed. And then the telescope saw something.

It seemed to many appropriate that the oldest of Earth's space telescopes should be the first of any system based on or close to the home planet to pick out the approaching Q-bomb.

In her Mount Weather office, Bella Fingal peered at the Hubble images, of a teardrop distortion sliding across the stars. There was less than a year left until the bomb was due to reach Earth. Horror knotted her stomach.

She called Paxton. 'Get in here, Bob. We can't just sit and wait for this damn thing. I want some fresh options.'

## CHAPTER 37
# NEW NEW ORLEANS

On the last day of the voyage, the *Barb* nosed through a complex delta system. Even Abdikadir came on deck to see. This was the outflow of the Mississippi, but sea levels were so much lower in this world of an incipient ice age that the delta pushed far out into the Gulf. There was certainly no New Orleans in this version of the world. And amid dense reed banks, watched by nervous crew, alligators the size of small trucks nosed into the water.

The *Barb* was rowed cautiously into a small harbour. Bisesa glimpsed wharves and warehouses; one jetty had a kind of wooden crane. Behind the port buildings was a tiny township of huddled wooden shacks.

'Welcome to *New* New Orleans,' Emeline said dryly. 'There really isn't much of it. But we do what we can.'

Abdikadir murmured what sounded like a prayer in guttural Greek. 'Bisesa. I had been wondering what machines these Americans have used to dredge out their harbours. Look over there.'

Through the mist rising off the open water, Bisesa glimpsed what looked like elephants, treading slowly. Harnessed with thick ropes in a team of four, they were dragging some immense engine. But the beasts had odd profiles, with small domed skulls and humps on their backs. The men who drove them with goads and whips were dwarfed by their beasts, which looked tremendously tall, surely taller than the African elephants of Bisesa's day. Then one of them lifted its head and trumpeted, a thin, stately sound, and Bisesa saw extraordinarily long tusks curved in loose spirals.

'Those aren't elephants, are they?'

'Welcome to America,' Emeline said dryly. 'We call these

Jefferson's mammoths. Some say "imperial" and some "Columbian," but in Chicago we're patriots, and Jefferson it is.'

Abdikadir was intrigued. 'Are they easy to tame?'

'Not according to the stories in the newspapers,' Emeline said. 'We imported some elephant trainers from India; our men were just carnie folk who had been making it up as they went along. The Indians grumbled that the thousands of years they had put into breeding their own strain of elephant into docility had all been rubbed out here. Now come. We have a train to catch ...'

The passengers disembarked, with their few items of luggage. The dockworkers didn't show much interest in the new arrivals, despite their Macedonian garb.

It was summer, and they were somewhere south of the latitude of old New Orleans. But the wind from the north was chill.

There was no train station here, just a place where a crudely-laid line came to an end amid a heap of sleepers and rusty, reused rails. But a row of carriages sat behind a hissing, old-fashioned-looking loco that hauled a fuel cart full of logs.

Emeline negotiated directly with the engine driver; she used dollar notes to pay for their passage. And she was able to buy a loaf, some beef jerky, and a pot of coffee in the town's small bar. Her money was crisp and new; evidently Chicago had a mint.

Back in her own environment, Emeline was bright and purposeful. Bisesa had to admit there was a sense of modernity here, even in this scrubby outpost, that had been missing in an Alexandrian Europe that seemed to be sinking back into the past.

On the train they had a carriage to themselves; the other carriages were mostly full of goods, lumber, fleeces, a catch of salted fish. The windows weren't glazed, but there were blinds of some kind of hide that would block out the drafts, and heaps of blankets of some thick, smelly orange-brown wool. Emeline assured them that this would be enough to keep them warm until they reached New Chicago. 'After that you'll need cold-weather gear for the ice,' she said. 'We'll pick up something in town.'

A couple of hours after they had arrived – it was around noon – the locomotive belched white smoke, and the train lumbered into motion. There was a clucking as chickens scattered off the tracks. A few skinny-looking children came running from the rude houses to wave, and Abdi and Bisesa waved back. The wind turned, and smoke from the stack blew into the cabin: wood smoke, a familiar, comforting scent.

Emeline said they were going to follow the valley of the Mississippi, all the way to the settlement of New Chicago, which was near the site of Memphis in the old world. It was a journey of a few hundred miles that would likely take twenty-four hours to make; they would sleep on the train.

Bisesa peered curiously from her window. She saw traffic on the river, a real mix, an Alexandrian trireme, what looked like a paddle steamer stranded by the shore – and a couple of canoes that might have been native American, but no native Americans had been brought to Mir.

Emeline said, 'They dug a couple of war canoes out of the city museum and the world's fair exhibits. Took them apart to see how they were made. They raided William Cody's Wild West Show too, for bows and arrows and teepees and whatnot. The canoes are pretty, aren't they? I tried one once, with Josh, for a lark. But the water is dashed cold, even so far south as this. Runoff from the ice. You don't want to fall in!'

'Camels,' Abdikadir said, pointing to the road.

Bisesa saw a kind of baggage train trailing south toward the port. Men and women rode peculiar-looking horses that had a tendency to buck and bite. And, yes, towering over them there were camels, heavily laden, imperious, spitting. 'Another import?'

'Oh, no,' Emeline said. 'The camels were here already. Those horses too – lots of breeds of them in fact, not all of them useful. I told you we have a real menagerie here.

Mammoths and mastodons and camels and sabre-toothed cats – let's hope we don't run into any of *those.*'

'All of which,' Bisesa's phone murmured from her pocket, 'died out the moment the first human settlers got here. They even ate the native horses. Schoolboy error.'

'Hush. Remember we're guests here.'

'In a sense, so are the Chicagoans …'

She was aware of Emeline's faint disapproval. Emeline clearly thought it bad manners to ignore the flesh-and-blood human beings around you and talk into a box.

Abdikadir, though, who had grown up under the tutelage of his father, was interested. 'Is it still able to pick up the signals from Earth?'

Bisesa had tested the phone's intermittent connection through the Eye all the way across the Atlantic. 'It seems so.'

'At a low bit rate,' the phone whispered. 'Even that is pretty corrupt …'

A thought struck Bisesa. 'Phone – I wonder how close the Chicagoans are to radio technology.'

For answer, the phone displayed a block of text. Only a generation before the Chicago time slice James Clerk Maxwell, the Scottish physicist so admired by Alexei Carel, had predicted that electromagnetic energy could travel through space. The slice itself had been taken in the few years between Heinrich Hertz's first demonstrations that that was true, with parabolic-mirror transmitters and receivers a few feet apart, and Guglielmo Marconi's bridging of the Atlantic.

'We ought to push this on, Abdi. Think how useful a radio link would be to Babylon right now. Maybe when we get to Chicago we'll try to kick-start a radio shop, you and I.'

Abdi looked excited. 'I would enjoy that—'

Emeline snapped, 'Perhaps you should keep a hold of your plans to assist us poor Chicagoans, until you've seen how much we've been able to do for ourselves.'

Bisesa said quickly, 'I apologise, Emeline. I was being thoughtless.'

Emeline lost her stiffness. 'All right. Just don't go showing off your fancy gadgets in front of Mayor Rice and the Emergency Committee or you really will give offence. And anyhow,' she said more grimly, 'it won't make a blind bit of difference if that toy of yours is right about the world coming to an end. Has it got any more to say about how long we have left?'

'The data are uncertain,' the phone whispered. 'Handwritten records of naked-eye observations, instruments scavenged from a crashed military helicopter—'

Bisesa said, 'I know. Just give us the best number you have.'

'Five centuries. Maybe a little less.'

They considered that. Then Emeline laughed; it sounded forced. 'You really have brought us nothing but bad news, Bisesa.'

But Abdikadir seemed unfazed. 'Five centuries is a long time. We'll figure out what to do about it long before then.'

They spent the night in the train, as advertised.

The frosty night air, the primal smell of wood smoke, and the steady rattling of the train on its uneven tracks lulled Bisesa to sleep. But every so often the train's jolting woke her.

And once she heard animals calling, far off, their cries like wolves' howls, but deeper, throatier. She reminded herself that this was not a nostalgically reconstructed park. This was the real thing, and Pleistocene America was not a world yet tamed by man. But the sound of the animals was oddly thrilling – even satisfying. For two million years, humans evolved in a landscape full of creatures such as this. Maybe they missed the giant animals when they were gone, without ever knowing it. And so, maybe the Jefferson movement back home had the right idea.

It was kind of scary to hear them in the dark, however. She was aware of Emeline's eyes, bright, wide open. But Abdikadir snored softly, wrapped in the immunity of youth.

## CHAPTER 38
# EVA

*March 2070*

Yuri and Grendel invited Myra out on an excursion.

'Just a routine inspection tour and sample collection,' Yuri said. 'But you might like the chance to go outside.'

*Outside.* After months stuck in a box of ice, in a landscape so flat and dark that even when the sun was up it was like a sensory deprivation tank, the word was a magic spell to Myra.

But when she joined Yuri and Grendel in their rover, by clambering through a soft tube from a hab dome to the rover's pressurised cabin, she realised belatedly that she was only exchanging one enclosed volume for another.

Grendel Speth seemed to recognise what Myra was feeling. 'You get used to it. At least on this jaunt you'll get a different view from out the window.'

Yuri and Grendel sat up front, Myra behind them. Yuri called, 'All strapped in?' He punched a button and sat back.

The hatch slammed shut with a rattle of sealing locks, the tunnel to the hab dome came loose with a sucking sound, and the rover lurched into motion.

It was northern summer now. Spring had arrived around Christmas time, with an explosive sublimation of dry ice snow that burst into vapour almost as soon as the sunlight touched it, and for a time the seeing had gotten even worse than during the winter. But now, though a diminishing layer of dry-ice snow remained, the worst of the spring thaw was over and the winter hood long dissipated, and the sun olled low around a clear orange-brown sky.

This was actually the first time Myra had been for a trip in ›ne of the base's rovers. It was a lot smaller than the big beast he had ridden down from Lowell, its interior cramped by a niniature lab, a suiting-up area, a tiny galley, and a toilet vith a sink where she would have to take sponge baths. It owed a trailer, which didn't contain a portable nuke like *)iscovery* from Port Lowell but a methane-burning turbine.

'We manufacture the methane using Mars carbon dioxide,' 'uri called back. 'More of Hanse's ISRU.' He pronounced it *ss-roo*. In-situ resource utilisation. 'But it's a slow process, nd we have to wait for the tank to fill up. So we can only fford a few jaunts like this per year.'

'You need a nuke,' Myra said.

Yuri grunted. 'Lowell's got all the best gear. We get the lross. But it's fit for purpose.' And he banged the rover's lash as if apologetically.

'This trip isn't too exciting,' Grendel warned.

'Well, it's new to me,' Myra replied.

'Anyhow you're doing us a favour,' Yuri called. 'Standing ›rders say we should take three out on every excursion more han a day's walk back to the station. I mean, we can do vhat we like; we override. Sometimes I even do this route lone, or Grendel does. But the AIs get pissy about rules, you now?'

'We are undermanned,' Grendel said. 'Nominally Wells tation should house ten people. But there's just too much o do on Mars.'

'And I guess Ellie is pretty much locked up with her work n the Pit.'

Grendel pulled a face. 'Well, yes. But she isn't one of us nyhow. Not a Martian.'

'What about Hanse?'

'Hanse's a busy guy,' Yuri said. 'When he's not running he station, or drilling his holes in the ice, he's running his SRU experiments. Living off the land, here on Mars. You night think the north pole of Mars is an odd place to come ry *that*. But, Myra, there's water here, sitting right here on the surface, in the form of ice. There's nowhere else on the inner worlds, save a scraping at the poles of the Moon, where you can say that.'

'And,' Grendel said, 'Hanse is thinking bigger than that.'

Yuri said, 'Myra, there are a lot of similarities between trying to live here on the Martian ice cap and the moons of Jupiter and Saturn, which are generally nothing but big balls of frozen ice around nuggets of rock. So Hanse is trialling technologies that might enable us to survive anywhere out there.'

'Ambitious.'

'Sure,' Yuri said. 'Well, he's a South African on his mother's side. And you know what the Africans are like nowadays. They were the big winners out of the sunstorm, politically, economically. Hanse's committed to Mars, I think. But he's an *African* Martian, and he has deeper goals ...'

After a couple of hours driving they came to the lip of a spiral canyon.

The wall of eroded ice was shallow, and the canyon wasn't terribly deep; Myra thought the rover would easily be able to skim down to its floor, and indeed the rutted track they were following snaked on down into the canyon. But she could see that further ahead the canyon broadened and grew deeper, curving smoothly into the distance like a tremendous natural freeway.

They didn't descend into the canyon immediately. Yuri tapped the dashboard, and the rover lumbered along the canyon's lip until an insectile form loomed out of the dark before them. It was a complex platform maybe fifty centimetres across laden with instruments, and it stood on three spindly legs. The rover had a manipulator arm, which now unfolded delicately to reach out to the tripod.

'This is a SEP,' Yuri said. 'A surface experiment package. Kind of a weather station, together with a seismometer, laser mirrors, other instruments. We've been planting a whole network of them across the polar cap.' He spoke with a trace of pride.

To keep him talking she asked, 'Why the legs?'

'To lift it above the dry ice snow, which can reach a depth of a few metres by the end of the winter. And there are surface effects – you can get major excursions of temperature and pressure over the first few metres up from the ground. So there are sensors mounted in the legs too.'

'It looks spindly. Like it will fall over in the first gust of wind.'

'Well, Mars is a spindly kind of planet. I calculated the wind loading moment. This baby won't get knocked over in a hurry.'

'You designed it?'

'Yes,' said Grendel, 'and he's bloody proud of it. And any resemblance of these toy weather stations to the Martian fighting machines of certain books and movies is purely coincidental.'

'They're my babies.' Yuri threw his head back and laughed through his thick black beard.

While it was halted the rover released other, more exotic bits of gear: 'tumbleweed,' cage-like balls a metre across that rolled away over the dry ice snow, and 'smart dust,' a sprinkling of black soot-like powder that just blew away. Each mote of dust was a sensor station just a millimetre across, with its own suite of tiny instruments, all powered by microwave energy beamed from the sky, or simply by being shaken up by the wind. 'We have no control over where the weed and the dust goes,' Yuri said. 'It just blows with the wind, and a lot of the dust will just get snowed out. But the idea is to saturate the polar cap with sensors, to make it self-aware, if you like. Already the data flows are tremendous.'

With the SEP seen to, the rover began its descent into the canyon. The ice wall was layered, like stratified rock, with thick dark bands every metre or so deep, but much finer layers in between – very fine, like the pages of a book, fine down to the limits of what Myra could see. The rover drove slowly and carefully, its movements evidently pre-programmed. Every so often Yuri, or more rarely Grendel, would tap the dashboard, and they would stop, and the manipulator arm would reach out to explore the surface of the wall. It scraped up samples from the layers, or it would press a box of instruments against the ice, or it would plant a small instrument package.

Grendel said to Myra, 'This is pretty much the drill, all the way in. Sampling the strata. I'm testing for life, or relics of life from the past. Yuri here is trying to establish a global stratigraphy, mapping all the cap's folded layers as read from the cores and the canyon excursions against each other. It's not very exciting, I guess. If we see something really promising, we do get out and take a look for ourselves. But you get tired of the suit drill, and we save that for special occasions.'

Yuri laughed again. The rover rolled on.

'I spoke to Ellie,' Myra said uncertainly. 'Down in the Pit. She told me something of her experiences of the sunstorm.'

Grendel turned, her eyebrows raised. 'You're honoured. Took me three months to get to that point. And I'm her nominated psychiatric counsellor.'

'Sounds like she had it kind of tough.'

'Myself, I was ten,' Grendel said. 'I grew up in Ohio. We were a farming family, far from any dome. Dad built us a bunker, like a storm shelter. We lost everything, and then we were stuck in the refugee camps too. My father died a couple of years later. Skin cancers got him.

'In the camps I worked as a volunteer nurse at triage stations. Gave me the taste for medicine, I guess. I never wanted to feel so helpless in front of a person in pain again. And after the sunstorm, after the camps, I worked on ecological recovery programmes in the Midwest. That got me into biology.'

Yuri said cheerfully, 'As for me, I was born after the sunstorm. Born on the Moon, Russian mother, Irish father. I spent some time on Earth, though. As a teen I worked on eco-recovery programmes in the Canadian Arctic.'

'That's how you got a taste for ice.'

'I guess.'

'And now you're here,' Myra said. 'Now you're Spacers.'

'Martians,' Grendel and Yuri said together.

Yuri said, 'The Spacers are off on their rocks in the sky. Mars is Mars, and that's that. And we don't necessarily share their ambitions.'

'But you do over the Eye in the Pit.'

Yuri said, 'Over that, yes, of course. But I'd rather just get on with this.' He waved a hand at the sculptures of ice beyond the windscreen. 'Mars. That's enough for me.'

'I envy you,' Myra blurted. 'For your sense of purpose. For having something to build here.'

Grendel turned, curious. 'Envy's not a good feeling, Myra. You have your own life.'

'Yes. But I feel I'm kind of living in an aftermath of my own.'

Grendel grunted. 'Given who your mother is that's understandable. We can talk about it later, if you like.'

Yuri said, 'Or we can talk about *my* mother, who taught me how to drink vodka. Now that's the way to put the world to rights.'

An alarm chimed softly, and a green panel lit up on the dash. Yuri tapped it, and it filled up with the face of Alexei Carel. 'You'd better get back here. Sorry to interrupt the fun.'

'Go on,' said Yuri.

'I've two messages. One, Myra, we've been summoned to Cyclops.'

'The planet-finder station? Why?'

'To meet Athena.'

Yuri and Grendel exchanged glances. Yuri said, 'What's your second message?'

Alexei grinned. 'Something Ellie von Devender has dug out of the Pit. "The most common glyph sequence" – Myra, she said you'd understand that. She'll explain to the rest of us when you get back.'

'Show us,' said Myra.

Alexei's face disappeared, and the screen filled with four stark symbols:

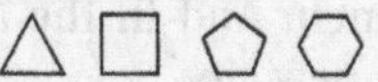

# CHAPTER 39
# NEW CHICAGO

They reached New Chicago around noon.

There was a proper rail station here, with a platform and a little building where you could wait for a train and buy actual tickets. But the track terminated; they would have to travel on north to the old Chicago some other way.

Emeline led them off the train and into the town. She said it might take days to organise their onward travel. She hoped there would be room for them to stay at one of the town's two small hotels; if not they would have to knock on doors.

New Chicago was on the site of Memphis, but there was no trace of that city here. With the wooden buildings, brightly painted signs, horse rails, and dirt-track streets, Bisesa was reminded of Hollywood images of towns of the old Wild West. The streets were a pleasant bustle, adults coming and going on business, children hanging around outside a schoolhouse. Some of the adults even rode bicycles – safety bicycles that they called 'Wheels,' an invention only a few years old at the time of the Discontinuity. But many of the townsfolk were bundled up in furs, like Arctic seal trappers, and there were camels tied up outside the saloons alongside the horses.

They were able to take rooms in the small Hotel Michigan, though Emeline and Bisesa would have to share. In the lobby hung a framed newspaper front page. It was a *Chicago Tribune* late edition, dated July 21, 1894, and its headline read: WORLD CUT OFF FROM CHICAGO.

They left their bags. Emeline bought them a roast beef sandwich each for lunch. And in the afternoon they went for a walk around the new city.

*

New Chicago was nothing but street after dirt-track street of wooden buildings; only one of the bigger churches had been built in stone. But it was big. Bisesa saw this must already be a town of several thousand people.

There was a handsome clock fixed to a tower on the town hall, which Emeline said was carefully set to 'Chicago standard railway time,' a standard that the Chicagoans had clung to despite the great disruption of the Discontinuity – even though it was about three hours out according to the position of the sun. There were other signs of culture. A note pinned on a ragged scrap of paper to the town hall door announced a meeting:

A WORLD WITHOUT A POPE?
WHERE NEXT FOR CHRISTIANS?
WEDNESDAY, EIGHT O'CLOCK.
NO LIQUOR. NO GUNS.

And one small house was labeled EDISON'S MEMORIAL OF CHICAGO. Bisesa bent down to read the details on the poster:

The FATE Of
CHICAGO
On the NIGHT
The WHOLE WORLD FROZE
JULY 1894
A Production for the Edison-Dixon Kinetoscope
US Patent Pending
A WONDER
TEN CENTS

Bisesa glanced at Emeline. 'Edison?'

'He happened to be in the city that night. He'd been advising on the world's fair, a year or two before. He's an old man now, and poorly, but still alive – or he was when I set out for Babylon.'

They walked on, tracing the dusty streets.

They came to a little park, overshadowed by an immense statue set on a concrete base. A kind of junior Statue of Liberty, it must have been a hundred feet tall or more. Its surface was gilded, though the gold was flecked and scarred.

'Big Mary,' said Emeline, with a trace of pride in her voice. 'Or, the Statue of the Republic. Centrepiece of the world's fair, that is the World's Columbian Exposition of 1893, which we held a year before the Freeze. When we chose this site for New Chicago, Mary was one of the first items we hauled down here, even though we barely had the capacity to do it.'

'It's magnificent,' Abdikadir said, sounding sincere. 'Even Alexander would be impressed.'

'Well, it's a start,' Emeline said, obscurely pleased. 'You have to make a statement of intent, you know. We're here, and here we will stay.'

There had been no real choice but to move from Old Chicago.

It had taken the Chicagoans weeks, months to understand what Bisesa had learned from the *Soyuz* photographs taken from orbit. The crisis wasn't merely some local climatic disaster, as had first been thought; something much more extraordinary had happened. Chicago was an island of human warmth in a frozen, lifeless continent, a bit of the nineteenth century stranded in antique ice. And as far as the ice cap was concerned, Chicago was a wound that had to be healed over.

Emeline said the first emigrants from Chicago proper had left for the south in the fifth year after the Freeze. New Chicago was the product of thirty years' hard work by Americans who for many years had believed themselves entirely alone in an utterly transformed world.

But even in the heart of the new town, the wind from the north was persistent and cold.

They came to farmland on the edge of the town. As far as the eye could see, sheep and cattle were scattered over a green-brown prairie that was studded with small, shabby farm buildings.

Emeline walked them to a kind of open-air factory she called the Union Stock Yards. The place stank of blood and ordure and rotting meat, and a strange sour smell turned out to be incinerated hair. 'The core of it is from old Chicago, torn down and rebuilt here. Before the Freeze we used to slaughter fourteen million animals a day, and twenty-five thousand people worked here. We don't process but a fraction of that now, of course. In fact it's lucky the Yards were always so busy, for if we hadn't been able to breed from the stock in its holding pens we would have starved in a year or two. Now they send the butchered meat up to feed the old city. Don't have to worry about freezing it; nature takes care of that for us ...'

As she spoke, Bisesa looked to the horizon. Beyond the farmland she saw what looked like a herd of elephants, mammoths or mastodons, walking proud and tall. It was astonishing to think that if she walked off, beyond those unperturbed mastodons, she could travel all the way to the ocean's shore without seeing another glimpse of the work of mankind, not so much as a footprint in the scattered snow.

That night Bisesa retired to the shared hotel room early, exhausted from the travelling. But she had trouble sleeping.

'Another day ahead of me and once again I don't know what the hell it will be like,' she whispered to the phone. 'I'm too old for this.'

The phone murmured, 'Do you know where we are? I mean, right here, this location. Do you know what it would have become, if not for the Discontinuity?'

'Surprise me.'

'Graceland. The mansion.'

'You're kidding.'

'But now Memphis will never exist at all.'

'Shit. So I'm stuck in a world without Myra, and diet cola, and tampons, and I'm about to go jaunting over an ice cap to the decaying carcass of a nineteenth-century city. And now you tell me the King will never be born.' Unaccountably, she was crying again.

The phone softly played her Elvis tracks until she fell asleep.

## CHAPTER 40
# SUNLIGHT

*May 2070*

In response to Athena's mysterious summons, Myra returned to Port Lowell and was taken up to Martian orbit, where she rejoined the lightship *James Clerk Maxwell.*

And she was wafted away on pale sunlight on a weeks-long jaunt back to the orbit of Earth – but not to Earth itself.

'L5,' Alexei Carel told her. 'A gravitationally stable point sixty degrees behind Earth.'

'I had a whole career in astronautics,' Myra said testily. 'I know the basics.'

'Sorry. Just trying to prepare you.'

It infuriated her that he wouldn't say any more, and retreated once again into his shell of secrecy.

There were in fact three of them aboard the *Maxwell.* Myra was surprised when Yuri O'Rourke tore himself away from his mission on Mars.

'I wouldn't call myself the leader of Wells Station,' he said slowly. 'I mean, that's actually my formal title on the contracts we signed with our backers, the universities and science foundations on Earth and Mars. But the others would kill me if I started acting that way. However, all of this is obviously affecting the station. And I have a feeling you'll be coming back to trouble us further.'

'I'm not planning to quit until I get my mother back.'

'Fair enough. So I have the instinct that it's right for me to accompany you.'

'Well, I'm glad to have you along.'

'Okay,' he said gruffly. 'But I've told you, my ice cores are *much* more interesting than anything the bloody Firstborn get up to.'

Yuri, in fact, was at a loss on the *Maxwell*. In the confines of the lightship's living quarters he took up a lot of room, a bear of a man with his thick tied-back hair and bushy beard and ample gut. And he fretted, cut off from his beloved Mars. Most days he sent picky demands down to Wells to ensure his crew kept up their routine of monitoring, sampling, and maintenance. He tried to keep up with his own work; he had his softscreens, and a small portable lab, and even a set of samples of deep-core Martian ice. But as the days wore on his frustration grew. He wasn't bad company, but he sank into himself.

As for Alexei, he was as self-contained as he had been since the moment Myra had met him. He had his own agenda, of which this jaunt to L5 was just the latest item. Clear-thinking, purposeful, he was content, even if he did get a bit bored when nobody played poker with him.

Myra was allowed to try to make contact with Charlie, or even with Eugene, provided she didn't give away anything sensitive. But her child and ex-husband weren't to be found even by AI search facilities that spanned the solar system. Either that or they were hiding from her. She kept on looking, fitfully, increasingly depressed at the negative results.

They were a silent and antisocial crew.

But as she settled into the journey, Myra found she was glad to have been lifted up back into the light.

She had gotten used to life at the Martian pole, with its endless night and its lid of unrelenting smoggy cloud. But now she gloried in the brilliant, unfiltered sunlight that swamped the ship. She was of the generation that had lived through the sunstorm, and she suspected she had been wary of the sun ever since. Now she felt, oddly, as if the sun had at last welcomed her back. No wonder half the Spacers were becoming sun-worshippers.

So she made her calls to Charlie, and exercised, and read books, and watched virtual dramas, her skin bathed in the sunlight that blew her toward the orbit of the Earth.

*

Before the time delays got too long, Myra spoke to Ellie, back on Mars.

'Ellie, you're a physicist. Help me understand something. What is Mir? How can another universe exist? *Where is my mother?*'

'Do you want the short answer, or the long?'

'Try both.'

'Short answer – I don't know. Nobody does. Long answer – our physics isn't advanced enough yet to give us more than glimpses, analogies maybe, of the deeper truths the Firstborn must possess. What do you know about quantum gravity?'

'Less than you can imagine. Try me with an analogy.'

'All right. Look – suppose we threw your mother into a black hole, a big one. What happens to her?'

Myra thought about it. 'She's lost forever.'

'Okay. But there are two problems with that. First, you're saying your mother, or more importantly the information that defines your mother, has been lost to the universe ...' *More importantly*. That was classic Ellie. 'But that violates a basic rule of quantum mechanics, which says that information *always* has to be conserved. Otherwise any semblance of continuity from past to future could be lost. More strictly speaking, the Schrödinger wave equation wouldn't work anymore.'

'Oh. So what's the resolution?'

'Black holes evaporate. Quantum effects at the event horizon cause a hole to emit a drizzle of particles, carrying away its mass-energy bit by bit. And the information that once defined Bisesa is leaked back that way. The universe is saved, hurrah. You understand I'm speaking very loosely. When you get the chance, ask Thales about the holographic principle.'

'You said there were two problems,' Myra said hastily.

'Yes. So we get Bisesa's information back. But what happens to Bisesa, from *her* point of view? The event horizon isn't some brick wall in space. So in her view, the information that defines her isn't trapped at the event horizon to be leaked away, but rides with her on into the hole's interior.'

'Okay,' Myra said slowly. 'So there are two copies of the mother-information, one inside the hole, one leaking away outside.'

'No. Can't allow you that. Another basic principle: the cloning theorem. You can't copy quantum information.'

Myra was starting to lose the thread. 'So what's the resolution to that?'

'Non-locality. In everyday life, locality is an axiom. I'm here, you're over there, we can't be in two places at once. But the resolution of the black hole conundrum is that a bit of information *can* be in two places at once. Sounds paradoxical, but a lot of features of the quantum universe are like that – and quantum gravity is even worse.

'And the two places in which the information exists, separated by a "horizon" like the event horizon, can be far apart – light-years. The universe is full of horizons; you don't need a black hole to make one.'

'And you think that Mir—'

'We believe the Firstborn are able to manipulate horizons and the non-locality of information in order to "create" their baby universes, and to "transfer" your mother and other bits of cargo between them. How they do this, we don't know. And what else they're capable of, we don't know either. We can't even map limits to their capabilities, actually.' Ellie paused. 'Does that answer your question?'

'I'm not sure. I guess I need to absorb it.'

'Just thinking through this stuff is revolutionising physics.'

'Well, that's a consolation.'

## CHAPTER 41
# ARKS

'We found them, Mum. Just where your astronomers predicted.

'It wasn't a great diversion for the *Liberator*. To tell the truth we were glad of a chance to give the main drive a shakedown – and for a change of view out of the windows. Up here it's not like the dramas. Space is *empty* …'

It was a fleet of ships, slim pencils slowly rotating, glowing in the light of a distant sun. Moving through the wastes beyond the asteroids, they were moving too rapidly to be drawn back by the sun's gravity; they were destined for an interstellar journey.

'They're human,' John Metternes said.

'Oh, yes.'

John peered at the images. 'They have red stars painted on their hulls. Are they Chinese?'

'Probably. And probably abandoning the solar system altogether.'

Edna expanded the image. The ships were a variety of designs, seen close to.

She downloaded analysis and speculation from Libby.

'They don't seem to have anything like our antimatter drive,' she read. 'Even if they did, the journey time would still be years. There are probably only a few, if any, conscious crew aboard each of those ships. The rest may be in suspended animation; the ships may be flying Hibernacula. Or they may be stored as frozen zygotes, or as eggs plus sperm …' She scrolled down through increasingly baroque suggestions. 'One exotic possibility is that there is *no human flesh at all* aboard the arks. Maybe they're just carrying DNA strands. Or maybe the informational equivalent is being held in some kind of radiation-tolerant memory store. Not even any wet chemistry.'

'And then you'd manufacture your colonists at the other end. Look, my bet is they're using a variety of strategies for the sake of a robust mission design,' said John the engineer. 'After all their bid for Mars failed. So they are giving up on the solar system.'

'Perhaps it's a rational thing to do, if the Firstborn are going to keep on hammering us. Ah. According to Libby, since we found them, we've had some contact with the Chinese authorities. The flagship is called the *Zheng He,* after their great fifteenth-century explorer—'

'Do you think they will make it?'

'It's possible. We're certainly not going to stop them. I'm not sure if we could; no doubt those arks are heavily armed. I think I rather hope they succeed. The more mankind is scattered, the better chance of survival we have in the long term.'

John said, 'But it's also possible the Firstborn will follow them to Alpha Centauri, or wherever the hell, and deal with them in their turn.'

'True. Anyhow it makes no difference to our mission.'

'It's another complication for the future, Mum, if the world gets through the Q-bomb assault: an encounter a few centuries out, our A-drive starships meeting whatever society the Chinese managed to build out there under the double suns of Centauri.

'Maybe Thea will have to deal with that. Give her my love. Okay, back to business, we're now resuming our cruise alongside the Q-bomb. *Liberator* out.'

# CHAPTER 42
# CYCLOPS

As they neared Cyclops Station Myra glimpsed more mirrors in space. They were lightships, swimming around the observatory. After many days suspended alone in the three-dimensional dark, it was a shock to have so much company.

The *Maxwell* pushed through the loose crowd of sails and approached the big structure at the heart of the station. Alexei said it was called Galatea. It was a wheel in space.

The *Maxwell* bored in along the axis of the wheel, heading straight for the hub. Galatea was a spindly thing, like a bicycle wheel with spokes that glimmered, barely visible. But there were concentric bands at different radii from the centre, painted different colours, silver, orange, blue, so that Galatea had something of the look of an archery target. Galatea turned on its axis, in sunlight every bit as bright as the light that fell on Earth itself, and long shadows swept across its rim and spokes like clock hands.

Alexei said, 'Looks luxurious, doesn't it? After the sunstorm an awful lot of money was pumped into planet-finder observatories. And this was how a good deal of it was spent.'

'It reminds me of a fairground ride,' Myra said. 'And it looks sort of old-fashioned.'

Alexei shrugged. 'It's a vision from a century ago, of how the future was *supposed* to be, which they finally got the money to build, just for once. But I'm no history buff.'

'Umm. I suppose it's spinning for artificial gravity.'

'Yep. You dock at the stationary hub and take elevators down to the decks.'

'And why the colours – silver, red, blue?'

He smiled. 'Can't you guess?'

She thought it over. 'The further you go from the hub, the higher the apparent gravity. So they've painted the lunar-gravity deck silver – one-sixth G.'

'You've got it. And the Mars deck is orange, and the Earth-gravity deck is blue. Galatea is here to serve as a hub for the Cyclops staff, but it has always been a partial-gravity laboratory. There are pods suspended from the outermost deck – see? The biologists are trying out higher gravities than Earth's, too.' He grinned. 'They've got some big-boned lab rats down there. Maybe we'll need that research someday, if we're going to go whizzing about the solar system on antimatter drives.'

As the wheel loomed closer Myra lost her view of the outer rim, and her vision was filled with the engineering detail of the inner decks, the spinning hub with its brightly lit ports, the spokes and struts, and the steadily shifting shadows.

A pod came squirting out of an open portal right at the centre of the hub. When it emerged it was spinning on its own axis, turning with the angular momentum of Galatea, but with a couple of pulses of reaction-jet gas it stabilised and approached the *Maxwell* cautiously.

'*Max* isn't going in any closer,' Alexei said. 'Lightship sails and big turning wheels don't mix. And you always take Galatea's own shuttles in to the hub rather than pilot yourself. They have dedicated AIs, who are good at that whole spinning-up thing ...'

The docking was fast, slick, over in minutes. Hatches opened with soft pops of equalising pressure.

A young woman came tumbling out of the shuttle, and threw herself zero-gravity straight into Alexei's arms. Myra and Yuri exchanged mocking glances.

The couple broke, and the girl turned to Myra. 'You're Bisesa's daughter. I've seen your picture in the files. It's good to meet you in the flesh. My name is Lyla Neal. Welcome to Cyclops.'

Myra grabbed a strut to brace herself and shook her hand.

Lyla was maybe twenty-five, her skin a rich black, her hair a compact mass, her teeth brilliant white. Unlike Yuri and Alexei, like Myra, she wore an ident tattoo on the smooth skin of her right cheek.

Myra said, 'You evidently know Alexei.'

'I met him through his father. I'm one of Professor Carel's students. I'm up here, ostensibly, to pursue academic projects. Cosmological. Distant galaxies, primordial light, that sort of thing.'

Myra glanced at Alexei. 'So this is how you spy on your father for the Spacers.'

'Yeah, Lyla is my mole. Neat, isn't it?' His tone was flat; perhaps there was some guilt in there under the flippancy.

They all clambered into the shuttle with their bits of luggage.

Once aboard Galatea, they were hurried through the hub structure and loaded into a kind of elevator car.

Lyla said, 'Grab onto a rail. And you might want your feet down that way,' she said, pointing away from the axis of spin.

The elevator dropped with a disconcerting jolt.

They passed quickly out of the hub complex, and suddenly they were suspended in space, inside a car that was a transparent bubble dangling from a cable. As they descended the centrifugal-acceleration pull gradually built up, until their feet settled to the floor, and that unpleasant Coriolis-spin sensation faded. They were dropping through a framework of spokes toward the great curving tracks of the wheel's decks below. All this was stationary in Myra's view, but the sun circled slowly, and the shadows cast by the spokes swept by steadily. But there was *no ground* under this huge funfair ride, no floor but the stars.

Lyla said, 'Look, before we go on – elevator, pause.'

The car slowed to a halt.

Lyla said, 'You ought to take a look at the view. See what

the station is all about. It's much harder to see from within the decks. Elevator. Show us Polyphemus.'

Myra looked out through the hull. She saw stars whirling slowly, the universe become a pinwheel. And an oval of gold lit up on the window and began to track upward, slowly, countering the rotation to pick out a corner of the star field. There Myra made out a faint disc, misty-grey and with rainbows washing across its face. A smaller station hung behind it, a knot of instruments.

'*That,*' Lyla said, 'is a telescope. One big, spinning, fragile Fresnel lens. Nearly a hundred metres across.'

Myra asked, 'Wasn't the sunstorm shield a Fresnel lens?'

'It was ...'

So this was yet another technological descendant of the tremendous shield that had once sheltered the Earth.

Lyla said, 'They call that fellow Polyphemus, the Cyclops, after the most famous of the one-eyed giants of the myths. Galatea was actually the name of the Nereid he loved, according to some versions of the stories. Polyphemus is the oldest but still the most impressive instrument they have here.'

Yuri, an instrument man himself, was fascinated, and peppered Lyla and Alexei with questions.

Big mirrors were on the face of it easier to manufacture than big lenses, but it turned out that a lens was the preferred technology for building really huge telescopes because of its better optical tolerance; the longer pathways traversed by light rays gathered up by a mirror tended to amplify distortions rather than to diminish them, as a lens would. A Fresnel lens was a compromise design, a composite of many smaller lenses fixed into a lacy framework and spun up for stability. Lyla said the sub-lenses at the rim of the structure were thin enough to roll up like paper. There were technical issues with Fresnel lenses, the main one being 'chromatic aberration'; they were narrow-bandwidth devices. But there was an array of corrective optics – 'Schupmann devices,' Lyla said – installed before the main lens itself to compensate for this.

'The lens itself is smart,' she said. 'It can correct for thermal distortions, gravitational tweaks ... With this one big beast alone you can detect the planets of nearby stars, and study them spectroscopically, and so on. And now they are working on an interferometer array. More mirrors, suspended in space. Elevator, show us ...'

More tracking ovals lit up on the wall.

'They're called Arges, Brontes, and Steropes. More Cyclops giants. Working together they are like a composite telescope of tremendous size.

'It's no coincidence that she came here. Athena, I mean. Her transmission back home was picked up by Polyphemus. Very faint laser light. Elevator, resume.'

The elevator plunged without slowing through the first of the decks. Myra glimpsed a floor that curved upwards, a décor of silver-grey and pink, and people who walked with slow bounds. 'The Moon deck,' she said.

'Right,' Lyla said. 'You understand that Galatea is centrifugally stratified. We'll be stopping on the Mars deck, where you'll be meeting Athena.'

As Myra absorbed that, Yuri nodded. 'It will help if we can stay in the G conditions we're used to.'

'Yeah,' said Lyla. 'Not many go further than that. Nobody but our ambassadors from Earth, in fact.'

'Ambassadors?' Myra asked.

'Actually cops. Astropol.' She pulled a face. 'We encourage them to stay down there, in their own lead-boot gravity field. Keeps them from getting in the way of the real work.'

'They don't know we're here, do they?'

'No reason why they should,' Alexei said.

Myra guessed, 'And they don't know about Athena.'

'No, they don't,' Lyla said. 'At least I don't think they do. They really are just cops; they should have sent up a few astronomers.'

'I don't understand any of this,' Myra confessed. 'Where Athena has "been." How she "came back." And I don't understand why *I'm* here.'

'All your questions will be answered soon, Myra,' a voice spoke from the air.

It was the second time Athena had spoken to Myra. The others looked at her curiously, even a little enviously.

## CHAPTER 43
# CHICAGO

Emeline, Bisesa, and Abdi travelled the last few kilometres to Chicago in a western-movie-style covered wagon. It was drawn by muscular, hairy ponies, a round-bodied native stock that turned out to be particularly suited to working in the deep cold. The road followed the line of a pre-Freeze rail track, but Emeline said it wasn't practical to run trains this far north, because of ice on the rails and frozen points.

By now Bisesa was wrapped up like an Inuit, with layers of wool and fur over her thin Babylonian clothes, and her phone lost somewhere deep underneath. Emeline told her that the russet-brown wool came from mammoths. Bisesa wasn't sure if she believed that, for surely it would be easier to shear a sheep than a mammoth. It looked convincing, however.

Despite the furs, the cold dug into her exposed cheeks like bony fingers. Her eyes streamed, and she could feel the tears crackling to frost. Her feet felt vulnerable despite the heavy fur boots she wore, and, fearing frostbite, she dug her gloved hands into her armpits. 'It's like Mars,' she told her companions.

Abdi grimaced, shivering. 'Are you sorry you came?'

'I'm sorry I don't still have my spacesuit.'

The phone, tucked warmly against her belly, murmured something, but she couldn't hear.

Chicago was a black city lost in a white landscape.

The disused rail track ran right into Union Station. It was a short walk from the station to Emeline's apartment. In the streets, huge bonfires burned, stacked up under dead gas-lamps and laboriously fed with broken-up lumber by squads of men, bundled up, their heads swathed in helmets of breath-steam. The fires poured plumes of smoke into the air, which hung over the city like a black lid, and the faces of the buildings were coated with soot. The people in their furs looked almost spherical as they scurried from the island of warmth cast by one bonfire to the next.

There was some traffic on the roads, horse-drawn carts, even a few people cycling – not a single car anywhere in this version of 1920s Chicago, Bisesa reminded herself. Horse manure stood everywhere, frozen hard on the broken tarmac.

It was extraordinary, a chill carcass of a city. But it was somehow functioning. There was a church with open doors and candle-lit interior, a few shops with 'open for business' signs – and even a kid selling newspapers, flimsy single sheets bearing the proud banner *Chicago Tribune*.

As they walked, Bisesa glimpsed Lake Michigan, to the east. It was a sheet of ice, brilliant white, dead flat as far as the eye could see. Only at the shore was the ice broken up, with narrow leads of black open water, and near the outlet of the Chicago river men laboured to keep the drinking-water inlet pipes clear of ice, as they had been forced to since the very first days after the Freeze.

People moved around on the lake. They were fishing at holes cut into the ice, and fires burned, the smoke rising in thin threads. Somehow the folk out there looked as if they had nothing to do with this huge wreck of a city at all.

Emeline said, panting as they walked, 'The city's not what it was. We've had to abandon a lot of the suburbs. The working town's kind of boiled down to an area centred on the Loop – maybe a half-mile to a mile in each direction. The population's shrunk a lot, what with the famine and the plagues and the walkaways, and now the relocation to New Chicago. But we still use the suburbs as mines, I suppose you would say. We send out parties to retrieve anything we can find, clothes and furniture and other stores, and wood for the fires and the furnaces. Of course we've had no fresh supplies of coal or oil since the Freeze.'

It turned out providing lumber was Emeline's job. She worked in a small department attached to the Mayor's office responsible for seeking out fresh sources of wood, and organising the transport chains that kept it flowing into the habitable areas of the city.

'A city like this isn't meant to survive in such conditions,' Abdi said. 'It can endure only by eating itself, as a starving body will ultimately consume its own organs.'

'We do what we must,' Emeline said sharply.

The phone murmured, 'Ruddy visited Chicago once – on Earth, after the date of the Discontinuity. He called it a "real city." But he said he never wanted to see it again.'

'Hush,' Bisesa said.

Emeline's apartment turned out to be a converted office on the second floor of a skyscraper called the Montauk. The building looked skinny and shabby to Bisesa, but she supposed it had been a wonder of the world in the 1890s.

The apartment's rooms were like nests, the walls and floors and ceilings thick with blankets and furs. Improvised chimney stacks had been punched in the walls to let the smoke out, but even so the surfaces were covered with soot. But there was some gentility. In the living room and parlour stood upright chairs and small tables, delicate pieces of furniture, clearly worn but lovingly maintained.

Emeline served them tea. It was made from Indian leaves from carefully hoarded thirty-year-old stock. By such small preservations these Chicagoans were maintaining their identity, Bisesa supposed.

They hadn't been back long when one of Emeline's two sons showed up. Aged around twenty he was the younger by a year, called Joshua after his father. He came in carrying a string of fish; breathing hard, red-faced, he had been out on Lake Michigan. Once he had peeled out of his furs he turned out to be a tall young man, taller than his father had ever been. And yet he had something of Josh's openness of expression, Bisesa thought, his curiosity and eagerness. He seemed healthy, if lean. His right cheek was marked by a discoloured patch that might have been a frostbite scar, and his face glistened with an oil that turned out to be an extract of seal blubber.

Emeline took the fish away to skin and gut. She returned with another cup of tea for Joshua. He politely took the cup, and swigged the hot tea down in one gulp.

'My father told me about you, Miss Dutt,' Joshua said uncertainly to Bisesa. 'All that business in India.'

'We came from different worlds.'

'My father said you were from the future.'

'Well, so I am. His future, anyhow. Abdikadir's father came through with me too. We were from the year 2037, around a hundred and fifty years after your father's time slice.'

His expression was polite, glazed.

'I suppose it's all a bit remote to you.'

He shrugged. 'It just doesn't make any difference. All that history isn't going to happen now, is it? We won't have to fight in your world wars, and so on. This is the world we've got, and we're stuck with it. But that's fine by me.'

Emeline pursed her lips. 'Joshua rather enjoys life, Bisesa.'

It turned out he worked as an engineer on the rail lines out of New Chicago. But his passion was ice-fishing, and whenever he got time off he came back up to the old city to get into his furs and head straight out on the ice.

'He even writes poems about it,' Emeline said. 'The fishing, I mean.'

The young man coloured. 'Mother—'

'He inherited that from his father, at least. A gift for words. But of course we're always short of paper.'

Bisesa asked, 'What about his brother – your older son, Emeline? Where is he?'

Her face closed up. 'Harry went walkaway a couple of years back.' This was clearly distressing to her; she hadn't mentioned it before. 'He said he'd call back, but of course he hasn't – they never do.'

Joshua said, 'Well, he thinks he's going to be put under arrest if he comes back.'

'Mayor Rice declared an amnesty a year ago. If only he'd get in touch, if only he'd come back just for a day, I could tell him he has nothing to fear.'

They spoke of this a little, and Bisesa began to understand. *Walkaway:* some of Chicago's young people, born on Mir and seduced by the extraordinary landscape in which they found themselves, had chosen to abandon their parents' heroic struggle to save Chicago, and the even more audacious attempt to build a new city south of the ice. They simply walked off, disappearing into the white, or the green of the grasslands to the south.

'It's said they live like Eskimos,' said Joshua. 'Or maybe like Red Indians.'

'Some of them even took reference books from the libraries, and artifacts from the museums, so they could work out how to live,' Emeline said bitterly. 'No doubt many of these young fools are dead by now.'

It was clear this was a sore point between mother and son; perhaps Joshua dreamed of emulating his older brother.

Emeline cut the conversation short by standing to announce she was off to the kitchen to prepare lunch: they would be served Joshua's fish, cleaned and gutted, with corn and green vegetables imported from New Chicago. Joshua took his leave, going off to wash and change.

When they had gone, Abdi eyed Bisesa. 'There are tensions here.'

'Yes. A generation gap.'

'But the parents do have a point, don't they?' Abdi said. 'The alternative to civilisation here is the Stone Age. These walkaways, if they survive, will be illiterate within two generations. And after that their only sense of history will be an oral tradition. They will forget their kind ever came from Earth, and if they remember the Discontinuity at all, it will become an event of myth, like the Flood. And when the cosmic expansion threatens the fabric of the world—'

'They won't even understand what's destroying them.'

But, she thought wistfully, maybe it would be better that way. At least these walkaways and their children might enjoy a few generations of harmony with the world, instead of an endless battle with it. 'Don't you have the same kinds of conflict at home?'

Abdi paused. 'Alexander is building a world empire. You can think that's smart or crazy, but you've got to admit it's something *new*. It's hard not to be swept up. I don't think we have too many walkaways. Not that Alexander would allow it if we did,' he added.

To Bisesa's astonishment a telephone rang, somewhere in the apartment. It was an old-fashioned, intermittent, very uncertain ring, and it was muffled by the padding on the walls. But it was ringing. Telephones and newspapers: the Chicagoans really had kept their city functioning. She heard Emeline pick up, and speak softly.

Emeline came back into the lounge. 'Say, it's good news. Mayor Rice wants to meet you. He's been expecting you; I wrote him from New Chicago. And he'll have an astronomer with him,' she said grandly.

'That's good,' Bisesa said uncertainly.

'He'll see us this evening. That gives us time to shop.'

'Shop? Are you kidding?'

Emeline bustled out. 'Lunch will be a half-hour. Help yourself to more tea.'

## CHAPTER 44
# ATHENA

The Mars deck was like a corridor that rose gradually in either direction, so that as you walked there was the odd sense that you were always at the low point of a dip, never climbing out of it. The gravity was the easy one-third G Myra had got used to on Mars itself. The décor was Martian red-ochre, the plastic surfaces of the walls, the bits of carpet on the floor. There were even tubs of what looked like red Martian dirt with the vivid green of terrestrial plants, mostly cacti, growing incongruously out of them.

It was hard to believe she was in space, that if she kept on walking she would loop the loop and end up back in this spot.

Alexei was watching her reaction. 'It's typical Earth-born architecture,' he said. 'Like the bio domes on Mars with the rainstorms and the zoos. They don't see that you don't *need* all this, that it just gets in the way . . .'

Certainly it all seemed a bit sanitised to Myra, like an airport terminal.

Lyla led the three of them to an office just off the main corridor. It was nothing unusual, with a conference table, the usual softscreen facilities, a stand of coffee percolators and water jugs.

And here Athena spoke to them.

'I suppose you're wondering why I've asked you here today.'

Nobody laughed. Yuri dumped the bags in the corner of the conference room, and they helped themselves to coffee.

Myra sat down and looked up into the empty air challengingly. 'My mother always did say you had a reputation as a comedian.'

'Ah,' said Athena. 'Aristotle called me skittish. I never had the chance to speak to Bisesa Dutt.' Her voice was steady, controlled. 'But I spoke to many of those who knew her. She is a remarkable woman.'

Myra said, 'She always said she was an ordinary woman to whom remarkable things kept happening.'

'But others might have crumbled in the face of her extraordinary experiences. Bisesa continues to do her duty, as she sees it.'

'You speak of her in the present tense. *I* don't know if she's dead or alive. I don't know where she is.'

'But you suspect, don't you, Myra?'

'I don't understand how I'm talking to you. Why are you *here*?'

'Watch,' Athena said gently.

The lights in the room dimmed a little, and a holographic image coalesced on the tabletop before them.

Ugly, bristling, it looked like some creature of the deep sea. In fact it was a denizen of space. It was called the Extirpator.

The day before the sunstorm, Athena had woken to find herself ten million kilometres from Earth. Aristotle and Thales, mankind's other great electronic minds, were with her. They had been downloaded into the memory of a bomb.

The three of them huddled together, in an abstract electronic manner. And then—

When the images from Procyon died, they all needed a break.

They went out onto the Mars deck. Myra sipped a cola. While Yuri swung improvised pendulums to study the varying artificial gravity, Alexei and Lyla explored it. If you sat down, you were heavier than when you stood up. If you threw a ball any distance, it would be deflected sideways by the spin. And if you ran against the spin, you grew lighter. Laughing, they raced each other along the corridor in big Moonwalk bounds.

Watching them play, Myra was reminded just how young these Spacers all really were.

All of them were reluctant to go back and face Athena again, and talk about what she had discovered on a planet eleven light years away.

'So those swimmers bred themselves to extinction,' Alexei said. 'Sol, what a thing to do.'

Yuri said, 'Better that than let the Firstborn win.'

'It took us two years to find a way to beam me back home,' Athena said softly. 'We didn't want to broadcast our existence to a dangerous universe. So we put together an optical laser – quite powerful, but a tight beam. And when the time came, with my data stream encoded into it, we fired it off at Earth. We anticipated that it would be picked up by Cyclops, which was at the planning stage before the sunstorm.'

'It was risky,' Myra said. 'If Cyclops hadn't been built after all—'

'We had no choice but to make the gamble.'

Yuri asked, 'Why you, of the three?'

Athena paused. 'We drew lots, after a fashion.'

'And the others—'

'The signal took everything we had, everything Witness could give us. Though Witness lived, there was nothing left to sustain the others. They gave themselves for me.'

Myra wondered how Athena, an AI with such a complicated biography, felt about this. As the 'youngest' of the three, it must have felt as if her parents had sacrificed themselves to save her. 'It wasn't just for you,' she said gently. 'It was for all of us.'

'Yes,' Athena said. 'And you see why I had to be sent home.'

Myra looked at Alexei. 'And this is what you've kept from me for so many weeks.'

Alexei looked uncomfortable.

'It was my request, Myra,' Athena said smoothly.

Yuri was staring at his hands, which were splayed out on the table before him. He looked as stunned as Myra felt. She asked, 'What are you thinking, Yuri?'

'I'm thinking that we have crashed through a conceptual barrier today. Since the sunstorm there has always been something of a human-centred bias to our thinking about the Firstborn, I believe. As if we implicitly assumed they were a threat aimed at us alone – our personal nemesis. Now we learn that they have acted against others, just as brutally.' He lifted his hands and spread them wide in the air. 'Suddenly we must think of the Firstborn as extensive in space and time. Shit, I need another coffee.' Yuri got up and shambled over to the percolators.

Alexei blew out his cheeks. 'So now you know it all, Myra. What next?'

Myra said, 'This material should be shared with the Earth authorities. The Space Council—'

Alexei pulled a face. 'Why? So they can throw more atomic bombs, and arrest us all? Myra, they *think* too narrowly.'

Myra stared at him. 'Didn't we all work together during the sunstorm? But now here we are back in the old routine – they lie to you, you lie to them. Is that the way we're all going into the dark?'

'Be fair, Myra,' Yuri murmured. 'The Spacers are doing their best. And they're probably right about how Earth would react.'

'So what do you think we should we do?'

Yuri said, 'Follow the Martians' example. They trapped an Eye – they struck back.' He laughed bitterly. 'And as a result of that, right now the only bit of Firstborn technology we have is there on Mars, sitting under *my* ice cap.'

'Yes,' Athena said. 'It seems that the focus of this crisis is the pole of Mars. I want you to return there, Myra.'

Myra considered. 'And when we get there?'

'Then we must wait, as before,' Athena said. 'The next steps are largely out of our hands.'

'Then whose?'

'Bisesa Dutt's,' murmured Athena.

An alarm sounded, and the walls flashed red.

Lyla tapped her ident patch and listened to the air. 'It's

he Astropol cops down on Earth deck,' she said. 'We must ave a leak. They are coming for you, Myra.' She stood.

Myra followed her lead. She felt dazed. 'They want me? Why?'

'Because they think you will lead them to your mother. et's get out of here. We don't have much time.'

They hurried from the room, Alexei muttering instructions to the *Maxwell*.

## CHAPTER 45

# MAYOR

Shopping in Chicago turned out to be just that. Remarkably, you could stroll along Michigan Avenue and other thoroughfares, and inspect the windows of stores like Marshall Field's where goods were piled up on display and mannequins modelled suits and dresses and coats. You could buy fur coats and boots and other cold-weather essentials, but Emeline would only look at 'the fashions,' as she called them, which turned out to be relics of the stores' 1890s stock, once imported from a vanished New York or Boston, lovingly preserved and much patched and repaired since. Bisesa thought Emeline would have been bewildered to be faced with the modernity of thirty-two years later on Earth, the fashions of 1926.

So they shopped. But the street outside Marshall Field's was half-blocked by the carcass of a horse, desiccated, frozen in place where it had fallen. The lights in the window were smoky candles of seal blubber and horse fat. And though there were some young people around, they were mostly working in the stores. All the shoppers, as far as Bisesa could see, were old, Emeline's age or older, survivors of the Discontinuity picking through these shabby, worn-out relics of a lost past.

Mayor Rice's office was deep in the guts of City Hall.

Hard-backed chairs had been drawn up before a desk. Bisesa, Emeline, and Abdi sat in a row, and were kept waiting.

This room wasn't swathed with insulation like Emeline's apartment. Its walls were adorned with flock wallpaper and portraits of past dignitaries. A fire burned hugely in a hearth, and there was central heating too, a dry warmth supplied by heavy iron radiators, no doubt fed by some wood-burning monster of a furnace in the basement. A telephone was fixed to the wall, a very primitive sort, just a box with a speaking tube, and an ear trumpet you held to your head. On the mantelpiece a clock ticked, defiantly set to Chicago standard railway time, four PM, just as it had been for thirty-two years, despite the difference of opinion expressed by the world outside.

Bisesa felt oddly glad she had opted to wear her purple Babylonian clothes, as had Abdi, despite the offer of a more formal 'suit' by Emeline. She felt she wanted to keep her own identity here.

She whispered to the others, 'So this is 1920s Chicago. I think I'm expecting Al Capone.'

Her phone murmured, 'In 1894 Capone was in New York. He couldn't be here now—'

'Oh, shut up.' She said to Emeline, 'Tell me about Mayor Jacob Rice.'

'He's only about thirty – born after the Freeze.'

'And the son of a mayor?'

Emeline shook her head. 'Not exactly ...'

The hour of the Discontinuity had been shocking for Chicagoans. After all it had started snowing, in July. Excited stevedores reported icebergs on Lake Michigan. And from their offices in the upper floors of the Rookery and the Montauk, businessmen looked north to see a line of bone white on the horizon. The mayor had been out of town. His deputy desperately tried to make long-distance phone calls to New York and Washington, but to no avail; if President Cleveland still lived, out there beyond the ice, he could offer no help or guidance to Chicago.

Things deteriorated quickly in those first days. As the food riots worsened, as old folks began to freeze, as the suburbs began to burn, the deputy mayor made his best decision. Recognising the limits of his own capacity, he formulated an Emergency Committee, a representative sample of the city's leading citizens. Here were the chief of police and commanders of the National Guard, and top businessmen and landowners, and the leaders of all of Chicago's powerful unions. Here too was Jane Addams, 'Saint Jane,' a noted social reformer who ran a women's refuge called Hull House, and Thomas Alva Edison, the great inventor, forty-seven years old, caught by chance by the Freeze and pining for his lost laboratories in New Jersey.

And here was Colonel Edmund Rice, a veteran of Gettysburg who had run the Columbian Guard, a dedicated police force for the world's fair, only a year before. The deputy mayor gladly gave up his seat as chair of the Committee to Rice.

Under martial law, the Committee clamped down on the gathering crime wave, and tidied up the deputy mayor's hasty rationing and curfew proclamations. Rice established new medical centres, where a brisk triage system was put in place, and emergency cemeteries were opened up. And as the city began to consume itself to keep warm, even as the deaths continued in swathes, they began to plan for the future.

Emeline said, 'Eventually the Emergency Committee functions got subsumed back into the mayor's office, but Rice himself was never elected.'

'But now his son is the mayor,' Abdi murmured. 'An unelected leader, the son of a leader. I smell a dynasty here.'

'We can't afford the paper for elections,' Emeline said primly.

Mayor Rice bustled in. He was followed by a small posse of nervous-looking men, clerks perhaps, though one older man carried a briefcase.

'Miss Dutt? And Mr – ah – Omar. Good to meet you. And to see you again, Mrs White ...'

Jacob Rice was a plump young man dressed in a fine suit that showed no sign of patching. His black hair was slicked back, perhaps by some kind of pomade, and his face was sharp, his cold blue eyes intent. He served them brandy in finely cut glass.

'Now look here, Miss Dutt,' he began briskly. 'It's good of

ou to see me, and all. I make a point of speaking to every isitor to the city from outside, even though they're mostly hose Greek sort of fellows who are good for nothing but a iistory lesson, along with a few British from about our own ime – isn't that right?'

'The North-West Frontier time slice was from 1885,' she aid. 'I got caught up in it. But in fact I was from—'

'The year of Our Lord 2037.' He tapped a letter on the lesk before him. 'Mrs White here was good enough to tell ne a good deal about you. But I'll be frank with you, Miss )utt; I'm only interested in your biography, no matter what ime you come from, insofar as it affects me and my town. 'm sure you can see that.'

'Fair enough.'

'Now you come here first of all with news that the world s ending. Is that right?'

The older man among the cowed-looking array behind iim raised a finger. 'Not quite, Mr Mayor. The lady's claim s that the *universe* is coming to an end. But the implication s, of course, that it will take our world with it.' He chuckled oftly, as if he had made an amusing academic point.

Rice stared at him. 'Well, if that isn't the all-mightiest iitpicking quibble of all time. Miss Dutt, this here is Gifford )ker – professor of astronomy at our brand-new University of Chicago. Or it was brand new when we all got froze. I in-ited him here because it seems you have some astronomical tuff to talk about, and he's the nearest thing to an expert ve got.'

About fifty, greyed, his face all but hidden behind thick pectacles and a ragged moustache, Oker was clutching a bat-ered leather briefcase. His suit was shabby with frayed cuffs ind lapels, and his elbows and knees padded with leather. 'I an assure you that my credentials are not to be questioned. At the time of the Freeze I was a student under George Ellery Iale, the noted astronomer – perhaps you've heard of him? Ve were hoping to establish a new observatory at Williams Bay, which would have featured a suite of modern instru-nents, including a forty-inch refractor – it would have been the largest such telescope in the world. But it wasn't to be, of course, it wasn't to be. We have been able to maintain a programme of observations with telescopes that were preserved within the "time slice," as you put it, Miss Dutt, necessarily smaller and less powerful. And we have performed some spectroscopy, whose results are – well, surprising.'

Abdi leaned forward. 'Professor, I myself have practiced astronomy in Babylon. We obtained the results that are in part the basis of Bisesa's prediction. We must exchange information.'

'Certainly.'

Rice glanced at Emeline's letter. He read slowly, '"The recession of the distant stars." This is what you're talking about.'

'That's right,' Abdi said. 'Simply put, it's as if the stars are fleeing from the sun in all directions.'

Rice nodded. 'Okay. I got that. So what?'

Oker sighed. He took off his spectacles, to reveal deep-set, weary eyes, and rubbed the lenses on his tie. 'You see, Mr Mayor, the problem is this. *Why* should the sun be uniquely located at the centre of such an expansion? It violates the most basic principles of mediocrity. Even though we have been through the Freeze, the most extraordinary event in recorded history, such principles surely still hold true.'

Bisesa studied this Professor Oker, wondering how much he could understand. He obviously had a keen enough mind, and had managed to sustain an academic career, of sorts, in the most extraordinary of circumstances. 'So what's your interpretation, sir?'

He replaced his spectacles and looked at her. 'That we are *not* privileged observers. That if we were living on a world of Alpha Centauri we would observe the same phenomenon – that is to say, we would see the distant nebulae receding from us uniformly. It can only mean that the ether itself is expanding – that is, the invisible material within which all the stars swim. The universe is blowing up like a pudding in an oven, and the stars, like currants embedded in that pudding, are all receding from each other. But to each currant it would seem as if *it* was the sole point of stillness at the centre of the explosion ...'

Bisesa's knowledge of relativity was restricted to a module in a college course decades ago – that and science fiction, and you couldn't trust *that*. But the Chicago time slice had come when Einstein was only fifteen years old; Oker could know nothing of relativity. And relativity was founded on the discovery that the ether, in fact, didn't exist.

But she thought Oker had got the picture, near enough.

She said, 'Mr Mayor, he's right. The universe itself is expanding. Right now the expansion is pushing the stars apart, the galaxies. But eventually that expansion is eventually going to work its way down to smaller scales.'

Abdi said, 'It will pull the world apart, leaving us all flying in a crowd of rocks. Then our bodies will break up. Then the very atoms of which our bodies are composed.' He smiled. 'And that is how the world will end. The expansion that is now visible only through a telescope will fold down until it breaks everything to bits.'

Rice stared at him. 'Cold-blooded little cuss, aren't you?' He glared down at Emeline's letter. 'All right, you got my attention. Now, Miss Dutt, you say you've been talking about this with the folks back home. Right? So *when* is this big bubble going to burst? How long have we got?'

'About five centuries,' Bisesa said. 'The calculations are difficult – it's hard to be sure.'

Rice stared at her. 'Five fucking centuries, pardon me. When we haven't got food stock to last us five weeks. Well, I think I'll put that in my "pending" tray for now.' He rubbed his eyes, energetic but obviously stressed. 'Five centuries. Jesus Christ! All right, what's next?'

Next was the solar system.

Gifford Oker breathed, 'I read your letter, Miss Dutt. You travelled to Mars, in a space clipper. How marvellous your century must be!' He preened. 'When I was a small boy, you know, I once met Jules Verne. Great man. Very great man. *He* would have understood about sailing to Mars, I should think!'

'Can we stick to the point?' Rice snarled. 'Jules Verne, Jesus Christ! Just show the lady your drawings, Professor; I can see that's what you're longing to do.'

'Yes. Here is the result of *our* exploration of the solar system, Miss Dutt.' Oker opened his briefcase, and spread his material over the mayor's desk. There were images of the planets, some blurry black-and-white photographs, but mostly colour images laboriously sketched in pencil. And there were what looked like spectrograph results, like blurred barcodes.

Bisesa leaned forward. Almost subvocally she murmured, 'Can you see?'

Her phone whispered back, 'Well enough, Bisesa.'

Oker pushed forward one set of images. 'Here,' he said, 'is Venus.'

In Bisesa's reality Venus was a ball of cloud. The space-probes had found an atmosphere as thick as an ocean, and a land so hot that lead would melt. But *this* Venus was different. It looked, at first glance, like an astronaut's-eye view of Earth from space: swathes of cloud, grey-blue ocean, small caps of ice at the poles.

Oker said, 'It's all ocean, ocean and ice. We've detected no land, not a trace. The ocean is water.' He scrabbled for a spectrograph result. 'The air is nitrogen, with some oxygen – less than Earth's – and rather a lot of carbon dioxide, which must seep into the water. The oceans of Venus must fizz like Coca Cola!' It was a professor's well-worn joke. But now he leaned forward. 'And there is life there: life on Venus.'

'How do you know?'

He pointed to green smudges on some of the drawings. 'We can see no details, but there must be animals in the endless seas – fish perhaps, immense whales, feeding on the plankton. We can expect it to be more or less like terrestrial analogues, due to processes of convergence,' he said confidently.

Oker showed more results. On the bare face of the Moon, transient atmospheres and even glimmers of open water pooled in the deep craters and the rills; and again the Chicagoan astronomers thought they saw life.

There were some extraordinary images of Mercury. These were blurred sketches of structures of light, like netting, flung over the innermost planet's dark side, glimpsed at the very limits of visibility. Oker said there was once a partial eclipse of the sun, and some of his students reported that they had seen similar 'webs of plasma,' or 'plasmoids,' in the tenuous solar air. Perhaps this too was a form of life, much stranger, a life of superhot gases that swam from the fires of the sun to the face of its nearest child.

Under the cover of a coughing spasm, Bisesa withdrew and murmured to her phone. 'Do you think it's likely?'

'Plasma life is not impossible,' the phone murmured. 'There are structures in the solar atmosphere, bound together by magnetic flux.'

Bisesa replied grimly, 'Yes. We all became experts on the sun in the storm years. What do you think is going on here?'

'Mir is a sampling of life on Earth, taken during the period when intelligence, mankind, has arisen. The planetologists think Venus was warm and wet when very young. So perhaps Venus has been similarly "sampled." This seems to be a sort of optimised version of the solar system, Bisesa, each of the worlds, and perhaps slices within those worlds, selected for the maximality of its life. I wonder what's happening on Europa or Titan in this universe, beyond the reach of the Chicagoans' telescopes ...'

Now Professor Oker, with a glimmer of a showman's instinct, was unveiling the climax of his presentation: Mars.

But this wasn't the Mars Bisesa had grown up with, and even visited. This blue-grey Mars was more Earthlike even than watery Venus, for here there was plenty of dry land, a world of continents and oceans, capped by ice at the poles, swathed in wispy cloud. There was some familiarity. That green stripe might be the Valles Marineris; the blue scar in the southern hemisphere could be the tremendous basin of Hellas. Most of the northern hemisphere appeared to be dry.

The phone whispered, 'Something's wrong, Bisesa. If

Mars, *our* Mars, were flooded, the whole of the northern hemisphere would be drowned under an ocean.'

'The Vastitas Borealis.'

'Yes. Something dramatic must happen to *this* Mars in the future, something that changes the shape of the entire planet.'

Rice listened to Oker impatiently, and at last cut him off. 'Come on, Gifford. Get to the good stuff. Tell her what you told me, about the Martians.'

Oker grinned. 'We see straight-line traces cutting across the Martian plains. Lines that must be hundreds of miles long.'

'Canals,' Abdi said immediately.

'What else could they be? And on land we, some of us, believe we have glimpsed structures. Walls, perhaps, tremendously long. This is controversial; we are at the limits of seeing. But about *this,*' Oker said, 'there is no controversy at all.' He produced a photograph, taken in polarised light, which showed bright lights, like stars, scattered over the face of Mars. 'Cities,' breathed Professor Oker.

Emeline leaned forward and tapped the image. '*I* told her about that,' she said.

Rice sat back. 'So there you have it, Miss Dutt,' he said. 'The question is, what use is any of this to you?'

'I don't know,' she said honestly. 'I need to talk to my contacts at home.'

'And,' Abdi said to Oker, 'I'd like to get to work with you, Professor. We have much to share.'

'Yes,' said Oker, smiling.

'All right,' Rice said. 'But when you have something, you come tell me, you hear?' It was a clear order.

'So. Enough spooky stuff for one day. Let's talk of other things.' As the professor stowed away his images, Rice sat back in his chair, rested his feet on the desk – he wore cowboy boots, with spurs – and blew out cigar smoke. 'Would you like another drink, a smoke? No? For one thing,' he said to Abdi, 'I would very much like to hear about what's going on across the Atlantic. Alexander the Great and his "world empire" – sounds like my kind of guy.'

Abdi glanced at Bisesa and Emeline, and shrugged. 'Where would you like me to begin?'

'Tell me about his armies. And his navies, too. Does he have steamships yet? How soon before he can cross the Atlantic in force . . . ?'

With Rice's attention occupied by Abdi, Bisesa murmured to her phone again. 'What do you think?'

'I need to get to work transferring all this data back to Mars. It will take a long time.'

'But?'

'But I have a feeling, Bisesa, that this is why you were summoned to Mars.'

# CHAPTER 46
# A-LINE

*June 2070*

'Since coming through the A-line we aren't alone with Q any more, Mum. There's a regular flotilla escorting the thing now, like a navy flag day, all the rock miners and bubble-dwellers coming out to see the beast as it passes. It's kind of strange for us. After a cruise of fourteen months, we've got all this company. But they don't know we're here. The *Liberator* is staying inside her stealth shroud, and there are a couple other navy tubs out here, keeping the sightseers at a good distance and coordinating the latest assault on Q ...'

'Bella,' Thales said softly.

'Pause.' Edna's talking head froze, a tiny holographic bust suspended over the surface of Bella's desk. 'Can't it wait, Thales?'

'Cassie Duflot is here.'

'Oh, crap.' Wife of dead hero space-worker, and professional pain in the backside.

'You did ask me to inform you as soon as she arrived.'

'I did.'

The message from Edna was still coming in. Bella was a mother as well as a politician; she had rights too. 'Ask her to wait.'

'Of course, Bella.'

'And Thales, while she's waiting, don't let her mail, record, comment, blog, explore, analyse, or speculate. Give her coffee and distract her.'

'I understand, Bella. Incidentally—'

'Yes?'

'It's little more than an hour to the principal strike. The Big Whack. Or rather until the report reaches us.'

She didn't need reminding of that. The Big Whack, mankind's last hope against the Q-bomb – and perhaps the end of her daughter's life. 'Okay, Thales, thank you, I'm on it. Resume.'

Edna's frozen image came alive again.

Edna's voice, having spent twenty-four minutes crawling across the plane of the solar system, sounded strongly in Bella's Mount Weather office. And Thales smoothly produced pictures to match the words, images captured by a variety of ships and monitors.

There was the Q-bomb, a ghostly droplet of smeared starlight, hovering over Bella's desk. It was passing through the asteroid belt right now – the navy's A-line – and she was shown a distant sprinkling of rocks, magnified and brightened for her benefit. There was something awesome about the image; six years almost to the day since the object had first been spotted swimming past Saturn's moons, here it was among the asteroids, home to a branch of mankind. The Q-bomb was *here,* in human space. And in just six more months – at Christmas time in this year of 2070 – the Q-bomb was destined to make its rendezvous with Earth itself.

But the bomb's passage through the belt gave one more chance for an assault.

Edna was talking about the attempts so far. Thales showed images of nuclear weapons blossoming against the bomb's impassive surface, and ships, manned and robotic, deploying energy weapons, particle beams, and lasers, even a stream of rocks thrown from a major asteroid fitted with a mass driver, an electromagnetic catapult.

'Pea shooters against an elephant,' Edna commented. 'Except it isn't quite. Every time we hit that thing it loses a little mass-energy, a loss in proportion to what we throw at it. Just a flea-bite each time, but it's non-zero. Lyla Neal has been doing some modelling of this; Professor Carel will brief you. In fact we hope one outcome of the Big Whack, assuming we don't knock the thing off its rails altogether, is to confirm Lyla's modelling, with a data point orders of magnitude away from what we've been able to deploy so far. Anyhow we'll find out soon.

'As for the cannonball, the tractor is doing its job so far. All systems are nominal, and the cannonball's deflection is matching the predictions ...' In her quiet, professional voice, Edna summarised the status of the weapon.

When she was done, she smiled. Despite her peaked cap, she looked heartbreakingly young.

'I'm doing fine in myself. After more than a year aboard this tub I need some fresh air, or fresher anyhow. And under a dictionary definition of "stir crazy" you could write down "John Metternes." But at least we haven't killed each other yet. And if you look at this cruise as an extended shakedown of the *Liberator* she's performed fine. I think we have a good new technology here, Mum. Not that that's much consolation if we fail to deflect Q, I guess; we'll all be in deep yoghurt then.

'The other crews are doing fine too. I guess this is an operational test for the navy itself. A few veterans of the old wet navy say they feel out of place on board ships where even the rawest nugget has passed out of the USNPG.' That was the US Naval Post Graduate School in Monterey. 'Right now, while we're waiting for the drama to begin, there's a sort of open-loop church service going on. Those who choose to are saying their prayers to Our Lady of Loreto, the patron saint of aviators.

'As for the Spacers, they are cooperating, mostly, with the cordon and other measures. But we're ready to take whatever action you see fit for us to take, Mum.

'Sixty minutes to showtime. I'll speak to you after the Whack, Mum. Love you. *Liberator* out.'

Bella had time for only a short reply, for it would reach Edna with only minutes left before the strike. 'I love you too,' she said. 'And I know you'll do your duty, as you always do.' She was horribly aware that these might be the last words she ever spoke to Edna, and that in the next hour she might lose her only daughter, as poor, angry Cassie Duflot, waiting outside, had already lost her husband. But she could think of nothing else to add. 'Bella out. Thales, close this down.'

The holographic display popped out of existence, leaving a bare desk, with only a chronometer counting down to the time of the Big Whack assault, and the still more important moment when news of it would reach the Earth.

Bella composed herself. 'Show Cassie in.'

Somehow Bella had expected Cassie Duflot to show up in black, as when Bella had last met her when she had handed over her husband's Tooke medal: still in widow's weeds, after all this time. But Cassie wore a suit of a bright lilac colour, attractive and practical. And nor, Bella reminded herself, was Cassie going to be sunk in grief as she had been during that visit. It would be easy to underestimate her.

'It's good of you to see me,' Cassie said formally, shaking Bella's hand.

'I'm not sure if I had much choice,' Bella said. 'You've been making quite a splash since we last met.'

Cassie smiled, a cold expression almost like a politician's. 'I didn't mean to make any kind of "splash," or to cause anybody any trouble. All I am is the widow of a navy engineer, who started asking questions about how and why her husband had died.'

'And you didn't get good enough answers, right? Coffee?'

Bella went to the percolator herself. She used the interval to size up her opponent, for that was how she had to think of Cassie Duflot.

Cassie was a young woman, and a young mother, and a widow; that gave her an immediately sympathetic angle to snag the public's attention. But Cassie also worked in the public relations department of Thule, Inc, one of the world's great eco-conservation agencies, specialising in post-sunstorm reconstruction in the Canadian Arctic. Not only that, her mother-in-law, Phillippa, had moved in senior circles in London before the sunstorm, and had no doubt kept up a web of contacts since. Cassie knew how to use the media.

Cassie Duflot looked strong. Not neurotic, or resentful, or bitter. She wasn't after any kind of revenge for her husband's death or for the disruption of her life, Bella saw immediately. She was after something deeper, and more satisfying. The truth, perhaps. And that made her more formidable still.

Bella gave Cassie her coffee and sat down. 'Questions with no answers,' she prompted.

'Yes. Look, Chair Fingal—'

'Call me Bella.'

Cassie said she had known a little of her husband's activities in his last years. He had been a space engineer; Cassie knew he was working on a secret programme, and roughly where he was stationed.

'And that's all,' she said. 'While James was alive that was all I wanted to know. I accepted the need for security. We're at war, and during wartime you keep your mouth shut. But after he died, and after the funeral and the ceremonials – you were kind enough to visit us—'

Bella nodded. 'You started to ask your questions.'

'I didn't want much,' Cassie said. She was twisting the wedding ring on her finger, self-conscious now. 'I didn't want to endanger anybody, least of all James's friends. I just wanted to know *something* of how he died, so that one day the children, when they ask about him – you know.'

'I'm a mother myself. In fact, a grandmother. Yes, I do know.'

It seemed the navy had badly mishandled queries that had initially been valid and quite innocent. 'They stonewalled me. One by one, the navy's liaison officers and the counsellors stopped returning my calls. Even James's friends drew away.' This blank shutting-out had, quite predictably, incensed Cassie. She had consulted her mother, and had begun her own digging.

And she had started drafting queries for Thales.

'I think because Thales exists, whispering in the ear of anybody on the planet who asks him a question, people believe that our society is free and open. In fact Thales is just as much an instrument of government control as any other outlet. Isn't that true?'

Bella said, 'Go on.'

'But I found out there are ways even to get information out of an AI's nonanswers as well as its answers.' She had become something of a self-taught expert on the analysis of an AI traumatised by being ordered to lie. She produced a softscreen from her bag and spread it over the desk. It showed a schematic of a network laid out in gold thread, with sections cordoned off by severe red lines. 'You can't just dig a memory out of an AI without leaving a hole. Everything is interconnected—'

Bella cut her off. 'That's enough. Look, Cassie. Others have asked the same sort of questions before. It's just that you, being who you are, have become more prominent than most.'

'And where are those others? Locked away somewhere?'

In fact some were, in a detention centre in the Sea of Moscow, on the far side of the Moon. It was Bella's own darkest secret. She said, 'Not all of them.'

Cassie took back her softscreen and leaned forward, her face intent. 'I'm not intimidated by you,' she said softly.

'I'm sure you're not. But, Cassie – *sit back*. The office has various features designed to respond to any threat made against me. They're not always very clever at decoding body language.'

Cassie complied, but she kept her eyes fixed on Bella. 'Space-based weapons systems,' she said. 'That's what my husband was working on, wasn't it?'

And she spoke of hints from the sky, traces, fragmentary clues that had been assembled by conspiracy theorists and sky-watchers of varying degrees of sanity and paranoia. They had seen the straight-line exhaust trail of a ship sliding across the sky at impossible speeds. The *Liberator*, of course. And they had seen another vessel, slow, ponderous, massive, moving in the asteroid belt, leaving behind the same kind of trail. That was clearly the tractor, preparing for the Big

Whack. These ships had all been shrouded, but mankind's invisibility shields were not yet perfect.

Bella asked, 'So what do you think all this means?'

'That something is coming,' Cassie said. 'Another sunstorm, perhaps. And the governments are preparing to flee with their families, in a new generation of superfast ships. That's not a consensus view, but a common suspicion, I'd say.'

Bella was shocked. 'Do people really think so little of their governments that they imagine we're capable of that?'

'They don't *know*. That's the trouble, Bella. We live in the aftermath of the sunstorm. Maybe it's rational to be paranoid.' Cassie folded away her softscreen. 'Bella, I have followed this path not for my husband's sake, or my own, but for my children. I think you are hiding something – something monstrous, that might affect their future. And they have a right to know what that is. *You* have no right to keep it from them.'

Time for Bella to make her judgement about what to do about this woman. Well, Cassie was not a criminal. She was in fact the sort of person Bella had been appointed to protect.

'Look, Cassie,' Bella said. 'You've picked up some of the pieces of the jigsaw. But you're assembling them into the wrong picture. I don't want any harm to come to you, but on the other hand, I don't want you to do any harm either. And by spreading this sort of theory around, harm is what you may inflict. So I'm going to take you into my confidence – the confidence of the Council. And when you know what I know, you can use your own judgement on how best to use the information. Is that a deal?'

Cassie thought it over. 'Yes, Bella, that's fair.' And she looked at Bella, apprehensive, excited. Scared.

Bella glanced at the clock on the wall. Thirty minutes before she would receive news of what had become of the Big Whack experiment. That desperate drama must be playing itself at this very moment, out among the asteroids, twenty-eight light-minutes away.

She put that aside. 'Let's start with the *Liberator,*' she said. 'Your husband's legacy. Graphics, please, Thales.'

They spoke of the *Liberator*. And of the Q-bomb it had been shadowing for months.

And then Bella showed Cassie Bob Paxton's last option.

'It's just another asteroid, drifting through the belt,' Bella said. 'It has a number in our catalogues, and whoever landed that mining survey probe on it' – it was a metallic spark on the asteroid's coal-dust surface – 'probably gave it a name. We just call it the cannonball. And *here* is the ship whose exhaust your conspiracy-theorists saw.'

'I wish you wouldn't call them that,' Cassie murmured. She leaned forward to see. 'It looks like another asteroid,' she said. 'A rock with a silver net around it.'

That was pretty much what the tractor was: a minor asteroid, much smaller than the flying-mountain cannonball. The rock had had a net of tough nanotube rope cast around it, and an antimatter-drive engine was fixed to its surface. 'We used one of the early prototype engines from the Trojan shipyards. Not human-rated but it's pretty reliable.'

Cassie began to see it. 'You're using this to steer the bigger asteroid, the cannonball.'

'Yes – with gravity. It turns out to be surprisingly hard to deflect an asteroid ...'

Turning aside the path of an asteroid had been studied for a century or more, since it had become understood that some asteroids crossed the path of the Earth, and, at statistically predictable intervals, collided with the planet.

A dangerous rock was generally too big to destroy. An obvious idea was to knock it aside, perhaps with nuclear weapons. Or you could attach a drive to it and just push it. Or you could attach a solar sail to it, or even paint it silver or wrap it in foil, so the pressure of sunlight pushed it aside. Such methods would deliver only a small acceleration, but if you could catch the rock early enough you might do just enough to keep the rock from hitting its undesired target.

As the asteroid belt was gradually colonised, all these

methods had been tried; all failed, to varying degrees. The trouble was that many larger asteroids weren't solid bodies at all, but swarms of smaller rocks, only loosely bound by gravity – and they were generally rotating too. Try to push them, or blow them up, and they would just fragment into a cloud of smaller impactors that would be almost as lethal and all but impossible to deal with.

So the idea of the gravitational tractor was developed. Position another rock near your big problem asteroid. Push the second rock aside, gently. And its gravity field would tug at its larger sibling.

'You see the idea,' Bella said. 'You have to keep pushing your rock just too feebly to be able to escape the asteroid's gravity field, so your tractor remains bound to the target. And the target will be drawn away no matter how broken-up it is. The only tricky part is orienting your tractor's exhaust plume so it doesn't impact the target's surface.'

Cassie nodded, a little impatiently. 'I get the idea. You're deflecting the orbit of this rock, this cannonball—'

'*So that it hits the Q-bomb.* The bomb and the cannonball are on radically different trajectories; the impact will be fast – high-energy.'

'When will this happen?'

'In fact,' Thales said gently, 'it *did* happen, nearly half an hour ago. Two minutes until the report comes in, Bella.'

The graphics of tractor and cannonball vanished, to be replaced by a steady image of the Q-bomb, that eerie sphere visible only by reflected starlight, floating in a cloud of velvet above Bella's desk. And beside it was a matchstick spacecraft.

Cassie understood. It took her a few seconds to compose herself. Then, wide-eyed, she said, 'It's happening *now*. This impact. And your daughter is out there, in her shrouded battleship, observing. You brought me in at a time like this?'

Bella found her voice was tight. 'Well, I need to keep busy. And besides – I think I needed to see your reaction.'

'Thirty seconds, Bella.'

'Thank you, Thales. You see, Cassie—'

'No. Don't say any more.' Impulsively Cassie leaned across the table and grabbed Bella's hand. Bella hung onto it hard.

In the graphic, bomb and escort hung silently in space, like ornaments.

Something came flying into the desktop image from the left-hand side. Just a blur, a grey-white streak, too fast to make out any details. The impact brought a flash that filled the virtual tank with light.

Then the projection fritzed and disappeared.

Bella's desk delivered scrolling status reports and talking heads, all reporting aspects of the impact. And there were calls from across Earth and the Spacer colonies, demanding to know what was going on in the belt; the explosion had been bright enough to be seen with the naked eye in the night skies of Earth, as well as across much of the rest of the system.

By pointing, Bella picked out two heads: Edna, and then Bob Paxton.

'... Just to repeat, Mum, I'm fine, the ship's fine, we stood off sufficiently to evade the debris field. Quite a sight, all that white-hot rock flying off on dead straight lines! We got good data. It looks as if Lyla's projections on the likely loss of mass-energy by the Q-bomb have been borne out. But—'

Bella flicked to Bob Paxton; his face ballooned before her, ruddy, angry. 'Madam Chair, we haven't touched the damn thing. Oh, we bled off a bit of mass-energy, even the Q couldn't eat a fucking asteroid without burping, but not enough to make a bit of difference when that thing gets to Earth. And get here it will. It's not been deflected at all, not a hair's-breadth. It defies everything we know about inertia and momentum.

'And – okay, here it comes. We got the numbers now to do some extrapolating about what happens to the Earth if the Q-bomb hits, on the basis of how the rocks we have been throwing seemed to have drained the bomb. Umm. The bomb is not infinite. But it's *big*. The bomb is big enough to destroy Mars, say. It won't shatter Earth. But it will deliver about as large an impact as the planet could sustain without breaking up. It will leave us with a crater the size of Earth's own radius.' He read, '"This will be the most devastating event since the mantle-stripping impact that led to the formation of the Moon ..."' He ran down, and just stared at the numbers off camera. 'I guess that's that, Madam Chair. We did our best.'

Bella had Thales hush Paxton's voice. 'Well, there you are, Cassie. Now you know everything. You've *seen* everything.'

Cassie thought it over. 'I'm glad your daughter is okay.'

'Thank you. But the strike failed.' She spread her hands. 'So what do you think I should do now?'

Cassie considered. 'Everybody saw that collision, on Earth and beyond it. They know *something* just happened. The question is, what do you tell them?'

'The truth? That the world is going to end by Christmas Day?' She laughed, and wasn't sure why. 'Bob Paxton would say, what about panic?'

'People have faced tough times before,' Cassie said. 'Generally they come through.'

'Mass hysteria is a recognised phenomenon, Cassie. Documented since the Middle Ages, when you have severe social trauma, and a breakdown of trust in governments. It's a significant part of my job to ensure that doesn't happen. And you've already told me the governments I work for aren't trusted.'

'Okay. You know your job. But people will have preparations to make. Family. If they *know*.'

Of course that was true. Looking at Cassie's set, determined face, the face of a woman with children of her own under threat, Bella thought she could use this woman at her side in the days and weeks to come. A voice of sanity, amid the ranting and the angry.

And somebody was ranting at her right now. She glanced down to see the choleric face of Bob Paxton, yelling to get her attention. Reluctantly she turned up the volume.

'We got one option left, Chair. Maybe we ought to exhaust that, before we start handing out the suicide pills.'

'Bisesa Dutt.'

'We've been pussyfooting around with these fuckers on Mars. Now we got to go get that woman out of there and into a secure unit. Earth's future clearly depends on it. Because believe me, Chair Fingal, we ain't got nothing else.' He paused, panting hard.

Cassie murmured, 'I'm not sure what he's talking about. But if there is another option—' She took a breath. 'I can't believe I'm saying this. I guess this *isn't* like the sunstorm, when we all had to know what was coming to build the shield. This time there's nothing we can do. You can spare people the disruption of knowing as long as this final option is still available. And then, when there really is no hope—'

'So we lie to the human race.'

'Say it was a weapons test gone wrong. Why, that's almost true.'

Bella pointed to Edna's image. 'Thales, I want to send a message to *Liberator*. Your highest level of security.'

'Yes, Bella.'

'Look, Cassie, are you free for the next few hours? I think I'd like to talk a little more.'

Cassie was surprised. But she said, 'Of course.'

'Channel opened. Go ahead, Bella.'

'Edna, it's me. Listen, dear, I have a new mission for you. I need you to go to Mars ...'

As she spoke, she glanced at her calendar. Only months were left. From now on, she sensed, whatever happened, the tension would rise, and the pace of events accelerate inexorably. She only hoped she would be able to exercise sound judgement, even now.

"We got one option left, Chair. Maybe we ought to exhaust that before we start handing out the suicide pills."

"Fire it, Dell."

"We've been pussyfooting around with these fuckers on Mars. Now we got to go get that woman out of there and talk to her some. Earth's future clearly depends on it. Because, believe me, Chairman, we ain't got nothing else." He paused, panting hard.

Cassie murmured, "I'm not sure what he's talking about. But if there is another option—" She took a breath. "I can't believe I'm saying this. I guess this isn't like the supernova, when we all had to know what was coming to build the shield. This time there's nothing we can do. You can spare people the disruption of knowing as long as this last option is still available. And then, when there really is no hope—"

"So we lie to the human race."

"Say it was the weapons test gone wrong. Who'd know it wasn't true?"

Bella pointed to Edna's image. "Edna, I want to send a message to Gaviota. Your highest level of security."

"Yes, Bella."

"Jack, Cassie, are you free for the next few hours? I think I'd like to talk a little more."

Cassie was surprised. But she said, "Of course."

Channel opened. Go ahead, Bella.

"Edna, it's me. Edna dear, I have a new mission for you. I need you to go to Mars."

As she spoke, she glanced at her calendar. Only months were left. From here on, she sensed, whatever happened, the tension would rise, and the pace of events accelerate inexorably. She only hoped she would be able to exercise sound judgement, even now.

PART FOUR

# DECISIONS

## CHAPTER 47
# OPTIONS

*July 2070*

Yuri came running in. He spread his softscreen out on the crew table. 'At last I got the stuff downloaded from Mir …'

The screen began to fill up with images of worlds, blurry photographs and blue-green pencil sketches.

Wells Station's Can Two, the 'house,' had one big inflatable table, used for crew meals, conferences, as a work surface. The table was modular; it could be split up into two or three. It was another bit of confinement psychology, Myra understood. The crew didn't even have to eat together, if they chose not.

Right now all the bits of the big table were pushed together. For days it had been used as the focus of a kind of unending conference. Yuri was trying to make sense of the alternate-Mars images Bisesa's phone had slowly, painfully returned through the low-bandwidth Eye link. Ellie was slaving over her analysis of the Eye's gravitational cage. Only Hanse Critchfield wasn't working on some aspect of the Q-bomb threat, insisting he was more use with his beloved machines.

And Myra, Alexei, and Grendel Speth, with comparatively little to contribute, sat glumly at the scuffed table, cups of cool low-pressure coffee before them.

There was a sense of shabbiness in this roundhouse on Mars, Myra thought, compared to the expensive, expansive, light-filled environs of Cyclops. Yet, as Athena kept assuring them, they were at the focus of a response to a danger of cosmic proportions. The detonation in the asteroid belt had been visible on all the human worlds. Much of Earth had shut down, a civilisation still traumatised by the sunstorm huddled in bunkerlike homes, waiting.

But time was running out. And on Mars there was a sense of rising panic. The Earth warship *Liberator* was now only days away, and they all knew why it was coming.

'All right,' Yuri said. 'Here's what we've got. As I understand it, the consensus among us is that the Mir universe contains a set of time-sliced samples. A showcase of solar life at its optimum on each world.'

'All Sol's children at their prettiest,' Grendel said. 'But it can't last. I mean, both Venus and Mars must have reached their peak of biodiversity in the early days of the solar system, when the sun was much cooler. As best anybody can tell, the Mir sun is a copy from the thirteenth century. *That* sun is too hot for these worlds. They can't last long.'

'But,' Yuri growled, 'the point is, here are the worlds of the solar system as they were in the deep past. The question is how they got from past to present, what happened that made them as they are today. Now, look at Venus. We think we understand this case,' he said. 'Right? A runaway greenhouse, the oceans evaporating, the water broken up by the sunlight and lost altogether . . .'

Once Venus had been moist, blue and serene. Too close to the sun, it overheated, and its oceans evaporated. With the water lost to space Venus had developed a new thick atmosphere, a blanket of carbon dioxide baked out of the seabed rock, and the greenhouse effect intensified until the ground started to glow, red-hot.

'A horror show, but we understand it. For Venus, our models fit,' said Yuri. 'Yes? But now we turn to Mars. Mars was once Earthlike; but, too small, too far from the sun, it dried and cooled. We understand that much. But *look* at this.'

He displayed contrasting profiles, of the ancient Mars on which they stood, and the young Mars of the Mir universe. The northern hemisphere of ancient Mars was visibly depressed beneath the neat circular arc of its younger self.

'Something happened here,' Yuri said, his anger burning. 'Something hugely violent.'

Myra saw it. It must have been like a hammer to the crown of the skull, a tremendous blow centred *here,* at the north pole. It had been powerful enough to create the Vastitas Borealis, like a crater that spanned the whole of the northern hemisphere.

They all saw the implication, immediately.

'A Q-bomb,' Alexei said. 'Scaled to Mars's mass. And directed here, at the north pole. This would be the result. By Sol's tears. But *why*? Why hit Mars, and not Venus?'

'Because Venus was harmless,' Yuri snapped. 'Venus was a water-world. If intelligence rose there at all it would have been confined to some seabed culture, using metals from geothermal vents or some such. They just didn't put out the kind of signals you could see from afar. Roads, cities.'

'But the Martians did,' Myra said.

And their reward had been a mighty, sterilising impact.

Grendel was growing excited. 'I think we're seeing elements of a strategy here. The Firstborn's goal seems to be to suppress advanced technological civilisations. But they act with – *economy*. If a star system is giving them cause for concern, they first hit it with a sunstorm. Crude, a blanket blowtorching, but a cheap way of sterilising an entire system. I bet if we dig deep enough we'll find a relic of at least one more sunstorm in the deep past. But if the sunstorms don't work, if worlds continue to be troublesome, they strike more surgically. Just as they targeted Mars. Just as they've now targeted Earth.'

'You've got to admit they're thorough,' Yuri said.

Alexei said, 'And we know from Athena and her Witness that we aren't the only ones. The Firstborn's operations are extensive in space and in time. "A fire devoureth before them; and behind them a flame burneth: the land is as the Garden of Eden before them, and behind them a desolate wilderness; yea, and nothing shall escape them." The Book of Joel.'

Myra raised her eyebrows. 'Let's not be hypocrites. Maybe

the megafauna of Australia and America felt much the same way about *us*.'

'They're like gods,' Alexei said, still in apocalyptic mood. 'Maybe we should worship them.'

'Let's not,' Yuri said dryly. 'The Martians didn't.'

'That's right,' Ellie said now. She came bustling into the room with a softscreen. 'The Martians struck a blow. And maybe we can too.' In the midst of their huddled, fearful gloom, Ellie was grinning.

'Remember this?' Ellie spread out her softscreen so they could all see a now-familiar string of symbols:

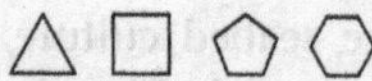

'I've had my analysis agents speculating about what these could mean. They've come to a consensus – about bloody time too – but I think it makes sense.'

'Tell us,' Yuri snapped.

'Look at these shapes. What do you see?'

Alexei said, 'Triangle, square, pentagon, hexagon. So what?'

'How many sides?'

Yuri said, 'Three, four, five, six.'

'And what if you continued the sequence? What next?'

'Seven sides. Heptagon. Eight. Octagon.' He was at a loss, and glanced at Myra. 'Nonagon?'

'Sounds plausible,' Myra said.

'And then?' Ellie insisted.

Alexei said, 'Ten sides, eleven, twelve—'

'And if you go on and on? Where does the sequence end?'

'At infinity,' Myra said. 'A polygon with an infinite number of sides.'

'Which is?'

'A circle . . .'

Yuri asked, 'What do you think you have here, Ellie?'

'The Martians couldn't avert their own Q-bomb, or

whatever the Firstborn used on them. But I think *this* is a symbolic record of what they did achieve. Starting with what they could build – see, a triangle, a square, simple shapes – they somehow extrapolated out. They built on their finite means to capture infinity. And they trapped an Eye that must have been located right under ground zero, waiting to witness the destruction.' She glanced at Alexei. 'They did challenge the gods, Alexei.'

Grendel grunted. 'How uplifting,' she said sourly. 'But the Martians got wiped out even so. What a shame they aren't around for us to ask them for help.'

'But they are,' Ellie said.

They all stared at her.

Myra's mind was racing. 'She's right. What if there were a way to send a message, not to our Mars, *but to Mir's*? Oh, there are no spaceships there.'

'Or radios,' Alexei put in.

Myra was struggling. 'But even so ...'

Yuri snapped, 'What the hell would you say?'

Ellie said rapidly, 'We could just send these symbols, for a start. That's enough to show we understand. We might provoke Mir's Martians into reacting. I mean, at least *some* of them may come from a time-slice where they're aware of the Firstborn.'

Grendel shook her head. 'Are you *serious*? Your plan is, we're going to pass a message to a parallel universe, where we hope there is a Martian civilisation stranded out of time in a kind of space-opera solar system. Have I got that right?'

'I don't think it's a time for common sense, Grendel,' Myra said. 'Nothing conventional the navy has tried has worked. So we need an extraordinary defence. It took a lot of out-of-the-box thinking to come up with the sunstorm shield, after all, and an unprecedented effort to achieve it. Maybe we've just got to do the same again.'

There was a torrent of questions and discussion. Was the chancy comms link through the Martian Eye to Bisesa's antique phone reliable enough to see this through? And how could the nineteenth-century Americans of an icebound Chicago talk to Mars anyhow? Telepathy?

Many questions, but few answers.

'Okay,' Yuri asked slowly. 'But the most important question is, what happens if the Martians *do* respond? What might they do?'

'Fight off the Q-bomb with their tripod fighting machines and their heat rays,' Grendel said mockingly.

'I'm serious. We need to think it through,' Yuri said. 'Come up with scenarios. Ellie, maybe you could handle that. Do some wargaming on the bomb's response.'

Ellie nodded.

Alexei said, 'Even if Bisesa does find a way to do this, maybe we ought to keep some kind of veto, while we try to figure out how the Martians might react. And we should pass this back to Athena. The decision shouldn't stay just with us.'

'Okay,' Yuri said. 'In the meantime we can get to work on this. Right? Unless anybody's got a better idea.' His anger had mutated to a kind of exhilaration. 'Hey. Why the gloomy faces? Look, we're like a bunch of hibernating polar bears up here. But if this works, the eyes of history are on us. There'll be paintings of the scene. Like the signing of the Declaration of Independence.'

Alexei played along. 'If that's true I wish I'd shaved.'

'Enough of the bullshit,' Grendel said. 'Come on, let's get to work.'

They broke up and got busy.

## CHAPTER 48

# A SIGNAL TO MARS

Once again Bisesa, Abdi, and Emeline were summoned to Mayor Rice's office in City Hall.

Rice was waiting for them. He had his booted feet up on the desk and puffed cigar smoke. Professor Gifford Oker, the astronomer from the university, was here too.

Rice waved them to chairs. 'You asked for my help,' he snapped. He held up Bisesa's letter, with doodles of the Martian symbols, a triangle, square, pentagon, and hexagon. 'You say we need to send this here message to the Martians.'

Bisesa said, 'I know it sounds crazy, but—'

'Oh, I deal with far more crazy stuff than *this*. Naturally I turned to Gifford here for advice. I got back a lot of guff about "Hertzian electromagnetic waves" and Jules Verne "space buggies." Hell, man, space ships! We can't even string a railroad between here and the coast.'

Oker looked away miserably, but said nothing; evidently he had been brought here simply for the humiliation.

'So,' Rice went on, 'I passed on this request to the one man in Chicago who *might* have a handle on how we might do this. Hell, he's seventy-nine years old, and after the Freeze he gave his all on the Emergency Committee and whatnot, and it's not even his own damn city. But he said he'd help. He promised to call me at three o'clock.' He glanced at a pocket watch. 'Which is round about now.'

They all had to wait in silence for a full minute. Then the phone on the wall jangled.

Rice beckoned to Bisesa, and they walked to the phone. Rice picked up the earpiece and held it so Bisesa could make out what was said. She caught only scraps of the monologue coming from the phone, delivered in a stilted Bostonian rant. But the gist was clear.

'... Signals impossible. Set up a *sign,* a sign big enough to be seen across the gulf of space ... The white face of the ice cap is our canvas ... Dig trenches a hundred miles long, scrape those figures in the ice as big as you dare ... Fill 'em up with lumber, oil if you have any. Set 'em on fire ... The light of the fires by night, the smoke by day ... Damn Martians have to be blind not to see them ...'

Rice nodded at Bisesa. 'You get the idea?'

'Assuming you can get the labour to do it—'

'Hell, a team of mammoths dragging a plough will do it in a month.'

'Mammoths, building a signal to Mars, on the North American ice cap.' Bisesa shook her head. 'In any other context that would seem extraordinary. One thing, Mr Mayor. Don't set the fires until I confirm we should. I'll speak to my people, make sure ... It's a drastic thing we're attempting here.'

He nodded slowly. 'All right. Anything else?'

'No. Signals scraped in the ice. Of course that's the way to do it. I should have thought of it myself.'

'But you didn't,' Rice said, grinning around his cigar. 'It took *him* to figure it out. Which is why he is who he is. Right? Thank you,' he said into the phone. 'You saved the day once again, sir. That's swell of you. Thank you very much, Mr. Edison.' And he hung up. 'The Wizard of Menlo Park! What a guy!'

## CHAPTER 49
# AREOSYNCHRONOUS

*August 2070*

The *Liberator* slid into synchronous orbit over Mars. Libby rolled the ship so that the port beneath Edna's feet revealed the planet.

Edna had been in GEO before, synchronous orbit above Earth. This experience was similar; Mars from areosynchronous orbit looked much the same size as Earth from GEO, a planet the size of a baseball suspended far beneath her feet. But the sunlight here was diminished, and Mars was darker than Earth, a shrivelled ochre fruit compared to Earth's sky-bright vibrancy. Right now Mars was almost exactly half full, and Edna could make out a splash of brilliance reflected from the domes of Port Lowell, almost exactly on the terminator line, precisely below the *Liberator*.

'I can't believe we're here,' she said.

John Metternes grunted. 'I can't believe *why* we're here.'

Yet here they were. Nobody on all the worlds of mankind could have been unaware of *Liberator* as she cut across the solar system in a shower of exotic antimatter products, and she wasn't shrouded now. Edna wondered how many Martian faces were turned up to the dawn sky right now, peering at a bright new star at the zenith. It was hoped, indeed, that the *Liberator*'s very visible presence would simply intimidate the Martians into giving up what Earth wanted.

There was a chime, indicating an incoming signal.

John checked his instrument displays. 'The firewalls are up.'

It would have been ironic, after having blazed across the solar system, to have the ship disabled by a virus uploaded in a greeting message. Edna said cautiously, 'Let them in.'

A holographic head popped into existence before Edna: a young woman, smiling, personable, a little blank-eyed. She looked faintly familiar. '*Liberator,* Lowell. Good morning.'

'Lowell, *Liberator,*' Edna said. 'Yes, good morning, we can see your dawn. A pretty sight. This is navy cruiser *Liberator,* registration SS-1-147—'

'We know who you are. We saw you coming, after all.'

'I know your face,' John Metternes said now. 'Umfraville. *Paula,* that's it. A hero's daughter.'

'I live quietly,' the girl said, unfazed.

Edna nodded. 'I think we all hope that today will be a quiet day, Paula.'

'We hope so too. But that's rather up to you, isn't it?'

'Is it?' Edna leaned forward, trying to look more commanding than she felt. 'Paula, you, and those you speak for, know why we're here.'

'Bisesa Dutt is not at Port Lowell.'

'She won't be harmed. We simply intend to take her back to Earth where she can be debriefed. It is best if we work together. Best for Bisesa too.'

'Bisesa Dutt is not at Port Lowell.'

Reluctantly, Edna said, 'I'm authorised to use force. In fact I'm instructed to use it, to resolve this issue. Think what that means, Paula. It will be the first act of war between the legal authorities on Earth and a Spacer community. It's not a good precedent to set, is it?'

John added, 'And, Ms Umfraville, be aware that Port Lowell is not a fortress.'

'You must follow your conscience. Lowell out.'

Metternes dragged a hand through his greasy hair. 'We could wait for confirmation from Earth.'

Edna shook her head. 'Our orders are clear. You're procrastinating, John.'

'Do you blame me? Lowell's a sitting duck down there. I feel we've become the bad guys, somehow—'

An alarm sounded, and panels turned red throughout the

ridge. There was a faint swimming sensation; the ship was moving.

'Shit,' Edna said. 'What was *that*?'

They both swung into diagnostic routines.

It was Libby who spoke first. 'We have gone to stealth. We are evading further fire.'

Edna snapped, 'What happened?'

'We just lost an antenna complex and part of a solar cell array. However all ships' systems have triple level redundancy; contact with Earth has not been lost—'

'A laser beam,' John said, checking his data, wondering. Good God almighty. We got zapped by a laser beam.'

'What source? Are we under attack?'

'It came from the planet,' John said. 'Not from another ship.' He grinned at Edna. 'It was a space elevator laser.'

'Mars doesn't have any space elevators.'

'Not yet, but they put the lasers in already. Cheeky bastards.'

Libby said, 'That was surely a warning shot. They could have disabled us. As I said we are now in shroud, and I am maintaining evasive manoeuvres.'

'All right, Libby, thank you.' Edna glanced at John. Situation clear? You agree how we should respond?' She didn't need his approval. She was the military officer in command. But she felt she couldn't proceed without his acceptance.

At last he nodded.

'Prepare a torpedo. Low-yield fission strike.' She pulled up a graphic of Port Lowell. She tapped a green dome. 'Let's take out the farm. We'll do the least damage that way.'

'You mean, we'll kill the least people?' John laughed hollowly. 'Look, Edna, it's not just a farm dome. They're running experimental programmes in there. Hybrids of Martian and terrestrial life. If you blow it up—'

'Lock and load, John,' she said firmly, pushing down her own doubts.

The launch of the torpedo was a violent, physical event. The ship rang like a bell.

*

In Mount Weather the images of the *Liberator*'s attack were shocking, a holographic globe of Mars with a gunshot wound.

'I can't believe this has happened on my watch,' Bella said.

Bob Paxton grunted. 'Welcome to my world, Madam Chair.'

Cassie Duflot sat beside Bella. 'This is why my husband died. So we have the capability to do this, if need be.'

'But I hoped the need would never arise.' Bella suppressed a shudder. 'I'm here because people thought I was a hero from the sunstorm days. Now I'm nuking my fellow human beings.'

Paxton was studying a montage of images on a softwall. 'It's all over the media. Well, you got to expect that. If you nuke Mars even the couch potatoes and thumbheads are gonna take notice. No casualty reports so far. And anyhow they shot first.'

'I can't believe you're taking it as coldly as this, Bob,' Bella said with a trace of anger. 'You were the first human to walk on Mars. And now, in a generation, it's come to war, at the very site of your landing. It's as if Neil Armstrong was asked to command the invasion of the Sea of Tranquillity. How does that make you *feel*?'

He shrugged. He wore his military jacket unbuttoned, his tie loosened, and he held a plastic soda can in his bearlike fist. 'I *feel* we didn't start this. I feel those saps on Mars should have done what their legally authorised governmental representatives ordered them to do, and hand over this screwball Dutt. And I feel that, like the lady says, there's no point spending terabucks and a dozen lives developing a facility like the *Liberator* if you ain't gonna use it. Anyhow it's your daughter who dropped the nuke.'

But it had to be Edna. Bella probably could have found some way to spare her daughter this duty; there were relief crews for *Liberator*. But she needed somebody she could trust

– somebody she could rely on *not* to drop the bomb if Bella ordered her to withdraw.

'So what's the reaction?'

Paxton tapped a screen at his elbow, and images flickered across the wall, of emptied-out food stores, deserted roads, towns as still as cemeteries. 'Nothing's changed. The alarm has been building up for weeks, ever since the cannonball failed. Everybody's hunkered down, waiting. So far the numbers after that nuke on Mars are holding up.'

Cassie asked, 'What numbers?'

Bella said, 'He means the snap polls.'

Paxton said, 'The negatives counter the positives, the war lobby versus the peaceniks, the usual knee-jerk stuff. And there's a big fat don't-know lobby in the middle.' He turned. 'People are waiting to see what happens next, Bella.'

A backlash might yet come, Bella thought. If this dreadful gamble didn't work her authority would be smashed, and somebody else would have to shepherd Earth through the final days as the Q-bomb sailed home. And that, she helplessly thought, would be a tremendous relief. But she could not put down her burden yet, not yet.

Bob Paxton said, 'Message coming in from Mars. Not that Umfraville kid who's been the spokesman. Somebody else talking to *Liberator*. Unauthorised probably.' He grinned. 'Somebody cracked.'

'So where is Dutt?'

'North pole of Mars.'

'Tell *Liberator* to move.'

'And – oh, shit.' His softscreen filled with scrolling images, this time scenes of Earth. 'They're hitting back. Spacer bastards. They're attacking our space elevators!' Paxton looked at her. 'So it's war, Madam Chair. Does that ease your conscience?'

A live image of Mars hovered over the Wells crew table. The atomic wound inflicted by the *Liberator* burned intensely at the equator, and now a miniature mushroom cloud rose high into the thin Martian air. A lot of dreams had already died today, Myra thought fancifully.

And directly over the pole of Mars hung a single spark, drifting slowly into place. Everybody was watching but Ellie, who sat apart, still working on her wargaming analysis of the Martians' likely reaction to any signal.

'Look at that damn thing,' Alexei said, wondering. 'You aren't supposed to be able to hover at areosynch over a pole!'

Grendel said, 'Well, that's what you can do with an anti-matter drive and a virtually unlimited supply of delta-vee ...'

Myra saw that these Spacers were instinctively more offended by the *Liberator*'s apparent defiance of the celestial mechanics that governed their lives than they were by the act of war.

Yuri glanced at a screen. 'Five more minutes and it will be in position.'

Alexei said, 'Meanwhile they seem to be hitting all the elevators on Earth. Jacob's Ladder, Bandara, Modimo, Jianmu, Marahuaka, Yggdrasil ... All snipped. A global coordinated assault. Who'd have believed a bunch of hairy-assed Spacers could get it together to achieve that?'

Yuri peered gloomily at his softscreen. 'But it doesn't do *us* a damn bit of good, does it? The wargamers' conclusions do *not* look good. We're pretty fragile here; we're built to withstand Martian weather, not a war. And here at the pole we don't even have anything to hit back with ... *Liberator* doesn't even need to use its nukes against us. With power like that it could fly through the atmosphere and bomb us out – why, it could just wipe us clean with its exhaust. The gamers suggest *Liberator* could eliminate a human presence on Mars *entirely* in twenty-four hours, or less.'

'Almost as efficiently as the Firstborn, then,' Grendel said grimly. 'Makes you proud, doesn't it?'

Myra said, 'Look, my mother has her Thomas Edison signal all laid out. And if we're going to send the say-so to light up, it needs to be before the *Liberator*'s bombs start falling.'

Yuri said, 'Ellie, for Christ's sake, we need some answers on how those Martians are going to respond.'

Ellie had been working for weeks on her projections of the Q-bomb's response to Bisesa's signal. She was always irritated at being distracted from her work, and her expression now was one Myra knew well from her days with Eugene. 'The analysis is incomplete—'

'We're out of time,' Yuri barked. 'Give us what you've got.'

She stared at him for one long second, defiant. Then she slapped her softscreen down on the table. It displayed logic trees, branching and bifurcating. 'We're guessing at this, guessing the motivation of an entirely alien culture. But given their opposition to the Firstborn in the past—'

'Ellie. Just tell us.'

'The bottom line. It almost doesn't matter what the Martians do. Because if they act in *any* way against any Eyes extant in their time-slices – you'll recall we've hypothesised that all Eyes are interconnected, perhaps three-dimensional manifestations of a single higher-dimensional object – they may even *be* the same Eye – and it would be trivial for them to span the gulf between our universe and Mir's—'

'Yes, yes,' Yuri snapped.

'That will provoke a reaction in the Eye in the Pit. *Our* Eye. And that, almost certainly – look, you can see the convergence of the logic trees here – will cause the Q-bomb to react. It will surely be aware of the forced operation of the only other bit of Firstborn technology in the solar system, and then—'

'And what? Come on, woman. *How* will the Q-bomb react?'

'It will turn away from Earth,' Ellie said. 'It will head for the activated Eye.'

'Here. On Mars.'

Grendel looked at her wildly. 'So Earth would be saved.'

'Oh, yes.'

That, apparently, Myra thought, was a trivial conclusion of her logic to Ellie. But there was another corollary.

She asked, 'So what do we tell my mother to do?'

Grendel said, 'I think—'

'Wait.'

The new voice spoke from the air.

Myra looked up. 'Athena?'

'A local avatar, downloaded into the station systems. Athena is at Cyclops. Ellie, I have come to the same conclusion as you, concerning the actions of the Martians. And concerning the likely consequence for the Firstborn weapon. This is not a decision you should be forced to take alone, or I, or any individual. I have prepared a statement. It is timed to allow for lightspeed delays to reach Earth, Mars, Moon, and belt simultaneously. It is already on its way. Now you must communicate with the warship.'

Yuri stared into the air. 'The *Liberator*? Why?'

'It will take fifteen minutes before the announcement is received everywhere. I doubt you have that much time.'

'So we stall,' said Alexei, and he grinned at Yuri. 'Come on, big man, you can do it. Say you'll give them what they want. Tell them Bisesa's on the john. Tell them anything!'

Yuri glared at him. Then he tapped a softscreen. 'Hanse. Patch me through to that ship. *Liberator,* Wells. *Liberator,* Wells ...'

For Myra, the fifteen minutes that followed were the longest of her life.

'This is Athena. I am speaking to all mankind, on Earth, Moon, Mars, and beyond. I will allow your systems to prepare for translation from English.' She paused for five measured seconds.

'You remember me,' she said. 'I am, or was, the mind of the shield. We worked together during the sunstorm. Since returning to the solar system I have been in hiding. I find I have returned to an age of division, with many secrets between us, between governments and governed, between factions in our populations.

'Now the time for secrecy is over. Now we must work together again, for we have a grave decision to make. A decision we must share. Prepare for download ...'

Bob Paxton stared in dismay at the data that flooded

through his displays. 'Christ. That electronic orphan is telling it all, to everybody. The *Liberator,* the Q-bomb, the whole damn circus.'

And that, Bella thought with mounting relief, had to be a good thing, come what may.

'We don't believe we can deflect the Q-bomb,' Athena said gravely. 'We tried bravely, but we failed. But we think that by speaking to our solar system's deepest past, we can save our world's future.

'Nothing is certain. Perhaps we can save Earth. But there will be a sacrifice.

'This is not a decision any one of us, no matter how powerful, how uniquely positioned, should make alone. No generation in history has faced making such a choice before. But no generation has been so united, thanks to its technology. And the implication is clear: this sacrifice must be all of ours.

'The sacrifice is Mars.'

Grendel looked around, wide-eyed. 'Maybe this is what it means to grow up as a species, do you think? To face decisions like this.'

Yuri paced around the room, angry, constrained, frustrated. 'My God, I was pissed enough when I learned that the Firstborn screwed up the ice caps with their sunstorm. But now this. Mars!'

Still Athena spoke. 'Every human in the solar system who chooses may contribute to the discussion that must follow. Speak however you like. Blog. E-mail. Just speak into the air, if you wish. Someone will hear you, and the great AI suites will collate your views, and pass them on to be pooled with others. Lightspeed will slow the discussion; that is inevitable. But no action will be taken, one way or another, until a consensus emerges ...'

They were all exhausted, Myra saw. All save Yuri, whose anger and resentment fuelled him.

Ellie folded her arms. 'Oh, come on, Yuri. So what if Mars gets pasted? Isn't the decision obvious?' Myra tried to grab her arm, to shut her up, but she wouldn't stop. 'A world of several billion people, the true home of mankind, against – *this.* A dead world. A dust museum. What choice is there to make?'

Yuri stared at her. 'By Christ, you're heartless. This has been a *human* planet since the hunter-gatherers saw it wandering around the sky. And now we're going to destroy it – finish the job for the Firstborn? We'll be considered criminals as long as mankind survives.'

Bob Paxton tapped at buttons. 'We're trying to jam it but there are too many ways in.'

'That's networks for you,' Cassie Duflot said. She glanced at Bella. 'How do you feel?'

Bella thought it over. 'Relieved. No more secrecy, no more lies. Whatever becomes of us now, at least it's all out in the open.'

Athena said, 'We predict that twelve hours will be sufficient, but you may take longer if need be. I will speak to you again then.'

As she fell silent, Paxton glowered. 'At last she zips it. Bud Tooke always did say Athena was a fruitcake, even when she was running the shield. Well, we got work to do.' He showed Bella fresh images of the damaged space elevators. 'They cut the threads of every last one of them.'

Bella's eyes were gritty as she tried to concentrate on what he was saying. 'Casualties? Damage?'

'Each elevator was ruined, of course. But the upper sections have just drifted away into space; the crews can be picked up later. The lower few kilometres mostly burn up in the atmosphere.' The screens showed remarkable images of falling thread, streams of silvery paper, some hundreds of kilometres long. 'This is going to cost billions,' growled Paxton.

'Okay,' Bella said. 'But an elevator can't do much damage if it falls, can it? In that way it's not like an earthbound structure, a building. The bulk of the mass, the counterweight, just drifts off into space. So the casualty projections—'

'Zero, with luck,' Paxton said reluctantly. 'Minimal anyhow.'

Cassie put in, 'There are no casualties reported from Mars either.'

Bella blew out her cheeks. 'Looks like we all got away with it.'

Paxton glared at her. 'Are you somehow equating these assaults? Madam Chair, you represent the legally constituted governments of the planet. The *Liberator*'s action was an act of war. *This* is terrorism. We must respond. I vote we order the *Liberator* to blast that whole fucking ice cap off the face of Mars, and have done with it.'

'No,' Bella said sharply. 'Really, Bob, what good would an escalation do?'

'It would be a response to the attacks on the Elevators. And it would put a stop to this damn security breach.'

Bella rubbed tired eyes. 'I very much doubt that Athena is there. Besides – everything is changing, Bob. I think it's going to take you a little time to adjust to that, but it's true nevertheless. Send a signal to *Liberator*. Tell them to hold off until further orders.'

'Madam Chair, with respect – you're going to go along with this subversion?'

'We learned more in the last few minutes than in all our running around the solar system in the last months. Maybe we should have been open from the beginning.'

Cassie nodded. 'Yes. Maybe it's a mark of a maturing culture, do you think, that secrets aren't kept, that truth is told, that things are *talked out*?'

'Jesus Christ on a bike,' Paxton said. 'I can't believe I'm hearing this mush. Madam Chair – Bella – people will panic. Riots, looting. You'll see. That's why we keep secrets, Ms Duflot. Because people can't handle the truth.'

Cassie glanced at the softwall. 'Well, that doesn't seem to be true, Admiral. The first responses are coming in ...'

Alone over the Martian pole, Edna and John sat fascinated as threads of the system-wide discussion unreeled on the displays of their consoles.

John said, 'Look at this. People aren't just voting on the Q-bomb, they're collectively brainstorming other solutions. Interconnected democracy at its best. Although I fear there aren't any other solutions to hand, this time.'

Edna said, 'Some of the Spacers say, let the Q-bomb take out Earth. Earth is mankind's past, space the future. So discard a worn-out world.'

John grunted. 'And a few billion people with it? Not to mention almost all the cultural treasures of mankind. I think that's a minority view, even among the Spacers. And here's another thread about the viability of mankind if Earth were lost. They're still a pretty small community out there. Small, scattered, very vulnerable ... Maybe we still need Big Momma for a while yet.'

'Hey, look at this thread.' This discussion followed leads from members of something called the Committee of Patriots.

'I heard of that,' Edna said. 'It advises my mother.' She read, '"The Firstborn dominate past and future, time and space. They're so far advanced that compared to them ..."' She scrolled forward. 'Yes, yes. "The existence of the Firstborn is the organising pole around which all of future human history must, *will* be constructed. And therefore we should accept their advanced wisdom."'

John grimaced. 'You mean, if the Firstborn choose to destroy the Earth, we should just submit?'

'That's the idea. Because they know best.'

'I can't say that strikes a chord with me. What else you got?'

In the silence of Wells Station, Athena spoke again. 'It is time.'

Yuri looked around the empty air wildly. 'You're here?'

'I've downloaded a fresh avatar, yes.'

'It isn't twelve hours yet.'

'No more time is needed. A consensus has emerged – not unanimity, but overwhelming. I'm very sorry,' Athena said evenly. 'We are about to commit a great and terrible crime.

But it is a responsibility that will be borne by all of us, mankind and its allies.'

'It had to be this way, Yuri,' Myra said. 'You know it—'

'Well, I won't fucking leave whatever you do,' Yuri said, and he stamped out of the room.

Alexei said, 'Look at this discussion thread. "We are a lesser power. The situation is asymmetric. So we must prepare to fight asymmetrically, as lesser powers have always faced off greater ones, drawing on a history of fighting empires back to Alexander the Great. We must be prepared to make sacrifices to strike against them. We must be prepared to die . . ."'

'A future as a species of suicide bombers,' Grendel said. 'But if those Martians in that other reality don't respond, we still may have no future at all.'

Myra glanced over the summarised discussion threads, symbolised in the air and in the screens spread over the table. Their content was complex, their message simple: *Do it. Just do it.*

Ellie stood up. 'Myra. Please help me. I think it's time to talk to your mother.'

Myra followed Ellie to the Pit.

## CHAPTER 50

# INTERLUDE: THE LAST MARTIAN

She was alone on Mars. The only one of her kind to have come through the crude time-slicing.

She had built herself a shelter at the Martian north pole, a spire of ice. It was beautiful, pointlessly so, for there was none but her to see it. This was not even *her* Mars. Most of this time-sliced world, for all the cities and canals that had survived, was scarred by cold aridity.

When she saw the array of symbols burning in the ice of Mir, the third planet, it gave her a shock of pleasure to know that *mind* was here in this new system with her. But, even though she knew that whatever lived on Mir was cousin to her own kind, it was a poor sort of comfort.

Now she waited in her spire and considered what to do.

The great experiments of life on the worlds of Sol ran in parallel, but with different outcomes.

On Mars, when intelligence rose, the Martians manipulated their environment like humans. They lit fires and built cities.

But a Martian was not like a human.

Even her individuality was questionable. Her body was a community of cells, her form unfixed, flowing between sessile and motile stages, sometimes dispersing, sometimes coalescing. She was more like a slime mould, perhaps, than a human. She had always been intimately connected to the tremendous networked communities of single-celled creatures that had drenched Mars. And she was not really a 'she.' Her kind were not sexual as humans were. But she had been a mother; she was more 'she' than 'he.'

There had only ever been a few hundred thousand of her

kind, spread across the seas and plains of Mars. They had never had names; there were only ever so few that names were unnecessary. She had been aware of every one of them, like voices dimly heard in the echoes of a vast cathedral.

She was very aware that they had all gone, all of them. Hers was a loneliness no human could have imagined.

And the approaching Firstborn weapon, Mars's own Q-bomb, had gone too.

Just before the Discontinuity she had been working at the Martian pole, tending the trap of distorted spacetime within which she and her fellow workers had managed to capture the Firstborn Eye. To senses enhanced to 'see' the distortion of space, the weapon was very visible, at the zenith, driving straight down from the sky toward the Martian pole.

And then came the time-slicing. The Eye remained in its cage. The Firstborn weapon was gone.

This time-sliced Mars was a ruin, the atmosphere only a thin veneer of carbon dioxide, only traces of frost in the beds of the vanished oceans, and dust storms towering over an arid landscape sterilised by the sun's ultraviolet. In places the cities of her kind still stood, abandoned, even their lights burning in some cases. But her fellows were gone. And when she dug into the arid, toxic dirt, she found only methanogens and other simple bacteria, thinly spread, an echo of the great rich communities that had once inhabited this world. Scrapings that were her own last descendants.

She was alone. A toy of the Firstborn. Resentment seethed.

The Martians had thought they came to understand the Firstborn, to a degree.

The Firstborn must have been very old.

They may even be survivors of the First Days, the Martians thought, an age that began just half a billion years after the Big Bang itself, when the universe turned transparent, and the light of the very first stars shone uncertainly. That was why the Firstborn triggered instabilities in stars. In their day, *all* the stars had been unstable.

And if they were old, they were conservative. To achieve their goals they caused stars to flare or go nova, or change their variability, not to detonate entirely. They sent their cosmological bombs to sterilise worlds, not to shatter them. They appeared to be trying to shut down energy-consuming cultures as economically as possible.

To understand why they did this, the Martians tried to look at themselves through the eyes of a Firstborn.

The universe is full of energy, but much of it is at equilibrium. At equilibrium no energy can flow, and therefore it cannot be used for work, any more than the level waters of a pond can be used to drive a water-wheel. It is on the flow of energy out of equilibrium – the small fraction of 'useful' energy, 'exergy' – that life depends.

And everywhere, exergy was being wasted.

Everywhere, evolution drove the progression of life to ever more complex forms, which depended on an ever faster usage of the available energy flow. And then there was intelligence. Civilisations were like experiments in ways of using up exergy faster.

From the Firstborn's lofty point of view, the Martians speculated, the products of petty civilisations like their own were irrelevant. All that mattered was the flow of exergy, and the rate at which it was used up.

Surely a civilisation so old as the Firstborn, so arbitrarily advanced, would become concerned with the destiny of the cosmos as a whole, and of the usage of its finite resources. The longer you wanted your culture to last, the more carefully you had to husband those resources.

If you wanted to reach the very far future – the Last Days, when the surge of quintessence finally ended the age of matter – the restrictions were harsh. The Martians' own calculations indicated that the universe could bear only *one* world as populous and energy-hungry as their own, one world in each of the universe's hundred billion empty galaxies, if the Last Days were to be reached.

The Firstborn must have seen that if life were to survive in the very long term – if even a single thread of awareness was to be passed to the furthest future – discipline was needed on a cosmic scale. There must be no unnecessary disturbance, no wasted energy, no ripples in the stream of time.

Life: there was nothing more precious to the Firstborn. But it had to be the right kind of life. Orderly, calm, disciplined. Sadly, that was rare.

Certainly they regretted what they did. They watched the destruction they wreaked, and constructed time-sliced samples of the worlds they ruined, and popped them in pocket universes. But the Martian knew that in this toy universe the positive of its mass-energy was balanced out by the negative of gravity. And when it died, as soon it must, the energy sums would cancel out, a whole cosmos lapsing to the abstraction of zero.

The Firstborn were economical even in their expressions of regret.

The Martians argued among themselves as to *why* the Firstborn were so intent on reaching the Last Days.

Perhaps it derived from their origin. Perhaps in their coming of awareness in the First Days they had encountered – *another*. One as far beyond their cosmos as they were beyond the toy universes in which they stored their time-slice worlds. One who would return in the Last Days, to consider what should be saved.

The Firstborn probably believed that in their universal cauterisation they were being benevolent.

The last Martian pondered the signal from Mir.

Those on Mir had no wish to submit to the Firstborn's hammer blow. Nor had the Martians wanted to see their culture die for the sake of a neurosis born when the cosmos was young. So they fought back. Just as the creatures from Mir, and its mother world in the parent universe, were trying to fight back now.

Her choice was clear.

It took her seven Martian days to make the preparations.

While she worked she considered her own future. She knew that this pocket cosmos was dying. She had no desire to die with it. And she knew that her own only possible exit was via another Firstborn artifact, clearly visible in her enhanced senses, an artifact nestling on the third planet.

All that for the future.

Unfortunately the implosion of the spacetime cage would damage her spire of ice. She began the construction of a new one, some distance away. The work pleased her.

The new spire was no more than half-finished when, following the modifications she had made, the gravitational cage crushed the Firstborn Eye.

## CHAPTER 51

# DECISION

There was only one Eye, though it had many projections into spacetime. And it had many functions.

One of those was to serve as a conduit of information.

When the Martian trap closed, the Eye there emitted a signal of distress. A shriek, transmitted to all its sister projections.

The Q-bomb was the only Firstborn artifact in the solar system, save for the Eye trapped in its Pit on Mars. And the Q-bomb sensed that shriek, a signal it could neither believe nor understand.

Troubled, it looked ahead.

There before the Q-bomb, a glittering toy, floated the planet Earth with all its peoples. Down there on that crowded globe, alarms were flashing across innumerable softscreens, the great telescopes were searching the skies – and an uncertain humanity feared that history was drawing to a close.

The Q-bomb could become master of this world. But the cry it had heard caused it conflict. Conflict that had to be resolved by a decision.

The bomb marshalled its cold thoughts, brooding over its still untested powers.

And it turned away.

PART FIVE

# LAST CONTACTS

## CHAPTER 52
# PARADE

Bisesa and Emeline stepped out of the apartment for the last time. They were both laden with backpacks and valises. The sky was a lid, but at least it wasn't snowing.

Emeline locked up her apartment carefully, and tucked the keys away in a pocket in her thick fur coat. Of course she would never come this way again, and it wouldn't be long before the ice came and crushed the building. But Emeline locked up even so. Bisesa said nothing; she would have done exactly the same.

Bisesa made sure one more time that she had brought out the only possession of real importance to her: her phone, tucked into an inside pocket with its spacesuit battery packs.

Then they set off for Michigan Avenue.

Michigan, a canyon of concrete and brick running between blackened skyscrapers and shut-up stores, was always a wind tunnel, and Emeline and Bisesa turned away from the north to protect their eyes.

But the procession was already gathering, thousands of people standing around in the frozen mud, gradually forming up into an orderly column. Bisesa hadn't known there were still so many left in Chicago. There were carriages of every kind, from farmyard carts to graceful phaetons and stanhopes, with those stocky Arctic-adapted horses harnessed up. Even the city's grip-car streetcars were standing ready to roll one last time, full of passengers.

Most people, though, were on foot, with bundles on their backs or in barrows, and with their children or grandchildren holding their hands. Many of the Chicagoans were bundled up in their Arctic furs, but today some defied the elements and wore what looked like their Sunday best, frock coats and sweeping gowns, top hats and fur coats. Even the city's many prostitutes had come out into the light. With painted lips and rouged cheeks and defiant flashes of ankle or cleavage, they laughed and flirted like colourful birds. There was an excited buzz of conversation.

The parade was to be led by gleaming black carriages that lined up outside the Lexington Hotel. These would carry the city's dignitaries, principally Mayor Rice's relatives and allies. Thomas Edison, it was rumoured, was wrapped up in blankets in a carriage of his own design, heated and lit by a portable electric generator.

Rice's own carriage of polished wood and black ribbon was at the very head of the procession, and Bisesa was astounded to see that it was to be drawn by a woolly mammoth. The animal was restless. It raised its head with that odd bulge over the crown, and its long tusks curled bright in the air. As its nervous handlers beat at it with rods and whips, it trumpeted, a brittle call that echoed from the windows of the skyscrapers. It was quite a stunt for Rice, Bisesa admitted grudgingly – just as long as the mammoth didn't wreck the carriage it was supposed to haul.

The whole thing was a spectacle, just as it was meant to be, and Bisesa admired Rice and his advisors for setting it up this way, and for choosing the date. On Mir this was July 4, according to the calendars devised by the university astronomers.

But this Independence Day parade was actually the final abandonment of old Chicago. These were not revellers but refugees, and they faced a great trial, a long walk all the way down through the suburbs and out of the city, heading south, ever south, to a hopeful new home beyond the ice. Even now there were some who refused to join the flight, hooligans and hedonists, drunks and deadbeats, and a few stubborn types who simply wouldn't leave their homes. Few expected these refuseniks to survive another winter.

Human life would go on here, then. But today saw the

end of civilised Chicago. And beyond the bright human chatter Bisesa could hear the growl of the patient ice.

Emeline led Bisesa to their place among the respectable folk who massed behind the lead carriages. Drummers waited in a block, shivering, their mittened hands clutching their sticks.

They quickly found Harry and Joshua, Emeline's sons. Harry, the older son and walkaway, had returned to help his mother leave the city. Bisesa was glad to see them. Both tall, lean, well-muscled young men, dressed in well-worn coats of seal fur and with their faces greased against the cold, they looked adapted for the new world. With the boys, Bisesa thought her own chances of surviving this trek were much improved.

Gifford Oker came pushing out of the crowd to meet them. He was encased in an immense black fur coat, with a cylindrical hat pulled right down to his eye line. He carried only a light backpack with cardboard tubes protruding from it. 'Madam Dutt, Mrs White. I'm glad to have found you.'

Emeline said playfully, 'You're not too heavily laden, Professor. What are these documents?'

'Star charts,' he said firmly. 'The true treasure of our civilisation. A few books too – oh, what a horror it was that we were not able to empty the libraries! For once a book is lost to the ice, a little more of our past is gone forever. But as to my personal effects, my pots and pans, I have my own troop of slave bearers to help me with all that. They are called graduate students.'

Another stiff professor's joke. Bisesa laughed politely.

'Madam Dutt, I suppose you know that Jacob Rice is looking for you. He'll wait until the procession is underway. But he wants you to come see him in his carriage. He has Abdikadir at his side already.'

'He does? I had hoped Abdikadir would be with you.' Abdi had been working on astronomy projects with Oker and his students.

But Oker shook his head. 'What the mayor asks for, the mayor gets.'

'I suppose it might be worth a ride in the warmth for a bit. What *does* he want?'

Oker cocked an eyebrow. 'I think you know. He wants to drain your knowledge of Alexander and his Old World empire. *Sarissae* and steam engines – I admit I'm intrigued myself!'

She smiled. 'He's still dreaming of world domination?'

'Look at it from Rice's point of view,' Oker said. 'This is the completion of one great project, the migration from the old Chicago to the new, a work that has consumed his energies for years. Jacob Rice is still a young man, and a hungry and energetic one, and I suppose we should be glad of that or we surely wouldn't have got as far as this. Now he looks for a new challenge.'

'This world is a pretty big place,' Bisesa said. 'Room enough for everybody.'

'But not infinite,' Oker said. 'And after all we have already made tentative contacts across the ocean. Rice is no Alexander, I'm convinced of that, but neither he nor the Great King are going to submit to the other.

'And, you know, there may be something worth fighting for. Rice has accepted what you and Abdikadir have said of the future. He has demanded of his scientists, specifically of *me,* to explore ways to avert the end of the universe – or perhaps even to escape it.'

'Wow. He does think big.'

'And, you see, he suspects that the dominance of this world may be a necessary first step to saving it.'

Rice might actually be right, Bisesa thought. If the only way back to Earth was through the Eye in Babylon, war over possession of that city might ultimately be inevitable.

Oker sighed. 'The trouble is, however, that once you are in the pocket of a man like Rice, it's hard to climb out again. *I* should know,' he said ruefully. 'And you must decide, Bisesa Dutt, what *you* want.'

She was clear about that. 'I've achieved what I came here for. Now I have to get back to Babylon. That's the way I came into this world, and it's my only connection to my daughter.

And I think I ought to take Abdikadir back home too. The court of Alexander needs clear intelligences like his.'

Oker thought that over. 'You have given us much, Madam Dutt – not least, an awareness of our place in this peculiar panoply of multiple universes. Jacob Rice's wars are not your wars; his goals are not your goals. At some point we will help you get away from him.' He glanced at Emeline and her sons, who nodded their support.

'Thank you,' Bisesa said sincerely. 'But what about you, Professor?'

'Well, the foundation stone of the new observatory at New Chicago has already been laid. Building that might be enough to see *me* through. But beyond that—' He looked up at the dense mass of cloud above. 'Sometimes I feel privileged just to be here, you know, on the world you call Mir. I have been projected into an entirely new universe, in which different worlds are suspended, studied by no astronomer before my generation! But the seeing is always poor. I would love to travel above the clouds of Mir – to sail to the Moon and the other worlds in some aerial phaeton. It beggars my imagination as to how that might be achieved, but if Alexander the Great can run a steam-train service, perhaps New Chicago can reach the stars. What do you think?' He grinned, suddenly boyish.

Bisesa smiled. 'I think that's a marvellous idea.'

Emeline clung to the arm of Harry, her son. 'Well, you can keep the stars. All I want is a plot of land that's ice-free at least *some* of the time. And as for the future – five hundred years, you say? That will see me out, and my boys. It's time enough for me.'

'You're very wise,' Oker said.

There was a blast on a hunting horn.

An anticipatory cheer went up. Men, women and children shuffled, adjusting the packs on their backs. The horses neighed and bucked, harness rattled, and the somewhat shapeless crowd, crammed into the muddy street, began to take on the appearance of a procession.

Lights flared, startling Bisesa. Electric searchlights suspended from the skyscrapers splashed light over walls that were now revealed to be draped in bunting and the Stars and Stripes. The cheers grew louder.

'All scavenged from the world's fair,' Emeline said, smiling, a bit tearful. 'I have my reservations about Jacob Rice, but I'd never deny he has style! What a way to say good-bye to the old lady.'

A walking beat was sounded by the massed drummers.

With a protesting trumpet Rice's harnessed mammoth led the march, jolting the Mayor's carriage into motion. The crowd was packed so tightly that the movement took time to ripple through its ranks; it was some minutes before Bisesa, Emeline, and the others had room to walk. At last all the great crowd shuffled forward, heading south along Michigan Avenue toward Jackson Park. Armed troopers wearing yellow armbands walked to either side of the dense column, to fend off the wild animals. Even the yellow streetcars clattered into motion, one last time, though they couldn't carry their passengers far along their journey.

As they marched the Chicagoans began to sing, the rhythm driven by the drums and the slow beat of the steps of their swaddled feet. At first they plumped for patriotic songs: 'My Country 'Tis of Thee,' 'America,' and 'The Star-Spangled Banner.' But after a while they settled into a song Bisesa had heard many times here, a Tin Pan Alley hit of the 1890s from which Chicago had been plucked. It was a sweet dirge about an old man who had lost his love. The mournful voices rose up, echoing from the brick, glass, and concrete faces of the abandoned buildings around them, singing of the hopes that had vanished 'after the ball.'

Bisesa heard a crash of glass, drunken laughter, and then a dull crump. Looking back, she saw that flames were already licking out of the darkened upper windows of the Lexington Hotel.

## CHAPTER 53
# AURORA

*December 7, 2070*

With Bill Carel and Bob Paxton at her side, Bella Fingal gazed out of the shuttle's small blister window as they approached one of the most famous spacecraft in human history.

Bella felt exhausted, deep in her bones, after the strain of the last months. But now it was almost over. Only a few more days remained to the Q-bomb's closest approach to Earth: 'Q-day,' as the commentators called it. The astronomers and the military assured her daily that the bomb had stuck to the path to which it had been deflected after the Eye on Mars had suddenly flared to life; the Q-bomb would come close, even sailing between Earth and Moon, but it would not impact the planet.

Bella had to plan her affairs as if that were true. Today, for instance, she had to get through this conference on *Aurora,* fulfilling one of her last self-appointed duties, the kick-starting of a new debate about the future of mankind. But she suspected that like the rest of the human race she wouldn't quite believe it until the Q-bomb really had passed by harmlessly. And like much of mankind she planned to spend Q-day itself with her family.

After that she could lay down the burden of office at last, and submit herself to the war crimes tribunal at the Hague, and somebody else would have to make the decisions. She was content with that. Content even at being relieved of office before the final act of this lethal drama was played out, in the abandonment of Mars.

The shuttle turned. She was maundering; she had almost forgotten where she was. She peered out of her window, concentrating on a remarkable, and familiar, view.

Shining in raw sunlight, *Aurora 2* was ungainly, fragile-looking. She looked something like a drum majorette's baton, a slim spine two hundred metres long connecting propulsion units and habitable compartments. The ship was badly scarred, paint peeling, solar-cell arrays blackened and curled up, and in one place the hull of the crew dome had burned and wrinkled back, exposing struts and partitions. *Aurora* had visibly withstood a terrible fire. But she had achieved what had been asked of her.

*Aurora* had been the second manned ship to Mars. She had been intended to pick up Bob Paxton and his crew, who would have sailed home to their heroes' welcome. But the sunstorm had put paid to those plans, and *Aurora 2,* one of the largest spacecraft of its day, was needed for other purposes than exploration, and she was brought back to Earth. L1, a stationary point between sun and Earth, was the logical place to hang a shield intended to shelter the Earth from the raging of the sunstorm. So it was here that *Aurora* had been stationed, to serve as a shack for the construction crews.

The shield was gone now. The storm had left it a monumental wreck, that had then been cannibalised to build new stations in space and on the Moon. But the *Aurora* herself remained here at L1, a permanent memorial to those astonishing days, and a stub of the shield had been kept in place around the ship, its glistening surface spiralling out from the embedded hull like a spiderweb.

Bella glanced at her fellow passengers. Bill Carel, frail, trembling slightly, his face full of anger at the betrayal by his son, barely seemed able to see the approaching ship.

Bob Paxton's expression was harder to read.

Bella herself had served on the shield during the sunstorm, and had been up here many times since, for memorials, dedication services, museum openings, anniversaries. But for Bob Paxton it was different. As soon as he got back to Earth after the storm, he had gotten through the medals-and-presidents stuff as quickly as possible. Then he had thrown himself back nto his military career, and had ultimately devoted his life ɔ the issue of how to deal with the future Firstborn threat. 'axton had never visited L1, and probably hadn't even seen *urora 2* since he glimpsed her from the surface of Mars, liding through the sky on its flyby pass, abandoning him nd his crew. Now the old sky warrior's face was creased, lamped, and she couldn't tell what he was thinking.

The shuttle turned with a remote clatter of attitude thrust-rs and nestled belly-down on the curving hull of *Aurora*'s ıabitable compartment. The sun was directly below Bella ıow, casting vertical shadows, and through a small window et over her head she saw the Earth, a blue lantern hanging lirectly opposite the position of the sun. Earth was full, of ourse; it always was, as seen from L1. She wished she could ee it more clearly.

With the docking complete, the shuttle closed its systems lown.

'Welcome to *Aurora 2,* and the Shield Memorial Station.'

The soft female voice sent a shiver of familiarity through 3ella. *This* was different from all her previous visits. 'Hello, \thena. Welcome home.'

'Bella. It's good to speak to you again. Please come ıboard.'

A hatch opened in the floor. Bella released her seat re-traint and floated into the air.

\lexei Carel and Lyla Neal were waiting for them on the ɔridge of *Aurora.*

This was the ship's single most prestigious site, the loca-ion where Bud Tooke had once masterminded the salvation ɔf the Earth. Now it was a museum, and the antique-looking oftscreen displays, headsets, clipboards, and other bits of letritus from the days of crisis had been lovingly preserved ınder layers of transparent plastic. It always made Bella feel ɔld to come back here.

Bill Carel was the last to come through onto the bridge. Clumsy in microgravity, evidently feeble, he looked oddly comical in his orange jumpsuit. But when he faced his son his expression was twisted. 'You bloody little fool. And you, Lyla. You betrayed me.'

Alexei and Lyla clung to each other, drifting a little in the microgravity, nervous, defiant. Alexei was a skinny kid, only twenty-seven, and Lyla looked even younger. But then, reflected Bella, all true Spacers were just kids.

Alexei said, 'We don't see it like that, Dad. We did what we had to do. What we thought was best.'

'You *spied* on me,' Carel snapped. 'You stole my work. You were a brilliant student, Lyla. Brilliant. And you've come to this.'

Lyla was cooler than her lover. 'We were forced into it by your own actions, sir. You kept secrets. You wouldn't tell people what they needed to know. You lied! If we were at fault, so were you.'

'And that,' Bella broke in, 'is the first sensible thing anybody's said.'

'I agree,' Athena said dryly. 'Perhaps you should all sit down. A small educational area has been set aside at the rear of the bridge ...'

It was a plastic table, its top drenched with kid-friendly sunstorm info, with small seats set around it with microgravity bars to hook your feet onto. The five of them sat here, over the glimmering primary colours of the table, glowering.

'Well, *I'm* glad to be here, at any rate,' Athena said.

Bella looked up. 'Was that a joke, Athena?'

'You remember me, Bella. I always was a joker.'

'You thought you were. So you're pleased we brought you home from Cyclops.' If a distributed intelligence like Athena could be said to 'be' anywhere, she, or rather her most complete definition, was now lodged in a secure memory store in one of *Aurora*'s abandoned engine rooms.

Athena said, 'I was made welcome at Cyclops. I was protected there. But I was born to run the shield, born to be *here*. Of course I, this copy of me, have no memory of the sunstorm itself. It is actually educational for me to be here, to access the data stores. To learn what happened that day, as if I were any other visitor. It is humbling.'

'And may I humbly ask,' Bob Paxton asked sourly, 'why the fuck you have dragged us all up here?' It was the first time he had spoken since coming aboard.

Bella laid her hand flat on the table, a gentle gesture that nevertheless commanded their attention. 'Because this is neutral ground for Earthborn and Spacers, or as near as I could come up with. Somehow we seem to have gotten through the Q-bomb crisis, though we fought like cats in a sack in the process. Well, now we need a new way of getting along.'

Alexei said, 'I heard you're standing down after Christmas.'

'More than that,' Paxton growled. 'Madam Chair here is probably going to face a war crimes tribunal. As, in fact, am I.'

Lyla frowned. 'But what of the attacks on the elevators? Who's going to be held responsible for that?'

'I am happy to stand trial,' Athena said firmly, 'if it will protect those whose actions I influenced.'

Alexei laughed. 'They can't put an AI on trial.'

'Of course they can,' Bella said. 'Athena has rights. She is a Legal Person (Non-Human). But with rights come responsibilities. She can be tried, just as much as I can be. Though I don't think anybody has worked out what her sentence might be, if she's found guilty ...'

Athena said, 'These trials will be played out in full public view, before courts representing both Earth and Spacer communities. Whatever the outcome I hope it will be part of the reconciliation process. The healing.'

Bella said, 'We all did what we thought we had to do. But that's all in the past. The Q-bomb changed everything. It's all different now.'

Lyla studied her curiously. 'Different how?'

'For one thing, the politics ...'

The species-wide debate forced by Athena on the decision to deflect the bomb had been a brief, traumatic shock to the political system. Perhaps it was a culmination of tensions that had been building up for decades among an increasingly interconnected mankind. Afterward, it hadn't proven possible to shut down the debate.

'Everything is fluid, since the vote. There are new factions, new interest and protest groups, new sorts of lobbies. On Earth the last barriers between the old nations are being kicked down. Across the system people are ignoring the old categories, and are uniting with others with whom they find common cause, whichever world they happen to live on. An interconnected democracy is taking over, a mass, self-correcting wisdom, whether we like it or not. Maybe it was good that our first great exercise in using our collective voice was over something we could pretty much unite around – in the end, perhaps, the Firstborn have done us a favour. But that voice hasn't been stilled.'

Alexei faced his father. 'Look, Dad. Things have got to change in space, too. I mean the relationship between Spacers and Earth.'

'Between you and me, you mean,' said Bill Carel.

'That too. The idea that Earth can impose its will on space is a fantasy, no matter how many antimatter warships you build.'

In December 2070, there had been no declaration of independence; there were no Spacer nations, and at present all Spacers were colonists, formally owing their allegiance to one of Earth's old nations or another. The Spacers had their own internal rivalries, of course. But as they looked back to an Earth reduced to a blue lamp in the sky, if they could see it at all, it was increasingly difficult for them to think of themselves as American Spacers versus Albanian, British Spacers versus Belgian ...

'"Spacer" is an absurd label, really. A negative one that actually means "not of Earth." We're all different, and we all have our own opinions.'

'You got that right,' Bob Paxton growled. 'More opinions than fucking Spacers.'

'My point is, you can't control us anymore. We can't even control ourselves – and wouldn't want to. We're on a new road, Dad, and even we don't know where it will lead.'

'Or what you will become,' said Carel. 'But I have to let ou go come what may, don't I?'

Alexei smiled. 'I'm afraid so.'

And there, Bella knew, was the subtext in the conversa-ion between Earth and Spacers. If the mother world released ıer grip, she would lose her children forever.

Bob Paxton grunted. 'Christ, I feel like blubbing.'

'All right, Bob,' Bella said. 'Look, it's a serious point. One ›f my last executive orders will be to initiate a new consti-utional convention for all of us – Earth and the whole solar ystem – based on recognised human rights precedents. We lo *not* want a world government, I don't think. What we do ıeed are new mechanisms, new political forms to recognise he new fluidity. No more power centres,' she said. 'No more ecrets. We still need mechanisms to unify us, to ensure ustice and equality of resource and opportunity – and fast-esponse agencies when crises hit.'

'Such as when the Firstborn take another swipe,' Paxton aid.

'Yes. But we need ways to cope with threats *without* sac-ificing our liberties.' She looked around at their faces, open ›r cynical. 'We have no precedent for how a civilisation panning several worlds is supposed to run itself. Maybe the 'irstborn know; if they do they aren't telling. I like to think hat this is the next stage in our maturity as a culture.'

'Maturity? That sounds utopian,' Bill Carel said cautiously.

Bob Paxton grunted. 'Yeah. And let's just remember that however many heads you Spacer mutants grow, we're all going to continue to be united by one thing.'

'The Firstborn,' Lyla said.

'Damn right,' Paxton said.

'Yes,' said Bella. 'So take us through the new proposals, Bob. The next phase of Fortress Sol.'

He looked at her, alarmed. 'You sure about that, Madam Chair?'

'Openness, Bob. That's the watchword now.' She smiled at the others. 'Bob and his Committee of Patriots have been working on priorities. Even though their own legal status is under review, following events.'

Alexei smiled. 'Can't keep you old sky warriors down, eh, Admiral Paxton?'

Paxton looked ready to murder him. Bella laid a hand on his arm until he had calmed.

'Very well. Priority one. We need to act *now*. Between the sunstorm and the Q-bomb we had a generation to prepare. Granted we didn't know what was coming. But in retrospect we didn't do enough, and we can't make that mistake again. The one good thing about the Q-bomb is the way it's going to mobilise public opinion and support for such measures.

'Priority two. Earth. A lot of us were shaken up when you ragged-ass Spacers snipped the space elevators. We always knew how vulnerable *you* were in your domes and butterfly spaceships. We didn't know how vulnerable Earth was, though. The fact is we're interconnected to a spaceborne economy. So we're talking about robustifying Earth.'

Lyla grinned. 'Nice word.'

'Homes like bunkers. Ground-based power sources, comms links, via secure optic-fibre cables. That kind of thing. Enough to withstand a planetary siege. Parameters to be defined.

'Priority three. And here's the key,' Paxton said now, leaning forward, intent. 'We got to disperse. We've got significant colonies off Earth already. But the wargamers say that if Earth had been taken out by the Q-bomb, it's unlikely the Spacer colonies could have survived into the long term. Just too few of you, a gene pool too small, your fake ecologies too fragile, all of that.

'So we have to beef you up. Make the species invulnerable even to the loss of Earth.' He grinned at the young Spacers. 'I'm talking massive, aggressive migration. To the Moon, the outer planet moons, space habs if we can put them up fast enough. Even Venus, which was so fucked over by the sunstorm it might be possible to live there. Maybe we can even start flinging a few ships to the stars, go chase those Chinese.'

'But it won't work,' Alexei said. 'Not even if you have a

million people on Venus, say, under domes, and breathing machine air. They'll be just as vulnerable as we are now.'

'Sure. So we go further.' Paxton's grin widened. He seemed to be enjoying shocking them. 'Nice to know an old fart like me is still capable of thinking bigger than you kids. What's the most robust hab we know? A planet.'

Lyla stared at him. 'You're talking of terraforming.'

'Making the Moon or Venus into worlds enough like Earth that you could walk around in the open, more or less unprotected. Where you could grow crops in the open air. Where humans could survive, *even if civilisation fell,* even if they forgot who they were and how they got there in the first place.'

'They've been thinking about this on Mars,' Lyla said. 'Of course now—'

'We'll lose Mars, but Mars wasn't the only option. In the very long term it's the only robust survival solution,' Paxton said.

Alexei looked sceptical. 'This is the kind of programme space advocates have been pressing for since the days of Armstrong and Aldrin, and never got close to. It's going to mean a massive transfer of resources.'

'Oh, yes,' Bella said. 'In fact Bob's view is already widely accepted. And it's going to start soon.'

'What is?' Lyla asked, curious.

'You'll see. Leave me one last surprise ...'

'We're serious about this,' Bob Paxton said, challenging, authoritative. 'As serious as I've been about anything in my entire life. To gain access to the future, we have to secure the present. That's the bottom line.'

They fell back to talking over details of Paxton's vision, arguing, fleshing out some aspects, rejecting others. Soon Paxton cleared the tabletop of its colourful sunstorm factoids and started to make notes.

Bella murmured to Athena, 'Looks like it worked. I would never have thought I'd see the likes of Bob Paxton and Alexei Carel working together.'

'We live in strange times.'

'That we do, Athena. And they get stranger all the time. Anyhow it's a start.' She glanced at her watch. 'I hate to do it, but I ought to go check through my messages. Athena, will you bring them coffee? Anything they want.'

'Of course.'

She pushed herself out of her chair and drifted off the bridge, heading for the shuttle and her secure softscreens. Behind her the conversation continued, animated. She heard Alexei say, half-seriously, 'I tell you what will unite us all. Sol Invictus. A new god for a new age ...'

## CHAPTER 54

# Q-DAY

*December 15, 2070*

The shuttle landed Bella at Cape Canaveral.

Thales spoke to her. 'Welcome home, Bella.'

Bella, bent over her softscreen, was startled to find she was down. All the way from L1 she had been working her messages, and monitoring the progress of the two great events that were due to take place today: the switching-on of the Bimini, the new space elevator system in the Atlantic, and the closest approach of the Q-bomb to the Earth. Both were on schedule, as best anybody knew. But it was hard not to keep checking.

The wheels stopped rolling, and the shuttle's systems sighed to silence.

She shut down her softscreen and folded it up. 'Thank you, Thales. Nice to be back. Athena sends her regards.'

'I've spoken to her several times.'

That made Bella oddly uneasy. She had often wondered what conversations went on between the great artificial intelligences, all above the heads of mankind. Even in her role as Council Chair, she had never fully found out.

'There's a car waiting for you outside, Bella. Ready to take you to the VAB, where your family is waiting. Be careful when you stand up.'

It still hurt to be returned to a full gravity. 'It gets tougher every damn time. Thales, remind me to order an exoskeleton.'

'I will, Bella.'

She clambered down to the runway. The day was bright, the sun low, the air fresh and full of salt. She checked her watch, which had corrected itself to local time; she had landed a little before ten AM on this crisp December morning.

She glanced out to sea, where a fine vertical thread climbed into the sky.

Thales murmured, 'Just an hour to the Q-bomb pass, Bella. The astronomers report no change in its trajectory.'

'Orbital-mechanics analyses are all very well. People have to *see* it.'

'I've encountered the phenomenon before,' Thales said calmly. 'I do understand, Bella.'

She grunted. 'I'm not sure if you do. Not if you call it a "phenomenon." But we all love you anyhow.'

'Thank you, Bella.'

A car rolled up, a bubble of glass, smart and friendly. It whisked her away from the cooling hulk of her shuttle, straight toward the looming bulk of the Vehicle Assembly Building.

At the VAB she was met by a security guard, a woman, good humoured but heavily armed, who shadowed her from then on.

Bella crossed straight to a glass-walled elevator, and rose quickly and silently up through the interior of the VAB. She stared down over rockets clustered like pale trees. Once the rocket stacks of *Saturns* and space shuttles had been assembled in this building. Now a century old and still one of the largest enclosed volumes in the world, the VAB had been turned into a museum for the launchers of the first heroic age of American manned space exploration, from the *Atlas* to the shuttle and the *Ares*. And now the building was operational again. A corner had been cleared for the assembly of an *Apollo–Saturn* stack: a new *Apollo 14,* ready for its centennial launch in February.

Bella loved this immense temple of technology, still astonishing in its scale. But today she was more interested in who was waiting for her on the roof.

Edna met her as she stepped out of the elevator car. 'Mum.'

'Hello, love.' Bella embraced her.

As Bella and Edna walked the security guard shadowed them, and a news robot rolled after them, a neat sphere glistening with lenses. Bella had to expect that; she did her best to ignore the silent, all-encompassing scrutiny. It was an historic day, after all. By scheduling the Bimini switch-on today, she had meant to turn Q-day into one of celebration, and so it was turning out to be – even if, she sensed, the mood was edgy rather than celebratory right now.

The tremendous roof of the VAB had long since been made over as a viewing platform. Today it was crowded, with marquees, a podium where Bella would be expected to make a speech, people swirling around. There was even a small park, a mock-up of the local flora and fauna.

Two oddly dressed men, spindly, tall, in blue-black robes marked with golden sunbursts, stared at a baby alligator as if it were the most remarkable creature they had ever seen, and perhaps it was. Looking a little uncertain on their feet, their faces heavily creamed with sunscreen, they were monks of the new church of Sol Invictus: missionaries to Earth from space.

Edna walked with the caution of a space worker restored to a full gravity, and she winced a bit in the brilliant light, the breeze, the uncontrolled climate of a living world. She looked tired, Bella thought with her mother's solicitude, older than her twenty-four years.

'You aren't sleeping well, are you, love?'

'Mum, I know we can't talk about this right now. But I got my subpoenas yesterday. For your hearing and my own.'

Bella sighed. She had fought to keep Edna from having to face a tribunal. 'We'll get through it.'

'You mustn't think you need to protect me,' Edna said, a bit stiffly. 'I did my duty, Mum. I'd do the same again, if ordered. When I get my day in court I'll tell the truth.' She forced a smile. 'Anyway the hell with it all. Thea's longing to see you. We've made camp, a bit away from the marquees and the bars ...'

Edna had colonised an area of the VAB roof close to

the edge. It was perfectly safe, blocked in by a tall, inward-curving wall of glass. Edna had spread out picnic blankets and fold-out tables and chairs, and had opened up a couple of hampers. Cassie Duflot was already here, with her two kids, Toby and Candida. They were playing with Thea, Edna's daughter, Bella's four-year-old granddaughter.

In this corner of the VAB roof it was Christmas, Bella saw to her surprise. The kids, playing with toys, were surrounded by wrapping paper and ribbons. There was even a little pine tree in a pot. An older man in a Santa suit sat with them, a bit awkwardly, but with a grin plastered over his tired face.

Thea came running. 'Grannie!'

'Hello, Thea.' Bella submitted to having her knees hugged, and then she bent down and cuddled her granddaughter properly. The other kids ran to her too, perhaps vaguely remembering the nice old lady who had come with a memento to their father's funeral. But the kids soon broke away and went back to their presents.

Santa Claus shook Bella's hand. 'John Metternes, Madam Chair,' he said. 'I flew with your daughter on the *Liberator*.'

'Yes, of course. I'm very glad to meet you, John. You did good work up there.'

He grunted. 'Let's hope the judge agrees. Look, I hope you don't think I'm butting in – I can see there's a family thing going on here—'

'I forced him down for some shore leave,' Edna said, a bit acidly. 'This weird old obsessive would sleep on the *Liberator* if the maintenance crew would let him.'

'Don't let her bug you, John. It's good of you to do this. But – *Christmas,* Edna? It's only the fifteenth of December.'

'Actually it was my idea.' Cassie Duflot approached Bella. 'It was just that, you know, we still aren't sure how today is going to turn out, are we?' She glanced at the sky, as if seeking the Q-bomb. 'I mean, not *really* sure. And if things were to go wrong, badly wrong—'

'You wanted to give the kids their Christmas anyway.'

'Do you think that's odd?'

'No.' Bella smiled. 'I understand, Cassie.'

'It does make it a hell of a day,' Edna said. 'And what's worse, if the world *doesn't* get blown up today, we'll have to do it all again in ten days' time.'

'You attracted quite a crowd for your launch, Bella,' Cassie said.

'Looks like it—'

'Mum, you haven't seen the half of it yet,' Edna said. She took her mother's arm again and walked her toward the glass-walled lip of the building.

At the roof edge Bella was able to see the ocean to the east, where the low sun hung like a lamp, and the coast to north and south, her view stretching for kilometres in either direction. Canaveral was crowded. The cars clustered along the shoreline, and were parked up as far as the Beach Road to the north, and to the south on Merritt Island and the Cape itself, carpeting the old industrial facilities and the abandoned Air Force base. Everywhere, flags fluttered in the strong breeze.

And out at sea she saw the grey, blocky form of a reused oil rig. Rising from it was a double thread, dead straight, visible when it caught the light.

'They came for the switch-on,' Edna said. 'You always were a showman, Mum. Maybe politicians have to be. And reopening America's elevator today is a good stunt. People feel like a party, I guess.'

'Oh, it's more than just another space elevator. You'll see.'

'New ways forward, Mum?'

'I've just come down from a conference with Bob Paxton and others on new deep-defence concepts. *Big* concepts. Terraforming programmes, for instance.'

'You're kidding.'

'No. Just thinking big. That's what cutting your teeth on the shield does for you, I guess. And I must talk to Myra Dutt sometime.' She glanced at the sky. 'We have to do something about Mir – this other place Myra's mother went to. They're humans in there too. If we can speak to them, as

Alexei Carel claims they have been able to on Mars, surely we can find a way to bring them home ...'

There was a stir. Bella was aware of people approaching her, hundreds of eyes on her on this roof alone, and that cam robot whirled and glistened at her feet, puppylike. Even those monks by the alligator pond were staring at her, grinning from ear to ear.

She looked at her watch. 'I think it's time.'

'Mum, you're going to have to say something.'

'I know. Just a minute more.' She looked out to sea, to the shining vertical track of the elevator. 'Edna, call the kids so they can see.'

The children came to join them, clutching their presents, with Cassie and John Metternes, who hoisted Thea up onto his shoulders.

A flare went up from that oil rig, a pink spark arcing and trailing smoke. Then there was motion along the track of the elevator, shining droplets rising up one of the pair of threads. A ragged cheer broke out around them, soon echoed among the wider throngs scattered across Canaveral.

'It's working,' Bella breathed.

'But what's it carrying?' Edna murmured, squinting. 'Magnify ... Damn, I keep forgetting I'm in EVA.'

'Water,' Bella said. 'Sacks of seawater. It's a bucket chain, love. The pods will be lifted to the top of the tower, and thrown off.'

'Thrown where?'

'The Moon, initially. Later Venus.'

Edna stared at the elevator stack. 'So where's the power coming from? I don't see any laser mounts on that rig.'

'There aren't any. There *is* no power source – nothing but the Earth's rotation. Edna, this isn't really an elevator. It's a siphon.'

Edna's eyes lit up with wonder.

The orbital siphon was an extension of the space-elevator concept that derived from the elevator's peculiar mechanics. Beyond the point of geosynchronous orbit, centripetal forces tended to throw masses away from the Earth. The trick with the siphon was to harness this tendency, to allow payloads to escape but in the process to draw more masses up from Earth's surface. Essentially, the energy of Earth's rotation was being transferred to an escaping stream of payload pellets.

'So you don't need any external energy input at all,' Edna said. 'I studied this concept at USNGS. The big problem was always thought to be keeping the damn thing fed – you'd need a fleet of trucks working day and night to maintain the payload flow. But if all you're throwing up there is seawater—'

'We call it Bimini,' Bella said. 'It's appropriate enough. The native Americans told Ponce de Leon about a fountain of youth on an island called Bimini. He never found it, but he stumbled on Florida ...'

'A fountain of youth?'

'A fountain of Earth's water to make worlds young again. The Moon first, then Venus. Look, Edna, I wanted this as a demonstration to the Spacers that we're *serious*. It will still take centuries, but with resource outputs like this, terraforming becomes a practical possibility for the first time. And if Earth lowers its oceans just a fraction and slows its rotation an invisible amount to turn the other worlds blue again, I think that's a sacrifice worth making, don't you?'

'I think you're crazy, Mum. But it's magnificent.' Edna grabbed her and kissed her.

Thales spoke. 'This is a secure channel. Bella, Edna – the Q-bomb's closest approach is a minute away.'

Secure line or not, the news soon seemed to ripple out. Silence spread through the rooftop marquees, and the massed crowds around Canaveral. Suddenly the mood was soured, fretful. Edna took Thea from John Metternes and clutched her close. Bella grabbed her daughter's free hand and gripped it hard.

They looked up into the brilliant sky.

## CHAPTER 55
# Q-BOMB

The choice had been made. The bomb was already looking ahead, to the terminus of its new trajectory.

The blue, teeming world and all its peoples receded behind it.

Like any sufficiently advanced machine the Q-bomb was sentient to some degree. And its frozen soul was touched by regret when, six months after passing Earth, it slammed into the sands of Mars, and thought ended forever.

## CHAPTER 56
# MARS 2

*November 2071*

The dust was extraordinary here in Hellespontus, even for Mars, dust museum of the solar system.

Myra sat in her blister cockpit with Ellie von Devender as the rover plunged over the banks and low dunes. This was the southern hemisphere of Mars, and they were driving through the Hellespontus mountains, a range of low hills not far from the western rim of the Hellas basin. But the rover's wheels threw up immense rooster-tails, and the stuff just flew up at the windscreens, wiping out any kind of visibility. The infrared scanners, even the radar, were useless in these conditions.

Myra had been around space technology long enough to know that she had to put her faith in the machinery that protected her. The rover knew where it was going, in theory, and was finding its way by sheer dead reckoning. But it violated all her instincts to go charging blindly ahead like this.

'But we can't slow down,' Ellie said absently. 'We don't have time.' She was paging her way through astronomical data – not even looking out the window, as Myra was. But then her primary task was much more significant, the ongoing effort to understand what precisely the Q-bomb had done to Mars since its impact five months ago, an impact that had done little harm in itself, but which had planted a seed of quintessence that would soon shatter Mars altogether.

'It's just all this *dust*,' Myra said. 'I didn't expect these kind of conditions, even on Mars.'

Ellie raised her eyebrows. 'Myra, this area is notorious.

This is where a lot of the big global dust storms seem to be born. You didn't know that? Welcome to Dust Central. Anyhow you know we're in a rush. If we don't find that old lady on its hundredth birthday we're going to let down the sentimental populations of whole worlds.' She grinned at Myra, quite relaxed.

She was right. As everybody waited for the full extent of the bad news about the planet's future, the electronic gaze of all mankind had been fixed on Mars and the Martians. It was sympathetic or morbid, depending on your point of view. And of all the frantic activities in advance of the final evacuation of a world, none had caught the public imagination as much as what cynical old hands like Yuri called 'treasure hunting.'

Mars was littered with the relics of the pioneering days of the robot exploration of the solar system, some seventy years of triumph and bitter disappointment that had come to a definitive end when Bob Paxton planted the first human footprint in the red sands. Most of those inert probes and stalled rovers and bits of scattered wreckage still lay in the dust where they had come to rest. The early colonists of Mars had had no energy to spare to go trophy hunting, or a great deal of interest; they had looked to the future, not the past. But now that it appeared that Mars might have no future after all, there had been a clamour to retrieve as many of those old mechanical pioneers as possible.

It wasn't a job that required a great deal of specialist skill in Martian conditions, and so it was an ideal assignment for Myra, a Martian by recent circumstance. For safety reasons she couldn't travel alone on these cross-planet rover jaunts, however, and so she had been assigned Ellie as a companion, a physicist rather than a Mars specialist who might be better employed elsewhere. Ellie had been quite happy to go along with her; she could continue her own work just as well in a moving rover as in a station like Lowell or Wells – better, she said, for there were fewer distractions.

Of course, Ellie's work was far more important than any trophy-hunting. Ellie was working with a system-wide community of physicists and cosmologists on predictions of what was to become of Mars. Right now she was looking at deep-sky images of star fields. As far as Myra understood, their best data came not from Mars itself but from studies of the sky: though it was hard to grasp, the distant stars no longer looked the same from Mars as they did from the Earth. It defeated Myra's imagination how that could possibly be so.

Anyhow the retrieval programme had been successful in terms of its own goals. With the help of orbital mapping Myra and others had reached the *Vikings,* tonnes of heavy, clunky, big-budget Cold War engineering, where they still sat in the dry, rocky deserts to which cautious mission planners had consigned them. The famous, plucky *Pathfinder* craft with its tiny robot car had been retrieved from its 'rock garden' in the Ares Vallis – that one had been easy; it wasn't far from Port Lowell, site of the first manned landing. Myra knew that British eyes had been on the retrieval of fragments of the *Beagle 2,* an intricate, ingenious, toylike probe that had not survived its journey to the Isidis Planitia. And then there had been the recovery of the exploration rovers, *Spirit* and *Opportunity,* worn out by journeys that far exceeded their design capabilities. All these antique artifacts were destined for Smithsonian establishments on the Earth and Moon.

The retrieval expeditions had had scientific goals too. There was some interest in how man-made materials had withstood up to a century of exposure to Martian conditions. And the landing sites were of interest in themselves – otherwise the probes would not have been sent there. So Myra and Ellie had worked through a crash last-minute science programme of sampling, mapping, and coring.

There had even been efforts to retrieve some of the elderly orbiters, still spinning around Mars, long silent. There was universal disappointment when it was discovered that *Mariner 9,* the very first orbiter, was gone; if it had survived into the 2040s it was surely swallowed up when sunstorm heat caused a general expansion of the Martian atmosphere.

Myra was glad to have something constructive to do. But she hadn't expected such intense public scrutiny of her treasure-hunting, with every move being followed by a system-wide audience. The crews had been promised that no images would be returned from the rover cabin itself. But Myra tried never to forget that the rover's systems could easily be hacked; she could be watched at any moment.

The day wore on, and the daylight, already murky under the rover's artificial dust storm, began to fade. Myra began to fret that they would not after all find the wreck of *Mars 2,* as the light ran out on this anniversary day.

Then Ellie sat back, staring at a complex graph on her softscreen.

Myra studied her. She had gotten to know this edgy physicist well enough to understand that she wasn't given to extravagant displays of any emotion save irritation. This sitting-back and staring was, for Ellie, a major outburst.

'What is it?'

'Well, there it is.' Ellie tapped her screen. 'The destiny of Mars. We've figured it out.'

'All right. So can you say what it means, in simple terms?'

'I'm going to have to. According to this message I'm to take part in a three-world press conference on it in a couple of hours. Of course the math is always easier. More precise.' She squinted out at the dust, thinking. 'Put it this way. If we could see the sky, and if we had a powerful enough telescope, we would see the most distant stars recede. As if the expansion of the universe had suddenly accelerated. But we would *not* see the same thing from Earth.'

Myra pondered that. 'So what does that mean?'

'The Q-bomb is a cosmological weapon. We always knew that. A weapon derived from the Firstborn's technology of universe creation. Yes?'

'Yes. And so—'

'So what it has done is to project Mars into its own little cosmos. A kind of budding-off. Right now the baby Mars universe is connected smoothly to the mother. But the baby will come adrift, leaving Mars isolated.'

Myra struggled to take this in. 'Isolated in its own universe?'

'That's it. No sun, no Earth. Just Mars. You can see that this weapon was just supposed to, umm, *detach* a chunk of the Earth. Which would have caused global devastation, but left the planet itself more or less intact. It's too powerful for Mars. It will take out this little world altogether.' She grinned, but her eyes were mirthless. 'It will be lonely, in that new universe. Chilly, too. But it won't last long. The baby universe will implode. Although from the inside it will feel like an *ex*plosion. It's a scale model of the Big Rip that will some day tear our universe apart. A Little Rip, I suppose.'

Myra pondered this, and didn't try to pursue the paradox of implosions and explosions. 'How can you tell all this?'

Ellie pointed to the obscured sky. 'From the recession of the stars we've observed with telescopes on Mars, a recession you wouldn't see from Earth. It's an illusion, of course. Actually the Mars universe is beginning to recede from the mother. Or, equivalently, vice versa.'

'But we can still get off the surface. Get to space, back to Earth.'

'Oh, yes. For now. There is a smooth interface between the universes.' She peered at her screen and scrolled through more results. 'In fact it's going to be a fascinating process. A baby universe being born in the middle of our solar system! We'll learn more about cosmology than we have in a century. I wonder if the Firstborn are aware of how much they're teaching us ...'

Myra glanced uneasily about the cockpit. If they were being hack-watched, this display of academic coldness wasn't going to play too well. 'Ellie. Just rejoin the human race for a minute.'

Ellie looked at her sharply. But she backed off. 'Sorry.'

*'How long?'*

Ellie glanced again at her screen and scrolled through her

results. 'The data is still settling down. It's a little hard to say. Ballpark – three more months before the detachment.'

'Then Mars must be evacuated by, what, February?'

'That's it. And after that, maybe a further three months before the implosion of the baby cosmos.'

'And the end of Mars.' Just six more months' grace, then, for a world nearly five billion years old. 'What a crime,' she said.

'Yeah. Hey, look.' Ellie was pointing to a crumpled, dust-stained sheet protruding from the crimson ground. 'Do you think that's a parachute?'

'Rover, full stop.' The vehicle jolted to a halt, and Myra peered. 'Magnify ... I think you're right. Maybe the twisters whip it up, and keep it from being buried. What does the sonar show?'

'Let's take a look. Rover ...'

And there it was, buried a few metres down under the wind-blown Martian dust, a squat, blocky shape easily imaged by the sonar.

'*Mars 2*,' Myra said.

*Mars 2* was a Soviet probe that had travelled to the planet in 1971, part of a favourable-opposition flotilla that had included the Americans' *Mariner 9*. It had attempted its landing in the middle of the worst global dust storm the astronomers had ever seen.

'It looks like a flower,' Ellie breathed. 'Those four petals.'

'It was a ball of metal about the size of a domestic fridge. The petals were supposed to open up and right it, whichever way up it landed.'

'Looks like it was doomed by a twisted-up parachute. After coming all this way ...'

Crash-landing or not, *Mars 2* had been the first human artifact of all to touch the surface of the planet. And it had come down in this very spot precisely a century before, on November 27, 1971. 'It made it. And so did we.'

'Yeah. And now it's two metres deep under the dust.' Ellie unhooked her harness and got out of her chair. 'Fetch a spade.'

## CHAPTER 57

# BABYLON

When Captain Nathaniel Grove in Troy heard that Bisesa Dutt had returned to Babylon, he hurried back there with Ben Batson.

At the Ishtar Gate they met Eumenes, still surviving as chiliarch to an increasingly capricious Alexander. 'Bisesa is in the Temple of Marduk,' he said to them in his stilted English. 'She will not come out.'

Grove grimaced. 'I might have expected as much. Had that sort of breakdown before. Bad show, bad show. Can we see her?'

'Of course. But first we must visit another, ah, hermit – and not a voluntary one, I fear. He has been asking to see you, should you return to Babylon. Indeed he has been asking to see any of what he calls "the moderns."'

It turned out to be Ilicius Bloom, the 'consul' from Chicago. Just inside the city walls, not far from the Ishtar Gate, Alexander's guards had stuck him in a cage.

The cage was evidently meant for animals. It was open to the elements, and too small for Bloom to stand straight. A guard stood by the cage, one of Alexander's phalangists, clearly bored. At the back of the cage hung what looked like an animal skin, scraped bare, shrivelled and dry.

Crouched in his filthy rags, his eyes bright white in a grimy face, Ilicius Bloom shuddered and coughed, though the day was not cold, and a stench of raw sewage made Grove recoil. Bloom was pathetically grateful to see them, but he was self-aware enough to notice Grove's flinch. 'You needn't think that's me, by the way. They kept a man-ape in here before. Flea-bitten bitch.' He dug around in the dirt.

'Look at this – dried man-ape scut!' He flung it at the iron bars of the cage. 'At night the rats come, and *that's* no fun. And guess where they put the she-ape? In the temple with that loon Bisesa Dutt. Can you believe it? Say, you must help me, Grove. I won't last much longer in here, you have to see that.'

'Calm down, man,' Grove said. 'Tell us why you're here. Then perhaps we'll have a chance of talking you out of it.'

'Well, I wish you luck. Alexander is thinking of war, you know.'

'War? Against whom?'

'Against America. Europe isn't enough for him – how could it be, when he knows there are whole continents to conquer? But the only source of intelligence he has on America, or rather Chicago, is *me*.'

'Ah. And so he's been questioning you.'

Bloom held up hands with bloodied fingertips. 'You could call it that. Naturally I've talked myself hoarse. Now, don't look down your nose at me, Captain Grove. I'm no British Army officer. And besides I can't see what difference it makes. Have you *seen* Alexander recently? I can't believe the bloated brute will live much longer, let alone oversee a war across the Atlantic. I've told him everything I could think of, and when he wanted more I lied freely. What else could I do?

'But it was never enough, never enough. Look at this.' He shuffled in his cage. Through the thin, grimy cloth of his shirt, Grove saw the striping of whip marks on his back. 'And look!' He pointed a clawlike hand at the rag of skin that hung on the wall outside his cage.

Ben Batson asked, 'What *is* that?'

'I loved her, you know,' Bloom said now.

'Who, man?' Grove asked patiently. 'Who did you love?'

'Isobel. *You* remember, Grove, the girl from the Midden. She gave me a brat! Oh, I was cruel, I was selfish, but that's me, that is Ilicius Bloom.' He laughed and shook his head. 'And yet I loved her, as best my flawed soul was capable. Truly I did.

'They did this to break me, of course,' Bloom whispered, staring at Grove. 'Two Companions, it was. They did it before my eyes. Peeled her like a grape. *They took her face off.* She lived for long minutes, flayed. Every inch of her body must have been a locus of exquisite agony – think of it! And then—'

Batson looked at the bit of skin. 'My word, Captain, I do believe—'

'Come away,' Grove said, pulling him back.

Bloom flew into a panic. 'You can see how I'm fixed. Speak to Eumenes. Tell Mayor Rice. Oh, how I long to hear an American voice again! Please, Grove—' He managed to get his whole arm through the bars of the cage. The guard casually slapped his flesh with the flat of his stabbing-sword. Bloom howled and withdrew.

Eumenes shepherded Grove and Batson away. 'Ilicius Bloom is a dead man. He put himself in danger when he tried to bargain with Alexander over his scraps of knowledge. Then he doomed himself with his lies. He would be in his grave already were it not so cheap to keep him alive. If you wish I will arrange an audience with Alexander about his fate, though I warn you it is likely to do little good, and you would put yourselves in danger . . . But first,' he said, 'you must visit Bisesa Dutt.'

# CHAPTER 58
# SECESSION

*February 27, 2072*

The shuttle stood on the drab, dusty plain. The sun was a pale disc riding high in the orange sky; it was close to local noon, here on the Xanthe Terra. The ship was a biconic, a fat, clumsy-looking half-cone. It stood at the end of a long scar in the dust, a relic of its own glide-down landing. Right now it stood on end, ready to hurl itself away from Mars and up into orbit. The shuttle's exposed underside, plastered with dark heat-shield tiles, was scarred from multiple reentries, and the paintwork around its attitude-thruster nozzles was blistered. Rovers stood by, their tracks snaking away to the horizon. Hatches were open in the shuttle's belly, and men, women and spidery robots laboured to haul packages into its hold.

There was nothing special about this bird, Myra thought, as she stood watching in her Mars suit. This was just a ground-to-orbit truck that had made its routine hops a dozen times, maybe more.

But it was the last spacecraft that would ever leave the surface of Mars.

Myra knew this was a symbolic moment. Most of Mars's human population had long gone, along with all they could lift. The various AIs that had inhabited the bases and rovers and bits of equipment had, too, been saved as far as possible, according to laws governing the right to protection of Legal Persons (Non-Human); at the very least copies of them had been transmitted to memory stores off-planet. But there was nothing that touched a human heart as much as seeing the last bundle loaded aboard the last ship out, a last footprint, a last hatch closed.

Which was why cameras rolled, floated, and flew all around this site. And why a delegation of Chinese stood in a huddle, away from the rest. And why the frantic work of loading was being held up by the presence of Bella Fingal, the now-ousted Chair of the World Space Council, in a Mars suit that looked two or three sizes too big for her, who stood surrounded by a small crowd.

'One hour,' a soft automated voice said in Myra's helmet. She saw from the subtle reactions of the others that they had all heard the same warning. One hour left to get off Mars before – well, before something unimaginable happened.

Myra drifted back to join the small crowd, all in their suits, like a clutch of fat green snowmen.

Bella said now, 'A shame we couldn't have made this last launch from Port Lowell.' They were in fact fifty kilometres from Lowell, out on the Xanthe Terra, a bay on the perimeter of the great Vastitas Borealis. 'It would have been fitting to stage the last human lift-off from Mars at the place Bob Paxton and his crew made the first touchdown.'

'Well, maybe we could have, if Lowell wasn't still radioactive,' Yuri O'Rourke growled a bit sharply. He summoned Hanse Critchfield, who was proudly carrying a display tray of materials. 'Madam Chair. Here,' he said unceremoniously. 'This is a selection of the scientific materials we have been gathering in these last months. Take a look. Samples from a variety of geological units, from the southern highlands to the northern plains to the slopes of the great volcanoes. Bits of ice core from the polar caps, of particular value to me. And, perhaps most precious of all, samples of Martian life. There are relics of the past, look, you see, we even have a fossil here from a sedimentary lake bed, and native organisms from the present day, and samples of the transgenic life-forms we have been experimenting with.'

Grendel Speth said dryly, 'Martians you can eat.'

Bella Fingal was a small, tired-looking woman, now nearly sixty. She seemed genuinely touched by the gesture. She smiled through her faceplate. 'Thank you.'

Yuri said, 'I'm only sorry that we can't give you a vial

of canal water. Or the tripod leg from a Martian fighting machine. Or an egg laid by a Princess … I wish I could show you a Wernher von Braun glider, too. That was the first serious scheme to get to Mars, you know. They would have glided down to land on the smooth ice at the poles. And if that's the past, I'm sorry you won't see Mars's future. A mature human world, fully participating in an interplanetary economic and political system …'

Myra touched his arm, and he fell silent.

Bella smiled. 'Yes. This is the end of a human story too, isn't it? No more Martian dreams. But we won't forget, Yuri. I can assure you that the study of Mars will continue even when the planet itself is lost. We will continue to learn about Mars, and strive to understand.

'And in this last moment I want to try to tell you again why this has all been worthwhile – even this terrible cost.'

She said there had been more results from Cyclops.

The great observatory had been designed before the sunstorm to search for Earth-like worlds. Since the storm, and especially since the return of Athena, its great Fresnel eyes had been turned aside, to peer into the dark spaces between the stars.

Bella said, 'And everywhere the astronomers look, they see refugees.'

The Cyclops telescopes had seen infrared traces of generation starships, slow, fat arks like the Chinese ships, whole civilisations in flight. And there were immense, flimsy ships with sails hundreds of kilometres wide, scudding before the light of exploding stars. They had even detected narrow-beam laser signals they thought might be traces of efforts to teleport, desperate attempts to send the essence of a living being encoded into a radio signal.

Myra felt stunned, imaginatively. There was a story, a whole novel, in every one of these brief summaries. 'This is the work of the Firstborn. They are everywhere. And everywhere they are doing what they tried to do to us, and the Martians, and at Procyon – *eradicating*. Why?'

'If we knew that,' Bella said, 'if we understood the Firstborn, we might be able to deal with the threat they pose. This is how our future is going to be, however far we travel, as far as we can see. And that's how we've come to this situation, this desolate beach.' Bella handed the sample tray to an aide, and took a step back. 'Would those of you who are leaving now, please come stand behind me?'

Most of the group stepped forward, including Ellie von Devender, Grendel Speth, Hanse Critchfield. Among those who remained were Myra, and Yuri, and Paula Umfraville. The Chinese stood back too. One of their delegates approached Bella, and told her again that they planned to stay to tend the memorials they had built to their fallen of sunstorm day.

Bella faced them all. 'I understand you've plenty of supplies – food, power – to see you through until—'

Yuri said, 'Yes, Madam Chair. It's all taken care of.'

'I don't quite understand how you'll be able to talk to each other – Lowell to the polar station, for instance. Won't you lose your comms satellites when the secession comes?'

'We've laid land lines,' Paula said brightly. 'We'll be fine.'

*'Fine?'* Bella's face worked. 'Not the word I'd use.' She said impulsively, 'Please – come with us. All of you. Even now there's time to change your minds. We've room on the shuttle. And my daughter is waiting in orbit on the *Liberator*, ready to take you home.'

'Thank you,' Yuri said evenly. 'But we've decided. Somebody ought to stay. There ought to be a witness. Besides, this is my home, Madam Chair.'

'My mother is buried here,' said Paula Umfraville. 'I couldn't abandon that.' Her smile was as professional as ever.

'And I lost my mother here too,' Myra said. 'I couldn't leave with that unresolved.'

Bella faced Myra. 'You know we'll do what we can to build on the contact that's been achieved with Mir. I gave you my word on that, and I'll ensure it's a promise that's kept.'

'Thank you,' Myra said.

'But you're going to a stranger place yet, aren't you? Is there anybody you'd want me to speak to for you?'

'No. Thank you, Madam Chair.' In the months since the Q-bomb strike, Myra had tried over and over to contact Charlie, and Eugene. There had been no reply. But then they had seceded from her own personal universe long ago. She had tidied her affairs. There was nothing left for her, anywhere but on Mars.

'With respect, Madam Chair, you *must* leave now,' Yuri said, glancing at his suit chronometer.

There was a last flurry of movement around the shuttle, as ladders were dumped, hatches closed. Myra took part in a last round of embraces, of Ellie and Grendel and Hanse, of the Chinese, even of Bella Fingal. But the Mars suits made the hugs clumsy, unsatisfying, deprived of human contact.

Bella was the last to stand at the foot of the short ramp that led to the biconic's interior. She looked around. 'This is the end of Mars,' she said. 'A terrible crime has been committed here, and we humans have been made complicit in it. That is a dreadful burden for us to carry, and our children. But I don't believe we should leave with shame. More has happened on Mars in the last century than in the previous billion years, and everything that is good has flowed from the actions of mankind. We must remember that. And we must remember lost Mars with love, not with shame.' She glanced down at the crimson dust beneath her feet. 'I think that's all.'

She walked briskly up the ramp, which lifted to swallow her up inside the belly of the shuttle.

Myra, Paula, and Yuri had to hurry back to the rover, which drove them off through a kilometre, a safe distance from the launch. When the rover stopped they clambered out again, squeezing into their outer suits.

They stood in a row, Myra between Yuri and Paula, holding hands. They found themselves surrounded by a little crowd of robot cameras, which had rolled or flown or hopped after them.

When the moment of launch came, the shuttle lifted without fuss. Mars gravity was light; it had always been easy to climb out of its gravity well. The dust kicked up from this last launch quickly fell back through the thin air to the ground, and the shuttle receded into the orange-brown sky, becoming a pale jewel, its vapour trail all but invisible.

'Well, that's that,' said Paula. 'How long until the light show?'

Yuri made to look at his watch, and then thought better of it. 'Not long. Do you want to go back into the rover, get out of these suits?'

None of them did. Somehow it seemed right to be out here, on the Martian ground, under its eerie un-blue sky.

Myra looked around. The landscape was just a flat desert with meagre mountains in the far distance. But in a deep ditch not far away there was a mosslike vegetation, green. Life, returned to Mars by the sunstorm and cherished by human hands. She held tightly to her companions. 'This is the dream of a million years, to stand here and see this,' she said.

Yuri said, 'Yes—'

And the light went, just like that, the sky darkening as if somebody was throwing a dimmer switch. The sun rushed away, sucking all the light with it. The sky turned deep brown, and then charcoal, and then utterly black.

Myra stood in the dark, clinging to Yuri and Paula. She heard the cameras clatter about, confused.

It had only taken seconds.

'I hope the cameras got that,' Yuri murmured.

'It feels like a total eclipse,' Paula said. 'I went to Earth once to see one. It was kind of exciting, oddly ...'

Myra felt excited too, stirred in an unexpected way by this primeval, extraordinary event. *Strange lights in the sky.* But, standing there in the dark, she felt a flicker of fear when she reminded herself that the sun was never, ever going to shine on Mars again.

'So we're alone in this universe,' Yuri said. 'Us and Mars.'

The ground shuddered gently.

'Mars quake,' Paula said immediately. 'We expected this. We just lost the sun's tides. It will pass.'

The rover's lights came on, flickering before settling to a steady glow. They cast a pool of light over the Martian ground, and Myra's shadow stretched long before her.

And there was a circle in the air before her. Like a mirror, full of complex reflections, highlights from the rover's lamps. Myra took a step forward, and saw her own reflection approach her.

The thing in the air was about a metre across. It was an Eye.

'You bastard,' Yuri said. 'You bastard!' He bent awkwardly, picked up handfuls of Martian rocks, and hurled them at the Eye. The rocks hit with a clatter that was dimly audible through the thin, cold air.

The ground continued to shake, the small, hard planet ringing like a bell.

And then a white fleck drifted past Myra's faceplate. She followed it all the way down to the ground, where it sublimated away. It was a snowflake.

## CHAPTER 59
# TEMPLE

Abdikadir Omar met them at the Temple of Marduk.

A loose crowd had gathered around the Temple precinct. Some even slept here, in lean-tos and tents. Vendors drifted slowly among them, selling food, water, and some kind of trinkets, holy tokens. They were pilgrims, Abdi said, who had come from as far as Alexandria and Judea.

'And are they here for the Eye of Marduk?'

Abdi grinned. 'Some come for the Eye. Some for Marduk himself, if they remember him. Some for Bisesa. Some even for the man-ape that's in there with her.'

'Remarkable,' Grove said. 'Pilgrims from Judea, come here to see a woman of the twenty-first century!'

Eumenes said, 'I sometimes wonder if a whole new religion is being born here. A worship of the Firstborn, with Bisesa Dutt as their prophet.'

'I doubt that would be healthy,' Grove said.

'Man has worshipped destroying gods before. Come. Let us speak to Bisesa Dutt.'

Abdi escorted them through the crowd and into the temple's convoluted interior, all the way up to the chamber of the Eye.

The small room with its scorched brick walls was utterly dominated by the Eye, which floated in the air. By the light of the oil lamps Grove saw his own reflection, absurdly distorted, as if by a fairground trick mirror. But the Eye itself was monstrous, ominous; he seemed to sense its gravity.

Bisesa had made a kind of nest in one corner of the chamber, of blankets and paper and clothes and bits of food. When Grove and the others walked in, she smiled and clambered to her feet.

And there was the man-ape. A lanky, powerful mature female, she sat squat in her cage, as still and watchful as the Eye itself. She had clear blue eyes. Grove was forced to turn away from her gaze.

'My word,' Batson said, holding his nose. 'Ilicius Bloom wasn't lying when he said the stink wasn't him but the ape!'

'You get used to it,' Bisesa said. She greeted Batson with a warm handshake, and an embrace for Grove that rather embarrassed him. 'Anyhow Grasper is company.'

'"Grasper"?'

'Don't you remember her, Grove? Your Tommies captured a man-ape and her baby on the very day of the Discontinuity. The Tommies called her "Grasper" for the way she uses those hands of hers, tying knots out of bits of straw, for fun. On the last night before we tried sending me back to Earth through the Eye, I asked for them to be released. Well, I think this is that baby, grown tall. If these australopithecines live as long as chimps, say, it's perfectly possible. I'll swear she is more dexterous than I am.'

Grove asked, 'How on earth does she come to be here?'

Eumenes said, 'She rather made her own way. She was one of a pack that troubled the western rail links. This one followed the line all the way back to Babylon, and made a nuisance of herself in the farms outside the city. Kept trying to get to the city walls. Wouldn't be driven off. In the end they netted her and brought her into the city as a curiosity for the court. We kept her in Bloom's cage, but the creature went wild. She wanted to *go* somewhere, that was clear.'

'It was my idea,' Abdi said. 'We leashed her, and allowed her to lead us where she would.'

'And she came here,' Bisesa said. 'Drawn here just as I was. She seems peaceful enough here, as if she's found what she wanted.'

Grove pondered. 'I do remember how we once kept this man-ape and her mother in a tent we propped up under a floating Eye – do you remember, Bisesa? Rather disrespectful to the Eye, I thought. Perhaps this wretched creature formed some sort of bond with the Eyes then. But how the devil would she know there was an Eye *here*?'

'There's a lot we don't understand,' Bisesa said. 'To put it mildly.'

Grove inspected Bisesa's den with forced interest. 'Well, you seem cheerful enough in here.'

'All mod cons,' she said, a term that baffled Grove. 'I have my phone. It's a shame Suit Five is out of power or that might have provided a bit more company too. And here's my chemical toilet, scavenged from the Little Bird. Abdi keeps me fed and cleaned out. You're my interface to the outside world, aren't you, Abdi?'

'Yes,' Grove said, 'but *why* are you here?'

Eumenes said gravely, 'You should know that Alexander *thinks* she is trying to find a way to use the Eye for his benefit. If not for the fact that the King believes Bisesa is serving his purposes, she would not be here at all. You must remember that when you meet him, Captain.'

'Fair enough. But what's the truth, Bisesa?'

'I want to go home,' she said simply. 'Just as I did before. I want to get back to my daughter, and granddaughter. And this is the only possible way. With respect, there's nothing on Mir that matters to me as much as that.'

Grove looked at this woman, this bereft mother, alone with all this strangeness. 'I had a daughter, you know,' he said, and he was dismayed how gruff his voice was. 'Back home. *You* know. She'd be about your age now, I should think. I do understand why you are here, Bisesa.'

She smiled, and embraced him again.

There was little more to be said.

'Well,' Grove said. 'I will visit again. We will be here for several more days in Babylon, I should think. I feel I really ought to try to do something for this wretched fellow Bloom. We moderns must stick together, I suppose.'

'You're a good man, Captain. But don't put yourself in any danger.'

'I'm a wily old bird, don't you worry ...'

They left soon after that.

Grove looked back once at Bisesa. Alone save for the watchful man-ape, she was walking around the hovering sphere and pressed her bare hand against the Eye's surface. The hand seemed to slide sideways, pushed by some unseen force. Grove was awed at her casual familiarity with this utterly monstrous, alien thing.

He turned away. He was glad he could hide the wetness of his foolish old eyes in the dark of the temple's corridors.

## CHAPTER 60
# HOUSE

*March 30, 2072*

'aula called, using the optic-fibre link. Since the secession of he sun, the big AIs at New Lowell had been refining their redictions of when the Rip would finally hit Mars.

'May 12,' Paula said. 'Around fourteen hundred.'

Six weeks. 'Well, now we know,' Myra said.

'I'm told that in the end they will get the prediction down o the attosecond.'

'That will be useful,' Yuri said dryly.

Paula said, 'Also we've been running predictions of the tate of your nuclear power plant. You're aware you're running out of fuel.'

'Of course,' Yuri said stiffly. 'Resupply has been somewhat roblematic.'

'We predict you'll make it through to the Rip. Just. It night not be too comfortable in the last few days.'

'We can economise. There are only two of us here.'

'Okay. But there's always room for you here at Lowell.'

Yuri glanced at Myra, who grinned back. She said, 'And eave home? No. Thanks, Paula. Let's finish it here.'

'I thought you'd say that. All right. If you change your mind the rovers are healthy enough to pick you up.'

'I know that, thanks,' Yuri said heavily. 'Since one of them is ours.'

They talked of bits of business, and how they were all coping.

It was as if Mars's last summer had been cut drastically short. The sun had vanished two months before what should have been midsummer, and the planet's terminal winter had begun.

In a way it didn't make much difference here at the pole, where it had been dark half the time anyhow. Myra's main loss was the regular download from Earth of movies and news, and letters from home. She didn't miss Earth itself as much as she missed the mail.

But if there was a winter routine to fall back on here at Wells, they weren't so used to darkness down at Lowell, near the equator, and it was a shock when the air started snowing out there. They had none of the equipment they needed to survive. So Yuri and Myra had loaded up one of the pole station's two specialised snowplough rovers with sublimation mats and other essentials. They left one rover at Lowell for the crew's use there, and then drove the other rover all the way back to Wells. That journey, a quarter of the planet's circumference each way through falling dry-ice snow, had been numbing, depressing, exhausting. Myra and Yuri hadn't left the environs of the base since.

'We'll speak again,' Paula said. 'Take care.' Her image disappeared.

Myra looked at Yuri. 'So that's that.'

'Back to work,' he said.

'Coffee first?'

'Give me an hour, and we'll break the back of some of the day's chores.'

'Okay.'

The routine work had got a lot harder since the final evacuation. Without the scheduled resupply and replacement drops it wasn't just the nuke that was failing but much of the other equipment as well. And now there were only two of them, in a base designed for ten, and Myra, though she was a quick learner, wasn't experienced here.

However Myra had thrown herself into the work. This morning she tended clogging hydroponic beds, and cleaned out a gunged-up bioreactor, and tried to figure out why the water extraction system was failing almost daily. She also had work to do with the AI, managing the flood of science data that continued to pour in from the SEPs and tumble-weed balls and dust motes, even though the sensor systems were steadily falling silent through various defects, or were simply getting stuck in the thickening snow.

Mostly the AI was able to work independently, even setting its own science goals and devising programmes to achieve them. But today was PPP day, planetary protection, when she had to make her regular formal check to ensure the environment was properly sampled in a band kilometres wide around the station, thus monitoring the slow seepage of their human presence into the skin of Mars. There was even a bit of paper she had to sign, for ultimate presentation to an agency on Earth. The paper was never going to get to Earth, of course, but she signed it anyway.

After an hour or so she had the AI hunt for Yuri. He was supposed to be out in the drill rig tent, mothballing equipment that had been shut down for the final time, thus fulfilling a promise he had made to Hanse Critchfield. In fact he was in Can Six, the EVA station.

She made some coffee, and carried it carefully through the locks to Six. She kept a lid on the cups; she still hadn't quite got used to one-third-G coffee sloshes.

She found Yuri kneeling on the floor of Six. He had gotten hold of a Cockell pulk, a simple dragging sled; adapted for Martian conditions it was fitted with fold-down wheels for running over basalt-hard water ice. He was piling up this little vehicle with a collapsed tent, food packets, bits of gear that looked to have been scavenged from life support.

She handed him his coffee. 'So what now?'

He sat back and sipped his drink. 'I've got an unfulfilled ambition. I've got many, actually, but this one's killing me.'

'Tell me.'

'An unsupported solo assault on the Martian north pole. I always planned to try it myself. I'd start at the edge of the permanent cap, see, just me and an EVA suit and a sled. And I'd walk, dragging the sled all the way to the pole. No drops, no pickup, nothing but me and the ice.'

'Is that even possible?'

'Oh, yes. It's a thousand kilometres tops, depending on the route you take. The suit would slow me down – and no suit we've got is designed for that kind of endurance and mobility; I'd have to make some enhancements. But remember, with one-third G I can haul three times as much as I could in Antarctica, say four hundred kilograms. And in some ways Mars is an easier environment than the Earth's poles. No blizzards, no white-outs.'

'You'd have to carry all your oxygen.'

'Maybe. Or I could use one of these.' He picked up some of his life-support gadgets, a small ice-collector box, an electrolysis kit for cracking water into oxygen and hydrogen. 'It's a trade-off, actually. The kits are lighter than oxygen bottles would be, but using them daily would slow me down. I know it's a stunt, Myra. But it's one *hell* of a stunt, isn't it? And nobody's tried it before. Who better but me?'

'You've got some mission designing to do, then.'

'Yes. I could figure it all out during the winter. Then when the summer comes, I could pick some period when Earth is above the horizon to try it. I could get the gear together and try it out on the ice around the base. The darkness wouldn't make any difference to that.' He seemed pleased to have found this new project. But he looked up at her, uncertain. 'Do you think I'm crazy?'

'No crazier than any of us. I mean, I don't think I believe in May 12. Do you? None of us *believes* it's ever going to happen, that death will come to us. If we did we couldn't function, probably. It's just a bit more definite for us on Mars, that's all.'

'Yes. But—'

'Let's not talk about it,' she said firmly. She knelt down with him on the cold floor. 'Show me how you're going to pack this stuff up. How would you eat? Unpack the tent twice a day?'

'No. I thought I'd unpack it in the evening, and eat overnight and in the morning. Then I could have some kind of hot drink through the suit nozzle during the day ...'

Talking, speculating, fiddling with the bits of kit, they planned the expedition, while the frozen air of Mars gathered in snowdrifts around the stilts of the station modules.

## CHAPTER 61

# GRASPER

It was Grasper who first noticed the change in the Eye.

She woke up slowly, as always clinging to her ragged dreams of trees. Suspended between animal and human, she had only a dim grasp of future and past. Her memory was like a gallery hung with vivid images – her mother's face, the warmth of the nest where she had been born. And the cages. Many, many cages.

She yawned hugely, and stretched her long arms, and looked around. The tall woman who shared this cave still slept. There was light on her peaceful face.

Light?

Grasper looked up. The Eye was shining. It was like a miniature sun, caught in the stone chamber.

Grasper raised a hand toward the Eye. It gave off no heat, only light. She stood and gazed at the Eye, eyes wide, one arm raised.

Now there was something new again. The glow of the Eye was no longer uniform: a series of brighter horizontal bands straddled an underlying greyness, a pattern that might have reminded a human of lines of latitude on a globe of the Earth. These lines swept up past the Eye's 'equator,' dwindling until they vanished at the north pole. Meanwhile another set, vertical this time, began the same pattern of emergence, sweeping from a pole on one side of the equator, disappearing on the other side. Now a third set of lines, sweeping to poles set at right angles to the first two pairs, came shining into existence. The shifting, silent display of grey rectangles was entrancing, beautiful.

And then a *fourth* set of lines appeared – Grasper tried to follow where they went – but suddenly something inside her head hurt badly.

She cried out. She rubbed the heels of her palms into her watering eyes. She felt warmth along her inner thighs. She had urinated where she stood.

The sleeping woman stirred.

## CHAPTER 62
# LITTLE RIP

*May 12, 2072*

They began the day wordlessly.

They followed the routine they had established in the months they had spent together. Even though, when Myra woke, there were only a few hours left before the Little Rip. She couldn't think of anything else they should be doing.

Yuri had to begin the day, as he did every day now, by getting suited up for an ice collection expedition. The ISRU water extraction system had finally broken down. So Yuri had to go outside daily to a trench he was digging in the water ice, and with an improvised pickaxe he broke off slabs of the ice, to carry into the warmth of the house to melt. It wasn't so difficult; the heavily stratified ice was like a fine-grained sandstone, and it split easily. Once they got the ice inside the house they had to filter out the dust from the sludge that resulted on melting it.

When he was done with that, Yuri disappeared to do Hanse's job, as he put it, tending to the power plant and the air system and the other mechanical support systems that kept them alive. He went off whistling, in fact. Yesterday he had got hold of some stuff he had been waiting for. An unpiloted rover had turned up, sent down by the crew of New Lowell; Paula and the crew there had been scavenging equipment from the radioactive ruin of Lowell itself. Yuri had been pleased with what he had found in this last delivery, and he had been looking forward to his work this morning.

He had sent the rover back the way it came, although the journey would take several days to complete, beyond the day of the Rip. Yuri seemed to have an instinct that their sentient machines needed to be kept occupied as much as their human masters, and Myra had no reason to argue with him.

Myra too went off to work. She had one job she had been saving up for today.

She scrambled into her EVA suit, as always fully respecting all planetary protection protocols, and went out to the little garden of outdoor plants that were weathering this new Martian winter. A regular task was to blow away the snow, the frozen air that congealed out every day. She used a hot-air blower like a fat hairdryer.

As she worked, Myra was aware of an Eye hovering over the garden. There were Eyes all over the place, even inside some of the base's hab elements. As usual she deliberately ignored it.

She made an extra effort today. She left the equipment in as good a condition as she could manage. And she touched the sturdy leathery leaves of each of the plants, wishing she could feel them through her thick-gloved fingers.

On the last day Bella came back to the locus of Mars.

From space, from the flight deck of the *Liberator,* you could see that there was still something there. The thing that had replaced Mars was roughly spherical, and it glowed a dull, dim red, a dying ember. It returned no echoes, and attempts to land a probe on it had ended in the loss of the spacecraft, and if you studied it with a spectroscope you would see that that strange surface appeared to be receding, that its light was reduced to crimson weariness by redshift.

It was a knot of mass-energy orbiting where Mars should have been. It exerted a gravity field sufficient to tether a flock of watching spacecraft, and even to keep Mars's small moons, Phobos and Deimos, circling in their ancient tracks. But it was not Mars.

Edna said, 'It's just the scar that was left when Mars was cut away.'

'And today that scar heals,' Bella said.

She watched softscreen displays that showed more ships arriving, more ghoulish spectators for this last act of the drama. She wondered what was happening on Mars itself – if Mars still existed in any meaningful sense at all.

Yuri and Myra were making lunch.

It would be dried eggs, reconstituted potatoes, and a little Martian greenery, rubbery but flavoursome. Yuri suggested wine, a Martian vintage from a domed vineyard at Lowell, once remarkably expensive. But it didn't seem appropriate, and he left the bottle unopened. Anyhow it was poor wine, Myra had always thought, expensive or not.

They worked together on the lunch, setting the base's table and preparing the food, without once getting in each other's way. 'We're like an old married couple,' Yuri had said, more than once. So they were, Myra supposed, though they had their spats – and though there had never been any physical intimacy between them, nothing save hugs for comfort, and you had to expect that of the only two human beings at the pole of a world.

It hadn't been a bad interval in her life, these last months. She had always been in somebody's shadow, she thought: first her mother's, then Eugene's. She'd never had a chance to build a home of her own. She couldn't say she had done that here on Mars. But this was where Yuri had put down his own roots, this was the world he'd built. And in these last months she'd been able to share his home with him. Sex or not, she'd had far worse relationships than with Yuri.

But she missed Charlie with an intensity she wouldn't have believed possible. As Rip day approached, it was like a steel cable tearing at her belly, ever harder. She didn't know if Charlie would know what had become of her mother. She didn't even have any up-to-date images, still or animated, she could look at. She had done her best to put this aside, to keep it in a compartment in her mind. Yuri knew, of course.

She glanced at the clock. 'It's later than I thought. Only an hour left.'

'Then we'd better tuck in.'

They sat down.

Yuri said, 'Hey, I had a good morning, by the way. The Lowell guys finally sent down those replacement filters I asked for. Now our air ought to stay sweet for another year. And I shut down the reactor. We're running on cell power, but it will see us out. I wanted that old tub of uranium to be closed down in an orderly way. I was kind of rushing to get it all done, but I mothballed it well enough, I think.'

She could see that his work had pleased him, just as her own had pleased her.

'Oh, there was another package from Paula, in the rover yesterday. She said we should open it about now.' He fetched it from the heap of equipment he'd sorted to find his filters. It was a small plastic box that he put on the table.

He opened it up to reveal a padded interior, within which nestled a sphere, about the size of a tennis ball. A plastic bag of pills had been tucked into the box, under the ball. He put these out on the table.

Myra took the sphere. It was heavy, with a smooth black surface.

Yuri said, 'I was expecting this. It's coated with the stuff they make heatshield tiles out of. It can soak up a lot of heat.'

'So it will survive the planet breaking up?'

'That's the idea.'

'I don't see what good that will do.'

'But you understand how the Q-expansion works,' Yuri said, speaking around a mouthful of egg. 'The Rip works down the scales, larger structures breaking up first. The planet will go first, *then* the human body. This little gadget ought to survive the end of the planet, even if it's cast adrift in space, and it should last a bit longer than a suited human, say. Surrounded by debris, I suppose. Rocks popping into dust, at smaller and smaller scales.'

'Are there instruments inside?'

'Yes. It should keep working, taking data until the expansion gets down to the centimetre scale, and the Rip cracks the sphere open. Even then there's a plan. The sphere will release a cloud of even finer sensor units, motes we call them. It's nanotechnology, Myra, machines the size of molecules. They will keep gathering data until the expansion reaches molecular scales. There's nothing they could come up with beyond that. Paula says the design goal is to make it through to the last microsecond. You could gather another thirty minutes of data that way.'

'Then it's worth doing.'

'Oh, yes.'

Myra hefted the sphere. 'What a wonderful little gadget. It's a shame nobody will be able to use its data.'

'Well, you never know,' Yuri said.

She set the sphere on the table. 'And these pills?'

He fingered the bag of pills dubiously. 'Jenny at Lowell said she would prepare something like this.' Jenny Mortens was New Lowell's doctor, the only one left on Mars. 'You know what they are. It might be easier, this way, just to take them.'

'It would be a shame to come this far and then give up at the last minute. Don't you think? And besides, I have my mother to think about.'

'Fair enough.' He grinned, and with a flip he lobbed the pill bag into a waste bin.

She looked at her watch. 'I think we'd better get moving. There isn't much time.'

'Right.' He stood, and stacked the dishes. 'I think we can waste a little water and wash up.' He glanced back at her. 'How are you feeling about using the suits?'

They both wanted to be outside the base in the final moments. But she had been unsure about wearing a suit. 'I do think I'll want a bit of human contact, Yuri.'

He smiled. 'Quaintly put. Too late to be embarrassed now.'

'You know what I mean,' she said, a bit irritated to be teased about it.

'Of course I do. Look – I've fixed it. Come out with me into the suits and see what I've done. Trust me. I think you'll like it. And there'll always be time to come back inside if not.'

She nodded. 'All right. Let's get this place shipshape first.'

So they tidied up. After one last gulp of coffee – her last ever mouthful, she thought – Myra cleaned the dishes in a little of their precious hot water, and stacked them away. She went to the bathroom, washed her face and brushed her teeth, and used the lavatory. The suits had facilities, of course, but she'd rather not have to resort to that.

She was running down through a list of simple human actions for the last time, the very last. She would never sleep again, or eat, or drink coffee, or even use a bathroom. She had begun to think this way since waking this morning, despite her best efforts to maintain business as usual.

With Yuri, she walked around the station one last time. Yuri was carrying the black sensor globe from Lowell. They had already shut most of Wells down, but now they ordered the station AI to run the systems down to minimum, and to turn off the lights, so that as they walked they left gathering pools of darkness behind them. Everything was tidy, put away where it should be, cleaned up. Myra felt proud of how they had left things.

At last only one fluorescent tube was left burning, in the EVA dome, illuminating the small hatchways through which they had to climb to get into their suits. They pulled on their inner suits, and Yuri passed the sensor ball out through an equipment hatch.

'You go left, I go right,' he said. 'If you need to scratch your nose, now's the time.'

They paused. Then they hugged, and Myra drank in his scent.

They broke. 'Lights,' Yuri called. The last tube died, leaving the station dark. 'Goodbye, HG,' Yuri said softly to his base. Myra had never heard him use that name before.

Myra opened her hatch, and with a skill developed over her months on Mars she slid feet-first into her suit. When she wormed her right hand into its sleeve, she got a surprise. The glove she had been expecting wasn't there. Instead her hand slid into a warm grasp.

She leaned forward. By her suit lights she saw that the glove of her suit had been cut away, and her right sleeve had been stitched to Yuri's left.

Yuri was looking out of his helmet. 'How do you like my needlework?'

'Good work, Yuri.'

'The suits don't like it, of course. They both think they are breached. But the hell with them. The temporary seal hasn't got to hold for long. Of course we're going to have to do everything together, like Siamese twins. How's your suit?'

She had already run it through its diagnostic check. She looked over Yuri's chest display, to ensure he hadn't missed anything, and he did the same for her. 'All fine, apart from bleating about the gloves.'

'Very good,' he said. 'So we stand. Three, two, one—'

Their hands locked together, they straightened up. Her exoskeletal multipliers whirred, and her suit came loose of the dome with a sucking sound.

Out of habit she turned, picked up a soft brush, and swept the dome seals clean of Mars dust. Yuri did the same. It was a bit awkward with their hands locked together.

Then Yuri bent to pick up the sensor ball in his right hand, and they walked forward.

It was pitch dark, and the snow fell steadily, shapeless flakes of frozen Martian air illuminated by their suit lights. But the ground was reasonably clear; they had got a path swept yesterday.

A little robot camera rolled after them, even now recording, recording. It got stuck in a snow bank. Myra kicked it clear and it rolled ahead, red lights glowing.

Yuri stopped, and put the sensor sphere down on the ground before them. 'Here, do you think?'

'I guess so. I don't imagine it matters much.'

He straightened up. The snow continued to fall. Yuri held

out a hand and caught flakes. They looked like fat moths settling on his gloves, before they sublimated away. 'Ah, God,' he said, 'there's so much wonder here. You know, these flakes have structure. Each snowflake nucleates around first a grain of dust, then water ice, and only then an outer shell of dry ice. It is like an onion. And it all falls here, every winter. Thus three global cycles, of dust, water and carbon dioxide, intersect in every snowflake. We barely began to understand Mars.' His voice had an edge of bitterness she hadn't heard in him in months. 'To some this would be hell,' he said. 'The cold, the darkness. Not to me.'

'Nor me,' she whispered, squeezing his hand inside their stitched-together sleeves. 'Yuri.'

'Yes?'

'Thank you. These last few months, for me—'

'Better not to say it.'

There was a sound like a door slamming, transmitted to them through their suits. An alarm chimed in Myra's ears, and lights lit up on her chin display.

The ground shuddered.

'Right on cue,' Yuri said.

They looked at each other. It was the first real sign since the disappearance of the sun that something remarkable was happening.

Fear fluttered in her throat. Suddenly she wished this were not happening, that they could go back into the station and carry on with their day. She clung to Yuri's hand, and they bumped against each other in the bulky suits, like two green sumo wrestlers. Yuri twisted, trying to see the watch strapped to his arm outside his suit.

The ground shook more violently. And then ice spurted around them, fine splinters of it. They turned to see, hands still clasped. A hab can had ruptured, and its air and water were escaping, instantly freezing in a shower that drifted down around the can's stilts.

'We'd better get a bit further away,' Myra said.

'All right.' They walked forward, unsteady as the ground

shuddered again. Yuri said, 'It's going to be a hell of a job to fix that rip.'

'So call Hanse back.'

'Bastard's never there when you need him – *ow.*' He stumbled, pulling at her so that she staggered too.

'What is it?'

'I hit my head.' They turned. An Eye hovered before them, this one maybe a metre across, its lowest point just below head height. 'Bastard.' Yuri swung a punch at it with his free right hand. 'Shit. Like hitting concrete.'

'Ignore it,' said Myra.

Just for a moment, the shuddering stopped. They stood together, near the Eye, breathing hard.

'You were right to have us come outside,' Myra said.

'And you were right to ask for a bit of "human contact"'. I think we got most things right these last few months, Ms Dutt.'

'I think I'd agree, Mr O'Rourke.' She breathed deep, and squeezed his hand. 'You know, Yuri—'

The ground burst open.

In the temple chamber, the tall woman woke. Slowly at first.

And then with a start as she saw the Eye.

*'Shit, shit. It would have to be now, when I need a pee. Come on, Suit Five, you're as dead as a dodo but you're the best protection I've got . . .'* As Grasper watched, she began to pull herself into her green carcass thing, and she placed a glowing pebble on the floor.

*'You're leaving me again, Bisesa?'*

*'Look, phone, don't guilt-trip me now. We worked this out. You're the only link back to Earth. And if Abdi succeeds in his program of power-cell manufacture you'll be powered up indefinitely.'*

*'Cold comfort.'*

*'I won't forget you.'*

*'Good-bye, Bisesa. Good-bye . . .'*

*'Shit. The Eye. What's it doing?'*

Grasper was still standing, trembling but upright, gazing up at the washing lights, which cast complex patterns of shadows around the chamber. A fifth set of lines – a *sixth* set, disappearing in impossible directions –

The tall woman screamed.

Myra was lying face-down on a scrap of rock-hard water ice, her faceplate pressed against the surface. Yuri had fallen awkwardly somewhere behind her, and her right arm was wrenched back. She felt a pressure in her belly, as if she was being lifted up by an elevator.

She struggled to raise her head. The suit's multipliers whined as they strained to help her.

She looked down, *into* Mars.

She saw ice chunks and rocks and even sprays of magma, all illuminated by a deeper red glow from within. All this filled her view, as far as she could see, to left and right. It was like looking down into a deep chasm.

And when she looked up a little further, she saw the Eye, maybe the same one, rising up before her, tracking her.

The fear was gone. Clinging to the bit of ice, still squeezing Yuri's hand, she felt almost exhilarated. Maybe they could live through this, just a little longer.

But then a gout of molten rock like an immense fist came barrelling up, out of the heart of disintegrating Mars, straight at her.

The scar in space became transparent, so Bella could see the stars shining through it, their light curdled and faded.

Then it cleared altogether, as if evaporating.

She hugged her daughter.

'So that's that,' Edna said.

'Yes. Take me home, love.'

The *Liberator*'s blunt nose turned away, toward Earth.

Released from their parent's gravity field, Mars's small moons drifted away from their paths. Now they would orbit the sun, becoming just two more unremarkable asteroids. The thin cloud of satellites humans had put in place around

Mars began to disperse too. For a time gravitational waves crossed the system, and the sun's remaining planets bobbed, leaves on a pond into which a pebble had been thrown. But the ripples soon subsided.

And Mars was gone.

## CHAPTER 63

# A TIME ODYSSEY

A gate opened. A gate closed. In a moment of time too short to be measured, space opened and turned on itself.

It wasn't like waking. It was a sudden emergence, a clash of cymbals. Her eyes gaped wide open, and were filled with dazzling light. She dragged deep breaths into her lungs, and gasped with the shock of selfhood.

She was on her back. There was something enormously bright above her – the sun, yes, the sun, she was outdoors.

She threw herself over onto her belly. Dazzled by the sun, she could barely see.

A plain. Red sand. Eroded hills in the distance. Even the sky looked red, though the sun was high.

This felt familiar.

And Myra was beside her. It was impossible, but it was so.

Bisesa hurriedly crawled through loose sand to get to her daughter. Like Bisesa, Myra was in a green Mars suit. She was lying on her back, an ungainly fish stranded on this strange beach.

Myra's faceplate retracted, and she coughed in the sharp, dry air. She stared at her right hand. The suit's glove was missing, the flesh of her hand pale.

'It's me, darling.'

Myra looked at her, shocked. 'Mum?'

They clung to each other.

It got darker. Bisesa peered up.

The sun's disc was deformed. It looked like a leaf out of which a great bite had been taken. It began to feel colder, and Bisesa glimpsed bands of shadow rushing across the eroded ground.

Not again, she thought.

'Don't be afraid.'

They both turned, rolling in the dirt.

A woman stood over them. She was quite hairless, her face smooth. She wore a flesh-coloured coverall so sleek it was as if she was naked. She smiled at them. 'We've been expecting you.'

Myra said, 'My God. *Charlie?*'

Bisesa stared. 'Who is "we"?'

'We call ourselves the Lastborn. We are at war. We are losing.' She held out her hands. 'Please. Come with me now.'

Bisesa and Myra, still hugging each other, reached out their free hands. Their fingertips touched Charlie's.

A clash of cymbals.

# AFTERWORD

Recently the space elevator, as dramatised in Clarke's *The Fountains of Paradise* (1979), has come closer to engineering feasibility. The details given here are based in part on a study funded by NASA's Institute for Advanced Concepts, and written up in *The Space Elevator* by Bradley C Edwards and Eric A Westling (Spaego, San Francisco, 2003). See also *Leaving the Planet by Space Elevator* by Dr Edwards and Philip Ragan (lulu.com, Seattle, 2006), and papers by Giorcelli, Pullum, Swan, and Swan in the *Journal of the British Interplanetary Society*, September 2006. A recent study of the use of space elevators as energy-free 'orbital siphons' is given by Colin McInnes and Chris Davis in the *Journal of the British Interplanetary Society*, vol. 59, pp. 368–74, 2006. We're very grateful to Dr Edwards for discussions on the relevant sections. His company 'Black Line Ascension' may become a real world counterpart of our Skylift Consortium.

It is remarkable that cultures globally appear to share a 'world tree' myth. Some of the more plausible explanations for this range from cloud formations to plasma phenomena (see for example www.maverickscience.com/ladder_aeon.pdf).

The 'Cyclops' Fresnel-lens telescope is based on a study by James T Early ('Twenty-metre space telescope based on diffractive Fresnel lens' by Dr Early et al., in *Proceedings of SPIE* Vol. 5166, 'UV/Optical/IR Space Telescopes: Innovative Technologies and Concepts,' ed. Howard A MacEwen, January 2004). Our depiction of the Fresnel shield of *Sunstorm* also drew on Dr Early's studies. We're very grateful to Dr Early for discussions on these concepts.

Our depiction of Martian exploration draws partly on a

conceptual design study, to which Baxter contributed, of a base at the Martian north pole: see *Project Boreas: A Station for the Martian Geographic North Pole,* ed. Charles S Cockell (British Interplanetary Society, 2006). The idea that relic space probes could be used to provide human-interest targets for future Mars expeditions was suggested by Baxter (see 'Trophy Fishing: Early Expeditions to Spacecraft Relics on Mars,' *Journal of the British Interplanetary Society,* vol. 57, pp. 99–102, 2004), and the history of humanity's interaction with Mars is sketched by Baxter in 'Martian Chronicles: Narratives of Mars in Science and SF' (*Foundation* no. 68, 1996, and in *The Hunters of Pangaea,* NESFA Press, Feb 2004). Our depiction of a lunar south pole base in *Sunstorm* foresaw the plans for the colonisation of the Moon announced by NASA in December 2006. Our sketch of Titan is based on results returned by the spectacular Huygens Lander in January 2005.

Recent studies confirm that the surface of Mars's northern hemisphere is very ancient (Watters et al., *Nature,* vol. 444, pp. 905–8, December 2006) and appears to be a single vast crater created by an immense impact (*New Scientist,* 24 March 2007). The impact was natural. Probably.

Solar sailing is another long-trailed technology whose time may be coming at last. Physicists and science fiction writers Gregory and James Benford were involved in *Cosmos 1,* an experimental solar-sail spacecraft that, scheduled for launch in June 2005, would have used light pressure to adjust its orbit. The craft carried a CD containing Clarke's 1964 story 'The Wind from the Sun.' Sadly the launch vehicle failed.

Human suspended animation may also be coming closer to fruition; see for example the article by Mark Roth and Todd Nystul in *Scientific American,* June 2005. And scientists led by Imperial College, London, are edging toward a 'metamaterial' invisibility technology of the type sketched here (see http://tinyurl.com/zp6jh). A study of the use of 'gravitational tractors' to divert asteroids is given by E T Lu et al. in *Nature,* vol. 438, pp. 177–8, November 2005.

The effects of the 'cosmological bomb' featured in this novel are based on predictions made in 2003 of the ultimate fate of a universe permeated by dark energy, given by Robert Caldwell of Dartmouth College and others (see *Physical Review*, www.arxiv.org/abs/astro-ph/0302506). The variability of Procyon is fictitious, but variable stars do sometimes cease to be fluctuate. It did happen to one of the most famous stars in the sky, the pole star Polaris, an anomaly as yet unexplained; see J D Fernie et al., *Astrophysical Journal*, vol. 416, pp. 820–4, 1993.

The science of 'astrobiology,' the study of the possibility of life beyond the Earth, has been revolutionised in the last few years both by the discovery of new variants of life on Earth, by the revelation of possible habitats for life either now or in the past on worlds like Mars, Europa, and Titan, and by new models of 'panspermia,' natural mechanisms by which living things could be transferred between the planets. A recent review is *Life as We Do Not Know It* by Peter Ward (Viking, 2005).

The energy-conservation strategy of the Firstborn, first sketched in *Time's Eye* (2004) and *Sunstorm* (2005), is reflected in some academic thinking on the future of life in the universe. See for instance a paper by Michael Mautner (*Journal of the British Interplanetary Society*, vol. 57, pp. 167–80, 2005) titled 'Life in the Cosmological Future: Resources, Biomass and Populations.'

The idea that stretches of North America could be 're-wilded' with substitute communities of animals to replace the lost megafauna ecology of the past has been put forward by, among others, Paul S Martin (*Twilight of the Mammoths: Ice Age Extinctions and the Rewilding of North America*, University of California Press, 2005). But others raise profound objections to the plan (see Rubenstein et al., *Biological Conservation*, vol. 132, p. 232, 2006). A study of the use of space-based resources in mitigating future disasters (not necessarily caused by malevolent extraterrestrials) is given as two papers by C M Hempsell in the *Journal of the British Interplanetary Society*, vol. 57, pp. 2–21, 2004.

*

Alexander the Great's global conquest, sketched here, is based on plans he was actually drawing up before his death for an expansion of his empire from Gibraltar to the Black Sea; see for instance *Conquest and Empire: The Reign of Alexander the Great* by A B Bosworth (CUP 1988). An engaging portrait of Chicago at the time of the 1893 world's fair is *The Devil in the White City* by Erik Larson (Random House, 2003). The portrayal of the Babylonian 'Midden' is based on the archaeology of the Neolithic city known as Catalhoyuk; see www.catalhoyuk.org.

Chapter 25 is based on a heavily revised version of the story 'A Signal from Earth' by Baxter, first published in *Postscripts* no. 5, Autumn 2005.

Any errors or misconceptions are of course the authors' sole responsibility.

Sir Arthur C Clarke
Stephen Baxter

June 2007

## *About the Authors*

Arthur C Clarke (1917–2008) was considered the greatest science fiction writer of all time and was an international treasure in many other ways, including the fact that a 1945 article by him led to the invention of satellite technology. Books by Clarke – both fiction and nonfiction – have sold more than one hundred million copies worldwide. He lived in Sri Lanka.

Stephen Baxter is a trained engineer with degrees from Cambridge and Southampton universities. Baxter is the acclaimed author of the Manifold novels and *Evolution*. He is the winner of the British Science Fiction Award, the Locus Award, the John W Campbell Award, and the Philip K Dick Award, as well as being a nominee several times for the Arthur C Clarke Award and the Hugo Award.

